JOURNEYS INTO MYSTERY

Travel and Mystery in a More Elegant Age

Edited by Greg Fowlkes

JOURNEYS INTO MYSTERY

Travel and Mystery in a More Elegant Age

© 2012 Resurrected Press
www.ResurrectedPress.com

Published by Resurrected Press

This classic book was handcrafted by Resurrected Press. Resurrected Press is dedicated to bringing high quality classic books back to the readers who enjoy them. These are not scanned versions of the originals, but, rather, quality checked and edited books meant to be enjoyed!

Please visit ResurrectedPress.com to view our entire catalogue!

ISBN 13: 978-1-937022-52-5

Printed in the United States of America

FOREWORD

They say that travel is broadening, and in no era was that more true than in the period before the First World War. The perfection of the railroad and steamship had transformed travel. No longer was a journey an arduous ordeal taking weeks or months. Instead, at least in the civilized world, travel had become an elegant mode of existence, at least for those who could afford to travel first class. One could board an overnight express in any of the capitols of Europe, have a first class meal in the dining car, sleep in comfortable private compartment, and arrive at one's destination in time for breakfast. For those wishing to travel between the Old and the New World, there were the great liners plying regular routes between the major ports. The rich and famous could dine in the luxurious first class dining salon, spend their days relaxing on deck or engaging in sport, or enjoy elegant diversions and music at night. And, in less than a week, arrive safely and promptly at their destination. And of course, once one arrived, there were the first class hotels ready to provide comfortable and luxurious accommodations complete with restaurants, chefs, maids, valets and all the other requirements of the wealthy traveler.

But, while travel may have become elegant, it was still travel. One could find oneself in the most unusual company. A foreign countess on one side, a retired military man on the other, a bishop or a diplomatic courier. But there were also other travelers with much more questionable pasts and occupations. The international jewel thief, the confidence man, the spy. The luxurious excursion might well turn into a journey into mystery.

It was only natural that writers of the day should set their pens to producing tales of such journeys, and this volume brings together three works by some of the best writers of the day. All of these writers were familiar with this world of travel, either as journalists, or in the case of Griffiths as a senior civil servant who served in a number of posts. They would have dined with lords and ladies, actresses and bishops. They would have stayed in the best hotels and traveled in first class railroad compartments and first class steamship staterooms. And so the portraits of travel that they provide their readers are ones based as much on experience as imagination.

And, if in the interest of entertainment, they populate their novels with the occasional embezzler, jewel-thief or murderer, we at least have the comfort of knowing that they are elegant embezzlers, sophisticated jewel-thieves, and impeccably dressed murderers. For theirs was a more elegant age.

Resurrected Press has as its mission the goal of bringing its readers some of the best, if now neglected, mystery fiction of past eras. With that in mind we welcome the reader into these *Journeys into Mystery*.

Greg Fowlkes
Editor-In-Chief
Resurrected Press
www.ResurrectedPress.com

RESURRECTED PRESS CLASSIC MYSTERY CATALOGUE

The Edwardian Detectives
Literary Sleuths of the Edwardian Era

Gems of Mystery
Lost Jewels from a More Elegant Age

E. C. Bentley
Trent's Last Case: The Woman in Black

Ernest Bramah
Max Carrados Resurrected:
The Detective Stories of Max Carrados

Agatha Christie
The Secret Adversary
The Mysterious Affair at Styles

Octavus Roy Cohen
Midnight

Freeman Wills Croft
The Ponson Case
The Pit Prop Syndicate

J. S. Fletcher
The Herapath Property
The Rayner-Slade Amalgamation
The Chestermarke Instinct
The Paradise Mystery
Dead Men's Money
The Middle of Things
Ravensdene Court
Scarhaven Keep
The Orange-Yellow Diamond
The Middle Temple Murder
The Tallyrand Maxim

Baroness Emma Orczy
The Old Man in the Corner

Edgar Allan Poe
The Detective Stories of Edgar Allan Poe

Arthur J. Rees
The Hampstead Mystery
The Shrieking Pit
The Hand In The Dark
The Moon Rock
The Mystery of the Downs

Mary Roberts Rinehart
Sight Unseen and The Confession

Dorothy L. Sayers
Whose Body?

Sir William Magnay
The Hunt Ball Mystery

Mabel and Paul Thorne
The Sheridan Road Mystery

Louis Tracy
The Strange Case of Mortimer Fenley
The Albert Gate Mystery
The Bartlett Mystery
The Postmaster's Daughter
The House of Peril
The Sandling Case: What Would You Have Done?
Charles Edmonds Walk
The Paternoster Ruby

John R. Watson
The Mystery of the Downs
The Hampstead Mystery

TABLE OF CONTENTS

THE ROME EXPRESS
BY ARTHUR GRIFFITHS

ORIGINALLY PUBLISHED 1907

EDITOR'S NOTES:
THE ROME EXPRESS
BY ARTHUR GRIFFITHS

The Rome Express, the very words conjure up a romantic time when travel, at least for those who could afford a compartment in a first class car, was elegant and refined. One could board the night train in Rome, dine along the way, sleep in comfortable accommodations and wake up at the station in Paris refreshed and ready to go.

In a scant half century railroads had covered the continent of Europe. Express lines connected the capitols and major cities covering distances in hours that would have taken days or weeks of arduous and dangerous travel by horse drawn coach before their advent. And it all ran like clockwork. One had only to consult one's copy of Bradshaw to find the schedules and connecting trains so that one could travel from anywhere to anywhere else with a minimum of fuss.

Train travel was indeed luxurious for those who had money, with sleeping cars, dining cars, smoking cars, stops at track side restaurants. First class passengers were shielded from the lower orders. Porters were available to provide services like hot water for washing, setting up the sleeping arrangements of the compartments, and making sure one was awake in time for arrival at the station.

This is the picture that Major Arthur Griffiths paints in *"The Rome Express."* Of course, not everything can be expected to run smoothly, especially when a body is discovered in one of the compartments. Then one must deal with officious foreign policemen and other inconveniences.

As a footnote, several films have been made based on the novel, *"Rome Express"* in 1932 and *"Sleeping Car to Trieste"* made after World War II.

About the Author

Major Arthur Griffiths (1838-1908) was born at an Indian garrison post, a descendent of a long line of military men. After serving as a Second Lieutenant during the Crimean War his regiment was posted to Halifax, Nova Scotia. He also served for a period at Gibraltar before retiring from the military to join the civil service where he held the post of Inspector of Prisons.

He wrote numerous books including *"Mysteries of Police and Crime"*, *"The Chronicles of Newgate"*, *"The Passenger from Calais"*, and *"The Rome Express"*.

THE ROME EXPRESS

CHAPTER I

The Rome Express, the *direttissimo*, or most direct, was approaching Paris one morning in March, when it became known to the occupants of the sleeping-car that there was something amiss, very much amiss, in the car.

The train was travelling the last stage, between Laroche and Paris, a run of a hundred miles without a stop. It had halted at Laroche for early breakfast, and many, if not all the passengers, had turned out. Of those in the sleeping-car, seven in number, six had been seen in the restaurant, or about the platform; the seventh, a lady, had not stirred. All had reentered their berths to sleep or doze when the train went on, but several were on the move as it neared Paris, taking their turn at the lavatory, calling for water, towels, making the usual stir of preparation as the end of a journey was at hand.

There were many calls for the porter, yet no porter appeared. At last the attendant was found–lazy villain!–asleep, snoring loudly, stertorously, in his little bunk at the end of the car. He was roused with difficulty, and set about his work in a dull, unwilling, lethargic way, which promised badly for his tips from those he was supposed to serve.

By degrees all the passengers got dressed, all but two,–the lady in 9 and 10, who had made no sign as yet; and the man who occupied alone a double berth next her, numbered 7 and 8.

As it was the porter's duty to call everyone, and as he was anxious, like the rest of his class, to get rid of his travellers as soon as possible after arrival, he rapped at each of the two closed doors behind which people presumably still slept.

The lady cried "All right," but there was no answer from No. 7 and 8.

Again and again the porter knocked and called loudly. Still meeting with no response, he opened the door of the compartment and went in.

It was now broad daylight. No blind was down; indeed, the one narrow window was open, wide; and the whole of the interior of the compartment was plainly visible, all and everything in it.

The occupant lay on his bed motionless. Sound asleep? No, not merely asleep—the twisted unnatural lie of the limbs, the contorted legs, the one arm drooping listlessly but stiffly over the side of the berth, told of a deeper, more eternal sleep.

The man was dead. Dead—and not from natural causes.

One glance at the blood-stained bedclothes, one look at the gaping wound in the breast, at the battered, mangled face, told the terrible story.

It was murder! Murder most foul! The victim had been stabbed to the heart.

With a wild, affrighted, cry the porter rushed out of the compartment, and to the eager questioning of all who crowded round him, he could only mutter in confused and trembling accents:

"There! There! In there!"

Thus the fact of the murder became known to everyone by personal inspection, for everyone (even the lady had appeared for just a moment) had looked in where the body lay. The compartment was filled for some ten minutes or more by an excited, gesticulating, polyglot mob of half a dozen, all talking at once in French, English, and Italian.

The first attempt to restore order was made by a tall man, middle-aged, but erect in his bearing, with bright eyes and alert manner, who took the porter aside, and said sharply in good French, but with a strong English accent:

"Here! It's your business to do something. No one has any right to be in that compartment now. There may be reasons—traces—things to remove; never mind what. But get them all out. Be sharp about it; and lock the door. Remember you will be held responsible to justice."

The porter shuddered, so did many of the passengers who had overheard the Englishman's last words.

Justice! It is not to be trifled with anywhere, least of all in France, where the uncomfortable superstition prevails that everyone who can be reasonably suspected of a crime is held to be guilty of that crime until his innocence is clearly proved.

All those six passengers and the porter were now brought within the category of the accused. They were all open to suspicion; they, and they alone, for the murdered man had been seen alive at Laroche, and the fell deed must have been done since then, while the train was in transit, that is to say, going at express speed, when no one could leave it except at peril of his life.

"Deuced awkward for us!" said the tall English general, Sir Charles Collingham by name, to his brother the parson, when he had reentered their compartment and shut the door.

"I can't see it. In what way?" asked the Reverend Silas Collingham, a typical English cleric, with a rubicund face and square-cut white whiskers, dressed in a suit of black serge, and wearing the professional white tie.

"Why, we shall be detained, of course; arrested, probably—certainly detained. Examined, cross-examined, bully-ragged—I know something of the French police and their ways."

"If they stop us, I shall write to the Times" cried his brother, by profession a man of peace, but with a choleric eye that told of an angry temperament.

"By all means, my dear Silas, when you get the chance. That won't be just yet, for I tell you we're in a tight place, and may expect a good deal of worry." With that he took out his cigarette-case, and his match-box, lighted his cigarette, and calmly watched the smoke rising with all the coolness of an old campaigner accustomed to encounter and face the ups and downs of life. "I only hope to goodness they'll run straight on to Paris," he added in a fervent tone, not unmixed with apprehension. "No! By jingo, we're slackening speed—."

"Why shouldn't we? It's right the conductor, or chief of the train, or whatever you call him, should know what has happened."

"Why, man, can't you see? While the train is travelling express, everyone must stay on board it; if it slows, it is possible to leave it."

"Who would want to leave it?"

"Oh, I don't know," said the General, rather testily. "Any way, the thing's done now."

The train had pulled up in obedience to the signal of alarm given by someone in the sleeping-car, but by whom it was impossible to say. Not by the porter, for he seemed greatly surprised as the conductor came up to him.

"How did you know?" he asked.

"Know! Know what? You stopped me."

"I didn't."

"Who rang the bell, then?"

"I did not. But I'm glad you've come. There has been a crime—murder."

"Good Heavens!" cried the conductor, jumping up on to the car, and entering into the situation at once. His business was only to verify the fact, and take all necessary precautions. He was a burly, brusque, peremptory person, the despotic, self-important French official, who knew what to do—as he thought—and did it without hesitation or apology.

"No one must leave the car," he said in a tone not to be misunderstood. "Neither now, nor on arrival at the station."

There was a shout of protest and dismay, which he quickly cut short.

"You will have to arrange it with the authorities in Paris; they can alone decide. My duty is plain: to detain you, place you under surveillance till then. Afterwards, we will see. Enough, gentlemen and madame"—

He bowed with the instinctive gallantry of his nation to the female figure which now appeared at the door of her compartment. She stood for a moment listening, seemingly greatly agitated, and then, without a word, disappeared, retreating hastily into her own private room, where she shut herself in.

Almost immediately, at a signal from the conductor, the train resumed its journey. The distance remaining to be traversed was short; half an hour more, and the Lyons station, at Paris, was reached, where the bulk of the passengers—all, indeed, but the occupants of the sleeper—descended and passed through the barriers. The latter were again desired to keep their places, while a posse of officials came and mounted guard. Presently they were told to leave the car one by one, but to take nothing with them. All their hand-bags, rugs, and belongings were to remain in the berths, just as they lay. One by one they were marched under escort to a large and bare waiting-room, which had, no doubt, been prepared for their reception.

Here they took their seats on chairs placed at wide intervals apart, and were peremptorily forbidden to hold any communication with each other, by word or gesture. This order was enforced by a fierce-looking guard in blue and red uniform, who stood facing them with his arms folded, gnawing his moustache and frowning severely.

Last of all, the porter was brought in and treated like the passengers, but more distinctly as a prisoner. He had a guard all to himself; and it seemed as though he was the object of peculiar suspicion. It had no great effect upon him, for, while the rest of the party were very plainly sad, and a prey to lively apprehension, the porter sat dull and unmoved, with the stolid, sluggish, unconcerned aspect of a man just roused from sound sleep and relapsing into slumber, who takes little notice of what is passing around.

Meanwhile, the sleeping-car, with its contents, especially the corpse of the victim, was shunted into a siding, and sentries were placed on it at both ends. Seals had been affixed upon the entrance doors, so that the interior might be kept inviolate until it could be visited and examined by the Chef de la Sûreté, or Chief of the Detective Service. Everyone and everything awaited the arrival of this all-important functionary.

CHAPTER II

M. Floçon, the Chief, was an early man, and he paid a first visit to his office about 7 A.M.

He lived just round the corner in the Rue des Arcs, and had not far to go to the Prefecture. But even now, soon after daylight, he was correctly dressed, as became a responsible ministerial officer. He wore a tight frock coat and an immaculate white tie; under his arm he carried the regulation portfolio, or lawyer's bag, stuffed full of reports, dispositions, and documents dealing with cases in hand. He was altogether a very precise and natty little personage, quiet and unpretending in demeanour, with a mild, thoughtful face in which two small ferrety eyes blinked and twinkled behind gold-rimmed glasses. But when things went wrong, when he had to deal with fools, or when scent was keen, or the enemy near, he would become as fierce and eager as any terrier.

He had just taken his place at his table and begun to arrange his papers, which, being a man of method, he kept carefully sorted by lots each in an old copy of the Figaro, when he was called to the telephone. His services were greatly needed, as we know, at the Lyons station and the summons was to the following effect:

"Crime on train No. 45. A man murdered in the sleeper. All the passengers held. Please come at once. Most important."

A fiacre was called instantly, and M. Floçon, accompanied by Galipaud and Block, the two first inspectors for duty, was driven with all possible speed across Paris.

He was met outside the station, just under the wide verandah, by the officials, who gave him a brief outline of the facts, so far as they were known, and as they have already been put before the reader.

"The passengers have been detained?" asked M. Floçon at once.

"Those in the sleeping-car only—"

"Tut, tut! They should have been all kept—at least until you had taken their names and addresses. Who knows what they might not have been able to tell?"

It was suggested that as the crime was committed presumably while the train was in motion, only those in the one car could be implicated.

"We should never jump to conclusions," said the Chief snappishly. "Well, show me the train card—the list of the travellers in the sleeper."

"It cannot be found, sir."

"Impossible! Why, it is the porter's business to deliver it at the end of the journey to his superiors, and under the law—to us. Where is the porter? In custody?"

"Surely, sir, but there is something wrong with him."

"So I should think! Nothing of this kind could well occur without his knowledge. If he was doing his duty—unless, of course, he—but let us avoid hasty conjectures."

"He has also lost the passengers' tickets, which you know he retains till the end of the journey. After the catastrophe, however, he was unable to lay his hand upon his pocket-book. It contained all his papers."

"Worse and worse. There is something behind all this. Take me to him. Stay, can I have a private room close to the other—where the prisoners, those held on suspicion, are? It will be necessary to hold investigations, take their depositions. M. le Juge will be here directly."

M. Floçon was soon installed in a room actually communicating with the waiting-room, and as a preliminary of the first importance, taking precedence even of the examination of the sleeping-car, he ordered the porter to be brought in to answer certain questions.

The man, Ludwig Groote, as he presently gave his name, thirty-two years of age, born at Amsterdam, looked such a sluggish, slouching, blear-eyed creature that M. Floçon began by a sharp rebuke.

"Now. Sharp! Are you always like this?" cried the Chief. The porter still stared straight before him with lack-lustre eyes, and made no immediate reply.

"Are you drunk? are you—Can it be possible?" he said, and in vague reply to a sudden strong suspicion, he went on: "What were you doing between Laroche and Paris? Sleeping?"

The man roused himself a little. "I think I slept. I must have slept. I was very drowsy. I had been up two nights; but so it is always, and I am not like this generally. I do not understand."

"Hah!" The Chief thought he understood. "Did you feel this drowsiness before leaving Laroche?"

"No, monsieur, I did not. Certainly not. I was fresh till then—quite fresh."

"Hum; exactly; I see;" and the little Chief jumped to his feet and ran round to where the porter stood sheepishly, and sniffed and smelt at him.

"Yes, yes." Sniff, sniff, sniff, the little man danced round and round him, then took hold of the porter's head with one hand, and with the other turned down his lower eyelid so as to expose the eyeball, sniffed a little more, and then resumed his seat.

"Exactly. And now, where is your train card?"

"Pardon, monsieur, I cannot find it."

"That is absurd. Where do you keep it? Look again—search—I must have it."

The porter shook his head hopelessly.

"It is gone, monsieur, and my pocket-book."

"But your papers, the tickets—"

"Everything was in it, monsieur. I must have dropped it."

Strange, very strange. However—the fact was to be recorded, for the moment. He could of course return to it.

"You can give me the names of the passengers?"

"No, monsieur. Not exactly. I cannot remember, not enough to distinguish between them."

"Fichtre! But this is most devilishly irritating. To think that I have to do with a man so stupid—such an idiot, such an ass!"

"At least you know how the berths were occupied, how many in each, and which persons? Yes? You can tell me that? Well, go on. By and by we will have the passengers in, and you can fix their places, after I have ascertained their names. Now, please! For how many was the car?"

"Sixteen. There were two compartments of four berths each, and four of two berths each."

"Stay, let us make a plan. I will draw it. Here, now, is that right?" and the Chief held up the rough diagram.

"Here we have the six compartments. Now take a, with berths 1, 2, 3, and 4. Were they all occupied?"

"No; only two, by Englishmen. I know that they talked English, which I understand a little. One was a soldier; the other, I think, a clergyman, or priest."

"Good! we can verify that directly. Now, b, with berths 5 and 6. Who was there?"

"One gentleman. I don't remember his name. But I shall know him by appearance."

"Go on. In c, two berths, 7 and 8?"

"Also one gentleman. It was he who—I mean, that is where the crime occurred."

"Ah, indeed, in 7 and 8? Very well. And the next, 9 and 10?"

"A lady. Our only lady. She came from Rome."

"One moment. Where did the rest come from? Did any embark on the road?"

"No, monsieur; all the passengers travelled through from Rome."

"The dead man included? Was he Roman?"

"That I cannot say, but he came on board at Rome."

"Very well. This lady—she was alone?"

"In the compartment, yes. But not altogether."

"I do not understand!"

"She had her servant with her."

"In the car?"

"No, not in the car. As a passenger by second class. But she came to her mistress sometimes, in the car."

"For her service, I presume?"

"Well, yes, monsieur, when I would permit it. But she came a little too often, and I was compelled to protest, to speak to Madame la Comtesse—"

"She was a countess, then?"

"The maid addressed her by that title. That is all I know. I heard her."

"When did you see the lady's maid last?"

"Last night. I think at Amberieux. about 8 p.m."

"Not this morning?"

"No, sir, I am quite sure of that."

"Not at Laroche? She did not come on board to stay, for the last stage, when her mistress would be getting up, dressing, and likely to require her?"

"No; I should not have permitted it."

"And where is the maid now, d'you suppose?"

The porter looked at him with an air of complete imbecility.

"She is surely somewhere near, in or about the station. She would hardly desert her mistress now," he said, stupidly, at last.

"At any rate we can soon settle that." The Chief turned to one of his assistants, both of whom had been standing behind him all the time, and said:

"Step out, Galipaud, and see. No, wait. I am nearly as stupid as this simpleton. Describe this maid."

"Tall and slight, dark-eyed, very black hair. Dressed all in black, plain black bonnet. I cannot remember more."

"Find her, Galipaud—keep your eye on her. We may want her—why, I cannot say, as she seems disconnected with the event, but still she ought to be at hand." Then, turning to the porter, he went on. "Finish, please. You said 9 and 10 was the lady's. Well, 11 and 12?"

"It was vacant all through the run."

"And the last compartment, for four?"

"There were two berths, occupied both by Frenchmen, at least so I judged them. They talked French to each other and to me."

"Then now we have them all. Stand aside, please, and I will make the passengers come in. We will then determine their places and affix their names from their own admissions. Call them in, Block, one by one."

CHAPTER III

The questions put by M. Floçon were much the same in every case, and were limited in this early stage of the inquiry to the one point of identity.

The first who entered was a Frenchman. He was a jovial, fat-faced, portly man, who answered to the name of Anatole Lafolay, and who described himself as a traveller in precious stones. The berth he had occupied was No. 13 in compartment f. His companion in the berth was a younger man, smaller, slighter, but of much the same stamp. His name was Jules Devaux, and he was a commission agent. His berth had been No. 15 in the same compartment, f. Both these Frenchmen gave their addresses with the names of many people to whom they were well known, and established at once a reputation for respectability which was greatly in their favour.

The third to appear was the tall, gray-headed Englishman, who had taken a certain lead at the first discovery of the crime. He called himself General Sir Charles Collingham, an officer of her Majesty's army; and the clergyman who shared the compartment was his brother, the Reverend Silas Collingham, rector of Theakstone-Lammas, in the county of Norfolk. Their berths were numbered 1 and 4 in a.

Before the English General was dismissed, he asked whether he was likely to be detained.

"For the present, yes," replied M. Floçon, briefly. He did not care to be asked questions. That, under the circumstances, was his business.

"Because I should like to communicate with the British Embassy."

"You are known there?" asked the detective, not choosing to believe the story at first. It might be a ruse of some sort.

"I know Lord Dufferin personally; I was with him in India. Also Colonel Papillon, the military attaché; we were in the same regiment. If I sent to the Embassy, the latter would, no doubt, come himself."

"How do you propose to send?"

"That is for you to decide. All I wish is that it should be known that my brother and I are detained under suspicion, and incriminated."

"Hardly that, Monsieur le General. But it shall be as you wish. We will telephone from here to the post nearest the Embassy to inform his Excellency–"

"Certainly, Lord Dufferin, and my friend, Colonel Papillon."

"Of what has occurred. And now, if you will permit me to proceed?"

So the single occupant of the compartment b, that adjoining the Englishmen, was called in. He was an Italian, by name Natale Ripaldi; a dark-skinned man, with very black hair and a bristling black moustache. He wore a long dark cloak of the Inverness order, and, with the slouch hat he carried in his hand, and his downcast, secretive look, he had the rather conventional aspect of a conspirator.

"If monsieur permits," he volunteered to say after the formal questioning was over, "I can throw some light on this catastrophe."

"And how so, pray? Did you assist? Were you present? If so, why wait to speak till now?" said the detective, receiving the advance rather coldly. It behooved him to be very much on his guard.

"I have had no opportunity till now of addressing any one in authority. You are in authority, I presume?"

"I am the Chief of the Detective Service."

"Then, monsieur, remember, please, that I can give some useful information when called upon. Now, indeed, if you will receive it."

M. Floçon was so anxious to approach the inquiry without prejudice that he put up his hand.

"We will wait, if you please. When M. le Juge arrives, then, perhaps; at any rate, at a later stage. That will do now, thank you."

The Italian's lip curled with a slight indication of contempt at the French detective's methods, but he bowed without speaking, and went out.

Last of all the lady appeared, in a long sealskin travelling cloak, and closely veiled. She answered M. Floçon's questions in a low, tremulous voice, as though greatly perturbed.

She was the Contessa di Castagneto, she said, an Englishwoman by birth; but her husband had been an Italian, as the name implied, and they resided in Rome. He was dead–she had been a widow for two or three years, and was on her way now to London.

"That will do, madame, thank you," said the detective, politely, "for the present at least."

"Why, are we likely to be detained? I trust not." Her voice became appealing, almost piteous. Her hands, restlessly moving, showed how much she was distressed.

"Indeed, Madame la Comtesse, it must be so. I regret it infinitely; but until we have gone further into this, have elicited some facts, arrived at some conclusions–But there, madame, I need not, must not say more."

"Oh, monsieur, I was so anxious to continue my journey. Friends are awaiting me in London. I do hope–I most earnestly beg and entreat you to spare me. I am not very strong; my health is indifferent. Do, sir, be so good as to release me from–"

As she spoke, she raised her veil, and showed what no woman wishes to hide, least of all when seeking the good-will of one of the opposite sex. She had a handsome face–strikingly so. Not even the long journey, the fatigue, the worries and anxieties which had supervened, could rob her of her marvellous beauty.

She was a brilliant brunette, dark-skinned; but her complexion was of a clear, pale olive, and as soft, as lustrous as pure ivory. Her great eyes, of a deep velvety brown, were saddened by near tears. She had rich red lips, the only colour in her face, and these, habitually slightly apart, showed pearly-white glistening teeth.

It was difficult to look at this charming woman without being affected by her beauty. M. Floçon was a Frenchman, gallant and impressionable; yet he steeled his heart. A detective must beware of sentiment, and he seemed to see something insidious in this appeal, which he resented.

"Madame, it is useless," he answered gruffly. "I do not make the law; I have only to support it. Every good citizen is bound to that."

"I trust I am a good citizen," said the Countess, with a wan smile, but very wearily. "Still, I should wish to be let off now. I have suffered greatly, terribly, by this horrible catastrophe. My nerves are quite shattered. It is too cruel. However, I can say no more, except to ask that you will let my maid come to me."

M. Floçon, still obdurate, would not even consent to that.

"I fear, madame, that for the present at least you cannot be allowed to communicate with any one, not even with your maid."

"But she is not implicated; she was not in the car. I have not seen her since–"

"Since?" repeated M. Floçon, after a pause.

"Since last night, at Amberieux, about eight o'clock. She helped me to undress, and saw me to bed. I sent her away then, and said I should not need her till we reached Paris. But I want her now, indeed I do."

"She did not come to you at Laroche?"

"No. Have I not said so? The porter,"–here she pointed to the man, who stood staring at her from the other side of the table,– "he made difficulties about her being in the car, saying that she came too often, stayed too long, that I must pay for her berth, and so on. I did not see why I should do that; so she stayed away."

"Except from time to time?"

"Precisely."

"And the last time was at Amberieux?"

"As I have told you, and he will tell you the same."

"Thank you, madame, that will do." The Chief rose from his chair, plainly intimating that the interview was at an end.

CHAPTER IV

He had other work to do, and was eager to get at it. So he left Block to show the Countess back to the waiting-room, and, motioning to the porter that he might also go, the Chief hastened to the sleeping-car, the examination of which, too long delayed, claimed his urgent attention.

It is the first duty of a good detective to visit the actual theatre of a crime and overhaul it inch by inch,—seeking, searching, investigating, looking for any, even the most insignificant, traces of the murderer's hands.

The sleeping-car, as I have said, had been side-tracked, its doors were sealed, and it was under strict watch and ward. But everything, of course, gave way before the detective, and, breaking through the seals, he walked in, making straight for the little room or compartment where the body of the victim still lay untended and absolutely untouched.

It was a ghastly sight, although not new in M. Floçon's experience. There lay the corpse in the narrow berth, just as it had been stricken. It was partially undressed, wearing only shirt and drawers. The former lay open at the chest, and showed the gaping wound that had, no doubt, caused death, probably instantaneous death. But other blows had been struck; there must have been a struggle, fierce and embittered, as for dear life. The savage truculence of the murderer had triumphed, but not until he had battered in the face, destroying features and rendering recognition almost impossible.

A knife had given the mortal wound; that was at once apparent from the shape of the wound. It was the knife, too, which had gashed and stabbed the face, almost wantonly; for some of these wounds had not bled, and the plain inference was that they had been inflicted after life had sped. M. Floçon examined the body closely, but without disturbing it. The police medical officer would wish to see it as it was found. The exact position, as well as the nature of the wounds, might afford evidence as to the manner of death.

But the Chief looked long, and with absorbed, concentrated interest, at the murdered man, noting all he actually saw, and conjecturing a good deal more.

The features of the mutilated face were all but unrecognizable, but the hair, which was abundant, was long, black, and inclined to curl; the black moustache was thick and drooping. The shirt was of fine linen, the drawers silk. On one finger were two good rings, the hands were clean, the nails well kept, and there was every evidence that the man did not live by manual labour. He was of the easy, cultured class, as distinct from the workman or operative.

This conclusion was borne out by his light baggage, which still lay about the berth,–hat-box, rugs, umbrella, brown morocco hand-bag. All were the property of someone well to do, or at least possessed of decent belongings. One or two pieces bore a monogram, "F.Q.," the same as on the shirt and under-linen; but on the bag was a luggage label, with the name, "Francis Quadling, passenger to Paris," in full. Its owner had apparently no reason to conceal his name. More strangely, those who had done him to death had been at no pains to remove all traces of his identity.

M. Floçon opened the hand-bag, seeking for further evidence; but found nothing of importance,–only loose collars, cuffs, a sponge and slippers, two Italian newspapers of an earlier date. No money, valuables, or papers. All these had been removed probably, and presumably, by the perpetrator of the crime.

Having settled the first preliminary but essential points, he next surveyed the whole compartment critically. Now, for the first time, he was struck with the fact that the window was open to its full height.

Since when was this? It was a question to be put presently to the porter and any others who had entered the car, but the discovery drew him to examine the window more closely, and with good results.

At the ledge, caught on a projecting point on the far side, partly in, partly out of the car, was a morsel of white lace, a scrap of feminine apparel; although what part, or how it had come there, was not at once obvious to M. Floçon. A long and minute inspection of this bit of lace, which he was careful not to detach as yet from the place in which he found it, showed that it was ragged, and frayed, and fast caught where it hung. It could not have been blown there by any chance air; it must have been torn from the article to which it belonged, whatever that might be,–head-dress, nightcap, night-dress, or handkerchief. The lace was of a kind to serve any of these purposes.

Inspecting further, M. Floçon made a second discovery. On the small table under the window was a short length of black jet beading, part of the trimming or ornamentation of a lady's dress.

These two objects of feminine origin–one partly outside the car, the other near it, but quite inside–gave rise to many conjectures. It led, however, to the inevitable conclusion that a woman had been at some time or other in the berth. M. Floçon could not but connect these two finds with the fact of the open window. The latter might, of course, have been the work of the murdered man himself at an earlier hour. Yet it is unusual, as the detective imagined, for a passenger, and especially an Italian, to lie under an open window in a sleeping-berth when travelling by express train before daylight in March.

Who opened that window, then, and why? Perhaps some further facts might be found on the outside of the car. With this idea, M. Floçon left it, and passed on to the line or permanent way.

Here he found himself a good deal below the level of the car. These sleepers have no foot-boards like ordinary carriages; access to them is gained from a platform by the steps at each end. The Chief was short of stature, and he could only approach the window outside by calling one of the guards and ordering him to make the small ladder (faire la petite echelle). This meant stooping and giving a back, on which little M. Floçon climbed nimbly, and so was raised to the necessary height.

A close scrutiny revealed nothing unusual. The exterior of the car was encrusted with the mud and dust gathered in the journey, none of which appeared to have been disturbed.

M. Floçon reentered the carriage neither disappointed nor pleased; his mind was in an open state, ready to receive any impressions, and as yet only one that was at all clear and distinct was borne in on him.

This was the presence of the lace and the jet beads in the theatre of the crime. The inference was fair and simple. He came logically and surely to this:

1. That some woman had entered the compartment.

2. That whether or not she had come in before the crime, she was there after the window had been opened, which was not done by the murdered man.

3. That she had leaned out, or partly passed out, of the window at some time or other, as the scrap of lace testified.

4. Why had she leaned out? To seek some means of exit or escape, of course.

But escape from whom? From what? The murderer? Then she must know him, and unless an accomplice (if so, why run from him?), she would give up her knowledge on compulsion, if not voluntarily, as seemed doubtful, seeing she (his suspicions were consolidating) had not done so already.

But there might be another even stronger reason to attempt escape at such imminent risk as leaving an express train at full speed. To escape from her own act and the consequences it must entail—escape from horror first, from detection next, and then from arrest and punishment.

All this would imperiously impel even a weak woman to face the worst peril, to look out, lean out, even try the terrible but impossible feat of climbing out of the car.

So M. Floçon, by fair process of reasoning, reached a point which incriminated one woman, the only woman possible, and that was the titled, high-bred lady who called herself the Contessa di Castagneto.

This conclusion gave a definite direction to further search. Consulting the rough plan which he had constructed to take the place of the missing train card, he entered the compartment which the Countess had occupied, and which was actually next door.

It was in the tumbled, untidy condition of a sleeping-place but just vacated. The sex and quality of its recent occupant were plainly apparent in the goods and chattels lying about, the property and possessions of a delicate, well-bred woman of the world, things still left as she had used them last—rugs still unrolled, a pair of easy-slippers on the floor, the sponge in its waterproof bag on the bed, brushes, bottles, button-hook, hand-glass, many things belonging to the dressing-bag, not yet returned to that receptacle. The maid was no doubt to have attended to all these, but as she had not come, they remained unpacked and strewn about in some disorder.

M. Floçon pounced down upon the contents of the berth, and commenced an immediate search for a lace scarf, or any wrap or cover with lace.

He found nothing, and was hardly disappointed. It told more against the Countess, who, if innocent, would have no reason to conceal or make away with a possibly incriminating possession, the need for which she could not of course understand.

Next, he handled the dressing-bag, and with deft fingers replaced everything.

Everything was forthcoming but one glass bottle, a small one, the absence of which he noted, but thought of little consequence, till, by and by, he came upon it under peculiar circumstances.

Before leaving the car, and after walking through the other compartments, M. Floçon made an especially strict search of the corner where the porter had his own small chair, his only resting-place, indeed, throughout the journey. He had not forgotten the attendant's condition when first examined, and he had even then been nearly satisfied that the man had been hocussed, narcotized, drugged.

Any doubts were entirely removed by his picking up near the porter's seat a small silver-topped bottle and a handkerchief, both marked with coronet and monogram, the last of which, although the letters were much interlaced and involved, were decipherable as S.L.L.C.

It was that of the Countess, and corresponded with the marks on her other belongings. He put it to his nostril, and recognized at once by its smell that it had contained tincture of laudanum, or some preparation of that drug.

M. Floçon was an experienced detective, and he knew so well that he ought to be on his guard against the most plausible suggestions, that he did not like to make too much of these discoveries. Still, he was distinctly satisfied, if not exactly exultant, and he went back towards the station with a strong predisposition against the Contessa di Castagneto.

Just outside the waiting-room, however, his assistant, Galipaud, met him with news which rather dashed his hopes, and gave a new direction to his thoughts.

The lady's maid was not to be found.

"Impossible!" cried the Chief, and then at once suspicion followed surprise.

"I have looked, monsieur, inquired everywhere; the maid has not been seen. She certainly is not here."

"Did she go through the barrier with the other passengers?"

"No one knows; no one remembers her; not even the conductor. But she has gone. That is positive."

"Yet it was her duty to be here; to attend to her service. Her mistress would certainly want her—has asked for her! Why should she run away?"

This question presented itself as one of infinite importance, to be pondered over seriously before he went further into the inquiry.

Did the Countess know of this disappearance?

She had asked imploringly for her maid. True, but might that not be a blind? Women are born actresses, and at need can assume any part, convey any impression. Might not the Countess have wished to be dissociated from the maid, and therefore have affected complete ignorance of her flight?

"I will try her further," said M. Floçon to himself.

But then, supposing that the maid had taken herself off of her own accord? Why was it? Why had she done so? Because—because she was afraid of something. If so, of what? No direct accusation could be brought against her on the face of it. She had not been in the sleeping-car at the time of the murder, while the Countess as certainly was; and, according to strong presumption, in the very compartment where the deed was done. If the maid was afraid, why was she afraid?

Only on one possible hypothesis. That she was either in collusion with the Countess, or possessed of some guilty knowledge tending to incriminate the Countess and probably herself. She had run away to avoid any inconvenient questioning tending to get her mistress into trouble, which would react probably on herself.

"We must press the Countess on this point closely; I will put it plainly to M. le Juge," said the detective, as he entered the private room set apart for the police authorities, where he found M. Beaumont le Hardi, the instructing judge, and the Commissary of the Quartier (arrondissement).

A lengthy conference followed among the officials. M. Floçon told all he knew, all he had discovered, gave his views with all the force and fluency of a public prosecutor, and was congratulated warmly on the progress he had made.

"I agree with you, sir," said the instructing judge: "we must have in the Countess first, and pursue the line indicated as regards the missing maid."

"I will fetch her, then. Stay, what can be going on in there?" cried M. Floçon, rising from his seat and running into the outer waiting-room, which, to his surprise and indignation, he found in great confusion.

The guard who was on duty was struggling, in personal conflict almost, with the English General. There was a great hubbub of voices, and the Countess was lying back half-fainting in her chair.

"What's all this? How dare you, sir?"

This to the General, who now had the man by the throat with one hand and with the other was preventing him from drawing his sword. "Desist–forbear! You are opposing legal authority; desist, or I will call in assistance and will have you secured and removed."

The little Chief's blood was up; he spoke warmly, with all the force and dignity of an official who sees the law outraged.

"It is entirely the fault of this ruffian of yours; he has behaved most brutally," replied Sir Charles, still holding him tight.

"Let him go, monsieur; your behaviour is inexcusable. What! you, a military officer of the highest rank, to assault a sentinel! For shame! This is unworthy of you!"

"He deserves to be scragged, the beast!" went on the General, as with one sharp turn of the wrist he threw the guard off, and sent him flying nearly across the room, where, being free at last, the Frenchman drew his sword and brandished it threateningly—from a distance.

But M. Floçon interposed with uplifted hand and insisted upon an explanation.

"It is just this," replied Sir Charles, speaking fast and with much fierceness: "that lady there—poor thing, she is ill, you can see that for yourself, suffering, overwrought; she asked for a glass of water, and this brute, triple brute, as you say in French, refused to bring it."

"I could not leave the room," protested the guard. "My orders were precise."

"So I was going to fetch the water," went on the General angrily, eying the guard as though he would like to make another grab at him, "and this fellow interfered."

"Very properly," added M. Floçon.

"Then why didn't he go himself, or call someone? Upon my word, monsieur, you are not to be complimented upon your people, nor your methods. I used to think that a Frenchman was gallant, courteous, especially to ladies."

The Chief looked a little disconcerted, but remembering what he knew against this particular lady, he stiffened and said severely, "I am responsible for my conduct to my superiors, and not to you. Besides, you appear to forget your position. You are here, detained—all of you"—he spoke to the whole room—"under suspicion. A ghastly crime has been perpetrated—by someone among you—"

"Do not be too sure of that," interposed the irrepressible General.

"Who else could be concerned? The train never stopped after leaving Laroche," said the detective, allowing himself to be betrayed into argument.

"Yes, it did," corrected Sir Charles, with a contemptuous laugh; "shows how much you know."

Again the Chief looked unhappy. He was on dangerous ground, face to face with a new fact affecting all his theories,—if fact it was, not mere assertion, and that he must speedily verify. But nothing was to be gained—much, indeed, might be lost—by prolonging this discussion in the presence of the whole party. It was entirely opposed to the French practice of investigation, which works secretly, taking witnesses separately, one by one, and strictly preventing all intercommunication or collusion among them.

"What I know or do not know is my affair," he said, with an indifference he did not feel. "I shall call upon you, M. le Général, for your statement in due course, and that of the others." He bowed stiffly to the whole room. "Everyone must be interrogated. M. le Juge is now here, and he proposes to begin, madame, with you."

The Countess gave a little start, shivered, and turned very pale.

"Can't you see she is not equal to it?" cried the General, hotly. "She has not yet recovered. In the name of—I do not say chivalry, for that would be useless—but of common humanity, spare madame, at least for the present."

"That is impossible, quite impossible. There are reasons why Madame la Comtesse should be examined first. I trust, therefore, she will make an effort."

"I will try, if you wish it." She rose from her chair and walked a few steps rather feebly, then stopped.

"No, no, Countess, do not go," said Sir Charles, hastily, in English, as he moved across to where she stood and gave her his hand. "This is sheer cruelty, sir, and cannot be permitted."

"Stand aside!" shouted M. Floçon; "I forbid you to approach that lady, to address her, or communicate with her. Guard, advance, do your duty."

But the guard, although his sword was still out of its sheath, showed great reluctance to move. He had no desire to try conclusions again with this very masterful person, who was, moreover, a general; as he had seen service, he had a deep respect for generals, even of foreign growth.

Meanwhile the General held his ground and continued his conversation with the Countess, speaking still in English, thus exasperating M. Floçon, who did not understand the language, almost to madness.

"This is not to be borne!" he cried. "Here, Galipaud, Block;" and when his two trusty assistants came rushing in, he pointed furiously to the General. "Seize him, remove him by force if necessary. He shall go to the violon–to the nearest lock-up."

The noise attracted also the Judge and the Commissary, and there were now six officials in all, including the guard, all surrounding the General, a sufficiently imposing force to overawe even the most recalcitrant fire-eater.

But now the General seemed to see only the comic side of the situation, and he burst out laughing.

"What, all of you? How many more? Why not bring up cavalry and artillery, horse, foot, and guns?" he asked, derisively. "All to prevent one old man from offering his services to one weak woman! Gentlemen, my regards!"

"Really, Charles, I fear you are going too far," said his brother the clergyman, who, however, had been manifestly enjoying the whole scene.

"Indeed, yes. It is not necessary, I assure you," added the Countess, with tears of gratitude in her big brown eyes. "I am most touched, most thankful. You are a true soldier, a true English gentleman, and I shall never forget your kindness." Then she put her hand in his with a pretty, winning gesture that was reward enough for any man.

Meanwhile, the Judge, the senior official present, had learned exactly what had happened, and he now addressed the General with a calm but stern rebuke.

"Monsieur will not, I trust, oblige us to put in force the full power of the law. I might, if I chose, and as I am fully entitled, commit you at once to Mazas, to keep you in solitary confinement. Your conduct has been deplorable, well calculated to traverse and impede justice. But I am willing to believe that you were led away, not unnaturally, as a gallant gentleman,–it is the characteristic of your nation, of your cloth,–and that on more mature consideration you will acknowledge and not repeat your error."

M. Beaumont le Hardi was a grave, florid, soft-voiced person, with a bald head and a comfortably-lined white waistcoat; one who sought his ends by persuasion, not force, but who had the instincts of a gentleman, and little sympathy with the peremptory methods of his more inflammable colleague.

"Oh, with all my heart, monsieur," said Sir Charles, cordially. "You saw, or at least know, how this has occurred. I did not begin it, nor was I the most to blame. But I was in the wrong, I admit. What do you wish me to do now?"

"Give me your promise to abide by our rules,–they may be irksome, but we think them necessary,–and hold no further converse with your companions."

"Certainly, certainly, monsieur,–at least after I have said one word more to Madame la Comtesse."

"No, no, I cannot permit even that–"

But Sir Charles, in spite of the warning finger held up by the Judge, insisted upon crying out to her, as she was being led into the other room:

"Courage, dear lady, courage. Don't let them bully you. You have nothing to fear."

Any further defiance of authority was now prevented by her almost forcible removal from the room.

CHAPTER VI

The stormy episode just ended had rather a disturbing effect on M. Floçon, who could scarcely give his full attention to all the points, old and new, that had now arisen in the investigation. But he would have time to go over them at his leisure, while the work of interrogation was undertaken by the Judge.

The latter had taken his seat at a small table, and just opposite was his greffier, or clerk, who was to write down question and answer, verbatim. A little to one side, with the light full on the face, the witness was seated, bearing the scrutiny of three pairs of eyes—the Judge first, and behind him, those of the Chief Detective and the Commissary of Police.

"I trust, madame, that you are equal to answering a few questions?" began M. le Hardi, blandly.

"Oh, yes, I hope so. Indeed, I have no choice," replied the Countess, bravely resigned.

"They will refer principally to your maid."

"Ah!" said the Countess, quickly and in a troubled voice, yet she bore the gaze of the three officials without flinching.

"I want to know a little more about her, if you please."

"Of course. Anything I know I will tell you." She spoke now with perfect self-possession. "But if I might ask—why this interest?"

"I will tell you frankly. You asked for her, we sent for her, and—"

"Yes?"

"She cannot be found. She is not in the station."

The Countess all but jumped from her chair in her surprise—surprise that seemed too spontaneous to be feigned.

"Impossible! it cannot be. She would not dare to leave me here like this, all alone."

"Parbleu! she has dared. Most certainly she is not here."

"But what can have become of her?"

"Ah, madame, what indeed? Can you form any idea? We hoped you might have been able to enlighten us."

"I cannot, monsieur, not in the least."

"Perchance you sent her on to your hotel to warn your friends that you were detained? To fetch them, perhaps, to you in your trouble?"

The trap was neatly contrived, but she was not deceived.

"How could I? I knew of no trouble when I saw her last."

"Oh, indeed? And when was that?"

"Last night, at Amberieux, as I have already told that gentleman." She pointed to M. Floçon, who was obliged to nod his head.

"Well, she has gone away somewhere. It does not much matter, still it is odd, and for your sake we should like to help you to find her, if you do wish to find her?"

Another little trap which failed.

"Indeed I hardly think she is worth keeping after this barefaced desertion."

"No, indeed. And she must be held to strict account for it, must justify it, give her reasons. So we must find her for you—"

"I am not at all anxious, really," the Countess said, quickly, and the remark told against her.

"Well, now, Madame la Comtesse, as to her description. Will you tell us what was her height, figure, colour of eyes, hair, general appearance?"

"She was tall, above the middle height, at least; slight, good figure, black hair and eyes."

"Pretty?"

"That depends upon what you mean by 'pretty.' Some people might think so, in her own class."

"How was she dressed?"

"In plain dark serge, bonnet of black straw and brown ribbons. I do not allow my maid to wear colours."

"Exactly. And her name, age, place of birth?"

"Hortense Petitpré, thirty-two, born, I believe, in Paris."

The Judge, when these particulars had been given, looked over his shoulder towards the detective, but said nothing. It was quite unnecessary, for M. Floçon, who had been writing in his note-book, now rose and left the room. He called Galipaud to him, saying sharply:

"Here is the more detailed description of the lady's maid, and in writing. Have it copied and circulate it at once. Give it to the station-master, and to the agents of police round about here. I have an idea–only an idea–that this woman has not gone far. It may be worth nothing, still there is the chance. People who are wanted often hang about the very place they would not stay in if they were wise. Anyhow, set a watch for her and come back here."

Meanwhile, the Judge had continued his questioning.

"And where, madame, did you obtain your maid?"

"In Rome. She was there, out of a place. I heard of her at an agency and registry office, when I was looking for a maid a month or two ago."

"Then she has not been long in your service?"

"No; as I tell you, she came to me in December last."

"Well recommended?"

"Strongly. She had lived with good families, French and English."

"And with you, what was her character?"

"Irreproachable."

"Well, so much for Hortense Petitpré. She is not far off, I dare say. When we want her we shall be able to lay hands on her, I do not doubt, madame may rest assured."

"Pray take no trouble in the matter. I certainly should not keep her."

"Very well, very well. And now, another small matter. I see," he referred to the rough plan of the sleeping-car prepared by M. Floçon,–"I see that you occupied the compartment d, with berths Nos. 9 and 10?"

"I think 9 was the number of my berth."

"It was. You may be certain of that. Now next door to your compartment–do you know who was next door? I mean in 7 and 8?"

The Countess's lip quivered, and she was a prey to sudden emotion as she answered in a low voice:

"It was where–where–"

"There, there, madame," said the Judge, reassuring her as he would a little child. "You need not say. It is no doubt very distressing to you. Yet, you know?"

She bent her head slowly, but uttered no word.

"Now this man, this poor man, had you noticed him at all? No–no–not afterwards, of course. It would not be likely. But during the journey. Did you speak to him, or he to you?"

"No, no–distinctly no."

"Nor see him?"

"Yes, I saw him, I believe, at Modane with the rest when we dined."

"Ah! exactly so. He dined at Modane. Was that the only occasion on which you saw him? You had never met him previously in Rome, where you resided?"

"Whom do you mean? The murdered man?"

"Who else?"

"No, not that I am aware of. At least I did not recognize him as a friend."

"I presume, if he was among your friends–"

"Pardon me, that he certainly was not," interrupted the Countess.

"Well, among your acquaintances–he would probably have made himself known to you?"

"I suppose so."

"And he did not do so? He never spoke to you, nor you to him?"

"I never saw him, the occupant of that compartment, except on that one occasion. I kept a good deal in my compartment during the journey."

"Alone? It must have been very dull for you," said the Judge, pleasantly.

"I was not always alone," said the Countess, hesitatingly, and with a slight flush. "I had friends in the car."

"Oh–oh"–the exclamation was long-drawn and rather significant.

"Who were they? You may as well tell us, madame, we should certainly find out."

"I have no wish to withhold the information," she replied, now turning pale, possibly at the imputation conveyed. "Why should I?"

"And these friends were–?"

"Sir Charles Collingham and his brother. They came and sat with me occasionally; sometimes one, sometimes the other."

"During the day?"

"Of course, during the day." Her eyes flashed, as though the question was another offence.

"Have you known them long?"

"The General I met in Roman society last winter. It was he who introduced his brother."

"Very good, so far. The General knew you, took an interest in you. That explains his strange, unjustifiable conduct just now—"

"I do not think it was either strange or unjustifiable," interrupted the Countess, hotly. "He is a gentleman."

"Quite a preux cavalier, of course. But we will pass on. You are not a good sleeper, I believe, madame?"

"Indeed no, I sleep badly, as a rule."

"Then you would be easily disturbed. Now, last night, did you hear anything strange in the car, more particularly in the adjoining compartment?"

"Nothing."

"No sound of voices raised high, no noise of a conflict, a struggle?"

"No, monsieur."

"That is odd. I cannot understand it. We know, beyond all question, from the appearance of the body,—the corpse,—that there was a fight, an encounter. Yet you, a wretched sleeper, with only a thin plank of wood between you and the affray, hear nothing, absolutely nothing. It is most extraordinary."

"I was asleep. I must have been asleep."

"A light sleeper would certainly be awakened. How can you explain—how can you reconcile that?" The question was blandly put, but the Judge's incredulity verged upon actual insolence.

"Easily: I had taken a soporific. I always do, on a journey. I am obliged to keep something, sulphonal or chloral, by me, on purpose."

"Then this, madame, is yours?" And the Judge, with an air of undisguised triumph, produced the small glass vial which M. Floçon had picked up in the sleeping-car near the conductor's seat.

The Countess, with a quick gesture, put out her hand to take it.

"No, I cannot give it up. Look as near as you like, and say is it yours?"

"Of course it is mine. Where did you get it? Not in my berth?"

"No, madame, not in your berth."

"But where?"

"Pardon me, we shall not tell you—not just now."

"I missed it last night," went on the Countess, slightly confused.

"After you had taken your dose of chloral?"

"No, before."

"And why did you want this? It is laudanum."

"For my nerves. I have a toothache. I—I—really, sir, I need not tell you all my ailments."

"And the maid had removed it?"

"So I presume; she must have taken it out of the bag in the first instance."

"And then kept it?"

"That is what I can only suppose."

"Ah!"

When the Judge had brought down the interrogation of the Countess to the production of the small glass bottle, he paused, and with a long-drawn "Ah!" of satisfaction, looked round at his colleagues.

Both M. Floçon and the Commissary nodded their heads approvingly, plainly sharing his triumph.

Then they all put their heads together in close, whispered conference.

"Admirable, M. le Juge!" said the detective. "You have been most adroit. It is a clear case."

"No doubt," said the Commissary, who was a blunt, rather coarse person, believing that to take anybody and everybody into custody is always the safest and simplest course. "It looks black against her. I think she ought to be arrested at once."

"We might, indeed we ought to have more evidence, more definite evidence, perhaps?" The Judge was musing over the facts as he knew them. "I should like, before going further, to look at the car," he said, suddenly coming to a conclusion.

M. Floçon readily agreed. "We will go together," he said, adding, "Madame will remain here, please, until we return. It may not be for long."

"And afterwards?" asked the Countess, whose nervousness had if anything increased during the whispered colloquy of the officials.

"Ah, afterwards! Who knows?" was the reply, with a shrug of the shoulders, all most enigmatic and unsatisfactory.

"What have we against her?" said the Judge, as soon as they had gained the absolute privacy of the sleeping-car.

"The bottle of laudanum and the porter's condition. He was undoubtedly drugged," answered the detective; and the discussion which followed took the form of a dialogue between them, for the Commissary took no part in it.

"Yes; but why by the Countess? How do we know that positively?"

"It is her bottle," said M. Floçon.

"Her story may be true—that she missed it, that the maid took it."

"We have nothing whatever against the maid. We know nothing about her."

"No. Except that she has disappeared. But that tells more against her mistress. It is all very vague. I do not see my way quite, as yet."

"But the fragment of lace, the broken beading? Surely, M. le Juge, they are a woman's, and only one woman was in the car—"

"So far as we know."

"But if these could be proved to be hers?"

"Ah! if you could prove that!"

"Easy enough. Have her searched, here at once, in the station. There is a female searcher attached to the detention-room."

"It is a strong measure. She is a lady."

"Ladies who commit crimes must not expect to be handled with kid gloves."

"She is an Englishwoman, or with English connections; titled, too. I hesitate, upon my word. Suppose we are wrong? It may lead to unpleasantness. M. le Prefet is anxious to avoid complications possibly international."

As he spoke, he bent over, and, taking a magnifier from his pocket, examined the lace, which still fluttered where it was caught.

"It is fine lace, I think. What say you, M. Floçon? You may be more experienced in such matters."

"The finest, or nearly so; I believe it is Valenciennes—the trimming of some underclothing, I should think. That surely is sufficient, M. le Juge?"

M. Beaumont le Hardi gave a reluctant consent, and the Chief went back himself to see that the searching was undertaken without loss of time.

The Countess protested, but vainly, against this new indignity. What could she do? A prisoner, practically friendless,— for the General was not within reach,—to resist was out of the question. Indeed, she was plainly told that force would be employed unless she submitted with a good grace. There was nothing for it but to obey.

Mother Tontaine, as the female searcher called herself, was an evil-visaged, corpulent old creature, with a sickly, soft, insinuating voice, and a greasy, familiar manner that was most offensive. They had given her the scrap of torn lace and the débris of the jet as a guide, with very particular directions to see if they corresponded with any part of the lady's apparel.

She soon showed her quality.

"Aha! oho! What is this, my pretty princess? How comes so great a lady into the hands of Mother Tontaine? But I will not harm you, my beauty, my pretty, my little one. Oh, no, no, I will not trouble you, dearie. No, trust to me;" and she held out one skinny claw, and looked the other way. The Countess did not or would not understand. "Madame has money?" went on the old hag in a half-threatening, half-coaxing whisper, as she came up quite close, and fastened on her victim like a bird of prey.

"If you mean that I am to bribe you—"

"Fie, the nasty word! But just a small present, a pretty gift, one or two yellow bits, twenty, thirty, forty francs—you'd better." She shook the soft arm she held roughly, and anything seemed preferable than to be touched by this horrible woman.

"Wait, wait!" cried the Countess, shivering all over, and, feeling hastily for her purse, she took out several napoleons.

"Aha! oho! One, two, three," said the searcher in a fat, wheedling voice. "Four, yes, four, five;" and she clinked the coins together in her palm, while a covetous light came into her faded eyes at the joyous sound. "Five—make it five at once, d'ye hear me?—or I'll call them in and tell them. That will go against you, my princess. What, try to bribe a poor old woman, Mother Tontaine, honest and incorruptible Tontaine? Five, then, five!"

With trembling haste the Countess emptied the whole contents of her purse in the old hag's hand.

"Bon aubaine. Nice pickings. It is a misery what they pay me here. I am, oh, so poor, and I have children, many babies. You will not tell them—the police—you dare not. No, no, no."

Thus muttering to herself, she shambled across the room to a corner, where she stowed the money safely away. Then she came back, showed the bit of lace, and pressed it into the Countess's hands.

"Do you know this, little one? Where it comes from, where there is much more? I was told to look for it, to search for it on you;" and with a quick gesture she lifted the edge of the Countess's skirt, dropping it next moment with a low, chuckling laugh.

"Oho! aha! You were right, my pretty, to pay me, my pretty—right. And some day, to-day, to-morrow, whenever I ask you, you will remember Mother Tontaine."

The Countess listened with dismay. What had she done? Put herself into the power of this greedy and unscrupulous old beldame?

"And this, my princess? What have we here, aha?"

Mère Tontaine held up next the broken bit of jet ornament for inspection, and as the Countess leaned forward to examine it more closely, gave it into her hand.

"You recognize it, of course. But be careful, my pretty! Beware! If anyone were looking, it would ruin you. I could not save you then. Sh! say nothing, only look, and quick, give it me back. I must have it to show."

All this time the Countess was turning the jet over and over in her open palm, with a perplexed, disturbed, but hardly a terrified air.

Yes, she knew it, or thought she knew it. It had been—But how had it come here, into the possession of this base myrmidon of the French police?

"Give it me, quick!" There was a loud knock at the door. "They are coming. Remember!" Mother Tontaine put her long finger to her lip. "Not a word! I have found nothing, of course. Nothing, I can swear to that, and you will not forget Mother Tontaine?"

Now M. Floçon stood at the open door awaiting the searcher's report. He looked much disconcerted when the old woman took him on one side and briefly explained that the search had been altogether fruitless.

There was nothing to justify suspicion, nothing, so far as she could find.

The detective looked from one to the other—from the hag he had employed in this unpleasant quest, to the lady on whom it had been tried. The Countess, to his surprise, did not complain. He had expected further and strong upbraidings. Strange to say, she took it very quietly. There was no indignation in her face. She was still pale, and her hands trembled, but she said nothing, made no reference, at least, to what she had just gone through.

Again he took counsel with his colleague, while the Countess was kept apart.

"What next, M. Floçon?" asked the Judge. "What shall we do with her?"

"Let her go," answered the detective, briefly.

"What! do you suggest this, sir," said the Judge, slyly. "After your strong and well-grounded suspicions?"

"They are as strong as ever, stronger: and I feel sure I shall yet justify them. But what I wish now is to let her go at large, under surveillance."

"Ah! you would shadow her?"

"Precisely. By a good agent. Galipaud, for instance. He speaks English, and he can, if necessary, follow her anywhere, even to England."

"She can be extradited," said the Commissary, with his one prominent idea of arrest.

"Do you agree, M. le Juge? Then, if you will permit me, I will give the necessary orders, and perhaps you will inform the lady that she is free to leave the station?"

The Countess now had reason to change her opinion of the French officials. Great politeness now replaced the first severity that had been so cruel. She was told, with many bows and apologies, that her regretted but unavoidable detention was at an end. Not only was she freely allowed to depart, but she was escorted by both M. Floçon and the Commissary outside, to where an omnibus was in waiting, and all her baggage piled on top, even to the dressing-bag, which had been neatly repacked for her.

But the little silver-topped vial had not been restored to her, nor the handkerchief.

In her joy at her deliverance, either she had not given these a second thought, or she did not wish to appear anxious to recover them.

Nor did she notice that, as the bus passed through the gates at the bottom of the large slope that leads from the Lyons Station, it was followed at a discreet distance by a modest fiacre, which pulled up, eventually, outside the Hotel Madagascar. Its occupant, M. Galipaud, kept the Countess in sight, and, entering the hotel at her heels, waited till she had left the office, when he held a long conference with the proprietor.

CHAPTER VIII

A first stage in the inquiry had now been reached, with results that seemed promising, and were yet contradictory.

No doubt the watch to be set on the Countess might lead to something yet—something to bring first plausible suspicion to a triumphant issue; but the examination of the other occupants of the car should not be allowed to slacken on that account. The Countess might have some confederate among them—this pestilent English General, perhaps, who had made himself so conspicuous in her defence; or someone of them might throw light upon her movements, upon her conduct during the journey.

Then, with a spasm of self-reproach, M. Floçon remembered that two distinct suggestions had been made to him by two of the travellers, and that, so far, he had neglected them. One was the significant hint from the Italian that he could materially help the inquiry. The other was the General's sneering assertion that the train had not continued its journey uninterruptedly between Laroche and Paris.

Consulting the Judge, and laying these facts before him, it was agreed that the Italian's offer seemed the most important, and he was accordingly called in next.

"Who and what are you?" asked the Judge, carelessly, but the answer roused him at once to intense interest, and he could not quite resist a glance of reproach at M. Floçon.

"My name I have given you—Natale Ripaldi. I am a detective officer belonging to the Roman police."

"What!" cried M. Floçon, colouring deeply. "This is unheard of. Why in the name of all the devils have you withheld this most astonishing statement until now?"

"Monsieur surely remembers. I told him half an hour ago I had something important to communicate—"

"Yes, yes, of course. But why were you so reticent. Good Heavens!"

"Monsieur was not so encouraging that I felt disposed to force on him what I knew he would have to hear in due course."

"It is monstrous—quite abominable, and shall not end here. Your superiors shall hear of your conduct," went on the Chief, hotly.

"They will also hear, and, I think, listen to my version of the story,–that I offered you fairly, and at the first opportunity, all the information I had, and that you refused to accept it."

"You should have persisted. It was your manifest duty. You are an officer of the law, or you say you are."

"Pray telegraph at once, if you think fit, to Rome, to the police authorities, and you will find that Natale Ripaldi–your humble servant–travelled by the through express with their knowledge and authority. And here are my credentials, my official card, some official letters–"

"And what, in a word, have you to tell us?"

"I can tell you who the murdered man was."

"We know that already."

"Possibly; but only his name, I apprehend. I know his profession, his business, his object in travelling, for I was appointed to watch and follow him. That is why I am here."

"Was he a suspicious character, then? A criminal?"

"At any rate he was absconding from Rome, with valuables."

"A thief, in fact?"

The Italian put out the palms of his hands with a gesture of doubt and deprecation.

"Thief is a hard, ugly word. That which he was removing was, or had been, his own property."

"Tut, tut! do be more explicit and get on," interrupted the little Chief, testily.

"I ask nothing better; but if questions are put to me–"

The Judge interposed.

"Give us your story. We can interrogate you afterwards."

"The murdered man is Francis A. Quadling, of the firm of Correse & Quadling, bankers, in the Via Condotti, Rome. It was an old house, once of good, of the highest repute, but of late years it has fallen into difficulties. Its financial soundness was doubted in certain circles, and the Government was warned that a great scandal was imminent. So the matter was handed over to the police, and I was directed to make inquiries, and to keep my eye on this Quadling"–he jerked his thumb towards the platform, where the body might be supposed to be.

"This Quadling was the only surviving partner. He was well known and liked in Rome, indeed, many who heard the adverse reports disbelieved them, I myself among the number. But my duty was plain—"

"Naturally," echoed the fiery little detective.

"I made it my business to place the banker under surveillance, to learn his habits, his ways of life, see who were his friends, the houses he visited. I soon knew much that I wanted to know, although not all. But one fact I discovered, and think it right to inform you of it at once. He was on intimate terms with La Castagneto—at least, he frequently called upon her."

"La Castagneto! Do you mean the Countess of that name, who was a passenger in the sleeper?"

"Beyond doubt! it is she I mean." The officials looked at each other eagerly, and M. Beaumont le Hardi quickly turned over the sheets on which the Countess's evidence was recorded.

She had denied acquaintance with this murdered man, Quadling, and here was positive evidence that they were on intimate terms!

"He was at her house on the very day we all left Rome—in the evening, towards dusk. The Countess had an apartment in the Via Margutta, and when he left her he returned to his own place in the Condotti, entered the bank, stayed half an hour, then came out with one hand-bag and rug, called a cab, and was driven straight to the railway station."

"And you followed?"

"Of course. When I saw him walk straight to the sleeping-car, and ask the conductor for 7 and 8, I knew that his plans had been laid, and that he was on the point of leaving Rome secretly. When, presently, La Castagneto also arrived, I concluded that she was in his confidence, and that possibly they were eloping together."

"Why did you not arrest him?"

"I had no authority, even if I had had the time. Although I was ordered to watch the Signor Quadling, I had no warrant for his arrest. But I decided on the spur of the moment what course I should take. It seemed to be the only one, and that was to embark in the same train and stick close to my man."

"You informed your superiors, I suppose?"

"Pardon me, monsieur," said the Italian blandly to the Chief, who asked the question, "but have you any right to inquire into my conduct towards my superiors? In all that affects the murder I am at your orders, but in this other matter it is between me and them."

"Ta, ta, ta! They will tell us if you will not. And you had better be careful, lest you obstruct justice. Speak out, sir, and beware. What did you intend to do?"

"To act according to circumstances. If my suspicions were confirmed—"

"What suspicions?"

"Why—that this banker was carrying off any large sum in cash, notes, securities, as in effect he was."

"Ah! You know that? How?"

"By my own eyes. I looked into his compartment once and saw him in the act of counting them over, a great quantity, in fact—"

Again the officials looked at each other significantly. They had got at last to a motive for the crime.

"And that, of course, would have justified his arrest?"

"Exactly. I proposed, directly we arrived in Paris, to claim the assistance of your police and take him into custody. But his fate interposed."

There was a pause, a long pause, for another important point had been reached in the inquiry: the motive for the murder had been made clear, and with it the presumption against the Countess gained terrible strength.

But there was more, perhaps, to be got out of this dark-visaged Italian detective, who had already proved so useful an ally.

"One or two words more," said the Judge to Ripaldi. "During the journey, now, did you have any conversation with this Quadling?"

"None. He kept very much to himself."

"You saw him, I suppose, at the restaurants?"

"Yes, at Modane and Laroche."

"But did not speak to him?"

"Not a word."

"Had he any suspicion, do you think, as to who you were?"

"Why should he? He did not know me. I had taken pains he should never see me."

"Did he speak to any other passenger?"

"Very little. To the Countess. Yes, once or twice, I think, to her maid."

"Ah! that maid. Did you notice her at all? She has not been seen. It is strange. She seems to have disappeared."

"To have run away, in fact?" suggested Ripaldi, with a queer smile.

"Well, at least she is not here with her mistress. Can you offer any explanation of that?"

"She was perhaps afraid. The Countess and she were very good friends, I think. On better, more familiar terms, than is usual between mistress and maid."

"The maid knew something?"

"Ah, monsieur, it is only an idea. But I give it you for what it is worth."

"Well, well, this maid—what was she like?"

"Tall, dark, good-looking, not too reserved. She made other friends—the porter and the English Colonel. I saw the last speaking to her. I spoke to her myself."

"What can have become of her?" said the Judge.

"Would M. le Juge like me to go in search of her? That is, if you have no more questions to ask, no wish to detain me further?"

"We will consider that, and let you know in a moment, if you will wait outside."

And then, when alone, the officials deliberated.

It was a good offer, the man knew her appearance, he was in possession of all the facts, he could be trusted—

"Ah, but can he, though?" queried the detective. "How do we know he has told us truth? What guarantee have we of his loyalty, his good faith? What if he is also concerned in the crime—has some guilty knowledge? What if he killed Quadling himself, or was an accomplice before or after the fact?"

"All these are possibilities, of course, but—pardon me, dear colleague—a little far-fetched, eh?" said the Judge. "Why not utilize this man? If he betrays us—serves us ill—if we had reason to lay hands on him again, he could hardly escape us."

"Let him go, and send someone with him," said the Commissary, the first practical suggestion he had yet made.

"Excellent!" cried the Judge. "You have another man here, Chief; let him go with this Italian."

They called in Ripaldi and told him, "We will accept your services, monsieur, and you can begin your search at once. In what direction do you propose to begin?"

"Where has her mistress gone?"

"How do you know she has gone?"

"At least, she is no longer with us out there. Have you arrested her—or what?"

"No, she is still at large, but we have our eye upon her. She has gone to her hotel—the Madagascar, off the Grands Boulevards."

"Then it is there that I shall look for the maid. No doubt she preceded her mistress to the hotel, or she will join her there very shortly."

"You would not make yourself known, of course? They might give you the slip. You have no authority to detain them, not in France."

"I should take my precautions, and I can always appeal to the police."

"Exactly. That would be your proper course. But you might lose valuable time, a great opportunity, and we wish to guard against that, so we shall associate one of our own people with you in your proceedings."

"Oh! very well, if you wish. It will, no doubt, be best." The Italian readily assented, but a shrewd listener might have guessed from the tone of his voice that the proposal was not exactly pleasing to him.

"I will call in Block," said the Chief, and the second detective inspector appeared to take his instructions.

He was a stout, stumpy little man, with a barrel-like figure, greatly emphasized by the short frock coat he wore; he had smallish pig's eyes buried deep in a fat face, and his round, chubby cheeks hung low over his turned-down collar.

"This gentleman," went on the Chief, indicating Ripaldi, "is a member of the Roman police, and has been so obliging as to offer us his services. You will accompany him, in the first instance, to the Hotel Madagascar. Put yourself in communication with Galipaud, who is there on duty."

"Would it not be sufficient if I made myself known to M. Galipaud?" suggested the Italian. "I have seen him here, I should recognize him—"

"That is not so certain; he may have changed his appearance. Besides, he does not know the latest developments, and might not be very cordial."

"You might write me a few lines to take to him."

"I think not. We prefer to send Block," replied the Chief, briefly and decidedly. He did not like this pertinacity, and looked at his colleagues as though he sought their concurrence in altering the arrangements for the Italian's mission. It might be wiser to detain him still.

"It was only to save trouble that I made the suggestion," hastily put in Ripaldi. "Naturally I am in your hands. And if I do not meet with the maid at the hotel, I may have to look further, in which case Monsieur–Block? Thank you–would no doubt render valuable assistance."

This speech restored confidence, and a few minutes later the two detectives, already excellent friends from the freemasonry of a common craft, left the station in a closed cab.

CHAPTER IX

"What next?" asked the Judge.

"That pestilent English officer, if you please, M. le Juge," said the detective. "That fire-eating, swashbuckling soldier, with his blustering barrack-room ways. I long to come to close quarters with him. He ridiculed me, taunted me, said I knew nothing—we will see, we will see."

"In fact, you wish to interrogate him yourself. Very well. Let us have him in."

When Sir Charles Collingham entered, he included the three officials in one cold, stiff bow, waited a moment, and then, finding he was not offered a chair, said with studied politeness:

"I presume I may sit down?"

"Pardon. Of course; pray be seated," said the Judge, hastily, and evidently a little ashamed of himself.

"Ah! Thanks. Do you object?" went on the General, taking out a silver cigarette-case. "May I offer one?" He handed round the box affably.

"We do not smoke on duty," answered the Chief, rudely. "Nor is smoking permitted in a court of justice."

"Come, come, I wish to show no disrespect. But I cannot recognize this as a court of justice, and I think, if you will forgive me, that I shall take three whiffs. It may help me keep my temper."

He was evidently making game of them. There was no symptom remaining of the recent effervescence when he was acting as the Countess's champion, and he was perfectly—nay, insolently calm and self-possessed.

"You call yourself General Collingham?" went on the Chief.

"I do not call myself. I am General Sir Charles Collingham, of the British Army."

"Retired?"

"No, I am still on the active list."

"These points will have to be verified."

"With all my heart. You have already sent to the British Embassy?"

"Yes, but no one has come," answered the detective, contemptuously.

"If you disbelieve me, why do you question me?"

"It is our duty to question you, and yours to answer. If not, we have means to make you. You are suspected, inculpated in a terrible crime, and your whole attitude is–is–objectionable–unworthy–disgr–"

"Gently, gently, my dear colleague," interposed the Judge. "If you will permit me, I will take up this. And you, M. le Général, I am sure you cannot wish to impede or obstruct us; we represent the law of this country."

"Have I done so, M. le Juge?" answered the General, with the utmost courtesy, as he threw away his half-burned cigarette.

"No, no. I do not imply that in the least. I only entreat you, as a good and gallant gentleman, to meet us in a proper spirit and give us your best help."

"Indeed, I am quite ready. If there has been any unpleasantness, it has surely not been of my making, but rather of that little man there." The General pointed to M. Floçon rather contemptuously, and nearly started a fresh disturbance.

"Well, well, let us say no more of that, and proceed to business. I understand," said the Judge, after fingering a few pages of the dispositions in front of him, "that you are a friend of the Contessa di Castagneto? Indeed, she has told us so herself."

"It was very good of her to call me her friend. I am proud to hear she so considers me."

"How long have you known her?"

"Four or five months. Since the beginning of the last winter season in Rome."

"Did you frequent her house?"

"If you mean, was I permitted to call on her on friendly terms, yes."

"Did you know all her friends?"

"How can I answer that? I know whom I met there from time to time."

"Exactly. Did you often meet among them a Signor–Quadling?"

"Quadling–Quadling? I cannot say that I have. The name is familiar somehow, but I cannot recall the man."

"Have you never heard of the Roman bankers, Correse & Quadling?"

"Ah, of course. Although I have had no dealing with them. Certainly I have never met Mr. Quadling."

"Not at the Countess's?"

"Never–of that I am quite sure."

"And yet we have had positive evidence that he was a constant visitor there."

"It is perfectly incomprehensible to me. Not only have I never met him, but I have never heard the Countess mention his name."

"It will surprise you, then, to be told that he called at her apartment in the Via Margutta on the very evening of her departure from Rome. Called, was admitted, was closeted with her for more than an hour."

"I am surprised, astounded. I called there myself about four in the afternoon to offer my services for the journey, and I too stayed till after five. I can hardly believe it."

"I have more surprises for you, General. What will you think when I tell you that this very Quadling–this friend, acquaintance, call him what you please, but at least intimate enough to pay her a visit on the eve of a long journey–was the man found murdered in the sleeping-car?"

"Can it be possible? Are you sure?" cried Sir Charles, almost starting from his chair. "And what do you deduce from all this? What do you imply? An accusation against that lady? Absurd!"

"I respect your chivalrous desire to stand up for a lady who calls you her friend, but we are officials first, and sentiment cannot be permitted to influence us. We have good reasons for suspecting that lady. I tell you that frankly, and trust to you as a soldier and man of honour not to abuse the confidence reposed in you."

"May I not know those reasons?"

"Because she was in the car–the only woman, you understand–between Laroche and Paris."

"Do you suspect a female hand, then?" asked the General, evidently much interested and impressed.

"That is so, although I am exceeding my duty in revealing this."

"And you are satisfied that this lady, a refined, delicate person in the best society, of the highest character,–believe me, I know that to be the case,–whom you yet suspect of an atrocious crime, was the only female in the car?"

"Obviously. Who else? What other woman could possibly have been in the car? No one got in at Laroche; the train never stopped till it reached Paris."

"On that last point at least you are quite mistaken, I assure you. Why not upon the other also?"

"The train stopped?" interjected the detective. "Why has no one told us that?"

"Possibly because you never asked. But it is nevertheless the fact. Verify it. Everyone will tell you the same."

The detective himself hurried to the door and called in the porter. He was within his rights, of course, but the action showed distrust, at which the General only smiled, but he laughed outright when the still stupid and half-dazed porter, of course, corroborated the statement at once.

"At whose instance was the train pulled up?" asked the detective, and the Judge nodded his head approvingly.

To know that would fix fresh suspicion.

But the porter could not answer the question.

Someone had rung the alarm-bell–so at least the conductor had declared; otherwise they should not have stopped. Yet he, the porter, had not done so, nor did any passenger come forward to admit giving the signal. But there had been a halt. Yes, assuredly.

"This is a new light," the Judge confessed. "Do you draw any conclusion from it?" he went on to ask the General.

"That is surely your business. I have only elicited the fact to disprove your theory. But if you wish, I will tell you how it strikes me."

The Judge bowed assent.

"The bare fact that the train was halted would mean little. That would be the natural act of a timid or excitable person involved indirectly in such a catastrophe. But to disavow the act starts suspicion. The fair inference is that there was some reason, an unavowable reason, for halting the train."

"And that reason would be–"

"You must see it without my assistance, surely! Why, what else but to afford someone an opportunity to leave the car."

"But how could that be? You would have seen that person, some of you, especially at such a critical time. The aisle would be full of people, both exits were thus practically overlooked."

"My idea is–it is only an idea, understand–that the person had already left the car–that is to say, the interior of the car."

"Escaped how? Where? What do you mean?"

"Escaped through the open window of the compartment where you found the murdered man."

"You noticed the open window, then?" quickly asked the detective. "When was that?"

"Directly I entered the compartment at the first alarm. It occurred to me at once that someone might have gone through it."

"But no woman could have done it. To climb out of an express train going at top speed would be an impossible feat for a woman," said the detective, doggedly.

"Why, in God's name, do you still harp upon the woman? Why should it be a woman more than a man?"

"Because"–it was the Judge who spoke, but he paused a moment in deference to a gesture of protest from M. Floçon. The little detective was much concerned at the utter want of reticence displayed by his colleague.

"Because," went on the Judge with decision–"because this was found in the compartment;" and he held out the piece of lace and the scrap of beading for the General's inspection, adding quickly, "You have seen these, or one of them, or something like them before. I am sure of it; I call upon you; I demand–no, I appeal to your sense of honour, Sir Collingham. Tell me, please, exactly what you know."

The General sat for a time staring hard at the bit of torn lace and the broken beads. Then he spoke out firmly:

"It is my duty to withhold nothing. It is not the lace. That I could not swear to; for me—and probably for most men—two pieces of lace are very much the same. But I think I have seen these beads, or something exactly like them, before."

"Where? When?"

"They formed part of the trimming of a mantle worn by the Contessa di Castagneto."

"Ah!" it was the same interjection uttered simultaneously by the three Frenchmen, but each had a very different note; in the Judge it was deep interest, in the detective triumph, in the Commissary indignation, as when he caught a criminal red-handed.

"Did she wear it on the journey?" continued the Judge.

"As to that I cannot say."

"Come, come, General, you were with her constantly; you must be able to tell us. We insist on being told." This fiercely, from the now jubilant M. Floçon.

"I repeat that I cannot say. To the best of my recollection, the Countess wore a long travelling cloak—an ulster, as we call them. The jacket with those bead ornaments may have been underneath. But if I have seen them,—as I believe I have,—it was not during this journey."

Here the Judge whispered to M. Floçon, "The searcher did not discover any second mantle."

"How do we know the woman examined thoroughly?" he replied. "Here, at least, is direct evidence as to the beads. At last the net is drawing round this fine Countess."

"Well, at any rate," said the detective aloud, returning to the General, "these beads were found in the compartment of the murdered man. I should like that explained, please."

"By me? How can I explain it? And the fact does not bear upon what we were considering, as to whether any one had left the car."

"Why not?"

"The Countess, as we know, never left the car. As to her entering this particular compartment,—at any previous time,—it is highly improbable. Indeed, it is rather insulting her to suggest it."

"She and this Quadling were close friends."

"So you say. On what evidence I do not know, but I dispute it."

"Then how could the beads get there? They were her property, worn by her."

"Once, I admit, but not necessarily on this journey. Suppose she had given the mantle away—to her maid, for instance; I believe ladies often pass on their things to their maids."

"It is all pure presumption, a mere theory. This maid—she has not as yet been imported into the discussion."

"Then I would suggest that you do so without delay. She is to my mind a—well, rather a curious person."

"You know her—spoke to her?"

"I know her, in a way. I had seen her in the Via Margutta, and I nodded to her when she came first into the car."

"And on the journey—you spoke to her frequently?"

"I? Oh, dear, no, not at all. I noticed her, certainly; I could not help it, and perhaps I ought to tell her mistress. She seemed to make friends a little too readily with people."

"As for instance—?"

"With the porter to begin with. I saw them together at Laroche, in the buffet at the bar; and that Italian, the man who was in here before me; indeed, with the murdered man. She seemed to know them all."

"Do you imply that the maid might be of use in this inquiry?"

"Most assuredly I do. As I tell you, she was constantly in and out of the car, and more or less intimate with several of the passengers."

"Including her mistress, the Countess," put in M. Floçon. The General laughed pleasantly.

"Most ladies are, I presume, on intimate terms with their maids. They say no man is a hero to his valet. It is the same, I suppose, with the other sex."

"So intimate," went on the little detective, with much malicious emphasis, "that now the maid has disappeared lest she might be asked inconvenient questions about her mistress."

"Disappeared? You are sure?"

"She cannot be found, that is all we know."

"It is as I thought, then. She it was who left the car!" cried Sir Charles, with so much vehemence that the officials were startled out of their dignified reserve, and shouted back almost in a breath: "Explain yourself. Quick, quick. What in God's name do you mean?"

"I had my suspicions from the first, and I will tell you why. At Laroche the car emptied, as you may have heard; everyone except the Countess, at least, went over to the restaurant for early coffee; I with the rest. I was one of the first to finish, and I strolled back to the platform to get a few whiffs of a cigarette. At that moment I saw, or thought I saw, the end of a skirt disappearing into the sleeping-car. I concluded it was this maid, Hortense, who was taking her mistress a cup of coffee. Then my brother came up, we exchanged a few words, and entered the car together."

"By the same door as that through which you had seen the skirt pass?"

"No, by the other. My brother went back to his berth, but I paused in the corridor to finish my cigarette after the train had gone on. By this time everyone but myself had returned to his berth, and I was on the point of lying down again for half an hour, when I distinctly heard the handle turned of the compartment I knew to be vacant all through the run."

"That was the one with berths 11 and 12?"

"Probably. It was next to the Countess. Not only was the handle turned, but the door partly opened–"

"It was not the porter?"

"Oh, no, he was in his seat,–you know it, at the end of the car,–sound asleep, snoring; I could hear him."

"Did any one come out of the vacant compartment?"

"No; but I was almost certain, I believe I could swear that I saw the same skirt, just the hem of it, a black skirt, sway forward beyond the door, just for a second. Then all at once the door was closed again fast."

"What did you conclude from this? Or did you think nothing of it?"

"I thought very little. I supposed it was that the maid wished to be near her mistress as we were approaching Paris, and I had heard from the Countess that the porter had made many difficulties. But you see, after what has happened, that there was a reason for stopping the train."

"Quite so," M. Floçon readily admitted, with a scarcely concealed sneer.

He had quite made up his mind now that it was the Countess who had rung the alarm-bell, in order to allow of the escape of the maid, her confederate and accomplice.

"And you still have an impression that someone—presumably this woman—got off the car, somehow, during the stoppage?" he asked.

"I suggest it, certainly. Whether it was or could be so, I must leave to your superior judgment."

"What! A woman climb out like that? Bah! Tell that to someone else!"

"You have, of course, examined the exterior of the car, dear colleague?" now said the Judge.

"Assuredly, once, but I will do it again. Still, the outside is quite smooth, there is no foot-board. Only an acrobat could succeed in thus escaping, and then only at the peril of his life. But a woman—oh, no! it is too absurd."

"With help she might, I think, get up on to the roof," quickly remarked Sir Charles. "I have looked out of the window of my compartment. It would be nothing for a man, nor much for a woman if assisted."

"That we will see for ourselves," said the detective, ungraciously.

"The sooner the better," added the Judge, and the whole party rose from their chairs, intending to go straight to the car, when the policeman on guard appeared at the door, followed close by an English military officer in uniform, whom he was trying to keep back, but with no great success. It was Colonel Papillon of the Embassy.

"Halloa, Jack! you are a good chap," cried the General, quickly going forward to shake hands. "I was sure you would come."

"Come, sir! Of course I came. I was just going to an official function, as you see, but his Excellency insisted, my horse was at the door, and here I am."

All this was in English, but the attaché turned now to the officials, and, with many apologies for his intrusion, suggested that they should allow his friend, the General, to return with him to the Embassy when they had done with him.

"Of course we will answer for him. He shall remain at your disposal, and will appear whenever called upon." He returned to Sir Charles, asking, "You will promise that, sir?"

"Oh, willingly. I had always meant to stay on a bit in Paris. And really I should like to see the end of this. But my brother? He must get home for next Sunday's duty. He has nothing to tell, but he would come back to Paris at any time if his evidence was wanted."

The French Judge very obligingly agreed to all these proposals, and two more of the detained passengers, making four in all, now left the station.

Then the officials proceeded to the car, which still remained as the Chief Detective had left it.

Here they soon found how just were the General's previsions.

The three officials went straight to where the still open window showed the particular spot to be examined. The exterior of the car was a little smirched and stained with the dust of the journey, lying thick in parts, and in others there were a few great splotches of mud plastered on.

The detective paused for a moment to get a general view, looking, in the light of the General's suggestion, for either hand or foot marks, anything like a trace of the passage of a feminine skirt, across the dusty surface.

But nothing was to be seen, nothing definite or conclusive at least. Only here and there a few lines and scratches that might be encouraging, but proved little.

Then the Commissary, drawing nearer, called attention to some suspicious spots sprinkled about the window, but above it towards the roof.

"What is it?" asked the detective, as his colleague with the point of his long fore-finger nail picked at the thin crust on the top of one of these spots, disclosing a dark, viscous core.

"I could not swear to it, but I believe it is blood."

"Blood! Good Heavens!" cried the detective, as he dragged his powerful magnifying glass out of his pocket and applied it to the spot. "Look, M. le Juge," he added, after a long and minute examination. "What say you?"

"It has that appearance. Only medical evidence can positively decide, but I believe it is blood."

"Now we are on the right track, I feel convinced. Someone fetch a ladder."

One of these curious French ladders, narrow at the top, splayed out at the base, was quickly leaned against the car, and the detective ran up, using his magnifier as he climbed.

"There is more here, much more, and something like–yes, beyond question it is–the print of two hands upon the roof. It was here she climbed."

"No doubt. I can see it now exactly. She would sit on the window ledge, the lower limbs inside the car here and held there. Then with her hands she would draw herself up to the roof," said the Judge.

"But what nerve! what strength of arm!"

"It was life and death. Within the car was more terrible danger. Fear will do much in such a case. We all know that. Well! what more?"

By this time the detective had stepped on to the roof of the car.

"More, more, much more! Footprints, as plain as a picture. A woman's feet. Wait, let me follow them to the end," said he, cautiously creeping forward to the end of the car.

A minute or two more, and he rejoined his colleagues on the ground level, and, rubbing his hands, declared joyously that it was all perfectly clear.

"Dangerous or not, difficult or not, she did it. I have traced her; have seen where she must have lain crouching ever so long, followed her all along the top of the car, to the end where she got down above the little platform exit. Beyond doubt she left the car when it stopped, and by arrangement with her confederate."

"The Countess?"

"Who else?"

"And at a point near Paris. The English General said the halt was within twenty minutes' run of the station."

"Then it is from that point we must commence our search for her. The Italian has gone on the wrong scent."

"Not necessarily. The maid, we may be sure, will try to communicate with her mistress."

"Still, it would be well to secure her before she can do that," said the Judge. "With all we know now, a sharp interrogation might extract some very damaging admissions from her," went on the detective, eagerly. "Who is to go? I have sent away both my assistants. Of course I can telephone for another man, or I might go myself."

"No, no, dear colleague, we cannot spare you just yet. Telephone by all means. I presume you would wish to be present at the rest of the interrogatories?"

"Certainly, you are right. We may elicit more about this maid. Let us call in the porter now. He is said to have had relations with her. Something more may be got out of him."

The more did not amount to much. Groote, the porter, came in, cringing and wretched, in the abject state of a man who has lately been drugged and is now slowly recovering. Although sharply questioned, he had nothing to add to his first story.

"Speak out," said the Judge, harshly. "Tell us everything plainly and promptly, or I shall send you straight to gaol. The order is already made out;" and as he spoke, he waved a flimsy bit of paper before him.

"I know nothing," the porter protested, piteously.

"That is false. We are fully informed and no fools. We are certain that no such catastrophe could have occurred without your knowledge or connivance."

"Indeed, gentlemen, indeed—"

"You were drinking with this maid at the buffet at Laroche. You had more drink with her, or from her hands, afterwards in the car."

"No, gentlemen, that is not so. I could not—she was not in the car."

"We know better. You cannot deceive us. You were her accomplice, and the accomplice of her mistress, also, I have no doubt."

"I declare solemnly that I am quite innocent of all this. I hardly remember what happened at Laroche or after. I do not deny the drink at the buffet. It was very nasty, I thought, and could not tell why, nor why I could not hold my head up when I got back to the car."

"You went off to sleep at once? Is that what you pretend?"

"It must have been so. Yes. Then I know nothing more, not till I was aroused."

And beyond this, a tale to which he stuck with undeviating persistence, they could elicit nothing.

"He is either too clever for us or an absolute idiot and fool," said the Judge, wearily, at last, when Groote had gone out. "We had better commit him to Mazas and hold him there in solitary confinement under our hands. After a day or two of that he may be less difficult."

"It is quite clear he was drugged, that the maid put opium or laudanum into his drink at Laroche."

"And enough of it apparently, for he says he went off to sleep directly he returned to the car," the Judge remarked.

"He says so. But he must have had a second dose, or why was the vial found on the ground by his seat?" asked the Chief, thoughtfully, as much of himself as of the others.

"I cannot believe in a second dose. How was it administered— by whom? It was laudanum, and could only be given in a drink. He says he had no second drink. And by whom? The maid? He says he did not see the maid again."

"Pardon me, M. le Juge, but do you not give too much credibility to the porter? For me, his evidence is tainted, and I hardly believe a word of it. Did he not tell me at first he had not seen this maid after Amberieux at 8 P.M.? Now he admits that he was drinking with her at the buffet at Laroche. It is all a tissue of lies, his losing the pocket-book and his papers too. There is something to conceal. Even his sleepiness, his stupidity, are likely to have been assumed."

"I do not think he is acting; he has not the ability to deceive us like that."

"Well, then, what if the Countess took him the second drink?"

"Oh! oh! That is the purest conjecture. There is nothing whatever to suggest or support that."

"Then how explain the finding of the vial near the porter's seat?"

"May it not have been dropped there on purpose?" put in the Commissary, with another flash of intelligence.

"On purpose?" queried the detective, crossly, foreseeing an answer that would not please him.

"On purpose to bring suspicion on the lady?"

"I don't see it in that light. That would imply that she was not in the plot, and plot there certainly was; everything points to it. The drugging, the open window, the maid's escape."

"A plot, no doubt, but organized by whom? These two women only? Could either of them have struck the fatal blow? Hardly. Women have the wit to conceive, but neither courage nor brute force to execute. There was a man in this, rest assured."

"Granted. But who? That fire-eating Sir Collingham?" quickly asked the detective, giving rein once more to his hatred.

"That is not a solution that commends itself to me, I must confess," declared the Judge. "The General's conduct has been blameworthy and injudicious, but he is not of the stuff that makes criminals."

"Who, then? The porter? No? The clergyman? No? The French gentlemen?—well, we have not examined them yet; but from what I saw at the first cursory glance, I am not disposed to suspect them."

"What of that Italian?" asked the Commissary.

"Are you sure of him? His looks did not please me greatly, and he was very eager to get away from here. What if he takes to his heels?"

"Block is with him," the Chief put in hastily, with the evident desire to stifle an unpleasant misgiving. "We have touch of him if we want him, as we may."

How much they might want him they only realized when they got further in their inquiry!

CHAPTER XII

Only the two Frenchmen remained for examination. They had been left to the last by pure accident. The exigencies of the inquiry had led to the preference of others, but these two well-broken and submissive gentlemen made no visible protest. However much they may have chafed inwardly at the delay, they knew better than to object; any outburst of discontent would, they knew, recoil on themselves. Not only were they perfectly patient now when summoned before the officers of justice, they were most eager to give every assistance to the law, to go beyond the mere letter, and, if needs be, volunteer information.

The first called in was the elder, M. Anatole Lafolay, a true Parisian bourgeois, fat and comfortable, unctuous in speech, and exceedingly deferential.

The story he told was in its main outlines that which we already know, but he was further questioned, by the light of the latest facts and ideas as now elicited.

The line adroitly taken by the Judge was to get some evidence of collusion and combination among the passengers, especially with reference to two of them, the two women of the party. On this important point M. Lafolay had something to say.

Asked if he had seen or noticed the lady's maid on the journey, he answered "yes" very decisively and with a smack of the lips, as though the sight of this pretty and attractive person had given him considerable satisfaction.

"Did you speak to her?"

"Oh, no. I had no opportunity. Besides, she had her own friends— great friends, I fancy. I caught her more than once whispering in the corner of the car with one of them."

"And that was–?"

"I think the Italian gentleman; I am almost sure I recognized his clothes. I did not see his face, it was turned from me–towards hers, and very close, I may be permitted to say."

"And they were friendly?"

"More than friendly, I should say. Very intimate indeed. I should not have been surprised if–when I turned away as a matter of fact–if he did not touch, just touch, her red lips. It would have been excusable–forgive me, messieurs."

"Aha! They were so intimate as that? Indeed! And did she reserve her favours exclusively for him? Did no one else address her, pay her court on the quiet—you understand?"

"I saw her with the porter, I believe, at Laroche, but only then. No, the Italian was her chief companion."

"Did anyone else notice the flirtation, do you think?"

"Possibly. There was no secrecy. It was very marked. We could all see."

"And her mistress too?"

"That I will not say. The lady I saw but little during the journey."

A few more questions, mainly personal, as to his address, business, probable presence in Paris for the next few weeks, and M. Lafolay was permitted to depart.

The examination of the younger Frenchman, a smart, alert young man, of pleasant, insinuating address, with a quick, inquisitive eye, followed the same lines, and was distinctly corroborative on all the points to which M. Lafolay spoke. But M. Jules Devaux had something startling to impart concerning the Countess.

When asked if he had seen her or spoken to her, he shook his head.

"No; she kept very much to herself," he said. "I saw her but little, hardly at all, except at Modane. She kept her own berth."

"Where she received her own friends?"

"Oh, beyond doubt. The Englishmen both visited her there, but not the Italian."

"The Italian? Are we to infer that she knew the Italian?"

"That is what I wish to convey. Not on the journey, though. Between Rome and Paris she did not seem to know him. It was afterwards; this morning, in fact, that I came to the conclusion that there was some secret understanding between them."

"Why do you say that, M. Devaux?" cried the detective, excitedly. "Let me urge you and implore you to speak out, and fully. This is of the utmost, of the very first, importance."

"Well, gentlemen, I will tell you. As you are well aware, on arrival at this station we were all ordered to leave the car, and marched to the waiting-room, out there. As a matter of course, the lady entered first, and she was seated when I went in. There was a strong light on her face."

"Was her veil down?"

"Not then. I saw her lower it later, and, as I think, for reasons I will presently put before you. Madame has a beautiful face, and I gazed at it with sympathy, grieving for her, in fact, in such a trying situation; when suddenly I saw a great and remarkable change come over it."

"Of what character?"

"It was a look of horror, disgust, surprise,—a little perhaps of all three; I could not quite say which, it faded so quickly and was followed by a cold, deathlike pallor. Then almost immediately she lowered her veil."

"Could you form any explanation for what you saw in her face? What caused it?"

"Something unexpected, I believe, some shock, or the sight of something shocking. That was how it struck me, and so forcibly that I turned to look over my shoulder, expecting to find the reason there. And it was."

"That reason—?"

"Was the entrance of the Italian, who came just behind me. I am certain of this; he almost told me so himself, not in words, but the mistakable leer he gave her in reply. It was wicked, sardonic, devilish, and proved beyond doubt that there was some secret, some guilty secret perhaps, between them."

"And was that all?" cried both the Judge and M. Floçon in a breath, leaning forward in their eagerness to hear more.

"For the moment, yes. But I was made so interested, so suspicious by this, that I watched the Italian closely, awaiting, expecting further developments. They were long in coming; indeed, I am only at the end now."

"Explain, pray, as quickly as possible, and in your own words."

"It was like this, monsieur. When we were all seated, I looked round, and did not at first see our Italian. At last I discovered he had taken a back seat, through modesty perhaps, or to be out of observation—how was I to know? He sat in the shadow by a door, that, in fact, which leads into this room. He was thus in the background, rather out of the way, but I could see his eyes glittering in that far-off corner, and they were turned in our direction, always fixed upon the lady, you understand. She was next me, the whole time.

"Then, as you will remember, monsieur, you called us in one by one, and I, with M. Lafolay, was the first to appear before you. When I returned to the outer room, the Italian was still staring, but not so fixedly or continuously, at the lady. From time to time his eyes wandered towards a table near which he sat, and which was just in the gangway or passage by which people must pass into your presence.

"There was some reason for this, I felt sure, although I did not understand it immediately.

"Presently I got at the hidden meaning There was a small piece of paper, rolled up or crumpled up into a ball, lying upon this table, and the Italian wished, nay, was desperately anxious, to call the lady's attention to it. If I had had any doubt of this, it was quite removed after the man had gone into the inner room. As he left us, he turned his head over his shoulder significantly and nodded very slightly, but still perceptibly, at the ball of paper.

"Well, gentlemen, I was now satisfied in my own mind that this was some artful attempt of his to communicate with the lady, and had she fallen in with it, I should have immediately informed you, the proper authorities. But whether from stupidity, dread, disinclination, a direct, definite refusal to have any dealings with this man, the lady would not—at any rate did not—pick up the ball, as she might have done easily when she in her turn passed the table on her way to your presence.

"I have no doubt it was thrown there for her, and probably you will agree with me. But it takes two to make a game of this sort, and the lady would not join. Neither on leaving the room nor on returning would she take up the missive."

"And what became of it, then?" asked the detective in breathless excitement. "I have it here." M. Devaux opened the palm of his hand and displayed the scrap of paper in the hollow rolled up into a small tight ball.

"When and how did you become possessed of it?"

"I got it only just now, when I was called in here. Before that I could not move. I was tied to my chair, practically, and ordered strictly not to move."

"Perfectly. Monsieur's conduct has been admirable. And now tell us—what does it contain? Have you looked at it?"

"By no means. It is just as I picked it up. Will you gentlemen take it, and if you think fit, tell me what is there? Some writing— a message of some sort, or I am greatly mistaken."

"Yes, here are words written in pencil," said the detective, unrolling the paper, which he handed on to the Judge, who read the contents aloud—

"Be careful. Say nothing. If you betray me, you will be lost too."

A long silence followed, broken first by the Judge, who said at last solemnly to Devaux:

"Monsieur, in the name of justice I beg to thank you most warmly. You have acted with admirable tact and judgment, and have rendered us invaluable assistance. Have you anything further to tell us?"

"No, gentlemen. That is all. And you—you have no more questions to ask? Then I presume I may withdraw?"

Beyond doubt it had been reserved for the last witness to produce facts that constituted the very essence of the inquiry.

CHAPTER XIII

The examination was now over, and, the dispositions having been drawn up and signed, the investigating officials remained for some time in conference.

"It lies with those three, of course—the two women and the Italian. They are jointly, conjointly concerned, although the exact degrees of guilt cannot quite be apportioned," said the detective.

"And all three are at large!" added the Judge.

"If you will issue warrants for arrest, M. le Juge, we can take them—two of them at any rate—when we choose."

"That should be at once," remarked the Commissary, eager, as usual, for decisive action.

"Very well. Let us proceed in that way. Prepare the warrants," said the Judge, turning to his clerk. "And you," he went on, addressing M. Floçon, "dear colleague, will you see to their execution? Madame is at the Hotel Madagascar; that will be easy. The Italian Ripaldi we shall hear of through your inspector Block. As for the maid, Hortense Petitpré, we must search for her. That too, sir, you will of course undertake?"

"I will charge myself with it, certainly. My man should be here by now, and I will instruct him at once. Ask for him," said M. Floçon to the guard whom he called in.

"The inspector is there," said the guard, pointing to the outer room. "He has just returned."

"Returned? You mean arrived."

"No, monsieur, returned. It is Block, who left an hour or more ago."

"Block? Then something has happened—he has some special information, some great news! Shall we see him, M. le Juge?"

When Block appeared, it was evident that something had gone wrong with him. His face wore a look of hot, flurried excitement, and his manner was one of abject, cringing self-abasement.

"What is it?" asked the little Chief, sharply. "You are alone. Where is your man?"

"Alas, monsieur! how shall I tell you? He has gone—disappeared! I have lost him!"

"Impossible! You cannot mean it! Gone, now, just when we most want him? Never!"

"It is so, unhappily."

"Idiot! Triple idiot! You shall be dismissed, discharged from this hour. You are a disgrace to the force." M. Floçon raved furiously at his abashed subordinate, blaming him a little too harshly and unfairly, forgetting that until quite recently there had been no strong suspicion against the Italian. We are apt at times to expect others to be intuitively possessed of knowledge that has only come to us at a much later date.

"How was it? Explain. Of course you have been drinking. It is that, or your great gluttony. You were beguiled into some eating-house."

"Monsieur, you shall hear the exact truth. When we started more than an hour ago, our fiacre took the usual route, by the Quais and along the riverside. My gentleman made himself most pleasant"

"No doubt," growled the Chief.

"Offered me an excellent cigar, and talked—not about the affair, you understand—but of Paris, the theatres, the races, Longchamps, Auteuil, the grand restaurants. He knew everything, all Paris, like his pocket. I was much surprised, but he told me his business often brought him here. He had been employed to follow up several great Italian criminals, and had made a number of important arrests in Paris."

"Get on, get on! come to the essential."

"Well, in the middle of the journey, when we were about the Pont Henri Quatre, he said, 'Figure to yourself, my friend, that it is now near noon, that nothing has passed my lips since before daylight at Laroche. What say you? Could you eat a mouthful, just a scrap on the thumb-nail? Could you?'"

"And you—greedy, gormandizing beast!—you agreed?"

"My faith, monsieur, I too was hungry. It was my regular hour. Well—at any rate, for my sins I accepted. We entered the first restaurant, that of the 'Reunited Friends,' you know it, perhaps, monsieur? A good house, especially noted for tripe à la mode de Caen." In spite of his anguish, Block smacked his fat lips at the thought of this most succulent but very greasy dish.

"How often must I tell you to get on?"

"Forgive me, monsieur, but it is all part of my story. We had oysters, two dozen Marennes, and a glass or two of Chablis; then a good portion of tripe, and with them a bottle, only one, monsieur, of Pontet Canet; after that a beefsteak with potatoes and a little Burgundy, then a rum omelet."

"Great Heavens! you should be the fat man in a fair, not an agent of the Detective Bureau."

"It was all this that helped me to my destruction. He ate, this devilish Italian, like three, and I too, I was so hungry,—forgive me, sir,—I did my share. But by the time we reached the cheese, a fine, ripe Camembert, had our coffee, and one thimbleful of green Chartreuse, I was plein jusqu'au bec, gorged up to the beak."

"And what of your duty, your service, pray?"

"I did think of it, monsieur, but then, he, the Italian, was just the same as myself. He was a colleague. I had no fear of him, not till the very last, when he played me this evil turn. I suspected nothing when he brought out his pocketbook,—it was stuffed full, monsieur; I saw that and my confidence increased,—called for the reckoning, and paid with an Italian bank-note. The waiter looked doubtful at the foreign money, and went out to consult the manager. A minute after, my man got up, saying:

"'There may be some trouble about changing that bank-note. Excuse me one moment, pray.' He went out, monsieur, and piff-paff, he was no more to be seen."

"Ah, nigaud (ass), you are too foolish to live! Why did you not follow him? Why let him out of your sight?"

"But, monsieur, I was not to know, was I? I was to accompany him, not to watch him. I have done wrong, I confess. But then, who was to tell he meant to run away?"

M. Floçon could not deny the justice of this defence. It was only now, at the eleventh hour, that the Italian had become inculpated, and the question of his possible anxiety to escape had never been considered.

"He was so artful," went on Block in further extenuation of his offence. "He left everything behind. His overcoat, stick, this book—his own private memorandum-book seemingly—" "Book? Hand it me," said the Chief, and when it came into his hands he began to turn over the leaves hurriedly. It was a small brass-bound note-book or diary, and was full of close writing in pencil.

"I do not understand, not more than a word here and there. It is no doubt Italian. Do you know that language, M. le Juge?"

"Not perfectly, but I can read it. Allow me."

He also turned over the pages, pausing to read a passage here and there, and nodding his head from time to time, evidently struck with the importance of the matter recorded.

Meanwhile, M. Floçon continued an angry conversation with his offending subordinate.

"You will have to find him, Block, and that speedily, within twenty-four hours,–to-day, indeed,–or I will break you like a stick, and send you into the gutter. Of course, such a consummate ass as you have proved yourself would not think of searching the restaurant or the immediate neighbourhood, or of making inquiries as to whether he had been seen, or as to which way he had gone?"

"Pardon me, monsieur is too hard on me. I have been unfortunate, a victim to circumstances, still I believe I know my duty. Yes, I made inquiries, and, what is more, I heard of him."

"Where? how?" asked the Chief, gruffly, but obviously much interested.

"He never spoke to the manager, but walked out and let the change go. It was a note for a hundred lire, a hundred francs, and the restaurant bill was no more than seventeen francs."

"Hah! That is greatly against him indeed."

"He was much pressed, in a great hurry. Directly he crossed the threshold he called the first cab and was driving away, but he was stopped–"

"The devil! Why did they not keep him, then?"

"Stopped, but only for a moment, and accosted by a woman."

"A woman?"

"Yes, monsieur. They exchanged but three words. He wished to pass on, to leave her, she would not consent, then they both got into the cab and were driven away together."

The officials were now listening with all ears.

"Tell me," said the Chief, "quick, this woman—what was she like? Did you get her description?"

"Tall, slight, well formed, dressed all in black. Her face—it was a policeman who saw her, and he said she was good-looking, dark, brunette, black hair."

"It is the maid herself!" cried the little Chief, springing up and slapping his thigh in exuberant glee. "The maid! The missing maid!"

The joy of the Chief of Detectives at having thus come, as he supposed, upon the track of the missing maid, Hortense Petitpré, was somewhat dashed by the doubts freely expressed by the Judge as to the result of any search. Since Block's return, M. Beaumont le Hardi had developed strong symptoms of discontent and disapproval at his colleague's proceedings.

"But if it was this Hortense Petitpré how did she get there, by the bridge Henri Quatre, when we thought to find her somewhere down the line? It cannot be the same woman."

"I beg your pardon, gentlemen," interposed Block. "May I say one word? I believe I can supply some interesting information about Hortense Petitpré. I understand that someone like her was seen here in the station not more than an hour ago."

" Peste! Why were we not told this sooner?" cried the Chief, impetuously.

"Who saw her? Did he speak to her? Call him in; let us see how much he knows."

The man was summoned, one of the subordinate railway officials, who made a specific report.

Yes, he had seen a tall, slight, neat-looking woman, dressed entirely in black, who, according to her account, had arrived at 10.30 by the slow local train from Dijon.

"Fichtre!" said the Chief, angrily; "and this is the first we have heard of it."

"Monsieur was much occupied at the time, and, indeed, then we had not heard of your inquiry."

"I notified the station-master quite early, two or three hours since, about 9 A.M. This is most exasperating!"

"Instructions to look out for this woman have only just reached us, monsieur. There were certain formalities, I suppose."

For once the detective cursed in his heart the red-tape, roundabout ways of French officialism.

"Well, well! Tell me about her," he said, with a resignation he did not feel. "Who saw her?"

"I, monsieur. I spoke to her myself. She was on the outside of the station, alone, unprotected, in a state of agitation and alarm. I went up and offered my services. Then she told me she had come from Dijon, that friends who were to have met her had not appeared. I suggested that I should put her into a cab and send her to her destination. But she was afraid of losing her friends, and preferred to wait."

"A fine story! Did she appear to know what had happened? Had she heard of the murder?"

"Something, monsieur."

"Who could have told her? Did you?"

"No, not I. But she knew."

"Was not that in itself suspicious? The fact has not yet been made public."

"It was in the air, monsieur. There was a general impression that something had happened. That was to be seen on every face, in the whispered talk, the movement to and fro of the police and the guards."

"Did she speak of it, or refer to it?"

"Only to ask if the murderer was known; whether the passengers had been detained; whether there was any inquiry in progress; and then—"

"What then?"

"This gentleman," pointing to Block, "came out, accompanied by another. They passed pretty close to us, and I noticed that the lady slipped quickly on one side."

"She recognized her confederate, of course, but did not wish to be seen just then. Did he, the person with Block here, see her?"

"Hardly, I think; it was all so quick, and they were gone, in a minute, to the cab-stand."

"What did your woman do?"

"She seemed to have changed her mind all at once, and declared she would not wait for her friends. Now she was in quite a hurry to go."

"Of course! and left you like a fool planted there. I suppose she took a cab and followed the others, Block here and his companion."

"I believe she did. I saw her cab close behind theirs."

"It is too late to lament this now," said the Chief, after a short pause, looking at his colleagues. "At least it confirms our ideas, and brings us to certain definite conclusions. We must lay hands on these two. Their guilt is all but established. Their own acts condemn them. They must be arrested without a moment's delay."

"If you can find them!" suggested the Judge, with a very perceptible sneer.

"That we shall certainly do. Trust to Block, who is very nearly concerned. His future depends on his success. You quite understand that, my man?"

Block made a gesture half-deprecating, half-confident.

"I do not despair, gentlemen; and if I might make so bold, sir, I will ask you to assist? If you would give orders direct from the Prefecture to make the round of the cab-stands, to ask of all the agents in charge the information we need? Before night we shall have heard from the cabman who drove them what became of this couple, and so get our birds themselves, or a point of fresh departure."

"And you, Block, where shall you go?"

"Where I left him, or rather where he left me," replied the inspector, with an attempt at wit, which fell quite flat, being extinguished by a frigid look from the Judge.

"Go," said M. Floçon, briefly and severely, to his subordinate; "and remember that you have now to justify your retention on the force."

Then, turning to M. Beaumont le Hardi, the Chief went on pleasantly:

"Well, M. le Juge, it promises, I think; it is all fairly satisfactory, eh?"

"I am sorry I cannot agree with you," replied the Judge, harshly. "On the contrary, I consider that we—or more exactly you, for neither I nor M. Garraud accept any share in it—you have so far failed, and miserably."

"Your pardon, M. le Juge, you are too severe," protested M. Floçon, quite humbly.

"Well! Look at it from all points of view. What have we got? What have we gained? Nothing, or, if anything, it is of the smallest, and it is already jeopardized, if not absolutely lost."

"We have at least gained the positive assurance of the guilt of certain individuals."

"Whom you have allowed to slip through your fingers."

"Ah, not so, M. le Juge! We have one under surveillance. My man Galipaud is there at the hotel watching the Countess."

"Do not talk to me of your men, M. Floçon," angrily interposed the Judge. "One of them has given us a touch of his quality. Why should not the other be equally foolish? I quite expect to hear that the Countess also has gone, that would be the climax!"

"It shall not happen. I will take the warrant and arrest her now, at once, myself," cried M. Floçon.

"Well, that will be something, yet not much. Yes, she is only one, and not to my mind the most criminal. We do not know as yet the exact responsibility of each, the exact measure of their guilt; but I do not myself believe that the Countess was a prime mover, or, indeed, more than an accessory. She was drawn into it, perhaps involved, how or why we cannot know, but possibly by fortuitous circumstances that put an unavoidable pressure upon her; a consenting party, but under protest. That is my view of the lady."

M. Floçon shook his head. Prepossessions with him were tenacious, and he had made up his mind about the Countess's guilt.

"When you again interrogate her, M. le Juge, by the light of your present knowledge, I believe you will think otherwise. She will confess,–you will make her, your skill is unrivalled,–and you will then admit, M. le Juge, that I was right in my suspicions."

"Ah, well, produce her! We shall see," said the Judge, somewhat mollified by M. Floçon's fulsome flattery.

"I will bring her to your chamber of instruction within an hour, M. le Juge," said the detective, very confidently.

But he was doomed to disappointment in this as he was in other respects.

CHAPTER XV

Let us go back a little in point of time, and follow the movements of Sir Charles Collingham.

It was barely 11 A.M. when he left the Lyons Station with his brother, the Reverend Silas, and the military attaché, Colonel Papillon. They paused for a moment outside the station while the baggage was being got together.

"See, Silas," said the General, pointing to the clock, "you will have plenty of time for the 11.50 train to Calais for London, but you must hurry up and drive straight across Paris to the Nord. I suppose he can go, Jack?"

"Certainly, as he has promised to return if called upon."

And Mr. Collingham promptly took advantage of the permission.

"But you, General, what are your plans?" went on the attaché.

"I shall go to the club first, get a room, dress, and all that. Then call at the Hotel Madagascar. There is a lady there,—one of our party, in fact,—and I should like to ask after her. She may be glad of my services."

"English? Is there anything we can do for her?"

"Yes, she is an Englishwoman, but the widow of an Italian— the Contessa di Castagneto."

"Oh, but I know her!" said Papillon. "I remember her in Rome two or three years ago. A deuced pretty woman, very much admired, but she was in deep mourning then, and went out very little. I wished she had gone out more. There were lots of men ready to fall at her feet."

"You were in Rome, then, some time back? Did you ever come across a man there, Quadling, the banker?"

"Of course I did. Constantly. He was a good deal about—a rather free-living, self-indulgent sort of chap. And now you mention his name, I recollect they said he was much smitten by this particular lady, the Contessa di Castagneto."

"And did she encourage him?"

"Lord! how can I tell? Who shall say how a woman's fancy falls? It might have suited her too. They said she was not in very good circumstances, and he was thought to be a rich man. Of course we know better than that now."

"Why now?"

"Haven't you heard? It was in the Figaro yesterday, and in all the Paris papers. Quadling's bank has gone to smash; he has bolted with all the 'ready' he could lay hands upon."

"He didn't get far, then!" cried Sir Charles. "You look surprised, Jack. Didn't they tell you? This Quadling was the man murdered in the sleeping-car. It was no doubt for the money he carried with him."

"Was it Quadling? My word! What a terrible Nemesis. Well, nil nisi bonum, but I never thought much of the chap, and your friend the Countess has had an escape. But now, sir, I must be moving. My engagement is for twelve noon. If you want me, mind you send—207 Rue Miromesnil, or to the Embassy; but let us arrange to meet this evening, eh? Dinner and a theatre—what do you say?"

Then Colonel Papillon rode off, and the General was driven to the Boulevard des Capucines, having much to occupy his thoughts by the way.

It did not greatly please him to have this story of the Countess's relations with Quadling, as first hinted at by the police, endorsed now by his friend Papillon. Clearly she had kept up her acquaintance, her intimacy to the very last: why otherwise should she have received him, alone, been closeted with him for an hour or more on the very eve of his flight? It was a clandestine acquaintance too, or seemed so, for Sir Charles, although a frequent visitor at her house, had never met Quadling there.

What did it all mean? And yet, what, after all, did it matter to him?

A good deal really more than he chose to admit to himself, even now, when closely questioning his secret heart. The fact was, the Countess had made a very strong impression on him from the first. He had admired her greatly during the past winter at Rome, but then it was only a passing fancy, as he thought,—the pleasant platonic flirtation of a middle-aged man, who never expected to inspire or feel a great love. Only now, when he had shared a serious trouble with her, had passed through common difficulties and dangers, he was finding what accident may do—how it may fan a first liking into a stronger flame. It was absurd, of course. He was fifty-one, he had weathered many trifling affairs of the heart, and here he was, bowled over at last, and by a woman he was not certain was entitled to his respect.

What was he to do?

The answer came at once and unhesitatingly, as it would to any other honest, chivalrous gentleman.

"By George, I'll stick to her through thick and thin! I'll trust her whatever happens or has happened, come what may. Such a woman as that is above suspicion. She must be straight. I should be a beast and a blackguard double distilled to think anything else. I am sure she can put all right with a word, can explain everything when she chooses. I will wait till she does."

Thus fortified and decided, Sir Charles took his way to the Hotel Madagascar about noon. At the desk he inquired for the Countess, and begged that his card might be sent up to her. The man looked at it, then at the visitor, as he stood there waiting rather impatiently, then again at the card. At last he walked out and across the inner courtyard of the hotel to the office. Presently the manager came back, bowing low, and, holding the card in his hand, began a desultory conversation.

"Yes, yes," cried the General, angrily cutting short all references to the weather and the number of English visitors in Paris. "But be so good as to let Madame la Comtesse know that I have called."

"Ah, to be sure! I came to tell Monsieur le Général that madame will hardly be able to see him. She is indisposed, I believe. At any rate, she does not receive to-day."

"As to that, we shall see. I will take no answer except direct from her. Take or send up my card without further delay. I insist! Do you hear?" said the General, so fiercely that the manager turned tail and fled up-stairs.

Perhaps he yielded his ground the more readily that he saw over the General's shoulder the figure of Galipaud the detective looming in the archway. It had been arranged that, as it was not advisable to have the inspector hanging about the courtyard of the hotel, the clerk or the manager should keep watch over the Countess and detain any visitors who might call upon her.

Galipaud had taken post at a wine-shop over the way, and was to be summoned whenever his presence was thought necessary.

There he was now, standing just behind the General, and for the present unseen by him.

But then a telegraph messenger came in and up to the desk. He held the usual blue envelope in his hand, and called out the name on the address:

"Castagneto. Contessa Castagneto."

At sound of which the General turned sharply, to find Galipaud advancing and stretching out his hand to take the message.

"Pardon me," cried Sir Charles, promptly interposing and understanding the situation at a glance. "I am just going up to see that lady. Give me the telegram."

Galipaud would have disputed the point, when the General, who had already recognized him, said quietly:

"No, no, Inspector, you have no earthly right to it. I guess why you are here, but you are not entitled to interfere with private correspondence. Stand back;" and seeing the detective hesitate, he added peremptorily:

"Enough of this. I order you to get out of the way. And be quick about it!"

The manager now returned, and admitted that Madame la Comtesse would receive her visitor. A few seconds more, and the General was admitted into her presence.

"How truly kind of you to call!" she said at once, coming up to him with both hands outstretched and frank gladness in her eyes.

Yes, she was very attractive in her plain, dark travelling dress draping her tall, graceful figure; her beautiful, pale face was enhanced by the rich tones of her dark brown, wavy hair, while just a narrow band of white muslin at her wrists and neck set off the dazzling clearness of her skin.

"Of course I came. I thought you might want me, or might like to know the latest news," he answered, as he held her hands in his for a few seconds longer than was perhaps absolutely necessary.

"Oh, do tell me! Is there anything fresh?" There was a flash of crimson colour in her cheek, which faded almost instantly. "This much. They have found out who the man was."

"Really? Positively? Whom do they say now?"

"Perhaps I had better not tell you. It may surprise you, shock you to hear. I think you knew him—"

"Nothing can well shock me now. I have had too many shocks already. Who do they think it is?"

"A Mr. Quadling, a banker, who is supposed to have absconded from Rome."

She received the news so impassively, with such strange self-possession, that for a moment he was disappointed in her. But then, quick to excuse, he suggested:

"You may have already heard?"

"Yes; the police people at the railway station told me they thought it was Mr. Quadling."

"But you knew him?"

"Certainly. They were my bankers, much to my sorrow. I shall lose heavily by their failure."

"That also has reached you, then?" interrupted the General, hastily and somewhat uneasily.

"To be sure. The man told me of it himself. Indeed, he came to me the very day I was leaving Rome, and made me an offer—a most obliging offer."

"To share his fallen fortunes?"

"Sir Charles Collingham! How can you? That creature!" The contempt in her tone was immeasurable.

"I had heard—well, someone said that—"

"Speak out, General; I shall not be offended. I know what you mean. It is perfectly true that the man once presumed to pester me with his attentions. But I would as soon have looked at a courier or a cook. And now—"

There was a pause. The General felt on delicate ground. He could ask no questions—anything more must come from the Countess herself.

"But let me tell you what his offer was. I don't know why I listened to it. I ought to have at once informed the police. I wish I had."

"It might have saved him from his fate."

"Every villain gets his deserts in the long run," she said, with bitter sententiousness. "And this Mr. Quadling is—But wait, you shall know him better. He came to me to propose—what do you think?—that he—his bank, I mean—should secretly repay me the amount of my deposit, all the money I had in it. To join me in his fraud, in fact–"

"The scoundrel! Upon my word, he has been well served. And that was the last you saw of him?"

"I saw him on the journey, at Turin, at Modane, at–Oh, Sir Charles, do not ask me any more about him!" she cried, with a sudden outburst, half-grief, half-dread. "I cannot tell you–I am obliged to–I–I–"

"Then do not say another word," he said, promptly.

"There are other things. But my lips are sealed–at least for the present. You do not–will not think any worse of me?"

She laid her hand gently on his arm, and his closed over it with such evident good-will that a blush crimsoned her cheek. It still hung there, and deepened when he said, warmly:

"As if anything could make me do that! Don't you know–you may not, but let me assure you, Countess–that nothing could happen to shake me in the high opinion I have of you. Come what may, I shall trust you, believe in you, think well of you– always."

"How sweet of you to say that! and now, of all times," she murmured quite softly, and looking up for the first time, shyly, to meet his eyes.

Her hand was still on his arm, covered by his, and she nestled so close to him that it was easy, natural, indeed, for him to slip his other arm around her waist and draw her to him.

"And now–of all times–may I say one word more?" he whispered in her ear. "Will you give me the right to shelter and protect you, to stand by you, share your troubles, or keep them from you–?"

"No, no, no, indeed, not now!" She looked up appealingly, the tears brimming up in her bright eyes. "I cannot, will not accept this sacrifice. You are only speaking out of your true-hearted chivalry. You must not join yourself to me, you must not involve yourself–"

He stopped her protests by the oldest and most effectual method known in such cases. That first sweet kiss sealed the compact so quickly entered into between them.

And after that she surrendered at discretion. There was no more hesitation or reluctance; she accepted his love as he had offered it, freely, with whole heart and soul, crept up under his sheltering wing like a storm-beaten dove reentering the nest, and there, cooing softly, "My knight—my own true knight and lord," yielded herself willingly and unquestioningly to his tender caresses.

Such moments snatched from the heart of pressing anxieties are made doubly sweet by their sharp contrast with a background of trouble.

CHAPTER XVI

They sat there, these two, hand locked in hand, saying little, satisfied now to be with each other and their new-found love. The time flew by far too fast, till at last Sir Charles, with a half-laugh, suggested:

"Do you know, dearest Countess—"

She corrected him in a soft, low voice.

"My name is Sabine—Charles."

"Sabine, darling. It is very prosaic of me, perhaps, but do you know that I am nearly starved? I came on here at once. I have had no breakfast."

"Nor have I," she answered, smiling. "I was thinking of it when—when you appeared like a whirlwind, and since then, events have moved so fast."

"Are you sorry, Sabine? Would you rather go back to—to—before?" She made a pretty gesture of closing his traitor lips with her small hand.

"Not for worlds. But you soldiers—you are terrible men! Who can resist you?"

"Bah! It is you who are irresistible. But there, why not put on your jacket and let us go out to lunch somewhere—Durand's, Voisin's, the Café de le Paix? Which do you prefer?"

"I suppose they will not try to stop us?"

"Who should try?" he asked.

"The people of the hotel—the police—I cannot exactly say whom; but I dread something of the sort. I don't quite understand that manager. He has been up to see me several times, and he spoke rather oddly, rather rudely."

"Then he shall answer for it," snorted Sir Charles, hotly. "It is the fault of that brute of a detective, I suppose. Still they would hardly dare—"

"A detective? What? Here? Are you sure?"

"Perfectly sure. It is one of those from the Lyons Station. I knew him again directly, and he was inclined to be interfering. Why, I caught him trying—but that reminds me—I rescued this telegram from his clutches."

He took the little blue envelope from his breast pocket and handed it to her, kissing the tips of her fingers as she took it from him.

"Ah!"

A sudden ejaculation of dismay escaped her, when, after rather carelessly tearing the message open, she had glanced at it.

"What is the matter?" he asked in eager solicitude. "May I not know?"

She made no offer to give him the telegram, and said in a faltering voice, and with much hesitation of manner, "I do not know. I hardly think–of course I do not like to withhold anything, not now. And yet, this is a business which concerns me only, I am afraid. I ought not to drag you into it."

"What concerns you is very much my business, too. I do not wish to force your confidence, still–"

She gave him the telegram quite obediently, with a little sigh of relief, glad to realize now, for the first time after many years, that there was someone to give her orders and take the burden of trouble off her shoulders.

He read it, but did not understand it in the least. It ran: "I must see you immediately, and beg you will come. You will find Hortense here. She is giving trouble. You only can deal with her. Do not delay. Come at once, or we must go to you.–Ripaldi, Hotel Ivoire, Rue Bellechasse."

"What does this mean? Who sends it? Who is Ripaldi?" asked Sir Charles, rather brusquely.

"He–he–oh, Charles, I shall have to go. Anything would be better than his coming here."

"Ripaldi? Haven't I heard the name? He was one of those in the sleeping-car, I think? The Chief of the Detective Police called it out once or twice. Am I not right? Please tell me–am I not right?"

"Yes, yes; this man was there with the rest of us. A dark man, who sat near the door–"

"Ah, to be sure. But what–what in Heaven's name has he to do with you? How does he dare to send you such an impudent message as this? Surely, Sabine, you will tell me? You will admit that I have a right to ask?"

"Yes, of course. I will tell you, Charles, everything; but not here—not now. It must be on the way. I have been very wrong, very foolish—but oh, come, come, do let us be going. I am so afraid he might—"

"Then I may go with you? You do not object to that?"

"I much prefer it—much. Do let us make haste!"

She snatched up her sealskin jacket, and held it to him prettily, that he might help her into it, which he did neatly and cleverly, smoothing her great puffed-out sleeves under each shoulder of the coat, still talking eagerly and taking no toll for his trouble as she stood patiently, passively before him.

"And this Hortense? It is your maid, is it not—the woman who had taken herself off? How comes it that she is with that Italian fellow? Upon my soul, I don't understand—not a little bit."

"I cannot explain that, either. It is most strange, most incomprehensible, but we shall soon know. Please, Charles, please do not get impatient."

They passed together down into the hotel courtyard and across it, under the archway which led past the clerk's desk into the street.

On seeing them, he came out hastily and placed himself in front, quite plainly barring their egress.

"Oh, madame, one moment," he said in a tone that was by no means conciliatory. "The manager wants to speak to you; he told me to tell you, and stop you if you went out."

"The manager can speak to madame when she returns," interposed the General angrily, answering for the Countess.

"I have had my orders, and I cannot allow her—"

"Stand aside, you scoundrel!" cried the General, blazing up; "or upon my soul I shall give you such a lesson you will be sorry you were ever born."

At this moment the manager himself appeared in reinforcement, and the clerk turned to him for protection and support.

"I was merely giving madame your message, M. Auguste, when this gentleman interposed, threatened me, maltreated me—"

"Oh, surely not; it is some mistake;" the manager spoke most suavely. "But certainly I did wish to speak to madame. I wished to ask her whether she was satisfied with her apartment. I find that the rooms she has generally occupied have fallen vacant, in the nick of time. Perhaps madame would like to look at them, and move?"

"Thank you, M. Auguste, you are very good; but at another time. I am very much pressed just now. When I return in an hour or two, not now."

The manager was profuse in his apologies, and made no further difficulty.

"Oh, as you please, madame. Perfectly. By and by, later, when you choose."

The fact was, the desired result had been obtained. For now, on the far side from where he had been watching, Galipaud appeared, no doubt in reply to some secret signal, and the detective with a short nod in acknowledgment had evidently removed his embargo.

A cab was called, and Sir Charles, having put the Countess in, was turning to give the driver his instructions, when a fresh complication arose.

Someone coming round the corner had caught a glimpse of the lady disappearing into the fiacre, and cried out from afar.

"Stay! Stop! I want to speak to that lady; detain her." It was the sharp voice of little M. Floçon, whom most of those present, certainly the Countess and Sir Charles, immediately recognized.

"No, no, no—don't let them keep me—I cannot wait now," she whispered in earnest, urgent appeal. It was not lost on her loyal and devoted friend.

"Go on!" he shouted to the cabman, with all the peremptory insistence of one trained to give words of command. "Forward! As fast as you can drive. I'll pay you double fare. Tell him where to go, Sabine. I'll follow—in less than no time."

The fiacre rattled off at top speed, and the General turned to confront M. Floçon.

The little detective was white to the lips with rage and disappointment; but he also was a man of promptitude, and before falling foul of this pestilent Englishman, who had again marred his plans, he shouted to Galipaud—

"Quick! After them! Follow her wherever she goes. Take this,"—he thrust a paper into his subordinate's hand. "It is a warrant for her arrest. Seize her wherever you find her, and bring her to the Quai l'Horloge," the euphemistic title of the headquarters of the French police.

The pursuit was started at once, and then the Chief turned upon Sir Charles. "Now it is between us," he said, fiercely. "You must account to me for what you have done."

"Must I?" answered the General, mockingly and with a little laugh.

"It is perfectly easy. Madame was in a hurry, so I helped her to get away. That was all."

"You have traversed and opposed the action of the law. You have impeded me, the Chief of the Detective Service, in the execution of my duty. It is not the first time, but now you must answer for it."

"Dear me!" said the General in the same flippant, irritating tone.

"You will have to accompany me now to the Prefecture."

"And if it does not suit me to go?"

"I will have you carried there, bound, tied hand and foot, by the police, like any common rapscallion taken in the act who resists the authority of an officer."

"Oho, you talk very big, sir. Perhaps you will be so obliging as to tell me what I have done."

"You have connived at the escape of a criminal from justice—"

"That lady? Psha!"

"She is charged with a heinous crime—that in which you yourself were implicated—the murder of that man on the train."

"Bah! You must be a stupid goose, to hint at such a thing! A lady of birth, breeding, the highest respectability—impossible!"

"All that has not prevented her from allying herself with base, common wretches. I do not say she struck the blow, but I believe she inspired, concerted, approved it, leaving her confederates to do the actual deed."

"Confederates?"

"The man Ripaldi, your Italian fellow traveller; her maid, Hortense Petitpré, who was missing this morning."

The General was fairly staggered at this unexpected blow. Half an hour ago he would have scouted the very thought, indignantly repelled the spoken words that even hinted a suspicion of Sabine Castagneto. But that telegram, signed Ripaldi, the introduction of the maid's name, and the suggestion that she was troublesome, the threat that if the Countess did not go, they would come to her, and her marked uneasiness thereat– all this implied plainly the existence of collusion, of some secret relations, some secret understanding between her and the others.

He could not entirely conceal the trouble that now overcame him; it certainly did not escape so shrewd an observer as M. Floçon, who promptly tried to turn it to good account.

"Come, M. le Général," he said, with much assumed bonhomie. "I can see how it is with you, and you have my sincere sympathy. We are all of us liable to be carried away, and there is much excuse for you in this. But now–believe me, I am justified in saying it –now I tell you that our case is strong against her, that it is not mere speculation, but supported by facts. Now surely you will come over to our side?"

"In what way?"

"Tell us frankly all you know–where that lady has gone, help us to lay our hands on her."

"Your own people will do that. I heard you order that man to follow her."

"Probably; still I would rather have the information from you. It would satisfy me of your good-will. I need not then proceed to extremities–"

"I certainly shall not give it you," said the General, hotly. "Anything I know about or have heard from the Contessa Castagneto is sacred; besides, I still believe in her–thoroughly. Nothing you have said can shake me."

"Then I must ask you to accompany me to the Prefecture. You will come, I trust, on my invitation." The Chief spoke quietly, but with considerable dignity, and he laid a slight stress upon the last word.

"Meaning that if I do not, you will have resort to something stronger?"

"That will be quite unnecessary, I am sure,–at least I hope so. Still–"

"I will go where you like, only I will tell you nothing more, not a single word; and before I start, I must let my friends at the Embassy know where to find me."

"Oh, with all my heart," said the little detective, shrugging his shoulders. "We will call there on our way, and you can tell the porter. They will know where to find us."

Sir Charles Collingham and his escort, M. Floçon, entered a cab together and were driven first to the Faubourg St. Honoré. The General tried hard to maintain his nonchalance, but he was yet a little crestfallen at the turn things had taken, and M. Floçon, who, on the other hand, was elated and triumphant, saw it. But no words passed between them until they arrived at the portals of the British Embassy, and the General handed out his card to the magnificent porter who received them.

"Kindly let Colonel Papillon have that without delay." The General had written a few words: "I have got into fresh trouble. Come on to me at the Police Prefecture if you can spare the time."

"The Colonel is now in the Chancery: will not monsieur wait?" asked the porter, with superb civility.

But the detective would not suffer this, and interposed, answering abruptly for Sir Charles:

"No. It is impossible. We are going to the Quai l'Horloge. It is an urgent matter."

The porter knew what the Quai l'Horloge meant, and he guessed intuitively who was speaking. Every Frenchman can recognize a police officer, and has, as a rule, no great opinion of him. "Very well!" now said the porter, curtly, as he banged the wicket-gate on the retreating cab, and he did not hurry himself in giving the card to Colonel Papillon.

"Does this mean that I am a prisoner?" asked Sir Charles, his gorge rising, as it did easily.

"It means, monsieur, that you are in the hands of justice until your recent conduct has been fully explained," said the detective, with the air of a despot.

"But I protest—"

"I wish to hear no further observations, monsieur. You may reserve them till you can give them to the right person."

The General's temper was sorely ruffled. He did not like it at all; yet what could he do? Prudence gained the day, and after a struggle he decided to submit, lest worse might befall him.

There was, in truth, worse to be encountered. It was very irksome to be in the power of this now domineering little man on his own ground, and eager to show his power. It was with a very bad grace that Sir Charles obeyed the curt orders he received, to leave the cab, to enter at a side door of the Prefecture, to follow this pompous conductor along the long vaulted passages of this rambling building, up many flights of stone stairs, to halt obediently at his command when at length they reached a closed door on an upper story.

"It is here!" said M. Floçon, as he turned the handle unceremoniously without knocking. "Enter."

A man was seated at a small desk in the centre of a big bare room, who rose at once at the sight of M. Floçon, and bowed deferentially without speaking.

"Baume," said the Chief, shortly, "I wish to leave this gentleman with you. Make him at home,"–the words were spoken in manifest irony,–"and when I call you, bring him at once to my cabinet. You, monsieur, you will oblige me by staying here."

Sir Charles nodded carelessly, took the first chair that offered, and sat down by the fire.

He was to all intents and purposes in custody, and he examined his gaoler at first wrathfully, then curiously, struck with his rather strange figure and appearance. Baume, as the Chief had called him, was a short, thick-set man with a great shock head sunk in low between a pair of enormous shoulders, betokening great physical strength; he stood on very thin but greatly twisted bow legs, and the quaintness of his figure was emphasized by the short black blouse or smock-frock he wore over his other clothes like a French artisan.

He was a man of few words, and those not the most polite in tone, for when the General began with a banal remark about the weather, M. Baume replied, shortly:

"I wish to have no talk;" and when Sir Charles pulled out his cigarette-case, as he did almost automatically from time to time when in any situation of annoyance or perplexity, Baume raised his hand warningly and grunted:

"Not allowed."

"Then I'll be hanged if I don't smoke in spite of every man jack of you!" cried the General, hotly, rising from his seat and speaking unconsciously in English.

"What's that?" asked Baume, gruffly. He was one of the detective staff, and was only doing his duty according to his lights, and he said so with such an injured air that the General was pacified, laughed, and relapsed into silence without lighting his cigarette.

The time ran on, from minutes into nearly an hour, a very trying wait for Sir Charles. There is always something irritating in doing antechamber work, in kicking one's heels in the waiting-room of any functionary or official, high or low, and the General found it hard to possess himself in patience, when he thought he was being thus ignominiously treated by a man like M. Floçon. All the time, too, he was worrying himself about the Countess, wondering first how she had fared; next, where she was just then; last of all, and longest, whether it was possible for her to be mixed up in anything compromising or criminal.

Suddenly an electric bell struck in the room. There was a table telephone at Baume's elbow; he took up the handle, put the tube to his mouth and ear, got his message answered, and then, rising, said abruptly to Sir Charles:

"Come."

When the General was at last ushered into the presence of the Chief of the Detective Police, he found to his satisfaction that Colonel Papillon was also there, and at M. Floçon's side sat the instructing judge, M. Beaumont le Hardi, who, after waiting politely until the two Englishmen had exchanged greetings, was the first to speak, and in apology.

"You will, I trust, pardon us, M. le Général, for having detained you here and so long. But there were, as we thought, good and sufficient reasons. If those have now lost some of their cogency, we still stand by our action as having been justifiable in the execution of our duty. We are now willing to let you go free, because—because—"

"We have caught the person, the lady you helped to escape," blurted out the detective, unable to resist making the point.

"The Countess? Is she here, in custody? Never!"

"Undoubtedly she is in custody, and in very close custody too," went on M. Floçon, gleefully. " Au secret, if you know what that means—in a cell separate and apart, where no one is permitted to see or speak to her."

"Surely not that? Jack–Papillon–this must not be. I beg of you, implore, insist, that you will get his lordship to interpose."

"But, sir, how can I? You must not ask impossibilities. The Contessa Castagneto is really an Italian subject now."

"She is English by birth, and whether or no, she is a woman, a high-bred lady; and it is abominable, unheard-of, to subject her to such monstrous treatment," said the General.

"But these gentlemen declare that they are fully warranted, that she has put herself in the wrong–greatly, culpably in the wrong."

"I don't believe it!" cried the General, indignantly. "Not from these chaps, a pack of idiots, always on the wrong tack! I don't believe a word, not if they swear."

"But they have documentary evidence–papers of the most damaging kind against her."

"Where? How?"

"He–M. le Juge–has been showing me a note-book;" and the General's eyes, following Jack Papillon's, were directed to a small carnet, or memorandum-book, which the Judge, interpreting the glance, was tapping significantly with his finger.

Then the Judge said blandly, "It is easy to perceive that you protest, M. le Général, against that lady's arrest. Is it so? Well, we are not called upon to justify it to you, not in the very least. But we are dealing with a brave man, a gentleman, an officer of high rank and consideration, and you shall know things that we are not bound to tell, to you or to any one."

"First," he continued, holding up the note-book, "do you know what this is? Have you ever seen it before?"

"I am dimly conscious of the fact, and yet I cannot say when or where."

"It is the property of one of your fellow travellers–an Italian called Ripaldi."

"Ripaldi?" said the General, remembering with some uneasiness that he had seen the name at the bottom of the Countess's telegram. "Ah! now I understand."

"You had heard of it, then? In what connection?" asked the Judge, a little carelessly, but it was a suddenly planned pitfall.

"I now understand," replied the General, perfectly on his guard, "why the note-book was familiar to me. I had seen it in that man's hands in the waiting-room. He was writing in it."

"Indeed? A favourite occupation evidently. He was fond of confiding in that note-book, and committed to it much that he never expected would see the light—his movements, intentions, ideas, even his inmost thoughts. The book—which he no doubt lost inadvertently is very incriminating to himself and his friends."

"What do you imply?" hastily inquired Sir Charles.

"Simply that it is on that which is written here that we base one part, perhaps the strongest, of our case against the Countess. It is strangely but convincingly corroborative of our suspicions against her."

"May I look at it for myself?" went on the General in a tone of contemptuous disbelief.

"It is in Italian. Perhaps you can read that language? If not, I have translated the most important passages," said the Judge, offering some other papers.

"Thank you; if you will permit me, I should prefer to look at the original;" and the General, without more ado, stretched out his hand and took the note-book.

What he read there, as he quickly scanned its pages, shall be told in the next chapter. It will be seen that there were things written that looked very damaging to his dear friend, Sabine Castagneto.

Ripaldi's diary—its ownership plainly shown by the record of his name in full, Natale Ripaldi, inside the cover—was a commonplace note-book bound in shabby drab cloth, its edges and corners strengthened with some sort of white metal. The pages were of coarse paper, lined blue and red, and they were dog-eared and smirched as though they had been constantly turned over and used.

The earlier entries were little more than a record of work to do or done.

"Jan. 11. To call at Café di Roma, 12.30. Beppo will meet me.

"Jan. 13. Traced M. L. Last employed as a model at S.'s studio, Palazzo B.

"Jan. 15. There is trouble brewing at the Circulo Bonafede; Louvaih, Malatesta, and the Englishman Sprot, have joined it. All are noted Anarchists.

"Jan. 20. Mem., pay Trattore. The Bestia will not wait. X. is also pressing, and Mariuccia. Situation tightens.

"Jan. 23. Ordered to watch Q. Could I work him? No. Strong doubts of his solvency.

"Feb. 10, 11, 12. After Q. No grounds yet.

"Feb. 27. Q. keeps up good appearance. Any mistake? Shall I try him? Sorely pressed. X. threatens me with Prefettura.

"March 1. Q. in difficulties. Out late every night. Is playing high; poor luck.

"March 3. Q. means mischief. Preparing for a start?

"March 10. Saw Q. about, here, there, everywhere."

Then followed a brief account of Quadling's movements on the day before his departure from Rome, very much as they have been described in a previous chapter. These were made mostly in the form of reflections, conjectures, hopes, and fears; hurry-scurry of pursuit had no doubt broken the immediate record of events, and these had been entered next day in the train.

"March 17 (the day previous). He has not shown up. I thought to see him at the buffet at Genoa. The conductor took him his coffee to the car. I hoped to have begun an acquaintance.

"12.30. Breakfasted at Turin. Q. did not come to table. Found him hanging about outside restaurant. Spoke; got short reply. Wishes to avoid observation, I suppose.

"But he speaks to others. He has claimed acquaintance with madame's lady's maid, and he wants to speak to the mistress. 'Tell her I must speak to her,' I heard him say, as I passed close to them. Then they separated hurriedly. "At Modane he came to the Douane, and afterwards into the restaurant. He bowed across the table to the lady. She hardly recognized him, which is odd. Of course she must know him; then why–? There is something between them, and the maid is in it.

"What shall I do? I could spoil any game of theirs if I stepped in. What are they after? His money, no doubt.

"So am I; I have the best right to it, for I can do most for him. He is absolutely in my power, and he'll see that–he's no fool–directly he knows who I am, and why I'm here. It will be worth his while to buy me off, if I'm ready to sell myself, and my duty, and the Prefettura–and why shouldn't I? What better can I do? Shall I ever have such a chance again? Twenty, thirty, forty thousand lire, more, even, at one stroke; why, it's a fortune! I could go to the Republic, to America, North or South, send for Mariuccia– no, cos petto! I will continue free! I will spend the money on myself, as I alone will have earned it, and at such risk.

"I have worked it out thus:

"I will go to him at the very last, just before we are reaching Paris. Tell him, threaten him with arrest, then give him his chance of escape. No fear that he won't accept it; he must, whatever he may have settled with the others. Altro! I snap my fingers at them. He has most to fear from me."

The next entries were made after some interval, a long interval, –no doubt, after the terrible deed had been done,–and the words were traced with trembling fingers, so that the writing was most irregular and scarcely legible.

"Ugh! I am still trembling with horror and fear. I cannot get it out of my mind; I never shall. Why, what tempted me? How could I bring myself to do it?

"But for these two women–they are fiends, furies–it would never have been necessary. Now one of them has escaped, and the other– she is here, so cold-blooded, so self-possessed and quiet–who would have thought it of her? That she, a lady of rank and high breeding, gentle, delicate, tender-hearted. Tender? the fiend! Oh, shall I ever forget her?

"And now she has me in her power! But have I not her also? We are in the same boat—we must sink or swim, together. We are equally bound, I to her, she to me. What are we to do? How shall we meet inquiry? Santissima Donna! why did I not risk it, and climb out like the maid? It was terrible for the moment, but the worst would have been over, and now—"

There was yet more, scribbled in the same faltering, agitated handwriting, and from the context the entries had been made in the waiting-room of the railroad station.

"I must attract her attention. She will not look my way. I want her to understand that I have something special to say to her, and that, as we are forbidden to speak, I am writing it herein—that she must contrive to take the book from me and read unobserved.

" Cos petto! she is stupid! Has fear dazed her entirely? No matter, I will set it all down."

Now followed what the police deemed such damaging evidence.

"Countess. Remember. Silence—absolute silence. Not a word as to who I am, or what is common knowledge to us both. It is done. That cannot be undone. Be brave, resolute; admit nothing. Stick to it that you know nothing, heard nothing. Deny that you knew him, or me. Swear you slept soundly the night through, make some excuse, say you were drugged, anything, only be on your guard, and say nothing about me. I warn you. Leave me alone. Or—but your interests are my interests; we must stand or fall together. Afterwards I will meet you—I must meet you somewhere. If we miss at the station front, write to me Poste Restante, Grand Hotel, and give me an address. This is imperative. Once more, silence and discretion."

This ended the writing in the note-book, and the whole perusal occupied Sir Charles from fifteen to twenty minutes, during which the French officials watched his face closely, and his friend Colonel Papillon anxiously.

But the General's mask was impenetrable, and at the end of his reading he turned back to read and re-read many pages, holding the book to the light, and seeming to examine the contents very curiously.

"Well?" said the Judge at last, when he met the General's eye.

"Do you lay great store by this evidence?" asked the General in a calm, dispassionate voice.

"Is it not natural that we should? Is it not strongly, conclusively incriminating?"

"It would be so, of course, if it were to be depended upon. But as to that I have my doubts, and grave doubts."

"Bah!" interposed the detective; "that is mere conjecture, mere assertion. Why should not the book be believed? It is perfectly genuine—"

"Wait, sir," said the General, raising his hand. "Have you not noticed—surely it cannot have escaped so astute a police functionary—that the entries are not all in the same handwriting?"

"What! Oh, that is too absurd!" cried both the officials in a breath.

They saw at once that if this discovery were admitted to be an absolute fact, the whole drift of their conclusions must be changed.

"Examine the book for yourselves. To my mind it is perfectly clear and beyond all question," insisted Sir Charles. "I am quite positive that the last pages were written by a different hand from the first."

For several minutes both the Judge and the detective pored over the note-book, examining page after page, shaking their heads, and declining to accept the evidence of their eyes.

"I cannot see it," said the Judge at last; adding reluctantly, "No doubt there is a difference, but it is to be explained."

"Quite so," put in M. Floçon. "When he wrote the early part, he was calm and collected; the last entries, so straggling, so ragged, and so badly written, were made when he was fresh from the crime, excited, upset, little master of himself. Naturally he would use a different hand."

"Or he would wish to disguise it. It was likely he would so wish," further remarked the Judge.

"You admit, then, that there is a difference?" argued the General, shrewdly. "But there is more than a disguise. The best disguise leaves certain unchangeable features. Some letters, capital G's, H's, and others, will betray themselves through the best disguise. I know what I am saying. I have studied the subject of handwriting; it interests me. These are the work of two different hands. Call in an expert; you will find I am right."

"Well, well," said the Judge, after a pause, "let us grant your position for the moment. What do you deduce? What do you infer therefrom?"

"Surely you can see what follows—what this leads us to?" said Sir Charles, rather disdainfully.

"I have formed an opinion—yes, but I should like to see if it coincides with yours. You think—"

"I know," corrected the General. "I know that, as two persons wrote in that book, either it is not Ripaldi's book, or the last of them was not Ripaldi. I saw the last writer at his work, saw him with my own eyes. Yet he did not write with Ripaldi's hand— this is incontestable, I am sure of it, I will swear it—ergo, he is not Ripaldi."

"But you should have known this at the time," interjected M. Floçon, fiercely. "Why did you not discover the change of identity? You should have seen that this was not Ripaldi."

"Pardon me. I did not know the man. I had not noticed him particularly on the journey. There was no reason why I should. I had no communication, no dealings, with any of my fellow passengers except my brother and the Countess."

"But some of the others would surely have remarked the change?" went on the Judge, greatly puzzled. "That alone seems enough to condemn your theory, M. le General."

"I take my stand on fact, not theory," stoutly maintained Sir Charles, "and I am satisfied I am right."

"But if that was not Ripaldi, who was it? Who would wish to masquerade in his dress and character, to make entries of that sort, as if under his hand?"

"Someone determined to divert suspicion from himself to others—"

"But stay—does he not plainly confess his own guilt?"

"What matter if he is not Ripaldi? Directly the inquiry was over, he could steal away and resume his own personality—that of a man supposed to be dead, and therefore safe from all interference and future pursuit."

"You mean—Upon my word, I compliment you, M. le Général. It is really ingenious! Remarkable, indeed! Superb!" cried the Judge, and only professional jealousy prevented M. Floçon from conceding the same praise.

"But how—what—I do not understand," asked Colonel Papillon in amazement. His wits did not travel quite so fast as those of his companions.

"Simply this, my dear Jack," explained the General: "Ripaldi must have tried to blackmail Quadling, as he proposed, and Quadling turned the tables on him. They fought, no doubt, and Quadling killed him, possibly in self-defence. He would have said so, but in his peculiar position as an absconding defaulter he did not dare. That is how I read it, and I believe that now these gentlemen are disposed to agree with me."

"In theory, certainly," said the Judge, heartily. "But oh! for some more positive proof of this change of character! If we could only identify the corpse, prove clearly that it is not Quadling. And still more, if we had not let this so-called Ripaldi slip through our fingers! You will never find him, M. Floçon, never."

The detective hung his head in guilty admission of this reproach.

"We may help you in both these difficulties, gentlemen," said Sir Charles, pleasantly. "My friend here, Colonel Papillon, can speak as to the man Quadling. He knew him well in Rome, a year or two ago."

"Please wait one moment only;" the detective touched a bell, and briefly ordered two fiacres to the door at once.

"That is right, M. Floçon," said the Judge. "We will all go to the Morgue. The body is there by now. You will not refuse your assistance, monsieur?"

"One moment. As to the other matter, M. le General?" went on M. Floçon. "Can you help us to find this miscreant, whoever he may be?"

"Yes. The man who calls himself Ripaldi is to be found—or, at least, you would have found him an hour or so ago—at the Hotel Ivoire, Rue Bellechasse. But time has been lost, I fear."

"Nevertheless, we will send there."

"The woman Hortense was also with him when last I heard of them."

"How do you know?" began the detective, suspiciously.

"Psha!" interrupted the Judge; "that will keep. This is the time for action, and we owe too much to the General to distrust him now."

"Thank you; I am pleased to hear you say that," went on Sir Charles. "But if I have been of some service to you, perhaps you owe me a little in return. That poor lady! Think what she is suffering. Surely, to oblige me, you will now set her free?"

"Indeed, monsieur, I fear—I do not see how, consistently with my duty"—protested the Judge.

"At least allow her to return to her hotel. She can remain there at your disposal. I will promise you that."

"How can you answer for her?"

"She will do what I ask, I think, if I may send her just two or three lines."

The Judge yielded, smiling at the General's urgency, and shrewdly guessing what it implied.

Then the three departures from the Prefecture took place within a short time of each other.

A posse of police went to arrest Ripaldi; the Countess returned to the Hotel Madagascar; and the Judge's party started for the Morgue,—only a short journey,—where they were presently received with every mark of respect and consideration.

The keeper, or officer in charge, was summoned, and came out bareheaded to the fiacre, bowing low before his distinguished visitors.

"Good morning, La Pêche," said M. Floçon in a sharp voice. "We have come for an identification. The body from the Lyons Station —he of the murder in the sleeping-car—is it yet arrived?"

"But surely, at your service, Chief," replied the old man, obsequiously. "If the gentlemen will give themselves the trouble to enter the office, I will lead them behind, direct into the mortuary chamber. There are many people in yonder."

It was the usual crowd of sightseers passing slowly before the plate glass of this, the most terrible shop-front in the world, where the goods exposed, the merchandise, are hideous corpses laid out in rows upon the marble slabs, the battered, tattered remnants of outraged humanity, insulted by the most terrible indignities in death.

Who make up this curious throng, and what strange morbid motives drag them there? Those fat, comfortable-looking women, with their baskets on their arms; the decent workmen in dusty blouses, idling between the hours of work; the riffraff of the streets, male or female, in various stages of wretchedness and degradation? A few, no doubt, are impelled by motives we cannot challenge—they are torn and tortured by suspense, trembling lest they may recognize missing dear ones among the exposed; others stare carelessly at the day's "take," wondering, perhaps, if they may come to the same fate; one or two are idle sightseers, not always French, for the Morgue is a favourite haunt with the irrepressible tourist doing Paris. Strangest of all, the murderer himself, the doer of the fell deed, comes here, to the very spot where his victim lies stark and reproachful, and stares at it spellbound, fascinated, filled more with remorse, perchance, than fear at the risk he runs. So common is this trait, that in mysterious murder cases the police of Paris keep a disguised officer among the crowd at the Morgue, and have thereby made many memorable arrests.

"This way, gentlemen, this way;" and the keeper of the Morgue led the party through one or two rooms into the inner and back recesses of the buildings. It was behind the scenes of the Morgue, and they were made free of its most gruesome secrets as they passed along.

The temperature had suddenly fallen far below freezing-point, and the icy cold chilled to the very marrow. Still worse was an all-pervading, acrid odour of artificially suspended animal decay. The cold-air process, that latest of scientific contrivances to arrest the waste of tissue, has now been applied at the Morgue to preserve and keep the bodies fresh, and allow them to be for a longer time exposed than when running water was the only aid. There are, moreover, many specially contrived refrigerating chests, in which those still unrecognized corpses are laid by for months, to be dragged out, if needs be, like carcasses of meat.

"What a loathsome place!" cried Sir Charles. "Hurry up, Jack! let us get out of this, in Heaven's name!"

"Where's my man?" quickly asked Colonel Papillon in response to this appeal.

"There, the third from the left," whispered M. Floçon. "We hoped you would recognize the corpse at once."

"That? Impossible! You do not expect it, surely? Why, the face is too much mangled for any one to say who it is."

"Are there no indications, no marks or signs, to say whether it is Quadling or not?" asked the Judge in a greatly disappointed tone.

"Absolutely nothing. And yet I am quite satisfied it is not him. For the simple reason that–"

"Yes, yes, go on."

"That Quadling in person is standing out there among the crowd."

M. Floçon was the first to realize the full meaning of Colonel Papillon's surprising statement.

"Run, run, La Pêche! Have the outer doors closed; let no one leave the place."

"Draw back, gentlemen!" he went on, and he hustled his companions with frantic haste out at the back of the mortuary chamber. "Pray Heaven he has not seen us! He would know us, even if we do not him."

Then with no less haste he seized Colonel Papillon by the arm and hurried him by the back passages through the office into the outer, public chamber, where the astonished crowd stood, silent and perturbed, awaiting explanation of their detention.

"Quick, monsieur!" whispered the Chief; "point him out to me."

The request was not unnecessary, for when Colonel Papillon went forward, and, putting his hand on a man's shoulder, saying, "Mr. Quadling, I think," the police officer was scarcely able to restrain his surprise.

The person thus challenged was very unlike any one he had seen before that day, Ripaldi most of all. The moustache was gone, the clothes were entirely changed; a pair of dark green spectacles helped the disguise. It was strange indeed that Papillon had known him; but at the moment of recognition Quadling had removed his glasses, no doubt that he might the better examine the object of his visit to the Morgue, that gruesome record of his own fell handiwork.

Naturally he drew back with well-feigned indignation, muttering half-unintelligible words in French, denying stoutly both in voice and gesture all acquaintance with the person who thus abruptly addressed him.

"This is not to be borne," he cried. "Who are you that dares–"

"Ta! ta!" quietly put in M. Floçon; "we will discuss that fully, but not here. Come into the office; come, I say, or must we use force?"

There was no escaping now, and with a poor attempt at bravado the stranger was led away.

"Now, Colonel Papillon, look at him well. Do you know him? Are you satisfied it is—"

"Mr. Quadling, late banker, of Rome. I have not the slightest doubt of it. I recognize him beyond all question."

"That will do. Silence, sir!" This to Quadling. "No observations. I too can recognize you now as the person who called himself Ripaldi an hour or two ago. Denial is useless. Let him be searched; thoroughly, you understand, La Pêche? Call in your other men; he may resist."

They gave the wretched man but scant consideration, and in less than three minutes had visited every pocket, examined every secret receptacle, and practically turned him inside out.

After this there could no longer be any doubt of his identity, still less of his complicity in the crime.

First among the many damning evidences of his guilt was the missing pocketbook of the porter of the sleeping-car. Within was the train card and the passengers' tickets, all the papers which the man Groote had lost so unaccountably. They had, of course, been stolen from his person with the obvious intention of impeding the inquiry into the murder. Next, in another inner pocket was Quadling's own wallet, with his own visiting-cards, several letters addressed to him by name; above all, a thick sheaf of bank-notes of all nationalities—English, French, Italian, and amounting in total value to several thousands of pounds.

"Well, do you still deny? Bah! it is childish, useless, mere waste of breath. At last we have penetrated the mystery. You may as well confess. Whether or no, we have enough to convict you by independent testimony," said the Judge, severely. "Come, what have you to say?"

But Quadling, with pale, averted face, stood obstinately mute. He was in the toils, the net had closed round him, they should have no assistance from him.

"Come, speak out; it will be best. Remember, we have means to make you—"

"Will you interrogate him further, M. Beaumont le Hardi? Here, at once?"

"No, let him be removed to the Prefecture; it will be more convenient; to my private office."

Without more ado a fiacre was called, and the prisoner was taken off under escort, M. Floçon seated by his side, one policeman in front, another on the box, and lodged in a secret cell at the Quai l'Horloge.

"And you, gentlemen?" said the Judge to Sir Charles and Colonel Papillon. "I do not wish to detain you further, although there may be points you might help us to elucidate if I might venture to still trespass on your time?"

Sir Charles was eager to return to the Hotel Madagascar, and yet he felt that he should best serve his dear Countess by seeing this to the end. So he readily assented to accompany the Judge, and Colonel Papillon, who was no less curious, agreed to go too.

"I sincerely trust," said the Judge on the way, "that our people have laid hands on that woman Petitpré. I believe that she holds the key to the situation, that when we hear her story we shall have a clear case against Quadling; and—who knows?— she may completely exonerate Madame la Comtesse."

During the events just recorded, which occupied a good hour, the police agents had time to go and come from the Rue Bellechasse. They did not return empty-handed, although at first it seemed as if they had made a fruitless journey. The Hotel Ivoire was a very second-class place, a lodging-house, or hotel with furnished rooms let out by the week to lodgers with whom the proprietor had no very close acquaintance. His clerk did all the business, and this functionary produced the register, as he is bound by law, for the inspection of the police officers, but afforded little information as to the day's arrivals.

"Yes, a man calling himself Dufour had taken rooms about midday, one for himself, one for madame who was with him, also named Dufour—his sister, he said;" and he went on at the request of the police officers to describe them.

"Our birds," said the senior agent, briefly. "They are wanted. We belong to the detective police."

"All right." Such visits were not new to the clerk.

"But you will not find monsieur; he is out; there hangs his key. Madame? No, she is within. Yes, that is certain, for not long since she rang her bell. There, it goes again."

He looked up at the furiously oscillating bell, but made no move.

"Bah! they do not pay for service; let her come and say what she needs."

"Exactly; and we will bring her," said the officer, making for the stairs and the room indicated.

But on reaching the door, they found it locked. From within? Hardly, for as they stood there in doubt, a voice inside cried vehemently:

"Let me out! Help! Help! Send for the police. I have much to tell them. Quick! Let me out."

"We are here, my dear, just as you require us. But wait; step down, Gaston, and see if the clerk has a second key. If not, call in a locksmith–the nearest. A little patience only, my beauty. Do not fear."

The key was quickly produced, and an entrance effected.

A woman stood there in a defiant attitude, with arms akimbo; she, no doubt, of whom they were in search. A tall, rather masculine-looking creature, with a dark, handsome face, bold black eyes just now flashing fiercely, rage in every feature.

"Madame Dufour?" began the police officer.

"Dufour! Rot! My name is Hortense Petitpré; who are you? La Rousse?" (Police.)

"At your service. Have you anything to say to us? We have come on purpose to take you to the Prefecture quietly, if you will let us; or–"

"I will go quietly. I ask nothing better. I have to lay information against a miscreant–a murderer–the vile assassin who would have made me his accomplice–the banker, Quadling, of Rome!"

In the fiacre Hortense Petitpré talked on with such incessant abuse, virulent and violent, of Quadling, that her charges were neither precise nor intelligible.

It was not until she appeared before M. Beaumont le Hardi, and was handled with great dexterity by that practised examiner, that her story took definite form.

What she had to say will be best told in the clear, formal language of the official disposition.

The witness inculpated stated:

"She was named Aglaé Hortense Petitpré, thirty-four years of age, a Frenchwoman, born in Paris, Rue de Vincennes No. 374. Was engaged by the Contessa Castagneto, November 19, 189–, in Rome, as lady's maid, and there, at her mistress's domicile, became acquainted with the Sieur Francis Quadling, a banker of the Via Condotti, Rome.

"Quadling had pretensions to the hand of the Countess, and sought, by bribes and entreaties, to interest witness in his suit. Witness often spoke of him in complimentary terms to her mistress, who was not very favourably disposed towards him.

"One afternoon (two days before the murder) Quadling paid a lengthened visit to the Countess. Witness did not hear what occurred, but Quadling came out much distressed, and again urged her to speak to the Countess. He had heard of the approaching departure of the lady from Rome, but said nothing of his own intentions.

"Witness was much surprised to find him in the sleeping-car, but had no talk to him till the following morning, when he asked her to obtain an interview for him with the Countess, and promised a large reward. In making this offer he produced a wallet and exhibited a very large number of notes.

"Witness was unable to persuade the Countess, although she returned to the subject frequently. Witness so informed Quadling, who then spoke to the lady, but was coldly received.

"During the journey witness thought much over the situation. Admitted that the sight of Quadling's money had greatly disturbed her, but, although pressed, would not say when the first idea of robbing him took possession of her. (Note by Judge—That she had resolved to do so is, however, perfectly clear, and the conclusion is borne out by her acts. It was she who secured the Countess's medicine bottle; she, beyond doubt, who drugged the porter at Laroche. In no other way can her presence in the sleeping-car between Laroche and Paris be accounted for—presence which she does not deny.)

"Witness at last reluctantly confessed that she entered the compartment where the murder was committed, and at a critical moment. An affray was actually in progress between the Italian Ripaldi and the incriminated man Quadling, but the witness arrived as the last fatal blow was struck by the latter.

"She saw it struck, and saw the victim fall lifeless on the floor.

"Witness declared she was so terrified she could at first utter no cry, nor call for help, and before she could recover herself the murderer threatened her with the ensanguined knife. She threw herself on her knees, imploring pity, but the man Quadling told her that she was an eye-witness, and could take him to the guillotine,—she also must die.

"Witness at last prevailed on him to spare her life, but only on condition that she would leave the car. He indicated the window as the only way of escape; but on this for a long time she refused to venture, declaring that it was only to exchange one form of death for another. Then, as Quadling again threatened to stab her, she was compelled to accept this last chance, never hoping to win out alive.

"With Quadling's assistance, however, she succeeded in climbing out through the window and in gaining the roof. He had told her to wait for the first occasion when the train slackened speed to leave it and shift for herself. With this intention he gave her a thousand francs, and bade her never show herself again.

"Witness descended from the train not far from the small station of Villeneuve on the line, and there took the local train for Paris. Landed at the Lyons Station, she heard of the inquiry in progress, and then, waiting outside, saw Quadling disguised as the Italian leave in company with another man. She followed and marked Quadling down, meaning to denounce him on the first opportunity. Quadling, however, on issuing from the restaurant, had accosted her, and at once offered her a further sum of five thousand francs as the price of silence, and she had gone with him to the Hotel Ivoire, where she was to receive the sum. Quadling had paid it, but on one condition, that she would remain at the Hotel Ivoire until the following day. Apparently he had distrusted her, for he had contrived to lock her into her compartment. As she did not choose to be so imprisoned, she summoned assistance, and was at length released by the police."

This was the substance of Hortense Petitpré's deposition, and it was corroborated in many small details.

When she appeared before the Judge, with whom Sir Charles Collingham and Colonel Papillon were seated, the former at once pointed out that she was wearing a dark mantle trimmed with the same sort of passementerie as that picked up in the sleeping-car.

L'Envoi .

Quadling was in due course brought before the Court of Assize and tried for his life. There was no sort of doubt of his guilt, and the jury so found, but, having regard to certain extenuating circumstances, they recommended him to mercy. The chief of these was Quadling's positive assurance that he had been first attacked by Ripaldi; he declared that the Italian detective had in the first instance tried to come to terms with him, demanding 50,000 francs as his price for allowing him to go at large; that when Quadling distinctly refused to be black-mailed, Ripaldi struck at him with a knife, but that the blow failed to take effect.

Then Quadling closed with him and took the knife from him. It was a fierce encounter, and might have ended either way, but the unexpected entrance of the woman Petitpré took off Ripaldi's attention, and then he, Quadling, maddened and reckless, stabbed him to the heart.

It was not until after the deed was done that Quadling realized the full measure of his crime and its inevitable consequences. Then, in a daring effort to extricate himself, he intimidated the woman Petitpré, and forced her to escape through the sleeping-car window.

It was he who had rung the signal-bell to stop the train and give her a chance of leaving it. It was after the murder, too, that he conceived the idea of personating Ripaldi, and, having disfigured him beyond recognition, as he hoped, he had changed clothes and compartments.

On the strength of this confession Quadling escaped the guillotine, but he was transported to New Caledonia for life.

The money taken on him was forwarded to Rome, and was usefully employed in reducing his liabilities to the depositors in the bank.

The other word.

Sometime in June the following announcement appeared in all the Paris papers:

"Yesterday, at the British Embassy, General Sir Charles Collingham, K. C. B., was married to Sabine, Contessa di Castagneto, widow of the Italian Count of that name."

THE VOICE IN THE FOG
BY HAROLD MACGRATH

ORIGINALLY PUBLISHED IN 1915

EDITOR'S NOTES:

THE VOICE IN THE FOG
BY HAROLD MACGRATH

More than one mystery has had its beginning in a dense fogs of London. In such a fog in becomes impossible for one to get ones bearings, and anything, or anyone, may appear from and disappear into the nearly solid walls that envelope one. In such a fog one can overhear conversations between strangers or find oneself in the wrong carriage. Such is the fog that begins Harold MacGrath's *The Voice in the Fog*.

The incidents in the fog, and there are more than one, lead the various characters on a trans-Atlantic journey by luxury steamship. And while some of them are free to partake of all that elegant mode of travel can offer, others find themselves forced to work for their passage. But that is part of the tale.

With its over-heard wager and theft of a priceless sapphire necklace, *The Voice in the Fog* offers more than its fair share of mystery, but as in many of MacGrath's works, there is also more than a little romance in evidence.

About the Author

Harold MacGrath (September 4, 1871-October 30, 1930) was an American novelist and writer of screenplays. Born in Syracuse, New York, he first worked as a journalist for the Syracuse Herald before turning to fiction. He wrote stories and novels of romance, mystery, espionage, and adventure, and in addition to having a number of top ten selling books he also wrote stories for many of the major magazines of the day. He was one of the first major authors to write for the film industry and over twenty of his stories and novels were turned into films.

THE VOICE IN THE FOG

CHAPTER I

Fog.

A London fog, solid, substantial, yellow as an old dog's tooth or a jaundiced eye. You could not look through it, nor yet gaze up and down it, nor over it; and you only thought you saw it. The eye became impotent, untrustworthy; all senses lay fallow except that of touch; the skin alone conveyed to you with promptness and no incertitude that this thing had substance. You could feel it; you could open and shut your hands and sense it on your palms, and it penetrated your clothes and beaded your spectacles and rings and bracelets and shoe-buckles. It was nightmare, bereft of its pillows, grown somnambulistic; and London became the antechamber to Hades, lackeyed by idle dreams and peopled by mistakes.

There is something about this species of fog unlike any other in the world. It sticks. You will find certain English cousins of yours, as far away from London as Hong-Kong, who are still wrapt up snugly in it. Happy he afflicted with strabismus, for only he can see his nose before his face. In the daytime you become a fish, to wriggle over the ocean's floor amid strange flora and fauna, such as ash-cans and lamp-posts and venders' carts and cab-horses and sandwich-men. But at night you are neither fish, bird nor beast.

The night was May thirteenth; never mind the year; the date should suffice: and a Walpurgis night, if you please, without any Mendelssohn to interpret it.

That happy line of Milton's--"Pandemonium, the high capital of Satan and his peers"--fell upon London like Elijah's mantle. Confusion and his cohort of synonyms (why not?) raged up and down thoroughfare and side-street and alley, east and west, danced before palace and tenement alike: all to the vast amusement of the gods, to the mild annoyance of the half-gods (in Mayfair), and to the complete rout of all mortals a-foot or a-cab. Imagine: militant suffragettes trying to set fire to the prime minister's mansion, *Siegfried* being sung at the opera, and a yellow London fog!

The press about Covent Garden was a mathematical problem over which Euclid would have shed bitter tears and hastily retired to his arbors and citron tables. Thirty years previous (to the thirteenth of May, not Euclid) some benighted beggar invented the Chinese puzzle; and tonight, many a frantic policeman would have preferred it, sitting with the scullery maid and the pantry near by. Simple matter to shift about little blocks of wood with the tip of one's finger; but cabs and carriages and automobiles, each driver anxious to get out ahead of his neighbor!--not to mention the shouting and the din and discord of horns and whistles and sirens and rumbling engines!

"It's hard luck," said Crawford, sympathetically. "It will be half an hour before they get this tangle straightened out."

"I shouldn't mind, Jim, if it weren't for Kitty," replied his wife. "I am worried about her."

"Well, I simply could not drag her into this coupé and get into hers myself. She's a heady little lady, if you want to know. As it is, she'll get back to the hotel quicker than we shall. Her cab is five up. If you wish, I'll take a look in and see if she's all right."

"Please do;" and she smiled at him, lovely, enchanting.

"You're the most beautiful woman in all this world!"

"Am I?"

Click! The light went out. There was a smothered laugh; and when the light flared up again, the aigrette in her copper-beech hair was all askew.

"If anybody saw us!"--secretly pleased and delighted, as any woman would have been who possessed a husband who was her lover all his waking hours.

"What! in this fog? And a lot I'd care if they did. Now, don't stir till I come back; and above all, keep the light on."

"And hurry right back; I'm getting lonesome already."

He stepped out of the coupé. Harlequin, and Colombine, and Humpty-Dumpty; shapes which came out of nowhere and instantly vanished into nothing, for all the world like the absurd pantomimes of his boyhood days. He kept close to the curb, scrutinizing the numbers as he went along. Never had he seen such a fog. Two paces away from the curb a headlight became an effulgence. Indeed, there were a thousand lights jammed in the street, and the fog above absorbed the radiance, giving the scene a touch of Brocken. All that was needed was a witch on a broomstick. He counted five vehicles, and stopped. The door-window was down.

"Miss Killigrew?" he said.

"Yes. Is anything wrong?"

"No. Just wanted to see if you were all right. Better let me take your place and you ride with Mrs. Crawford."

"Good of you; but you've had enough trouble. I shall stay right here."

"Where's your light?"

"The globe is broken. I'd rather be in the dark. Its fun to look about. I never saw anything to equal it."

"Not very cheerful. We'll be held up at least half an hour. You are not afraid?"

"What, I?" She laughed. "Why should I be afraid? The wait will not matter. But the truth is, I'm worried about mother. She would go to that suffragette meeting; and I understand they have tried to burn up the prime minister's house."

"Fine chance! But don't you worry. Your mother's a sensible woman. She'll get back to the hotel, if she isn't there already."

"I wish she had not gone. Father will be tearing his hair and twigging the whole Savoy force by the ears."

Crawford smiled. Readily enough he could conjure up the picture of Mr. Killigrew, short, thick-set, energetic, raging back and forth in the lobby, offering to buy taxicabs outright, the hotel, and finally the city of London itself; typically money-mad American that he was. Crawford wanted to laugh, but he compromised by saying: "He must be very careful of that hair of his; he hasn't much left."

"And he pulls out a good deal of it on my account. Poor dad! Why in the world should I marry a title?"

"Why, indeed!"

"Mrs. Crawford was beautiful tonight. There wasn't a beauty at the opera to compare with her. Royalties are frumps, aren't they? And that ruby! I don't see how she dares wear it!"

"I am not particularly fond of it; but it's a fad of hers. She likes to wear it on state occasions. I have often wondered if it is really the Nana Sahib's ruby, as her uncle claimed. Driver, the Savoy, and remember it carefully; the Savoy."

"Yes, sir; I understand, sir. But we'll all be some time, sir. Collision forward is what holds us, sir."

Alone again, Kitty Killigrew leaned back, thinking of the man who had just left her and of his beautiful wife. If only she might some day have a romance like theirs! Presently she peered out of the off-window. A brood of *Siegfried*-dragons prowled about, now going forward a little, now swerving, now pausing; lurid eyes and threatening growls.

Once upon a time, in her pigtail days, when her father was going to be rich and was only half-way between the beginning and the end of his ambition, Kitty had gone to a tent-circus. Among other things she had looked wonderingly into the dim, blurry glass-tank of the "human fish," who was at that moment busy selling photographs of himself. To-night, in searching for comparisons, this old forgotten picture recurred to her mind; blithely memory brought it forth and threw it upon the screen. All London had become a glass-tank, filled with human pollywogs.

She did not want to marry a title; she did not want to marry money; she did not want to marry at all. Poor kindly dad, who believed that she could be made happy only by marrying a title. As if she was not as happy now as she was ever destined to be!

Voices. Two men were speaking near the curb-door. She turned her head involuntarily in this direction. There were no lights in the frontage before which stood her cab, which intervened between the Brocken haze in the street, throwing a square of Stygian shadow against the fog, with right and left angles of aureola. She could distinguish no shapes.

"Cheer up, old top; you're in hard luck."

"I'm a bally ass."

"No, no; only a ripping good sporty game all the way through."

Oddly enough, Kitty sensed the irony. She wondered if the speaker's companion did.

"Well, a wager's a wager."

"And you're the last chap to welch a square bet. What's the odds? My word, I didn't urge you to change the stakes."

"Didn't you?"

The voice was young and pleasant; and Kitty was sure that the owner's face was even as pleasant as his voice. What had he wagered and lost?

"If you're really hard pressed. . . ."

"Hard pressed! Man, I've nothing in God's world but two guineas, six."

"Oh, I say now!"

"Its the truth."

"If a fiver will help you. . . ."

"Thanks. A wager's a wager. I've lost. I was a bally fool to play cards. Deserve what I got. Six months; that's the agreement. A madman's wager; but I'll stick."

"Six months; twelve o'clock, midnight, November thirteenth. It's the date, old boy; that's what hoodooed you, as the Americans say."

Kitty wasn't sure that the speaker was English; if he was, he had lost the insular significance of his vowels. Still, it was, in its way, as pleasant a voice as the other's. There was no doubt about the younger man; he was English to the core, English in his love of chance, English in his loyalty to his word; stupidly English. That he was the younger was a trifling matter to deduce: no young man ever led his elder into mischief, harmful or innocuous.

"Six months. It's a joke, my boy; a great big laugh for you and me, when there's nothing left in life but toddies and churchwardens. Six months."

"I dare say I can hang on till that time is over. Well, good night! No letters, no addresses."

"Exact terms. Six months from date I'll be cooling my heels in your ante-room."

"Cavenaugh, if it's anything else except a joke. . . ."

"Oh, rot! It was your suggestion. I tell you, it's a lark, nothing more. A gentleman's word."

"I'll start for my diggings."

"Ride home with me; my cab's here somewhere."

"No, thanks. I've got a little thinking to do and prefer to be alone. Good night."

"And good luck go with you. Deuce take it, if you feel so badly. . . ."

There was no reply; and Kitty decided that the younger man had gone on. Silence; or rather, she no longer heard the speakers. Then a low chuckle came to her and this chuckle broadened into ironic laughter; and she knew that Mephisto was abroad. What had been the wager; and what was the meaning of the six months? It is instinctive in woman to interpret the human voice correctly, especially when the eyes are not distracted by physical presentations. This man outside, whoever and whatever he was, deep in her heart Kitty knew that he was not going to play fair. What a disappointing world it was!--to set these human voices ringing in her ears, and then to take them out of her life forever!

Still the din of horns and whistles and sirens, still the shouting. Would they never move on? She was hungry. She wanted to get back to the hotel, to learn what had happened to her mother. Militant suffragettes, indeed! A pack of mad witches, who left their brooms behind kitchen doors when they ought to be wielding them about dusty corners. Woman never won anything by using brickbats and torches: which proved on the face of it that these militants were inefficient, irresponsible, and unlearned in history. Poor simpletons! Had not theirs always been the power behind the throne? What more did they want?

Her cogitations were peculiarly interrupted. The door opened, and a man plumped down beside her.

"Enid, it looks as if we'd never get out of this hole. Have you got your collar up?"

Numb and terrified, Kitty felt the man's hands fumbling about her neck.

"Where's your sable stole? You women beat the very devil for thoughtlessness. A quid to a farthing, you've left it in the box, and I'll have to go back for it, providing they'll let me in. And it's midnight, if a minute."

Pressing herself tightly into her corner, Kitty managed to gasp: "My name is not Enid, sir. You have mistaken your carriage."

"What? Good heavens!" Almost instantly a match sparkled and flared. His eyes, screened behind his hand, palm outward (a perfectly natural action, yet nicely calculated), beheld a pretty, charming face, large Irish blue eyes (a bit startled at this moment), and a head of hair as shiny-black as polished Chinese blackwood. The match, still burning, curved like a falling star through the window. "A thousand pardons, madam! Very stupid of me. Quite evident that I am lost. I beg your pardon again, and hope I have not annoyed you."

He was gone before she could form any retort. Where had she heard that voice before? With a little shudder--due to the thought of those cold strange fingers feeling about her throat-- her hands went up. Instantly she cried aloud in dismay. Her sapphires! They had vanished!

CHAPTER II

Daniel Killigrew, of Killigrew and Company (sugar, coffee and spices), was in a towering rage; at least, he towered one inch above his normal height, which was five feet six. Like an animal recently taken in captivity he trotted back and forth through the corridors, in and out of the office, to and from the several entrances, blowing the while like a grampus. All he could get out of these infernally stupid beings was "Really, sir!" He couldn't get a cab, he couldn't get a motor, he couldn't get anything. Manager, head-clerk, porter, doorman and page, he told them, one and all, what a dotty old spoof of a country they lived in; that they were all dead-alive persons, fit to be neither under nor above earth; that they wouldn't be one-two in a race with January molasses--"Treacle, I believe you call it here!" And what did they say to this scathing arraignment? Yes, what did they say? "Really, sir!" He knew and hoped it would happen: if ever Germany started war, it would be over before these Britishers made up their minds that there was a war. A hundred years ago they had beaten Napoleon (with the assistance of Spain, Austria, Germany and Russia), and were now resting.

Quarter to one, and neither wife nor daughter; outside there, somewhere in the fog; and he could not go to them. It was maddening. Molly might be arrested and Kitty lost. Served him right; he should have put his foot down. The idea of Molly being allowed to go with those rattle-pated women! Suffragettes! A "Bah!" exploded with a loud report. Hereafter he would show who voted in the Killigrew family. Poor man! He was made of that unhappy mental timber which agrees thoughtlessly to a proposition for the sake of peace and then regrets it in the name of war. His wife and daughter twisted him round their little fingers and then hunted cover when he found out what they had done.

He went out again to the main entrance and smoked himself headachy. He hated London. He had always hated it in theory, now he hated it in fact. He hated tea, buttered muffins, marmalade, jam, toast, cricket, box hedges three hundred years old, ruins, and the checkless baggage system, the wet blankets called newspapers. All the racial hatred of his forebears

(Tipperary born) surged hot and wrathful in his veins. At the drop of a hat he would have gone to war, individually, with all England. "Really, sir!" Nothing but that, when he was dying of anxiety!

A taxicab drew up before the canopy. He knew it was a taxicab because he could hear the sound of the panting engine. The curb-end of the canopy was curtained by the abominable fog. Mistily a forlorn figure emerged. The doorman started leisurely toward this figure. Killigrew pushed him aside violently. Molly, with her hat gone, her hair awry, her dress torn, her gloves ragged, her eyes puffed! He sprang toward her, filled with Berserker rage. Who had dared.

"Give the man five pounds," she whispered. "I promised it."

"Five. . . ."

"Give it to him! Good heavens, do I look as if I were joking? Pay him, pay him!"

Killigrew counted out five sovereigns, perhaps six, he was not sure. The chauffeur swooped them up, and set off.

"Molly Killigrew. . . ."

"Not a word till I get to the rooms. Hurry! Daniel, if you say anything I shall fall down!"

He led her to the lift. Curious glances followed, but these signified nothing. On a night such as this was there would be any number of accidents. Once in the living-room of the luxurious suite, Mrs. Killigrew staggered over to the divan and tumbled down upon it. She began to cry hysterically.

"Molly, old girl! Molly!" He put his arm tenderly across her heaving shoulders and kneeled. His old girl! Love crowded out all other thoughts. Money-mad he might be, but he never forgot that Molly had once fried his meat and peeled his potatoes and darned his socks. "Molly, what has happened? Who did this? Tell me, and I'll kill him!"

"Dan, when they started up the street for the prime minister's house, I could not get out of the crowd. I was afraid to. It was so foggy you had to follow the torches. I did not know what they were about till the police rushed us. One grabbed me, but I got away." All this between sobs. "Dan, I don't want to be a suffragette." Sob. "I don't want to vote." Sob.

And for the first time that night Killigrew smiled.

"Where's Kitty?"

He started to his feet. "She hasn't got back from the opera yet. She'll be the death of me, one of these fine days. You know her. Like as not she's stepped out of her cab to see what's going on, and has lost herself."

"But the Crawfords were with her."

"Would that make any difference with Kitty if she wanted to get out? I told her not to wear any jewels, but she wouldn't mind me. She never does. I haven't any authority except in my offices. You and Kitty. . . ."

"Don't scold!"

"All right; I won't. But, all the same, you and the girl need checking."

"Daniel, it was only because I wanted something to occupy myself with. It's no fun for me to sit still in my house and watch everybody else work. The butler orders the meals, the housekeeper takes charge of the linen, the footman the carriages. Why, I can't find a button to sew on anything any more. I only wanted something to do."

Killigrew did not smile this time. Here was the whole matter in a nutshell: she wanted something to do. And there were thousands of others just like her. Man-like, he forgot that women needed something more than money and attention from an army of servants. He had his offices, his stock-ticker, his warfare. Not because she wanted to vote, but because she wanted and needed something to do.

"Molly, old girl, I begin to see. I'm going to finance a home-bureau of charity. I mean it. Fifty thousand the year to do with as you like. No hospitals, churches, heathen; but the needy and deserving near by. You can send boys to college and girls to schools; and Kitty'll be glad to be your lieutenant. I never had a college education. Not that I ever needed it,"--with sudden truculence in his tone. "But it might be a good thing for some of the rising generations in my tenements. I'll leave the choice to you. And when it comes to voting, why, tell me which way to vote, and I'll do it. I'll be a bull moose, if you say so."

"You're the kindest man in the world, Dan, and I'm an old fool of a woman!"

Kitty burst into the room, star-eyed, pale. "Mother!" She sped to her mother's side. "Oh, I felt it in my bones that something was going to happen!"

"Think of it, Kitty dear; your mother, fighting with a policeman! Oh, it was frightful!"

"Never mind, mumsy," Kitty soothed. She rang for the maid, a thing her father had not thought to do. And when her mother was snug in bed, her head in cooling bandages, her face and hands bathed in refreshing cologne, Kitty returned to her father, "Dad, you mustn't say a word to mother about it, but I've been robbed."

"What?"

"My necklace. And I could not identify the thief if he stood before me this very minute. The interior light was out of order. He entered, pretending he had made a mistake. He called me Enid and told me to put up my collar; touched my neck with his hands. I was so astonished that I could not move. Finally I managed to explain that he had made a mistake. He apologized and got out; and it is quite evident that the necklace went with him."

"Can't you remember the least thing about him?"

"Nothing, absolutely nothing."

"Where were the Crawfords?"

"I did not wait to see them. My cab was ahead of theirs. What shall we do?"

"Notify the police; it's all we can do. They cost me an even ten thousand, Kitty. And I told you not to wear them on a night like this. I'm discouraged. I want to get out of this blasted country. I'm hoodooed." Killigrew walked the floor. He took out a cigar, eyed it thoughtfully, and returned it to his pocket. "Because they happen to be born in this smoke, they think the way they do things is the last word on the subject. I'd like to show them."

"Dad,"--with a bit of a smile,--"I know what the trouble is. You want to go home."

"And that's the truth. This is the first trip abroad I ever took with you and your mother, and it's going to be the last. I can't live out of my element, which is hurry and bustle and getting things done quickly. I'm a fish out of water. I want to go home; I want to see the Giants wallop the Cubs; and I want my two-weeks' bass fishing. But I'll hang on till the end of June as I promised. Ten thousand in sapphires you couldn't match in a hundred years, and Molly coming in banged up like a prize-fighter! . . . Someone at the door."

It proved to be Crawford.

"Glad you got back safely," he said relievedly.

"Had her necklace stolen," replied Killigrew briefly.

"You don't mean to say. . . ."

Kitty recounted her amazing adventure.

"And my wife's ruby is gone." Crawford made the disclosure simply. He was a quiet man; he had learned the futility of gestures, of wasting words in lamentation.

"Good gracious!" exclaimed Kitty.

"The windows of the cab were down. I stood outside, smoking to pass the time. Suddenly I heard Mrs. Crawford cry out. A hand had reached in from the off side, clutched the pendant, twisted it off, and was gone. All quicker than I can tell it. I tried to give chase, but it was utter folly. I couldn't see anything two feet away. Mrs. Crawford is a bit knocked up over it. Rather sinister stone, if its history is a true one: the Nana Sahib's ruby, you know. For the jewel itself I don't care. I never liked to see her wear it."

Killigrew threw up his hands. "And this is the London you've been bragging about to me! How much was the ruby worth?"

"Don't know; nobody does. It's one of those jewels you can't set a price on. He will not be able to dispose of it in its present shape. He'll break it up and sell the pieces, and that's the shame of it. Think of the infernal cleverness of the man! Two or three hundred vehicles stalled in the street, fog so thick you couldn't see your hand before your face. Simple game for a man with ready wit. And the police busy at the two ends of the block, trying to straighten out the tangle. Mrs. Crawford says that the hand was white, slender and well kept. It came in swiftly and accurately. The man had been watching and waiting. She was so unprepared for the act that she didn't even try to catch the hand. I have notified Scotland Yard. But you can't hunt down a hand. I'm willing to wager that we'll neither of us ever see the gems again."

"He must have come directly from your carriage to mine," said Kitty. "I am heart-broken."

"One of the tricks of fate. Glad you got back all right. We were mightily worried. Come over across the hall at nine to-morrow, all of you, for breakfast. Don't fuss up. And we'll talk over the affair and plan what's to be done. Good night."

"I like that young man," declared Killigrew emphatically. "He's the real article. American to the backbone; a millionaire who doesn't splurge. Well," sighing regretfully, "he was born to it, and I had to dig for mine. But I can't get it through my head why he wants to excavate mummies when he could dig up potatoes with some profit."

"Dad, find me an earl or a duke like Mr. Crawford, and I'll marry him just as fast as you like."

"Kittibudget, I'm not so strong for dukes as I was. Your mother will have a black eye in the morning, or I don't know a shindy when I see it. Now, hike off to bed. I'm all in."

"You poor old dad! I worry you to death."

She threw her lovely arms about his neck and kissed him.

"Well, you're worth it. Kitty, I've had a jolt to-night. You marry whom you blame please. I've been doing some tall thinking. Make your own romance, duke or dry-goods clerk. You'd never hook up with anything that wasn't a man. You're Irish. If he happens to be made, all well and good; if not, why, I'll undertake to make him. And that's a bargain. I don't want any alimony money in the Killigrew family."

She kissed him again and went into her bedroom. Kind-hearted, impulsive old dad! In a week's time he would forget all about this heart-to-heart talk, and shoo away every male who hadn't a title or a million, or who wasn't due to fall heir to one or the other. Nevertheless, she had long since made up her mind to build her own romance. That was her right, and she did not propose to surrender it to anybody. Her weary head on the pillow, she thought of the voices in the fog. "A wager's a wager."

The next morning the fog was not quite so thick; that is, in places there were holes and punctures. You saw a man's face and torso, but neither hat nor legs. Again, you saw the top of a cab bowling along, but no horse: phantasmally.

Breakfast in Crawford's suite was merry enough. Misfortune was turned into jest. At least, they made a fine show of it; which is characteristic of people who bow to the inevitable whenever confronted by it. Crawford was passing his cigars, when a page was announced. The boy entered briskly, carrying a tray upon which reposed a small package.

"By special messenger, sir. It was thought you might be liking to have it at once, sir." The page pocketed the shilling politely and departed.

"That's the first bit of live work I've seen anybody do in this hotel," commented Killigrew, striking a match.

"I have stopped here often," said Crawford, "and they are familiar with my wishes. Excuse me till I see what this is."

The quartet at the table began chatting again, about the fog, what they intended doing in Paris, sunshiny Paris. By and by Crawford came over quietly and laid something on the table before his wife's plate.

It was the Nana Sahib's ruby, so-called.

CHAPTER III

That same morning, at eleven precisely (when an insolent west wind sprang up and tore the fog into ribbons and scarves and finally blew it into smithereens, channelward) there stood before the windows of a famous haberdashery in the Strand a young man, twenty-four years of age, typically English, beardless, hair clipped neatly about his neck and temples, his skin fresh colored, his body carefully but thriftily clothed. Smooth-skinned he was about the eyes and nose and mouth, unmarked by dissipation; and he stood straight; and by the set of his shoulders (not particularly deep or wide) you would infer that when he looked at you he would look straight. Pity, isn't it, that you never really can tell what a man is inside by drawing up your brief from what he is outside. There is always the heel of Achilles somewhere; trust the devil to find that.

Of course you wish to know forthwith who returned the ruby, and why. As our statesmen say, regarding any important measure for public welfare, the time is not yet ripe. Besides, the young man I am describing had never heard of the Nana Sahib's ruby, unless vaguely in some Sepoy Mutiny tale.

His expression at this moment was rather mournful. He was regretting the thirty shillings the week he had for several years drawn regularly in this shop. Inside there he had introduced the Raglan shirt, the Duke of Westminster four-in-hand, and the Churchill batwing collar. He longed to enter and plead for reinstatement, but his new-found pride refused to budge his legs door-ward. Thirty shillings, twelve for his "third floor back," and the rest for clothes and books and simple amusements. What a whirl he had been in, this past fortnight!

He pulled at his chin, shook his head and turned away. No, he simply could not do it. What! suffer himself to be laughed at behind his back? Impossible, a thousand times no! At the first news stand he bought two or three morning papers, and continued on to his lodgings. He must leave England at once, but the question was--How?

It was a comfortable room, as "third floor backs" go. He read the "want" advertisements carefully, and at length paused at a paragraph which seemed to suit his fancy perfectly. "Cabin stewards wanted--White Star Line--New York and Liverpool."

He cut out the clipping, folded it and stored it away. Then he proceeded to pack up his belongings, not a very laborious affair.

Manuscripts. He riffled the pages ruefully. Sonnets and chant-royals and epics, fine and lofty in spirit; so fine indeed that they easily sifted through every editorial office in London. There was even a bulky romance. He had read so much about the enormous royalties which American authors received for their work, and English authors who were popular on the other side, that his ambition had been frenetically stirred. The fortunes such men as Maundering and Piffle and Drool made! And all he had accomplished so far had been the earnest support of the postal service. Far back at the beginning he had been unfortunate enough to sell a sonnet for ten shillings. Alack! You sell your first sonnet, you win your first hand at cards, and then the passion has you.

Poetry was a drug on the market. Nobody read it (or wrote it) these days; and any one who attempted to sell it was clearly mad. Oh, a jingle for Punch might pass, you know; something clever, with a snapper to it. But epic poetry? Sonnets? Why, didn't you know that there wasn't a magazine going that did not have some sub-editor who could whack out fourteen lines in fourteen minutes, whenever a page needed filling up? These things he had been told times without number. And Maundering, Piffle and Drool had long since cornered the romance market. The King's Highway had become No Thoroughfare.

America. He would go to the land of the brave (when occasion demanded) and the free (if you were imaginative). Having packed his trunk and valise, he departed for Liverpool. Besides, America was all that was left; he was at the end of his rope.

What a rollicking old fraud life was! Swung out of his peaceful orbit, by the legerdemain of death; no longer a humble steady star but a meteor; bumping as yet darkly against the planets; and then this monumental folly which had returned him to the old orbit but still in meteoric form, without peace or means of livelihood! An ass, indeed, if ever there was one.

He eventually arrived at his destination, lied blithely to the chief steward, and was assigned to the first-class cabins on the promenade deck, simply because his manner was engaging and his face pleasing to the eye. The sea? He had never been on it but once, and then only in a rowboat. A good sailor? Perhaps. Chicken and barley broths at eleven; the captain's table in the dining-saloon, breakfast, luncheon and dinner; cabin housekeeper and luggage man at the ports; and always a natty, stiffly starched jacket with a metal number; and "Yes, sir!" and "No, sir!" and "Thank you, sir!" his official vocabulary. Fine job for a poet!

It was all in the game he was going to play with fate. A chap who could sell flamingo ties to gentlemen with purple noses, and shirts with attached cuffs to coal-porters ought not to worry over such a simple employment as cabin-steward on board an ocean liner.

Early the next morning they left port, with only a few first-class passengers. The heavy travel was coming from the west, not going that way. The series of cabins under his stewardship were vacant. Therefore, with the thoroughness of his breed, he set about to learn "ship"; and by the time the first bugle for dinner blew, he knew port from starboard, boat-deck from main, and many other things, some unknown to the chief-steward who had made a hundred and twenty voyages on this very ship.

Beautiful weather; a mild southwest blow, with a moderate beam-sea; only the deck *would* come up smack against the soles of his boots in a most unexpected and aggravating manner. But after the third day out, he found his sea-legs and learned how to "lean." From two till five his time was his own, and a very good deal of this time he devoted to Henley and Morris and Walt Whitman, an ancient brier between his teeth and a canister of excellent tobacco at his elbow. Odd, isn't it, that an Englishman without his pipe is as incomplete as a Manx cat, which, as doubtless you know, has no tail. After all, does a Manx cat know that it is incomplete? Let me say, then, as incomplete as a small boy without pockets.

Toward his fellow stewards he was friendly without being companionable; and as they were of a decent sort, they let him go his way.

Several times during the voyage he opened his trunk and took out the manuscripts. Hang it, they weren't so bally bad. If he could still re-read them, after an hour or two with Henley, there must be some merit to them.

One afternoon he sat alone on the edge of his bunk. The sun was pouring into the porthole; intermittently it flashed over him. Suddenly and alertly he got up, looked out, listened intently, then stepped back into the cabin and locked the door. Again he listened. There was no sound except the steady heart-beats of the great engines below. He sat down sidewise, took out the chamois bag which hung around his neck, and poured the contents out on the blanket. Blue stones, rather dull at first; but ah! when the sun awoke the fires in them: blue as the flower o' the corn, the flame of burning sulphur. He gathered them up and slowly trickled them through his fingers. Sapphires, unset, beautiful as a woman's eyes. He replaced them in the chamois bag; and for the rest of the afternoon went about his affairs preoccupiedly, grave as a bishop under his miter. For, all said and done, he had much to be grave about.

In one of the panels of the partition which separated the cabin from the next, there was a crack. A human eye could see through it very well. And did.

My young poet had "signed on" under the name of Thomas Webb. It was not assumed. For years he had been known in the haberdashery as Webb. There was more to it, however; there was a tail to the kite. The English have an inordinate fondness for hyphens, for mother's family name and grandmother's family name and great-grandmother's, with the immediate paternal cognomen as a period. Thomas' full name was a rosary, if you like, of yeomen, of soldiers, of farmers, of artists, of gentle bloods, of dreamers. The latest transfusion of blood is always most powerful in effect upon the receiver; and as Thomas' father had died in penury for the sake of an idea, it was in order that the son should be something of a dreamer too. Poetry is but an expression of life seen through dreams.

His father had been a scholar, risen from the people; his mother had been gentle. From his seventh year the boy had faced life alone. He had never gone with the stream but had always found lodgment in the backwaters. There is no employment quieter, peacefuller than that of a clerk in a haberdashery. From Mondays till Saturdays, calm; a perfect environment for a poet. You would be surprised to learn of the vast army of poets and novelists and dramatists who dispense four-in-hands, collars, buttons and hosiery six days in the week and who go a-picnicking on the seventh, provided it does not rain.

Thomas had an idea. It was not a reflection of his lamented father's; it was wholly his own. He wanted to be loved. His father's idea had been to love; thus, humanity had laughed him into the grave. So it will be seen that Thomas' idea was the more sensible of the two.

The voyage was uneventful. Blue day followed blue day. When at length the great port of New York loomed in the distance, Thomas felt a thrilling in his spine. Perhaps yonder he might make his fortune; no matter what else he did, that remained to be accomplished, for he was a fortune-hunter, of the ancient type; that is, he expected to work for it. Shore leave would be his, and if during that time he found nothing, why, he was determined to finish the summer as a steward; and by fall he would have enough in wages and tips to give him a start in life. At present he could jingle but seven-and-six in his pocket; and jingle it frequently he did, to assure himself that it was not wearing away.

An important tug came bustling alongside. By the yellow flag he knew that it carried the quarantine officials, inspectors, and a few privileged citizens. Among others who came aboard Thomas noted a sturdy thick-chested man in a derby hat-- bowler, Thomas called it. Quietly this man sought the captain and handed him what looked to Thomas like a cablegram. The captain read it and shook his head. Thomas overheard a little of their conversation.

"You're welcome to look about, Mr. Haggerty; but I don't think you'll find the person you seek."

"If you don't mind, I'll take a prowl. Special case, Captain. Mr. Killigrew thought perhaps I'd see a face I knew."

"Valuable?"

"Fine sapphires. A chance that they may come int' this port. They haven't yet."

"Your customs inspectors ought to be able to help you," observed the captain, hiding a smile. "Nothing but motes can slip through their fingers."

"Sometimes they're tripped up," replied Haggerty. "A case like this is due t' slip through. I'll take a look."

Thomas heard no more. A detective. Unobserved, he went down to his stuffy cabin, took off the chamois bag and locked it in his trunk. So long as it remained on board, it was in British territory.

The following day he went into the great city of man-made cliffs. He walked miles and miles. Naturally he sought the haberdashers along Broadway. No employment was offered him: for the reason that he failed to state his accomplishments. But he was in nowise discouraged. He would go back to Liverpool. The ship would sail with full cabin strength, and this trip there would be tips, three sovereigns at least, and maybe more, if his charges happened to be generous.

He tied the chamois bag round his neck again, and turned in. He was terribly tired and footsore. He slept fitfully. At half after nine he sat up, fully awake. His cabin-mate (whom he rather disliked) was not in his bunk. Indeed, the bunk had not been touched. Suddenly Thomas' hand flew to his breast. The chamois bag was gone!

CHAPTER IV

Iambic and hexameter, farewell! In that moment the poet
died in Thomas; I mean, the poet who had to dig his expressions
of life out of ink-pots. Things boil up quickly and unexpectedly
in the soul; century-old impulses, undreamed of by the inheritor;
and when these bubble and spill over the kettle's lip, watch out.
There is an island in the South Seas where small mud-geysers
burst forth under the pressure of the foot. Fate had stepped on
Thomas.

As he sprang out of his bunk he was a reversion: the outlaw
in Lincoln-green, the Yeoman of the Guard, the bandannaed
smuggler of the southeast coast. Quickly he got into his
uniform. He went about this affair the right way, with foresight
and prudence; for he realized that he must act instantly. He
sought the purser, who was cordial.

"I'm not feeling well," began Thomas; "and the doctor is
ashore. Where's there an apothecary's shop?"

"Two blocks straight out from the pier entrance. You'll see
red and blue lights in the windows. Tummy?"

"I'm subject to dizzy spells. Where's Jameson?" Jameson
was the surly cabin-mate.

"Quit. Gone over to the Cunard. Fool. Like a little money
advanced? Here's a bill, five dollars."

"Thank you, sir." Twenty shillings, ten pence. "Doesn't
Jameson take his peg a little too often, sir?"

"He's a blighter. Glad to get rid of him. Hurry back. And
don't stop at Mike's or Johnny's,"--smiling.

"I never touch anything heavier than ale, sir." Mike's or
Johnny's; it saved him the trouble of asking. Tippling pubs
where stewards foregathered.

His uniform was his passport. Nobody questioned him as he
passed the barrier at a dog-trot. Outside the smelly pier (sugar,
coffee and spices, shipments from Killigrew and Company) he
paused to send a short prayer to heaven. Then he approached a
snoozing stevedore.

"Where's Mike's?"

"Lead y' there, ol' scout!"

"No; tell me where it is. Here's a shilling."

Explicit directions followed; and away went Thomas at a dog-trot again: the lust to punish, maim or kill in his heart. He was not a university man; he had not played cricket at Lord's or stroked the crew from Leander; but he was island-born, a chap for cold tubbings, calisthenics and long tramps into the country on pleasant Sundays. Thomas was slender, but sound and hard.

Jameson was not at Mike's nor at Johnny's; but there were dozens of other saloons. He did not ask questions. He went in, searched, and strode out. In the lowest kind of a drinking dive he found his man. A great wave of dizziness swept over Thomas. When it passed, only the bandannaed smuggler remained, cautious, cunning, patient.

The quarry was alone in a side-room, drinking gin and smiling to himself. For an hour Thomas waited. His palms became damp with cold sweat and his knees wabbled, but not in fear. Four glasses of ale, sipped slowly, tasting of wormwood. In the bar-mirror he could watch every move made by Jameson. No one went in. He had evidently paid in advance for the bottle of gin. Thomas ordered his fifth glass of ale, and saw Jameson's head sink forward a little. Thomas' sigh almost split his heart in twain. Jameson's head went up suddenly, and with a drunken smile he reached for the bottle and poured out a stiff potion. He drank it neat.

Thomas wiped his palms on his sleeves and ordered a cigar.

"Lonesome?" asked the swart bartender. This good-looking chap was rather a puzzle to him. He wasn't waiting for anybody, and he wasn't trying to get drunk. Five ales in an hour and not a dozen words; just an ordinary Britisher who didn't know how to amuse himself in Gawd's own country.

Jameson's head fell upon his arms. With assured step Thomas walked toward the corridor which divided the so-called wine-rooms. At the end of the corridor was a door. He did not care where it led so long as it led outside this evil-smelling den. He found the room empty opposite Jameson's. He went in quietly. The shabby waiter followed him, soft-footed as a cat.

"A bottle of Old Tom," said Thomas.

The waiter nodded and slipped out. He saw the sleeper in the other room, and gently closed the door.

"Gink in number two wants a bottle o' gin. He's th' kind. Layer o' ale an' then his quart. Th' real souse."

"So that's his game, huh?" said the bartender. "How's th' gink in number four?"

"Dead t' th' world."

"Tip th' Sneak. There may be a chancet t' roll 'em both. Here y' are. Soak 'im two-fifty."

Half an hour longer Thomas waited. Then he rose and tiptoed to the door, drawing it back without the least sound. Jameson's had not latched. Taking a deep long breath (strange, how one may control the heart by this process!) Thomas crossed the corridor and entered the other room; entered prepared for any emergency. If Jameson awoke, so much the worse for him. The gods owe it to the mortals they keep in bondage to bestow a grain of luck here and there along the way to Elysium or Hades. His cabin-mate's stentorian breathing convinced the trespasser that it was the stupidest, heaviest kind of sleep.

For a moment he looked down at the man contemptuously. To have befuddled his brain at such a time! Or was it because the wretch knew that he, Thomas, would not dare cry out over his loss? He stepped behind the sleeping man. He wanted to fall upon him, beat him with his fists. Ah, if he had not found him!

The night, fortunately, was warm and thick. Jameson had carelessly thrown open his coat and vest. Underneath he wore the usual sailor-jersey. Thomas steeled his arms. With one hand he pulled the roll collar away from the man's neck and with the other sought for the string: sought in vain. The light, the four drab walls, the haze of tobacco smoke, all turned red.

"Where is it, you dog? Quick!" Thomas shook the man. "Where is it? Quick, or I'll throttle you!"

"Lemme 'lone!" Jameson sagged toward the table again.

Thomas bent him back ruthlessly and plunged a hand into the inside pocket of the man's coat. The touch of the chamois-bag burned like fire. He pulled it out and transferred it to his own pocket and made for the door. He did not care now what happened. Found! Woe to any one who had the ill-luck to stand between him and the exit.

Outside the door stood the shabby waiter, grinning cheerfully. He was accompanied by a hulking, shifty-eyed creature.

"Roll 'im, ol' sport? Caught in th' act, huh?" gibed the waiter.

Thomas had the right idea. He struck first. The waiter crashed against the wall. The hulking, shifty-eyed one fared worse. He went down with his face to the cracks in the floor. Thomas dashed for the exit.

CHAPTER V

Outside he found himself in a kind of court. He ran about wildly, like a rat in a trap. He plumped into the alley, accidentally. Down this he fled, into the street. A voice called out peremptorily to him to stop, but he went on all the faster, swift as a hare. He doubled and circled through this street and that until at last he came out into a broad, brilliant thoroughfare. An iron-pillared railway reared itself skyward and trains clamored past. Bloomsbury: millions of years and miles away! He would wake up presently, with the sunlight (when it shone) pouring into his room, and the bright geraniums on the outside window-sill bidding him good morning.

He was on the point of rushing up the station stairway, when he espied a cab at the far corner. A replica of a London cab, something which smacked of home; he could have hugged for sheer joy the bleary-eyed cabby who touched his rusty high hat.

"Free?"

"Free 's th' air, bo. Where to?"

"Pier 60, White Star Line. How much?"--quite his old-time self again.

"Two dollars,"--promptly.

"All right. And hurry!" Thomas climbed in. He was safe.

As the crow flies it was less than a ten-minutes' jog from that corner to Pier 60. Thomas had not gone far; he had merely covered a good deal of ground. Cabby drove about for three-quarters of an hour and then drew up before the pier.

Back to his cabin once more, weak as a swimmer who had breasted a strong tide. He opened his trunk and rammed the chamois-bag into the toe of one of his patent-leather boots. In the daytime he would wear it about his neck, but each night back into the shoe it must go. He flung himself on the bunk, not to sleep, but to think and wonder.

Meantime there was great excitement in the dive. The waiter was rocking his body, wailing and holding his jaw. His companion was sitting on the floor. In the wine-room two policemen and a thick-set, black-mustached man in a derby hat were asking questions.

"Robbed!" moaned Jameson.

The man in the derby hat shook him roughly. "Robbed o' what, y' soak?"

"Robbed!"

"Mike," said the man in the derby, "put th' darbies on th' Sneak. We'll get something for our trouble, anyhow. An' tell that waiter t' put th' brakes on his yawp. Bring him in here. Now, you, what's happened?"

"Why, the gink in uniform comes in . . ."

The bartender interrupted. "A gink dressed like a ship-steward comes in an' orders ale. Drinks five glasses. Goes out int' th' wine-room 'cross th' hall an' orders a bottle o' gin. An' next I hears Johnny howlin' murder. Frame-up, Mr. Haggerty. Nothin' t' do with it, hones' t' Gawd! Th' boss ain't here."

Jameson lurched toward the bartender. "Young lookin'? Red cheeks? 'Old himself like a sojer?"

"That's 'im," agreed the bartender.

"What were y' robbed of?" demanded Haggerty.

Jameson looked into a pair of chilling blue eyes. His own wavered drunkenly. "Money."

"Y' lie! What was it?" Haggerty seized Jameson by the collar and swung him about. "Hurry up!"

"I tell you, my money. Paid off t'dy. 'E knew it. Sly." Jameson had become almost sober. Out of the muddle one thing loomed clearly: he could not be revenged upon his cabin-mate without getting himself into deep trouble. Money; he'd stick to that.

"Who is he?"

"Name's Webb; firs'-class steward on th' *Celtic*. Damn 'im!"

"Lock this fool up till morning," said Haggerty. "I'll find out what he's been robbed of."

"British subject!" roared Jameson.

"Not t'night. Take 'im away. Think I saw th' fellow running as I came by. Yelled at him, but he could run some. Take 'im away. Something fishy about this. I'll call on my friend Webb in th' morning. There might be something in this."

And Haggerty paid his call promptly; only, Thomas saw him first. The morning sun lighted up the rugged Irish face. Thomas not only saw him but knew who he was, and in this he had the advantage of the encounter. One of the first things a detective has to do is to surprise his man, and then immediately begin to bullyrag and overbear him; pretend that all is known, that the game is up. Nine times out of ten it serves, for in the same ratio there is always a doubtful confederate who may "peach" in order to save himself.

Thomas never stirred from his place against the rail. He drew on his pipe and pretended to be stolidly interested in the sweating stevedores, the hoist-booms and the brown coffee-bags.

A hand fell lightly on his shoulder. Haggerty had a keen eye for a face; he saw weak spots, where a hundred other men would have seen nothing out of the ordinary. The detective always planned his campaign upon his interpretation of the face of the intended victim.

"Webb?"

Thomas lowered his pipe and turned. "Yes, sir."

"Where were you between 'leven an' twelve last night?"

"What is that to you, sir?" (Yeoman of the Guard style.)

"What did Jameson take away from you?"

"Who are you, and what's your business with me?" The pipe-stem returned with a click to its ivory vise.

"My name is Haggerty, of th' New York detective force; American Scotland Yard, 'f that'll sound better. Better tell me all about it."

"I'm a British subject, on board a British ship."

"Nothing doing in m' lord style. When y' put your foot on that pier you become amenable t' th' laws o' th' United States, especially 'f you've committed a crime."

"A crime?"

"Listen here. You went int' Lumpy Joe's, waited till Jameson got drunk, an' then you rolled him."

"Rolled?"--genuinely bewildered.

"Picked his pockets, if you want it blunt. Th' question is, did he take it from you 'r you from him? I can arrest you, Mr. Webb, British subject 'r not. 'S up t' you t' tell me th' story. Don't be afraid of me; I don't eat up men. All y' got t' do is t' treat me on th' level. You won't lose anything 'f you're honest."

"Come with me, sir." (The smuggler was, in his day, a match in cunning for any or all of His Majesty's coast-guards.)

Haggerty followed the young man down the various companionways. Instinctively he knew what was coming, the pith of the matter if not the details. Thomas pulled out his trunk, unlocked it, threw back the lid, and picked up an old leather box.

"Look at this, sir. It was my mother's. And I'd be a fine chap, would I not, to let a drunken scoundrel steal it and get away with it."

It was a Neapolitan brooch, of pink coral, surrounded by small pearls. Haggerty balanced it on his palm and appraised it at three or found hundred dollars. He glanced casually into the leather box. Some faded tin-types, some letters, a very old Bible, and odds and ends of a young man's fancy: Haggerty shrugged. It looked as if he had stumbled into a mare's-nest.

"He said you took money."

"He lied,"--tersely.

"Do y' want t' appear against him?"

"No. We sail at seven to-morrow. So long as he missed his shot, let him go."

"Why didn't y' lodge a complaint against him?"

"I'm not familiar with your laws, Mr. Haggerty. So I took the matter in my own hands."

"Don't do it again. Sorry t' trouble you. But duty's duty. An' listen. Always play your game above board; it pays."

"Thanks."

Haggerty started to offer his hand, but the look in the gray eyes caused him to misdoubt and reconsider the impulse. So Thomas made his first mistake, which, later on, was to cost him dear. Coconnas shook hands with Caboche the headsman, and escaped the "question extraordinary." Truth is, Thomas was not an accomplished liar. He could lie to the detective, but he could not bring himself to shake hands on it.

On the way down the plank Haggerty mused: "An' I thought I had a hunch!"

Thomas sighed. "Play your game above board; it pays." Into what a labyrinth of lies he was wayfaring!

That same night, on the other side of the Atlantic, the ninth Baron of Dimbledon sailed for America to rehabilitate his fortunes. He did and he didn't.

CHAPTER VI

Thomas was a busy man up to and long after the hour of sailing. His cabins were filled with about all the variant species of the race: two nervous married women with their noisy mismanaged children, three young men on a lark, and an actress who was paying her husband's expenses and gladly announced the fact over and through the partitions. Three bells tingled all day long, and the only thing that saved Thomas from the "sickbay" was the fact that the bar closed at eleven. And a rough passage added to his labors. No Henley this voyage, no comfy loafing about the main-deck in the sunshine. A busy, miserable, dejected young man, who cursed his folly and yet clung to it with that tenacity which makes prejudice England's first-born.

Night after night, stretched out wearily on his bunk, the sordid picture of Lumpy Joe's returned to him. By a hair's breadth! It was always a source of amazement to recall how quickly and shrewdly his escape had been managed. He felt reasonably safe. Jameson would never dare tell what he knew, to incriminate himself for the sake of revenge. To have got the best of him and to have pulled the wool over the eyes of a keen American detective!

In Liverpool he deliberately threw away a full sovereign in motion-pictures and music-halls. But he drank nothing, not even his customary ale. Not so long ago he had tasted his first champagne; very expensive, something more than two hundred pounds. Stupid ass! And yet . . . The very life he had always been longing for, dreaming of, behind his counters: to be free, to rove at will, to seek adventure.

"Then," said Sir Tristram, "I will fight with you unto the uttermost." "I grant," said Sir Palomides, "for in a better quarrel keep I never to fight, for and I die of your hands, of a better knight's hands may I not be slain." . . .

Off for America again; and the Book of Marvelous Adventures, to be opened wide by a pair of Irish blue eyes, deep as the sea, glancing as the sunlight on its crests.

"You are my steward, I believe?"

In his soul of souls Thomas hoped so. "Yes, miss--indeed, yes, if you occupy this cabin."

"Here are the tickets"; and the young lady signed the slip of paper he gave her: Mr. and Mrs. Daniel Killigrew, Miss Killigrew and maid. "I shall probably keep you very busy." There was a twinkle in her eyes, but he was English and did not see it.

"That is what I am here for, miss." He smiled reassuringly.

"Never ask my father if he wishes tea and toast"--gravely.

"Yes, miss"--with honest gravity. Thomas knew nothing of women, young or old. With the habits and tastes of the male biped he was tolerably familiar. He was to learn.

"Hot water-bottles for my mother every night, and a pot of chocolate for myself. I shall always have my breakfast early in the saloon. I'm a first-rate sailor."

A rush, a whir.

"Kitty, you darling! They have put us on the other side of the ship."

Thomas was genuinely glad of it. With a goddess and a nymph to wait upon, heaven knew how many broken dishes he'd have to account for. Never in the park, never after the matinees, never in all wide London, had he seen two such lovely types: Titian and Greuse.

"No!" said the Greuse.

"Stupid mistake at the booking-office," replied the Titian. "Come up on deck. They are putting off."

"Just a moment. Put the small luggage, Mr. . . . ."

"Webb."

"Mr. Webb. Put the small luggage on the lounge. Never mind the straps. That is all."

"Yes, miss."

The two young women hurried off. Thomas stared after them, his brows bent in a mixture of perplexity, dazzlement and diffidence.

"A very good-looking steward."

"Kitty, you little wretch!"

"Why, he *is* good-looking."

"Princes, dukes, waiters, cabbies, stewards; all you do is look at them, and they become slaves. You've more mischief in you than a dozen kittens."

"I have met cabbies whom I much prefer to certain dukes."

"But I've a young man picked out for you. He's an artist."

"Good night!" murmured Kitty. "If there is one kind of person in the world dad considers wholly useless and incompetent, it's an artist or a poet."

"But this artist makes fifteen thousand and sometimes twenty thousand the year."

"Then he's no artist. What is his name?"

"Forbes, J. Mortimer Forbes."

"Oh. The pretty-cover man."

"My dear, he is one of the nicest young men in New York. His family is one of the best, and he goes everywhere. And but for his kindness. . . ."

"What?"

"Some day I'll tell you the story. Here we go! Good-by, England!"

"Good-by, sapphires!" said Kitty, so low that the other did not hear her.

At dinner Thomas was called to account by the chief steward for permitting his thumb to connect with the soup. But what would you, with Titian and Greuse smiling a soft "Thank you!" for everything you did for them?

* * * * * *

"Night, daddy."

"Good night, Kittibudget."

Crawford smiled after the blithe, buoyant figure as it swung confidently down the deck.

"I don't know what I'm going to do," mused Killigrew, looking across the rail at the careening stars.

"What about?"

"That child. I can't harness her."

"Somebody's bound to"--prophetically.

"It's got to be a whole man, or he'll wish he'd never been born. She's had her way so long that she's spoiled."

"Not a bit of it."

"Yes, she is. I told her not to wear those sapphires that night. And, by the way, I've been hoping they'd turn up like that ruby of yours. How do you account for that?"

The coal of Crawford's cigar waxed and waned and the ash lengthened.

"I've no doubt that you've been mighty curious since that morning. Perhaps you read the tale in the newspapers. I know of only one man who would return the Nana Sahib's ruby. Sentiment; for I believe the poor devil was really fond of me. A valet. With me for ten years. He was really my comrade; always my right-hand on my exploration trips; back-boned, fearless, reliable in a pinch, and a scholar in a way; though I can't imagine how and where he picked up his learning. He saved my life at least twice by his quick wit. In those days I was something of a stick; never went out. I hired him upon his word and because he looked honest. And he was for ten years. He gave his name as Mason, said he was born in central New York. We got along without friction of any sort. And I still miss him. Stole a hundred thousand dollars' worth of gems; hid them in the heels of my old shoes and nearly got away with them. Haggerty, the detective, thought for weeks that I was the man. I still believe that I was the innocent cause of Mason's relapse; for Haggerty was certain that somewhere in the past Mason had been a criminal. You see, I had a peculiar fad. I used to buy up old safes and open them for the sport of it. Crazy idea, but I found a good deal of amusement in it."

"You don't say!" gasped Killigrew, who had never heard of this phase before.

"It's my belief that Mason got his inspiration from watching me. I am devilish sorry."

"Then you believe that he is up to his old tricks again?"

"Yes,"--reluctantly. "The man who took my wife's ruby, took your daughter's sapphires. It needed a clever mind to conceive such a *coup*. Three other carriages were entered, with more or less success. In a dense fog; a needle in a haystack. And they'll never find him."

"It's up to you to put the detectives on the right track."

"I suppose I'll have to do it."

"If he returns to America he'll be caught. I'll give Haggerty the tip."

"I have my doubts of Mason committing any such folly. He picked up a small fortune that night. Strange mix-up."

"Here, try one of these," urged Killigrew, as the butt of Crawford's cigar went overboard.

"Thanks."

Thomas moved away from the ventilator. Mix-up, indeed! He stole down to the promenade deck, where the stewardess informed him that Miss Killigrew had just ordered her chocolate. He flew to the kitchens. It was a narrow escape. To have been found wanting the first night out!

"Come in," said a voice in answer to his knock.

He set the tray down on the stool, his heart insurgent and his fingers all thumbs. He might live to be a steward eighty years old, but he never would get over the awe, the embarrassment of these invasions by night. Each time he saw a woman in her peignoir or kimono he felt as though he had committed a sacrilege. True, he understood their attitude; he was merely a serving machine and for the time wiped off the roster of mankind.

A long blue coat of silk brocade enveloped Kitty from her throat to her sandals; sleeves which fell over her hands; buttoned by loops over corded knots. An experienced traveler could have told him that it was the peculiar garment which any self-respecting Chinaman would wear who was in mourning for his grandfather. Kitty wore it because of its beauty alone.

"Thank you," she said, as Thomas went out backward, court style. Kitty smiled across at her maid who was arranging the combs and brushes preparatory to taking down her mistress' hair. "He looked as if he were afraid of something, Celeste."

Celeste smiled enigmatically. "Ma'm'selle shoult haff been born in Pariss."

This was translatable, or not, as you pleased. Kitty sipped the chocolate and found it excellent. At length she dismissed the maid, switched off the lights, and then remembered that there was no water in the carafe. She rang.

Thomas replied so promptly that he could not have been farther off than the companionway. "You rang, miss?"

"Yes, Webb. Please fill this carafe."

"Is it possible that it was empty, miss?"

"I used it and forgot to ring for more."

All this in the dark.

Thomas hurried away, wishing he could find some magic spring on board. For what purpose he could not have told.

As for Kitty, she remained standing by the door, profoundly astonished.

CHAPTER VII

Third day out.

Kitty smiled at the galloping horizon; smiled at the sunny sky; smiled at the deck-steward as he served the refreshing broth; smiled at the tips of her sensible shoes, at her hands, at her neighbors: until Mrs. Crawford could contain her curiosity no longer.

"Kitty Killigrew, what have you been doing?"

"Doing?"

"Well, going to do?"--shrewdly.

Kitty gazed at her friend in pained surprise, her blue eyes as innocent as the sea--and as full of hidden mysterious things. "Good gracious! can't a person be happy and smile?"

"Happy I have no doubt you are; but I've studied that smile of yours too closely not to be alarmed by it."

"Well, what does it say?"

"Mischief."

Kitty did not reply to this, but continued smiling--at space this time.

On the ship crossing to Naples in February their chairs on deck had been together; they had become acquainted, and this acquaintance had now ripened into one of those intimate friendships which are really sounder and more lasting than those formed in youth. Crawford had heard of Killigrew as a great and prosperous merchant, and Killigrew had heard of Crawford as a millionaire whose name was very rarely mentioned in the society pages of the Sunday newspapers. Men recognize men at once; it doesn't take much digging. Before they arrived in Naples they had agreed to take the Sicilian trip together, then up Italy, through France, to England. The scholar and the merchant at play were like two boys out of school; the dry whimsical humor of the Scotsman and the volatile sparkle of the Irishman made them capital foils.

Killigrew dropped his *Rodney Stone*.

"Say, Crawford," he began, "after seeing ten thousand saints in ten thousand cathedrals, since February, I'd give a hundred dollars for a ringside ticket to a scrap like that one,"--indicating the volume on his knee.

Crawford lay back and laughed.

"Well," said his wife, with an amused smile, "why don't you say it?"

"Say what?"

"'So would I!'"

"Men are quite hopeless," sighed Mrs. Killigrew, when the laughter had subsided.

"You oughtn't object to a good shindy, Molly," slyly observed her husband. "You'll never forgive me that black eye."

"I'll never forgive the country you got it in,"--grimly. "But what's the harm in a good scrap between two husky fellows, trained to a hair to slam-bang each other?"

"It isn't refined, dad," said Kitty.

He sent a searching glance at her; he never was sure when that girl was laughing. "Fiddle-sticks! For four months now I've been shopping every day with you women, and you can't tell me prize-fights are brutal."

Crawford applauded gently.

"By the way, Crawford, you know something about direct charity." Killigrew threw back his rug and sat up. "I've got an idea. What's the use of giving checks to hospitals and asylums and colleges, when you don't know whether the cash goes right or wrong? I'm going to let Molly here start a home-bureau to keep her from voting; a lump sum every year to give away as she pleases. I'm strong for giving boys college education. Smooths 'em out; gives them a start in life; that is, if they are worth anything at the beginning. Like this: back the boy and screw up his honor and interest by telling him that you expect to be paid back when the time comes. There's no better charity in the world than making a man of a boy, making him want to stand on his own feet, independent. When you help inefficient people, you throw your money away. What do you think of the idea?"

"A first-rate one. I'd like to come in."

"No; this is all my own and Molly's. But how'll I start her off?"

"Get an efficient young man to act as private secretary; a fairly good accountant; no rich man's son, but some one who has had a chance to observe life. Make him a buffer between Mrs. Killigrew and the whining cheats. And above all, no young man who has social entrée to your house. That kind of a private secretary is always a fizzle."

"Any one in mind?"

"No."

"I have," said Kitty, rising and going toward the companion-ladder to the lower decks.

"What now?" demanded Killigrew.

"Let her be; Kitty has a sensible head on her shoulders, for all her foolery." Mrs. Killigrew laid a restraining hand on her husband's arm.

But Mrs. Crawford smiled a replica of that smile which had aroused her curiosity in regard to Kitty. And then her face grew serious.

Kitty had a mind like her father's. Her ideas were seldom nebulous or slow in forming. They sprang forth, full grown, like those mythological creatures: Minerva was an idea of Jove's, as doubtless Venus was an idea of Neptune's. Men with this quality become captains-general of armies or of money-bags. In a man it signifies force; in a woman, charm.

Kitty searched diligently and found the object of her quest on the main-deck, starboard, leaning against one of the deck supports and reading from a book which lay flat on the broad teak rail, in a blue shadow. The sea smiled at Kitty and Kitty smiled at the sea. Men are not the only adventurers; they have no monopoly on daring. And what Kitty proposed doing was daring indeed, for she did not know into what dangers it might eventually lead her.

"Mr. Webb?"

Thomas looked up. "You are wanting me, miss?"

"If you are not too busy."

"Really, no. I have been reading." He closed the book, loose-leafed from frequent perusals. "I am at your service."

"Do you read much, Mr. Webb?"

The reiteration of the prefix to his name awakened him to the marvelous fact that for the present he was no longer the machine; she was recognizing the man.

"Perhaps, for a man in my station, I read too much, Miss Killigrew."

Kitty's scarlet lips stirred ever so slightly. It was the first time he had added the name to the prefix: he in his turn was recognizing the woman. And this rather pleased her, for she liked to be recognized.

"May I ask what it is you are reading?"

He offered the book to her. *Morte d'Arthur.* Kitty's eyebrows, a hundred years or more ago, would have stirred to tender lyrics the quills of Prior and Lovelace and Suckling: arched when interested, a funny little twist to the inner points when angered, and when laughter possessed her. . . . Let Thomas indite the sonnet! Just now they were widely arched.

"I am very fond of the book," explained Thomas diffidently. "I love the pompous gallantry of these fairy chaps. How politely they used to hack each other into pieces!"

"Are you by chance a university man?"

"No. I am self-educated, if one may call it that. My father was a fellow at Trinity. For myself, I have always had to work."

"Do you like your present occupation?"

"It was the best I could find." How he would have liked to throw discretion to the winds and tell her the whole miserable story!

"Are you good at accounting?"

"Fairly." What was all this about? He began to riffle the leaves of the book, restively.

"Could you tell an honest man from a dishonest one?"

"I believe so." Thomas had eyebrows, too, but he did not know how to use them properly. Tell an honest man from a dishonest one, forsooth!

Kitty found the situation less easy than she had anticipated. The more questions she asked, the more embarrassed she grew; and it angered her because there was no clear reason why she should become embarrassed. And she also remarked his uneasiness. However, she went on determinedly.

"Have you ever had any contact with real poverty?"

"Yes,"--close-lipped. "Pardon me, Miss Killigrew, but . . ."

"Just a moment, Mr. Webb," she interrupted. "I dare say my questions seem impertinent, but they have a purpose back of them. My mother and I are looking for a private secretary for a charitable concern which we are going to organize shortly. We desire some one who is educated, who will be capable of guarding us from persons not worthy of benefactions, who will make recommendations, seek into the affairs of those considered worthy. We shall, of course, expect to find room for you. It will not be a chatter-tea-drinking affair. You will have the evenings to yourself and all of Sundays. The salary will be two hundred a month."

"Pounds?" gasped Thomas.

"Oh, no; dollars. I do not expect your answer at this moment. You must have time to think it over."

"It is not necessary, Miss Killigrew."

"You decline?"

"On the contrary, I accept with a good deal of gratitude. On condition," he added gravely.

"And that?"

"You will ask me no questions regarding my past."

Kitty looked squarely into his eyes and he returned the glance steadily and calmly.

"Very well; I accept the condition,"

Thomas was mightily surprised.

CHAPTER VIII

He had put forward this condition, perfectly sure that she would refuse to accept it. He could not understand.

"You accept that condition?"

"Yes." Having gone thus far with her plot, Kitty would have died rather than retreated; Irish temperament.

Thomas was moved to a burst of confidence. "I know that I am poor, and to the best of my belief, honest. Moreover, perhaps I should be compelled by the exigencies of circumstance to leave you after a few months. I am not a rich man, masquerading for the sport of it; I am really poor and grateful for any work. It is only fair that I should tell you this much, that I am running away from no one. Beyond the fact that I am the son of a very great but unknown scholar, a farmer of mediocre talents who lost his farm because he dreamed of humanity instead of cabbages, I have nothing to say." He said it gravely, without pride or veiled hauteur.

"That is frank enough," replied Kitty, curiously stirred. "You will not find us hard task-masters. Be here this afternoon at three. My father will wish to talk to you. And be as frank with him as you have been with me."

She smiled and nodded brightly, and turned away. He had a glimpse of a tan shoe and a slim tan-silk ankle, which poised birdlike above the high doorsill; and then she vanished into the black shadow of the companionway. She afterward confessed to me that her sensation must have been akin to that of a boy who had stolen an apple and beaten the farmer in the race to the road.

We all make the mistake of searching for our drama, forgetting that it arrives sooner or later, unsolicited.

Bewitched. Thomas should have been the happiest man alive, but the devil had recruited him for his miserables. Her piquant face no longer confronting and bewildering him, he saw this second net into which he had permitted himself to be drawn. As if the first had not been colossal enough! Where would it all end? Private secretary and two hundred the month--forty pounds--this was a godsend. But to take her orders day by day, to see her, to be near her. . . . Poverty-stricken wretch that he was, he should have declined. Now he could not; being a simple

Englishman, he had given his word and meant to abide by it. There was one glimmer of hope; her father. He was a practical merchant and would not permit a man without a past (often worse than a man with one) to enter his establishment.

Thomas was not in love with Kitty. (Indeed, this isn't a love story at all.) Stewards, three days out, are not in the habit of falling in love with their charges (Maundering and Drool notwithstanding). He was afraid of her; she vaguely alarmed him; that was all.

For seven years he had dwelt in his "third floor back"; had breakfasted and dined with two old maids, their scrawny niece, and a muscular young stenographer who shouted militant suffrage and was not above throwing a brickbat whenever the occasion arrived. There was a barmaid or two at the pub where he lunched at noon; but chaff was the alpha and omega of this acquaintance. Thus, Thomas knew little or nothing of the sex.

The women with whom he conversed, played the gallant, the hero, the lover (we none of us fancy ourselves as rogues!) were those who peopled his waking dreams. She was La Belle Isoude, Elaine, Beatrice, Constance; it all depended upon what book he had previously been reading. It is when we men are confronted with the living picture of some one of our dreams of them that women cease to dwell in the abstract and become issues, to be met with more or less trepidation. Back among some of his idle dreams there had been a Kitty, blue-eyed, black-haired, slender and elfish.

Kitty sat down in her chair. "Well," she said, "I have found him."

"Found whom?" asked Mrs. Crawford.

"The private secretary."

"What?" Killigrew swung his feet to the deck. "What the dickens have you been doing now? Who is it?"

"Webb."

"The steward?"

"Yes."

"Well, if that . . ." began Killigrew belligerently.

"Dad, either mother and I act as we please, or you may attend to the home-bureau yourself. Mother, it was agreed and understood that I should select any employee we might happen to need."

"It was, my dear."

"Very good. I want some one who will attend to the affairs honestly and painstakingly. There must be no idler about the house; and any young man . . ."

"Wouldn't an old one do?" suggested Killigrew.

"Whose set ideas would clash constantly with ours. And any young man we know would idle and look on the whole affair as a fine joke. I've had a talk with Webb. He's not a university man, but he's educated. I found him reading *Morte d'Arthur*."

"Ah!"--from Crawford.

"He became a steward because he could find nothing else to do at the present time. He has been poor, and I dare say he has known the pinch of poverty. You said only this morning, dad, that he was the most attentive steward you had ever met on shipboard. Besides, there is a case in point. Our butler was a steward before you engaged him, six years ago."

Killigrew began to smile. "How much have you offered him as a salary?"

"Two hundred a month, to be paid out of the funds."

"Janet," said Crawford, "it's a good thing I'm married, or I'd apply for the post myself."

"All right," agreed Killigrew; "a bargain's a bargain."

"A wager's a wager," thought Kitty.

"If you wake up some fine morning and find the funds gone . . ."

"Mother and I will attend to all checks, such as they are."

"Kitty, any day you say I'll take you into the firm as chief counsel. But before I approve of your selection, I'd like to have a talk with our friend Webb."

"He expects it. You are to see him on the main-deck at three this afternoon."

"Molly, how long have we been married?"

"Thirty years, Daniel."

"How old is Kitty?"

"Mother!"

"Twenty-two," answered Mrs. Killigrew relentlessly.

"Well, I was going to say that I've learned more about the Killigrew family in these four months of travel than in all those years together."

"Something more than ornaments," suggested Kitty dryly.

"Yes, indeed," replied her father amiably.

And when he returned to the boat-deck that afternoon for tea (which, by the way, he never drank, being a thorough-going coffee merchant), he said to Kitty: "You win on points. If Webb doesn't pan out, why, we can discharge him. I'll take a chance at a man who isn't afraid to look you squarely in the eyes."

At the precise time when Kitty retired and Thomas went aft for his good night pipe--eleven o'clock at sea and nine in New York--Haggerty found himself staring across the street at an old-fashioned house. Like the fisherman who always returns to the spot where he lost the big one, the detective felt himself drawn toward this particular dwelling. Crawford did not live there any more; since his marriage he had converted it into a private museum. It was filled with mummies and cartonnages, ancient pottery and trinkets.

What a game it had been! A hundred thousand in precious gems, all neatly packed away in the heels of Crawford's old shoes! And where was that man Mason? Would he ever return? Oh, well; he, Haggerty, had got his seven thousand in rewards; he was living now like a nabob up in the Bronx. He had no real cause to regret Mason's advent or his escape. Yet, deep in his heart burned the chagrin of defeat: his man had got away, and half the game (if you're a true hunter) was in putting your hand on a man's shoulder and telling him to "Come along."

He crossed the street and entered the, alley and gazed up at the fire-escape down which Mason had made his escape. What impelled the detective to leap up and catch the lower bars of the ground-ladder he could not have told you. He pulled himself up and climbed to the window.

Open!

Haggerty had nerves like steel wires, but a slight shiver ran down his spine. Open, and Crawford yet on the high seas. He waited, listening intently. Not a sound of any sort came to his ears. He stepped inside courageously and slipped with his back to the wall, where he waited, holding his breath.

Click! It seemed to come from his right.

"Come out o' that!" he snarled. "No monkey-business, or I'll shoot."

He flashed his pocket-lamp toward the sound, and aimed.

A blow on the side of the head sent the detective crashing against a cartonnage, and together the quick and the dead rolled to the floor. Instinctively Haggerty turned on his back, aimed at the window and fired.

Too late!

CHAPTER IX

When the constellation, which was not included among the accepted theories of Copernicus, passed away, Haggerty sat up and rubbed the swelling over his ear, tenderly yet grimly. Next, he felt about the floor for his pocket-lamp. A strange spicy dust drifted into his nose and throat, making him sneeze and cough. A mummy had reposed in the overturned cartonnage and the brittle bindings had crumbled into powder. He soon found the lamp, and sent its point of vivid white light here and there about the large room.

Pursuit of his assailant was out of the question. Haggerty was not only hard of head but shrewd. So he set about the accomplishment of the second best course, that of minute and particular investigation. Some one had entered this deserted house: for what? This, Haggerty must find out. He was fairly confident that the intruder did not know who had challenged him; on the other hand, there might be lying around some clue to the stranger's identity.

Was there light in the house, fluid in the wires? If so he would be saved the annoyance of exploring the house by the rather futile aid of the pocket-lamp, which stood in need of a fresh battery. He searched for the light-button and pressed it, hopefully. The room, with all its brilliantly decorated antiquities, older than Rome, older than Greece, blinded Haggerty for a space.

"Ain't that like these book chaps?" Haggerty murmured. "T' go away without turning off th' meter!"

The first thing Haggerty did was to scrutinize the desk which stood near the center of the room. A film of dust lay upon it. Not a mark anywhere. In fact, a quarter of an hour's examination proved to Haggerty's mind that nothing in this room had been disturbed except the poor old mummy. He concluded to leave that gruesome object where it lay. Nobody but Crawford would know how to put him back in his box, poor devil. Haggerty wondered if, after a thousand years, some one would dig him up!

Through all the rooms on this floor he prowled, but found nothing. He then turned his attention to the flight of stairs which led to the servants' quarters. Upon the newel-post lay the fresh imprint of a hand. Haggerty went up the stairs in bounds. There were nine rooms on this floor, two connecting with baths. In one of these latter rooms he saw a trunk, opened, its contents carelessly scattered about the floor. One by one he examined the garments, his heart beating quickly. Not a particle of dust on them; plenty of finger-prints on the trunk. It had been opened this very night--by one familiar, either at first-hand or by instruction. He had come for something in that trunk. What?

From garret to cellar, thirty rooms in all; nothing but the hand-print on the newel-post and the opened trunk. Haggerty returned to the museum, turned out all the lights except that on the desk, and sat down on a rug so as not to disturb the dust on the chairs. The man might return. It was certain that he, Haggerty, would come back on the morrow. He was anxious to compare the thumb-print with the one he had in his collection.

For what had the man come? Keep-sakes? Haggerty dearly wanted to believe that the intruder was the one man he desired in his net; but he refused to listen to the insidious whisperings; he must have proof, positive, absolute, incontestable. If it was Crawford's man Mason, it was almost too good to be true; and he did not care to court ultimate disappointment.

Proof, proof; but where? Why had the man not returned the clothes to the trunk and shut it? What had alarmed him? Everything else indicated the utmost caution. . . . A glint of light flashing and winking from steel. Haggerty rose and went over to the window. He picked up a bunch of keys, thirty or forty in all, on a ring, weighing a good pound. The detective touched the throbbing bump and sensed a moisture; blood. So this was the weapon? He weighed the keys on his palm. A long time since he had seen a finer collection of skeleton keys, thin and flat and thick and short, smooth and notched, each a gem of its kind. Three or four ordinary keys were sandwiched in between, and Haggerty inspected these curiously.

"H'm. Mebbe it's a hunch. Anyhow, I'll try it. Can't lose anything trying."

He turned out the desk light and went down to the lower hall, his pocket-lamp serving as guide. He unlatched the heavy door-chains, opened the doors and closed them behind him. He inserted one of the ordinary keys. It refused to work. He tried another. The door swung open, easily.

"Now, then, come down out o' that!" growled a voice at the foot of the steps. "Thought y'd be comin' out by-'n-by. No foolin' now, 'r I blow a hole through ye!"

Haggerty wheeled quickly. "'S that you, Dorgan? Come up."

"Haggerty?" said the astonished patrolman. "An' Mitchell an' I've been watchin' these lights fer an hour!"

"Some one's been here, though; so y' weren't wasting your time. I climbed up th' fire-escape in th' alley an' got a nice biff on th' coco for me pains. See any one running before y' saw th' lights?"

"Why, yes!"

"Ha! It's hard work t' get it int' your heads that when y' see a man running at this time o' night, in a quiet side-street it's up t' you t' ask him questions."

"Thought he was chasin' a cab."

"Well, listen here. Till th' owner comes back, keep your eyes peeled on this place. An' any one y' see prowling around, nab him an' send for me. On your way!"

Haggerty departed in a hurry. He had already made up his mind as to what he was going to do. He hunted up a taxicab and told the chauffeur where to go, advising him to "hit it up." His destination was the studio-apartment of J. Mortimer Forbes, the artist. It was late, but this fact did not trouble Haggerty. Forbes never went to bed until there was positively nothing else to do.

The elevator-boy informed Haggerty that Mr. Forbes had just returned from the theater. Alone? Yes. Haggerty pushed the bell-button. A dog bayed.

"Why, Haggerty, what's up? Come on in. Be still, Fritz!"

The dachel's growl ended in a friendly snuffle, and he began to dance upon Haggerty's broad-toed shoes.

"Bottle of beer? Cigar? Take that easy chair. What's on your mind tonight?" Forbes rattled away. "Why, man, there's a cut on the side of your head!"

"Uhuh. Got any witch-hazel?" The detective sat down, stretched out his legs, and pulled the dachel's ears.

Forbes ran into the bathroom to fetch the witch-hazel. Haggerty poured a little into his palm and dabbled the wound with it.

"Now, spin it out; tell me what's happened," said Forbes, filling his calabash and pushing the cigars across the table.

For a year and a half these two men, the antitheses of each other, had been intimate friends. This liking was genuine, based on secret admiration, as yet to be confessed openly. Forbes had always been drawn toward this man-hunting business; he yearned to rescue the innocent and punish the guilty. Whenever a great crime was committed he instantly overflowed with theories as to what the criminal was likely to do afterward. Haggerty enjoyed listening to his patter; and often there were illuminating flashes which obtained results for the detective, who never applied his energies in the direction of logical deduction. Besides, the chairs in the studio were comfortable, the imported beer not too cold, and the cigars beyond criticism.

Haggerty accepted a cigar, lighted it, and amusedly watched the eager handsome face of the artist.

"Any poker lately?"

"No; cut it out for six months. Come on, now; don't keep me waiting any longer."

"Mum's th' word?"--tantalizingly.

"You ought to know that by this time"--aggrieved.

Haggerty tossed the bunch of keys on the table.

"Ha! Good specimens, these," Forbes declared, handling them. "Here's a window-opener."

"Good boy!" said Haggerty, as a teacher would have commended a bright pupil.

"And a door-chain lifter. Nothing lacking. Did he hit you with these?"

"Ye-up."

"What are these regular keys for?"

"One o' them unlocks a door." Haggerty smoked luxuriously.

Forbes eyed the ordinary keys with more interest than the burglarious ones. Haggerty was presently astonished to see the artist produce his own key-ring.

"What now?"

"When Crawford went abroad he left a key with me. I am making some drawings for an Egyptian romance and wanted to get some atmosphere."

"Uhuh."

"Which key is it that unlocks a door?" asked Forbes, his eyes sparkling.

"Never'll get that out o' your head, will you?"

"Which key?"

"Th' round-headed one."

Forbes drew the key aside and laid it evenly against the one Crawford had left in his keeping.

"By George!"

"What's th' matter?"

"He's come back!"--in a whisper.

"You're a keen one! Ye-up; Crawford's valet Mason is visiting in town."

CHAPTER X

There are many threads and many knots in a net; these can not be thrown together haphazard, lest the big fish slip through. At the bottom of the net is a small steel ring, and here the many threads and the many knots finally meet. Forbes and Haggerty (who, by the way, thinks I'm a huge joke as a novelist) and the young man named Webb recounted this tale to me by threads and knots. The ring was of Kitty Killigrew, for Kitty Killigrew, by Kitty Killigrew, to paraphrase a famous line.

At one of the quieter hotels--much patronized by touring Englishmen--there was registered James Thornden and man. Every afternoon Mr. Thornden and his man rode about town in a rented touring car. The man would bundle his master's knees in a rug and take the seat at the chauffeur's side, and from there direct the journey. Generally they drove through the park, up and down Riverside, and back to the hotel in time for tea. Mr. Thornden drank tea for breakfast along with his bacon and eggs, and at luncheon with his lamb or mutton chops, and at five o'clock with especially baked muffins and apple-tarts.

Mr. Thornden never gave orders personally; his man always attended to that. The master would, early each morning, outline the day's work, and the man would see to it that these instructions were fulfilled to the letter. He was an excellent servant, by the way, light of foot, low of voice, serious of face, with a pair of eyes which I may liken to nothing so well as to a set of acetylene blow-pipes--bored right through you.

The master was middle-aged, about the same height and weight as his valet. He wore a full dark beard, something after the style of the early eighties of last century. His was also a serious countenance, tanned, dignified too; but his eyes were no match for his valet's; too dreamy, introspective. Screwed in his left eye was a monocle down from which flowed a broad ribbon. In public he always wore it; no one about the hotel had as yet seen him without it, and he had been a guest there for more than a fortnight.

He drank nothing in the way of liquor, though his man occasionally wandered into the bar and ordered a stout or an ale. After dinner the valet's time appeared to be his own; for he went out nearly every night. He seemed very much interested in shop-windows, especially those which were filled with curios. Mr. Thornden frequently went to the theater, but invariably alone.

Thus, they attracted little or no attention among the clerks and bell boys and waiters who had, in the course of the year, waited upon the wants of a royal duke and a grand duke, to say nothing of a maharajah, who was still at the hotel. An ordinary touring Englishman was, then, nothing more than that.

Until one day a newspaper reporter glanced carelessly through the hotel register. The only thing which escapes the newspaper man is the art of saving; otherwise he is omnipotent. He sees things, anticipates events, and often prearranges them; smells war if the secretary of the navy is seen to run for a street-car, is intimately acquainted with "the official in the position to know" and "the man higher up," "the gentleman on the inside," and other anonymous but famous individuals. He is tireless, impervious to rebuff, also relentless; as an investigator of crime he is the keenest hound of them all; often he does more than expose, he prevents. He is the Warwick of modern times; he makes and unmakes kings, sceptral and financial.

This particular reporter sent his card up to Mr. Thornden and was, after half an hour's delay, admitted to the suite. Mr. Thornden laid aside his tea-cup.

"I am a newspaper man, Mr. Thornden," said the young man, his eye roving about the room, visualizing everything, from the slices of lemon to the brilliant eyes of the valet.

"Ah! a pressman. What will you be wanting to see me about, sir?"--neither hostile nor friendly.

"Do you intend to remain long in America--incog?"

"Incog!" Mr. Thorndon leaned forward in his chair and drew down his eyebrow tightly against the rim of his monocle.

"Yes, sir. I take it that you are Lord Henry Monckton, ninth Baron of Dimbledon."

Master and man exchanged a rapid glance.

"Tibbets," said the master coldly, "you registered."

"Yes, sir."

"What did you register?"

"Oh," interposed the reporter, "it was the name Dimbledon caught my eye, sir. You see, there was a paragraph in one of our

London exchanges that you had sailed for America. I'm what we call a hotel reporter; hunt up prominent and interesting people for interviews. I'm sure yours is a very interesting story, sir." The reporter was a pleasant, affable young man, and that was why he was so particularly efficient in his chosen line of work.

"I was not prepared to disclose my identity so soon," said Lord Monckton ruefully. "But since you have stumbled upon the truth, it is far better that I give you the facts as they are. Interviewing is a novel experience. What do you wish to know, sir?"

And thus it was that, next morning, New York--and the continent as well--learned that Lord Henry Monckton, ninth Baron of Dimbledon, had arrived in America on a pleasure trip. The story read more like the scenario of a romantic novel than a page from life. For years the eighth Baron of Dimbledon had lived in seclusion, practically forgotten. In India he had a bachelor brother, a son and a grandson. One day he was notified of the death (by bubonic plague) of these three male members of his family, the baron himself collapsed and died shortly after. The title and estate went to another branch of the family. A hundred years before, a daughter of the house had run away with the head-gardener and been disowned. The great-great-grand-son of this woman became the ninth baron. The present baron's life was recounted in full; and an adventurous life it had been, if the reporter was to be relied upon. The interview appeared in a London journal, with the single comment--"How those American reporters misrepresent things!"

It made capital reading, however; and in servants' halls the newspaper became very popular. It gave rise to a satirical leader on the editorial page: "What's the matter with us republicans? Liberty, fraternity and equality; we flaunt that flag as much as we ever did. Yet, what a howdy-do when a title comes along! What a craning of necks, what a kotowing! How many earldoms and dukedoms are not based upon some detestable action, some despicable service rendered some orgiastic sovereign! The most honorable thing about the so-called nobility is generally the box-hedge which surrounds the manse. Kotow; pour our millions into the bottomless purses of spendthrifts; give them our most beautiful women. There is no remedy for human nature."

It was this editorial which interested Killigrew far more than the story which had given birth to it.

"That's the way to shout."

"Does it do any good?" asked Kitty. "If we had a lord for breakfast--I mean, at breakfast--would you feel at ease? Wouldn't you be watching and wondering what it was that made him your social superior?"

"Social superior? Bah!"

"That's no argument. As this editor wisely says, there's no remedy for human nature. When I was a silly schoolgirl I often wondered if there wasn't a duke in the family, or even a knight. How do you account for that feeling?"

"You were probably reading Bertha M. Clay," retorted her father, only too glad of such an opening.

"What is your opinion of titles, Mr. Webb?" she asked calmly.

"Mr. Webb is an Englishman, Kitty," reminded her mother.

"All the more reason for wishing his point of view," was the reply.

"A title, if managed well, is a fine business asset." Thomas stared gravely at his egg-cup.

"A humorist!" cried Killigrew, as if he had discovered a dodo.

"Really, no. I am typically English, sir." But Thomas was smiling this time; and when he smiled Kitty found him very attractive. She was leaning on her elbows, her folded hands propping her chin; and in his soul Thomas knew that she was looking at him with those boring critical blue eyes of hers. Why was she always looking at him like that? "It is notorious that we English are dull and stupid," he said.

"Now you are making fun of us," said Kitty seriously.

"I beg your pardon!"

She dropped her hands from under her chin and laughed. "Do you really wish to know the real secret of our antagonism, Mr. Webb?"

"I should be very glad."

"Well, then, we each of us wear a chip on our shoulder, simply because we've never taken the trouble to know each other well. Most English we Americans meet are stupid and caddish and uninteresting; and most of the Americans you see are boastful, loud-talking and money-mad. Our mutual impressions are wholly wrong to begin with."

"I have no chip on my shoulder," Thomas refuted eagerly.

"Neither have I."

"But I have," laughed her father. "I eat Englishmen for breakfast; fe-fo-fum style."

How democratic indeed these kindly, unpretentious people were! thought Thomas. A multimillionaire as amiable as a clerk; a daughter who would have graced any court in Europe with her charm and elfin beauty. Up to a month ago he had held all Americans in tolerant contempt.

It was as Kitty said: the real Englishman and the real American seldom met.

He did not realize as yet that his position in this house was unique. In England all great merchants and statesmen and nobles had one or more private secretaries about. He believed it to be a matter of course that Americans followed the same custom. He would have been wonderfully astonished to learn that in all this mighty throbbing city of millions--people and money--there might be less than a baker's dozen who occupied simultaneously the positions of private secretary and friend of the family. Mr. Killigrew had his private secretary, but this gentleman rarely saw the inside of the Killigrew home; it wasn't at all necessary that he should. Killigrew was a sensible man; his business hours began when he left home and ended when he entered it.

"Do you know any earls or dukes?" asked Killigrew, folding his napkin.

"Really, no. I have moved in a very different orbit. I know many of them by sight, however." He did not think it vital to add that he had often sold them collars and suspenders.

The butler and the second man pulled back the ladies' chairs. Killigrew hurried away to his offices; Kitty and her mother went up-stairs; and Thomas returned to his desk in the library. He was being watched by Kitty; nothing overt, nothing tangible, yet he sensed it: from the first day he had entered this house. It oppressed him, like a presage of disaster. Back of his chair was a fireplace, above this, a mirror. Once--it was but yesterday-- while with his back to his desk, day-dreaming, he had seen her in the mirror. She stood in the doorway, a hand resting lightly against the portiere. There was no smile on her face. The moment he stirred, she vanished.

Watched. Why?

CHAPTER XI

The home-bureau of charities was a success from the start; but beyond the fact that it served to establish Thomas Webb as private secretary in the Killigrew family, I was not deeply interested. I know that Thomas ran about a good deal, delving into tenements and pedigrees, judging candidates, passing or condemning, and that he earned his salary, munificent as it appeared to him. Forbes told me that he wouldn't have done the work for a thousand a week; and Forbes, like Panurge, had ten ways of making money and twelve ways of spending it.

The amazing characteristic about Thomas was his unaffected modesty, his naturalness, his eagerness to learn, his willingness to accept suggestions, no matter from what source. Haberdashers' clerks--at least, those I have known--are superior persons; they know it all, you can not tell them a single thing. I can call to witness dozens of neckties and shirts I shall never dare wear in public. But perhaps seven years among a clientele of earls and dukes, who were set in their ideas, had something to do with Thomas' attitude.

Killigrew was very well satisfied with the venture. He had had some doubts at the beginning: a man whose past ended at Pier 60 did not look like a wise speculation, especially in a household. But quite unconsciously Thomas himself had taken these doubts out of Killigrew's mind and--mislaid them. The subscriptions to all the suffragette weeklies and monthlies were dropped; and there were no more banners reading "Votes for Women" tacked over the doorways. Besides this, the merchant had a man to talk to, after dinner, he with his cigar and Thomas with his pipe, this privilege being insisted upon by the women folk, who had tact to leave the two men to themselves.

Thomas amused the millionaire. Here was a young man of a species with whom he had not come into contact in many years: a boy who did not know the first thing about poker, or bridge, or pinochle, who played outrageous billiards and who did not know who the latest reigning theatrical beauty was, and moreover, did not care a rap; who could understand a joke within reasonable time if he couldn't tell one; who was neither a nincompoop nor a mollycoddle. Thomas interested Killigrew more and more as the days went past.

Happily, the voice of conscience is heard by no ears but one's own.

After luncheons Thomas had a good deal of time on his hands; and, to occupy this time he returned to his old love, composition. He began to rewrite his romance; and one day Kitty discovered him pegging away at it. He rose from his chair instantly.

"Will you be wanting me, Miss Killigrew?"

"Only to say that father will be detained down-town to-night and that you will be expected to take mother and me to the theater. It is one of your English musical comedies; and very good, they say."

Thomas had been dreading such a situation. As yet there had been no entertaining at the Killigrew home; nearly all their friends were out of town for the summer; thus far he had escaped.

"I am sorry, Miss Killigrew, but I have no suitable clothes." Which was plain unvarnished truth. "And I do not possess an opera-hat." And never did.

Kitty laughed pleasantly. "We are very democratic in this house, as by this time you will have observed. In the summer we do not dress; we take our amusements comfortably. Ordinarily we would be at our summer home on Long Island; but delayed repairs will not let us into it till August. Then we shall all take a vacation. You will join us as you are; that is, of course, if you are not too busy with your own affairs."

"Never too busy to be of service to you, Miss Killigrew. I'm only scribbling."

"A book?"--interestedly.

"Bally rot, possibly. Would you like to read it?"--one of the best inspirations he had ever had. He was not one of those silly individuals who hem and haw when some one discovers they have the itch for writing, whose sole aim is to have the secret dragged out of them, with hypocritical reluctance.

"May I?" Her friendly aloofness fell away from her as if touched by magic. "I am an inveterate reader. Besides, I know several famous editors, and perhaps I could help you."

"That would be jolly."

"And you are writing a story, and never told us about it!"

"It never occurred to me to tell you. I shall be very glad to go to the theater with you and Mrs. Killigrew."

Kitty tucked the romance under her arm and flew to her room with it. This Thomas was as full of surprises as a Christmas-box.

He eyed the empty doorway speculatively. He rather preferred the friendly aloofness; otherwise some fatal nonsense might enter his head. He resumed his chair and transferred his gaze to the blotter. He added a few pothooks by the way: numerals in addition and subtraction (for he was of Scotch descent), a name which he scratched out and scrawled again and again scratched out. He examined the contents of his wallet. How many pounds did a dress-suit cost in this hurly-burly country? This question could be answered only in one way. He hastened out into the hall, put on his hat, made for the subway, and got out directly opposite the offices of Killigrew and Company, sugar, coffee and spices. London-bred, it did not take him long to find his way about. The racket disturbed him; that was all.

The building in which Killigrew and Company had its offices belonged to Killigrew personally. It had cost him a round million to build, but the office-rentals were making it a fine investment. These ornate office-buildings caused Thomas to marvel unceasingly. In London cubby-holes were sufficient. If merchants like Killigrew, generally these were along the water-front; creaky, old, dim-windowed. In this bewildering country a man conducted his business as from a palace. The warehouses were distinct establishments.

Thomas entered the portals, stepped cautiously into one of the express-elevators (so they insisted upon calling them here), and was shot up to the fourteenth floor, all of which was occupied by Killigrew and Company. It was Thomas' first venture in this district. And he learned the amazing fact that it was ordinarily as easy to see Mr. Killigrew as it was to see King George. Office-boys, minor clerks, head clerks, managers; they quizzed and buffeted him hither and thither. He never thought to state at the outset that he was Mrs. Killigrew's private secretary; he merely said that it was very important that he should see Mr. Killigrew at once.

"Mr. Killigrew is busy," he was informed by the assistant manager, at whose desk Thomas finally arrived. "If you will give me your card I'll have it sent in to him."

Thomas confessed that he had no card. The assistant manager grew distinctly chilling.

"If you will be so kind as to inform Mr. Killigrew that Mr. Webb, Mrs. Killigrew's private secretary . . ."

"Why didn't you say that at once, Mr. Webb? Here, boy; tell Mr. Killigrew that Mr. Webb wishes to see him. You might just as well follow the boy."

Killigrew was smoking, and perusing the baseball edition of his favorite evening paper. All this red-tape to approach a man who wasn't doing anything more vital than that! Thomas smiled. It was a wonderful people.

"Why, hello, Webb! What's the matter? Anything wrong at the house?"--anxiously.

"No, Mr. Killigrew. I came to see you on a personal matter."

Killigrew dropped the newspaper on his desk, a little frown between his eyes. He made no inquiry.

"Miss Killigrew tells me that you will not be home this evening, and that I am to take her and Mrs. Killigrew to the theater."

"Anything in the way to prevent you?" Killigrew appeared vastly relieved for some reason.

"As a matter of fact, sir, I haven't the proper clothes; and I thought you might advise me where to go to obtain them."

Killigrew laughed until the tears started. The very heartiness of it robbed it of all rudeness. "Good lord! and I was worrying my head off. Webb, you're all right. Do you need any funds?"

"I believe I have enough." Thomas appeared to be disturbed not in the least by the older man's hilarity. It was not infectious, because he did not understand it.

"Glad you came to me. Always come to me when you're in doubt about anything. I'm no authority on clothes, but my secretary is. I'll have him take you to a tailor where you can rent a suit for to-night. He'll take your measure, and by the end of the week . . ." He did not finish the sentence, but pressed one of the many buttons on his desk. "Clark, this is Mr. Webb, Mrs.

Killigrew's secretary. He wants some clothes. Take him along with you."

Alone again, Killigrew smiled broadly. The humor of the situation did not blind him to the salient fact that this Webb was a man of no small courage. He recognized in this courage a commendable shrewdness also: Webb wanted the right thing, honest clothes for honest dollars. A man like that would be well worth watching. And for a moment he had thought that Webb had fallen in love with Kitty and wanted to marry her! He chuckled. Clothes!

What a boy Kitty would have made! What an infallible eye she had for measuring a person! No servant-question ever dangled its hot interrogation point before his eyes. Kitty saw to that. She was the real manager of the household affairs, for all that he paid the bills. Some day she would marry a proper man; but heaven keep that day as far off as possible. What would he do without Kitty? Always ready to perch on his knee, to smooth the day-cares from his forehead, to fend off trouble, to make laughter in the house. He was not going to love the man who eventually carried her off. He was always dreading that day; young men about the house, the yacht and the summer home worried him. The whole lot of them were not worthy to tie the laces of her shoes, much as they might yearn to do so.

And all Webb wanted was a tailor! He would give a hundred for the right to tell this scare to the boys at the club, but Webb's ingenuous confidence did not merit betrayal. Still, nothing should prevent him from telling Kitty, who knew how to keep a secret. He picked up the newspaper and resumed his computation of averages (batting), chuckling audibly from time to time. Clothes!

At quarter to six Thomas returned to the house, laden with fat bundles which he hurried secretly to his room. He had never worn a dress-suit. He had often guilelessly dreamed of possessing one: between paragraphs, as another young man might have dreamed of vanquishing a rival. It was inborn that we should wish to appear well in public; to better one's condition, or, next best, to make the public believe one has. Thomas was deeply observant and quickly adaptive. Between the man who goes to school *with* books and the man who goes to school *in* books there is wide difference. What we are forced to learn seldom lifts us above the ordinary; what we learn by inclination plows our fields and reaps our harvests. It is as natural as breathing that we should like our tonics, mental as well as physical, sugar-coated.

Thomas had never worn a dress-suit; but in the matter of collars and cravats and shirts he knew the last word. But why should he wish to wear that mournfully conventional suit in which we are supposed to enjoy ourselves? She had told him not to bother about dress. Was it that very nonsense he dreaded, insidiously attacking the redoubts of his common sense?

That evening at dinner Kitty nor her mother appeared to notice the change. This gratified him; he knew that outwardly there was nothing left to desire or attain.

Kitty began to talk about the romance immediately. She had found the beginning very exciting; it was out of the usual run of stories; and if it was all as good as the first part, there would be some editors glad to get hold of it. So much for the confidence of youth. *The Black Veil,* as I have reason to know, lies at the bottom of Thomas' ancient trunk.

Long as he lived he would never forget the enjoyment of that night. The electric signs along Broadway interested him intensely; he babbled about them boyishly. Theater outside and theater within; a great drama of light and shadow, of comedy and tragedy; for he gazed upon the scene with all his poet's eyes. He enjoyed the opera, the color and music, the propinquity of Kitty. Sometimes their shoulders touched; the indefinable perfume of her hair thrilled him.

Kitty had seen all these things so many times that she no longer experienced enthusiasm; but his was so genuine, so un-English, that she found it impossible to escape the contagion. She did not bubble over, however; on the contrary, she sat through the performance strangely subdued, dimly alarmed over what she had done.

As they were leaving the lobby of the theater, a man bumped against Thomas, quite accidentally.

"I beg your pardon!" said the stranger, politely raising his hat and passing on.

Thomas' hand went clumsily to his own hat, which he fumbled and dropped and ran after frantically across the mosaic flooring.

A ghost; yes, sir, Thomas had seen a ghost.

I left Thomas scrambling about the mosaic lobby of the theater for his opera-hat. When he recovered it, it resembled one of those accordions upon which vaudeville artists play Mendelssohn's Wedding March and the latest ragtime (by request). Some one had stepped on it. Among the unanswerable questions stands prominently: Why do we laugh when a man loses his hat? Thomas burned with a mixture of rage and shame; shame that Kitty should witness his discomfiture and rage that, by the time he had retrieved the hat, the ghost had disappeared.

However, Thomas acted as a polished man of the world, as if eight-dollar opera-hats were mere nothings. He held it out for Kitty to inspect, smiling. Then he crushed it under his arm (where the broken spring behaved like an unlatched jack-in-the-box) and led the way to the Killigrew limousine.

"I am sorry, Mr. Webb," said Kitty, biting her lips.

"Now, now! Honestly, don't you know, I hated the thing. I knew something would happen. I never realized till this moment that it is an art all by itself to wear a high hat without feeling and looking like a silly ass."

He laughed, honestly and heartily; and Kitty laughed, and so did her mother. Subtle barriers were swept away, and all three of them became what they had not yet been, friends. It was worth many opera-hats.

"Kitty, I'm beginning to like Thomas," said her mother, later. "He was very nice about the hat. Most men would have been in a frightful temper over it."

"I'm beginning to like him, too, mother. It was cruel, but I wanted to shout with laughter as he dodged in and out of the throng. Did you notice how he smiled when he showed it to me? A woman stepped on it. When she screamed I thought there was going to be a riot."

"He's the most guileless young man I ever saw."

"He really and truly is," assented Kitty.

"I like him because he isn't afraid to climb up five flights of tenement stairs, or to shake hands with the tenants themselves. I was afraid at first."

"Afraid of what?"

"That you might have made a mistake in selecting him so casually for our secretary."

"Perhaps I have," murmured Kitty, under her breath.

Alone in her bedroom the smile left Kitty's face. A brooding frown wrinkled the smooth forehead. It was there when Celeste came in; it remained there after Celeste departed; and it vanished only under the soft, dispelling fingers of sleep.

There was a frown on Thomas' forehead, too; bitten deep. He tried to read, he tried to smoke, he tried to sleep; futilely. In the middle of the banquet, as it were, like a certain Assyrian king in Babylon, Thomas saw the Chaldaic characters on the wall: wherever he looked, written in fire--Thou fool!

CHAPTER XIII

Two mornings later the newspapers announced the important facts that Miss Kitty Killigrew had gone to Bar Harbor for the week, and that the famous uncut emeralds of the Maharajah of Something-or-other-apur had been stolen; nothing co-relative in the departure of Kitty and the green stones, coincidence only.

The Indian prince was known the world over as gem-mad. He had thousands in unset gems which he neither sold, wore, nor gave away. His various hosts and hostesses lived in mortal terror during a sojourn of his; for he carried his jewels with him always; and often, whenever the fancy seized him, he would go abruptly to his room, spread a square of cobalt-blue velvet on the floor, squat in his native fashion beside it, and empty his bags of diamonds and rubies and pearls and sapphires and emeralds and turquoises. To him they were beautiful toys. Whenever he was angry, they soothed him; whenever he was happy, they rounded out this happiness; they were his variant moods.

He played a magnificent game. Round the diamonds he would make a circle of the palest turquoises. Upon this pyramid of brilliants he would place some great ruby, sapphire, or emerald. Then his servants were commanded to raise and lower the window-curtains alternately. These shifting contra-lights put a strange life into the gems; they not only scintillated, they breathed. Or, perhaps the pyramid would be of emeralds; and he would peer into their cool green depths as he might have peered into the sea.

He kept these treasures in an ornamented iron-chest, old, battered, of simple mechanism. It had been his father's and his father's father's; it had been in the family since the days of the Peacock Throne, and most of the jewels besides. Night and day the chest was guarded. It lay upon an ancient Ispahan rug, in the center of the bedroom, which no hotel servant was permitted to enter. His five servants saw to it that all his wants were properly attended to, that no indignity to his high caste might be offered: as having his food prepared by pariah hands in the hotel kitchens, foul hands to make his bed. He was thoroughly

religious; the gods of his fathers were his in all their
ramifications; he wore the Brahmin thread about his neck.

He was unique among Indian princes. An Oxford graduate,
he persistently and consistently clung to the elaborate costumes
of his native state. And when he condescended to visit any one,
it was invariably stipulated that he should be permitted to bring
along his habits, his costumes and his retinue. In his suite or
apartments he was the barbarian; in the drawing-room, in the
ballroom, in the dining-room (where he ate nothing), he was the
suave, the courteous, the educated Oriental. He drank no wines,
made his own cigarettes, and never offered his hand to any one,
not even to the handsome women who admired his beautiful skin
and his magnificent ropes of pearls.

Some one had entered the bedroom, overpowered the guard,
and looted the bag containing the emeralds. The prince, the
lightest of sleepers, had slept through it all. He had awakened
with a violent headache, as had four of his servants. The big
Rajput who had stood watch was in the hospital, still
unconscious.

All the way from San Francisco the police had been waiting
for such a catastrophe. The newspapers had taken up and
published broadcast the story of the prince's pastime. Naturally
enough, there was not a crook in all America who was not
waiting for a possible chance. Ten emeralds, weighing from six
to ten carats each; a fortune, even if broken up.

Haggerty laid aside the newspaper and gravely finished his
ham and eggs.

"I'll take a peek int' this, Milly," he said to his wife. "We've
been waiting for this t' happen. A million dollars in jools in a
chest y' could open with a can-opener. Queer ginks, these
Hindus. We see lots o' fakers, but this one is the real article.
Mebbe a reward. All right; little ol' Haggerty can use th' money.
I may not be home t' supper."

"Anything more about Mr. Crawford's valet?"

Haggerty scowled. "Not a line. I've been living in gambling
joints, but no sign of him. He gambled in th' ol' days; some time
'r other he'll wander in somewhere an' try t' copper th' king. No
sign of him round Crawford's ol' place. But I'll get him; it's a
hunch. By-by!"

Later, the detective was conducted into the Maharajah's reception-room. The prince, in his soft drawling English (far more erudite and polished than Haggerty's, if not so direct), explained the situation, omitting no detail. He would give two thousand five hundred for the recovery of the stones.

"At what are they valued?"

"By your customs appraisers, forty thousand. To me they are priceless."

"Six t' ten carats? Why, they're worth more than that."

The prince smiled. "That was for the public."

"I'll take a look int' your bedroom," said Haggerty, rising.

"Oh, no; that is not at all necessary," protested the prince.

"How d' you suppose I'm going t' find out who done it, or how it was done, then?" demanded Haggerty, bewildered.

A swift oriental gesture.

The hotel manager soothed Haggerty by explaining that the prince's caste would not permit an alien to touch anything in the bedroom while it contained the prince's belongings.

"Well, wouldn't that get your goat!" exploded Haggerty. "That lets me out. You'll have to get a clairyvoint."

The prince suggested that he be given another suite. His servants would remove his belongings. He promised that nothing else should be touched.

"How long'll it take you?"

"An hour."

"All right," assented Haggerty. "Who's got th' suite across th' hall?" he asked of the manager, as they left the prince.

"Lord Monckton. He and his valet left this morning for Bar Harbor. Back Tuesday. A house-party of Fifth Avenue people."

"Uhuh." Haggerty tugged at his mustache. "I might look around in there while I'm waiting for his Majesty t' change. Did y'ever hear th' likes? Bug-house."

"But he pays a hundred the day, Haggerty. I'll let you privately into Lord Monckton's suite. But you'll waste your time."

"Sure he left this morning?"

"I'll phone the office and make sure. . . . Lord Monckton left shortly after midnight. His man followed early this morning. Lord Monckton went by his host's yacht. But the man followed by rail."

"What's his man look like?"

"Slim and very dark, and very quiet."

"Well, I'll take a look."

The manager was right. Haggerty had his trouble for nothing. There was no clue whatever in Lord Monckton's suite. There was no paper in the waste-baskets, in the fireplace; the blotters on the writing-desk were spotless. Some clothes were hanging in the closets, but these revealed only their fashionable maker's name. In the reception-room, on a table, a pack of cards lay spread out in an unfinished game of solitaire. All the small baggage had been taken for the journey. Truth to tell, Haggerty had not expected to find anything; he had not cared to sit idly twiddling his thumbs while the Maharajah vacated his rooms.

In the bathroom (Lord Monckton's) he found two objects which aroused his silent derision: a bottle of brilliantine and an ointment made of walnut-juice. Probably this Lord Monckton was a la-de-dah chap. Bah!

Once in the prince's vacated bedroom Haggerty went to work with classic thoroughness. Not a square foot of the room escaped his vigilant eye. The thief had not entered by the windows; he had come into the room by the door which gave to the corridor. He stood on a chair and examined the transom sill. The dust was undisturbed. He inspected the keyhole; sniffed; stood up, bent and sniffed again. It was an odor totally unknown to him. He stuffed the corner of his fresh handkerchief into the keyhole, drew it out and sniffed that. Barely perceptible. He wrapped the corner into the heart of the handkerchief, and put it back into his pocket. Some powerful narcotic had been forced into the room through the keyhole. This would account for the prince's headache. These Orientals were as bad as the Dutch; they never opened their windows for fresh air.

Beyond this faint, mysterious odor there was nothing else. The first step would be to ascertain whether this narcotic was occidental or oriental.

"Nothing doing yet," he confessed to the anxious manager. "But there ain't any cause for you t' worry. You're not responsible for jools not left in th' office."

"That isn't the idea. It's having the thing happen in this hotel. We'll add another five hundred if you succeed. Not in ten years has there been so much as a spoon missing. What do you think about it?"

"Big case. I'll be back in a little while. Don't tell th' reporters anything."

Haggerty was on his way to a near-by chemist whom he knew, when he espied Crawford in his electric, stalled in a jam at Forty-second and Broadway. He had not seen the archeologist since his return from Europe.

"Hey, Mr. Crawford!" Haggerty bawled, putting his head into the window.

"Why, Haggerty, how are you? Can I give you a lift?"

"If it won't trouble you."

"Not at all. Pretty hot weather."

"For my business. Wish I could run off t' th' seashore like you folks. Heard o' th' Maharajah's emeralds?"

"Yes. You're on that case?"

"Trying t' get on it. Looks blank jus' now. Clever bit o' work; something new. But I've got news for you, though. Your man Mason is back here again. I thought I wouldn't say nothing t' you till I put my hand on his shoulder."

"I'm sorry. I had hoped that the unfortunate devil would have had sense to remain abroad."

"Then you knew he was over there?"--quickly. "See him?"

"No. I shall never feel anything but sorry for him. You can not live with a man as I did, for ten years, and not regret his misstep."

"Oh, I understand your side. But that man was a born crook, an' th' cleverest I ever run up against. For all you know, he may have been back of a lot o' tricks Central never got hold of. I'll bet that each time that you went over with him, he took loot an' disposed of it. I may be pig-headed sometimes, but I'm dead sure o' this. Wait some day an' see. Say, take a whiff o' this an' tell me what y' think it is." Haggerty produced the handkerchief.

"I don't smell anything," said Crawford.

Haggerty seized the handkerchief and sniffed, gently, then violently. All he could smell was reminiscent of washtubs. The mysterious odor was gone.

This is not a story of the Maharajah's emeralds; only a knot in the landing-net of which I have already spoken. I may add with equal frankness that Haggerty, upon his own initiative, never proceeded an inch beyond the keyhole episode. It was one of his many failures; for, unlike the great fictional detectives who never fail, Haggerty was human, and did. It is only fair to add, however, that when he failed only rarely did any one else succeed. If ever criminal investigation was a man's calling, it was Haggerty's. He had infinite patience, the heart of a lion and the strength of a gorilla. Had he been highly educated, as a detective he would have been a fizzle; his mind would have been concerned with variant lofty thoughts, and the sordid would have repelled him: and all crimes are painted on a background of sordidness. In one thing Haggerty stood among his peers and topped many of them; in his long record there was not one instance of his arresting an innocent man.

So Haggerty had his failures; there are geniuses on both sides of the law; and the pariah-dog is always just a bit quicker mentally than the thoroughbred hound who hunts him; indeed, to save his hide he has to be.

Nearly every great fact is like a well-balanced kite; it has for its tail a whimsy. Haggerty, on a certain day, received twenty-five hundred dollars from the Hindu prince and five hundred more from the hotel management. The detective bore up under the strain with stoic complacency. "The Blind Madonna of the Pagan--Chance" always had her hand upon his shoulder.

Kitty went to Bar Harbor, her mother to visit friends in Orange. Thomas walked with a straight spine always; but it stiffened to think that, without knowing a solitary item about his past, they trusted him with the run of the house. The first day there was work to do; the second day, a little less; the third, nothing at all. So he moped about the great house, lonesome as a forgotten dog. He wrote a sonnet on being lonesome, tore it up and flung the scraps into the waste-basket. Once, he seated himself at the piano and picked out with clumsy forefinger *Walking Down the Old Kent Road.* Kitty could play. Often in the mornings, while at his desk, he had heard her; and oddly enough, he seemed to sense her moods by what she played.

(That's the poet.) When she played Chopin or Chaminade she went about gaily all the day; when she played Beethoven, Grieg or Bach, Thomas felt the presence of shadows.

There was a magnificent library, mostly editions de luxe. Thomas smiled over the many uncut volumes. True, Dickens, Dumas and Stevenson were tolerably well-thumbed; but the host of thinkers and poets and dramatists and theologians, in their hand-tooled Levant . . . ! Away in an obscure corner (because of its cheap binding) he came across a set of Lamb. He took out a volume at random and glanced at the fly-leaf--"Kitty Killigrew, Smith College." Then he went into the body of the book. It was copiously marked and annotated. There was something so intimate in the touch of the book that he felt he was committing a sacrilege, looking as it were into Kitty's soul. Most men would have gone through the set. Thomas put the book away. Thou fool, indeed! What a hash he had made of his affairs!

He saw Killigrew at breakfast only. The merchant preferred his club in the absence of his family.

Early in the afternoon of the fourth day, Thomas received a telephone call from Killigrew.

"Hello! That you, Webb?"

"Yes. Who is it?"

"Killigrew. Got anything to do to-night?"

"No, Mr. Killigrew."

"You know where my club is, don't you?"

"Yes."

"Well, be there at seven for dinner. Tell the butler and the housekeeper. Mr. Crawford has a box to the fight to-night, and he thought perhaps you'd like to go along with us."

"A boxing-match?"

"Ten rounds, light-weights; and fast boys, too. Both Irish."

"Really, I shall be glad to go."

"Webb?"

"Yes."

"Never use that word 'really' to me. It's un-Irish."

Thomas heard a chuckle before the receiver at the other end clicked on the hook. What a father this hearty, kindly, humorous Irishman would have made for a son!

In London Thomas' amusements had been divided into three classes. During the season he went to the opera twice, to the music-halls once a month, to a boxing-match whenever he could spare the shillings. He belonged to a workingmen's club not far from where he lived; an empty warehouse, converted into a hall, with a platform in the center, from which the fervid (and often misinformed) socialists harangued; and in one corner was a fair gymnasium. Every fortnight, for the sum of a crown a head, three or four amateur bouts were arranged. Thomas rarely missed these exhibitions; he seriously considered it a part of his self-acquired education. What Englishman lives who does not? Brains and brawn make a man (or a country) invincible.

At seven promptly Thomas called at the club and asked for Mr. Killigrew. He was shown into the grill, where he was pleasantly greeted by his host and Crawford and introduced to a young man about his own age, a Mr. Forbes. Thomas, dressed in his new stag-coat, felt that he was getting along famously. He had some doubt in regard to his straw hat, however, till, after dinner, he saw that his companions were wearing their Panamas.

Forbes, the artist, had reached that blasé period when, only upon rare occasions, did he feel disposed to enlarge his acquaintance. But this fresh-skinned young Britisher went to his heart at once, a kindred soul, and he adopted him forthwith. He and Thomas paired off and talked "fight" all the way to the boxing club.

There was a great crowd pressing about the entrance. There were eddies of turbulent spirits. A crowd in America is unlike any other. It is full of meanness, rowdyism, petty malice. A big fellow, smelling of bad whisky, shouldered Killigrew aside, roughly. Killigrew's Irish blood flamed.

"Here! Look where you're going!" he cried.

The man reached back and jammed Killigrew's hat down over his eyes. Killigrew stumbled and fell, and Crawford and Forbes surged to his rescue from the trampling feet. Thomas, however, caught the ruffian's right wrist, jammed it scientifically against the man's chest, took him by the throat and bore him back, savagely and relentlessly. The crowd, packed as it was, gave ground. With an oath the man struck. Thomas struck back, accurately. Instantly the circle widened. A fight outside was always more interesting than one inside the ropes. A blow ripped open Thomas' shirt. It became a slam-bang affair.

Thomas knocked his man down just as a burly policeman arrived. Naturally, he caught hold of Thomas and called for assistance. The wrong man first is the invariable rule of the New York police.

"Milligan!" shouted Killigrew, as he sighted one of the club's promoters.

Milligan recognized his millionaire patron and pushed to his side.

After due explanations, Thomas was liberated and the real culprit was forced swearing through the press toward the patrol-wagon, always near on such nights. Eventually the four gained Crawford's box. Aside from a cut lip and a torn shirt, Thomas was uninjured. If his fairy-godmother had prearranged this fisticuff, she could not have done anything better so far as Killigrew was concerned.

"Thomas," he said, as the main bout was being staged, the chairs and water-pails and paraphernalia changed to fresh corners, "I'll remember that turn. If you're not Irish, it's no fault of yours. I wish you knew something about coffee."

"I enjoy drinking it," Thomas replied, smiling humorously.

Ever after the merchant-prince treated Thomas like a son; the kind of a boy he had always wanted and could not have. And only once again did he doubt; and he longed to throttle the man who brought into light what appeared to be the most damnable evidence of Thomas' perfidy.

CHAPTER XV

We chaps who write have magic carpets.

Whiz!

A marble balcony, overlooking the sea, which shimmered under the light of the summer moon. Lord Henry Monckton and Kitty leaned over the baluster and silently watched the rush of the rollers landward and the slink of them back to the sea.

For three days Kitty had wondered whether she liked or disliked Lord Monckton. The fact that he was the man who had bumped into Thomas that night at the theater may have had something to do with her doddering. He might at least have helped Thomas in recovering his hat. Dark, full-bearded, slender, with hands like a woman's, quiet of manner yet affable, he was the most picturesque person at the cottage. But there was always something smoldering in those sleepy eyes of his that suggested to Kitty a mockery. It was not that recognizable mockery of all those visiting Englishmen who held themselves complacently superior to their generous American hosts. It was as though he were silently laughing at all he saw, at all which happened about him, as if he stood in the midst of some huge joke which he alone was capable of understanding: so Kitty weighed him.

He did not seem to care particularly for women; he never hovered about them, offering little favors and courtesies; rather, he let them come to him. Nor did he care for dancing. But he was always ready to make up a table at bridge; and a shrewd capable player he was, too.

The music in the ballroom stopped.

"Will you be so good, Miss Killigrew, as to tell me why you Americans call a palace like this--a cottage?" Lord Monckton's voice was pleasing, with only a slight accent.

"I'm sure I do not know. If it were mine, I'd call it a villa."

"Quite properly."

"Do you like Americans?"

"I have no preference for any people. I prefer individuals. I had much rather talk to an enlightened Chinaman than to an unenlightened white man."

"I am afraid you are what they call blasé."

"Perhaps I am not quite at ease yet. I was buffeted about a deal in the old days."

Lord Monckton dropped back into the wicker chair, in the deep shadow. Kitty did not move. She wondered what Thomas was doing. (Thomas was rubbing ointment on his raw knuckles.)

"I am very fond of the sea," remarked Lord Monckton. "I have seen some odd parts of it. Every man has his Odyssey, his Aeneid."

Aeneid. It seemed to Kitty that her body had turned that instant into marble as cold as that under her palms.

The coal of the man's cigar glowed intermittently. She could see nothing else.

Aeneid--Enid.

CHAPTER XVI

Thomas slammed the ball with a force which carried it far over the wire backstop.

"You must not drive them so hard, Mr. Webb; at least, not up. Drive them down. Try it again."

Tennis looked so easy from the sidelines that Thomas believed all he had to do was to hit the ball whenever he saw it within reach; but after a few experiments he accepted the fact that every game required a certain talent, quite as distinct as that needed to sell green neckties (old stock) when the prevailing fashion was polka-dot blue. How he loathed Thomas Webb. How he loathed the impulse which had catapulted him into this mad whirligig! Why had not fate left him in peace; if not satisfied with his lot, at least resigned? And now must come this confrontation, the inevitable! No poor rat in a trap could have felt more harassed. Mentally, he went round and round in circles, but he could find no exit. There is no file to saw the bars of circumstance.

That the lithe young figure on the other side of the net, here, there, backward and forward, alert, accurate, bubbling with energy . . . Once, a mad rollicking impulse seized and urged him to vault the net and take her in his arms and hold her still for a moment. But he knew. She was using him as an athlete uses a trainer before a real contest.

There was something more behind his stroke than mere awkwardness. It was downright savagery. Generally when a man is in anger or despair he longs to smash things; and these inoffensive tennis-balls were to Thomas a gift of the gods. Each time one sailed away over the backstop, it was like the pop of a safety-valve; it averted an explosion.

"That will be enough!" cried Kitty, as the last of a dozen balls sailed toward the distant stables.

The tennis-courts were sunken and round them ran a parapet of lawn, crisp and green, with marble benches opposite the posts, generally used as judges' stands. Upon one of these Kitty sat down and began to fan herself. Thomas walked over and sat down beside her. The slight gesture of her hand had been a command.

It was early morning, before breakfast; still and warm and breathless, a forerunner of a long hot summer day. A few hundred yards to the south lay the sea, shimmering as it sprawled lazily upon the tawny sands.

The propinquity of a pretty girl and a lonely young man has founded more than one story.

"You'll be enjoying the game, once you learn it."

"Do you think I ever will?" asked Thomas. He bent forward and began tapping the clay with his racket. How to run away!

Kitty, as she looked down at his head, knew that there were a dozen absurd wishes in her heart, none of which could possibly ever become facts. He was so different from the self-assertive young men she knew, with their silly flirtations, their inane small-talk, their capacity for Scotch whisky and long hours. For days she had studied him as through microscopic lenses; his guilelessness was real. It just simply could not be; her ears had deceived her that memorable foggy night in London. And yet, always in the dark his voice was that of one of the two men who had talked near her cab. Who was he? Not a single corner of the veil had he yet lifted, and here it was, the middle of August; and except for the week at Bar Harbor she had been with him day by day, laid she knew not how many traps, over which he had stepped serenely, warily or unconsciously she could not tell which. It made her heart ache; for, manly and simple as he appeared, honest as he seemed, he was either a rogue or the dupe of one, which was almost as bad. But to-day she was determined to learn which he was.

"What have you done with the romance?"

"I have put it away in the bottom of my trunk. The seventh rejection convinces me that I am not a story-teller."

He had a desperate longing to tell her all, then and there. It was too late. He would be arrested as a smuggler, turned out of the house as an impostor.

"Don't give up so easily. There are still ninety-three other editors waiting to read it."

"I have my doubts. Still, it was a pleasant pastime." He sat back and stared at the sea. He must go this day; he must invent some way of leaving.

Then came the Machiavellian way; only, he managed as usual to execute it in his blundering English style. Without warning he dropped his racket, caught Kitty in his arms tightly and roughly, kissed her cheek, rose, and strode swiftly across the courts, into the villa. It was done. He could go now; he knew very well he had to go.

His subsequent actions were methodical enough; a shower, a thorough rub-down, and then into his workaday clothes. He packed his trunk and hand-luggage, overlooked nothing that was his, and went down into the living-room where he knew he would find Killigrew with the morning papers. He felt oddly light-headed; but he had no time to analyze the cause.

"Good morning, Thomas," greeted the master of the house cordially.

"I am leaving, Mr. Killigrew. Will you be kind enough to let me have the use of the motor to the station?"

"Leaving! What's happened? What's the matter? Young man, what the devil's this about?"

"I am sorry, sir, but I have insulted Miss Killigrew."

"Insulted Kitty?" Killigrew sprang up.

"Just a moment, sir," warned Thomas. The tense, short but powerful figure of Kitty's father was not at that moment an agreeable thing to look at; and Thomas knew that those knotted hands were rising toward his throat. "Do not misinterpret me, sir. I took Miss Kitty in my arms and kissed her."

"You--kissed--Kitty?" Killigrew fell back into his chair, limp. For a moment there had been black murder in his heart; now he wondered whether to weep or laugh. The reaction was too sudden to admit of coherent thought. "You kissed Kitty?" he repeated mechanically.

"Yes, sir."

"What did she do?"

"I did not wait to learn, sir."

Killigrew got up and walked the length of the room several times, his chin in his collar, his hands clasped behind his back, under his coat-tails. The fifth passage carried him out on to the veranda. He kept on going and disappeared among the lilac hedges.

Thomas thought he understood this action, that his inference was perfectly logical; Killigrew, rather than strike the man who had so gratuitously insulted his daughter, had preferred to run away. (I know; for a long time I, too, believed Thomas the most colossal ass since Dobson.) Thomas gazed mournfully about the room. It was all over. He had burned his bridges. It had been so pleasant, so homelike; and he had begun to love these unpretentious people as if they had been his very own.

Except that which had been expended on clothes, Thomas had most of his salary. It would carry him along till he found something else to do. To get away, immediately, was the main idea; he had found a door to the trap. (The chamois-bag lay in his trunk, forgotten.)

"Your breakfast is ready, sir," announced the grave butler.

So Thomas ate his chops and potatoes and toast and drank his tea, alone.

And Killigrew, blinking tears, leaned against the stout branches of the lilacs and buried his teeth in his coat-sleeve. He was as near apoplexy as he was ever to come.

CHAPTER XVII

Meantime Kitty sat on the bench, stunned. Never before in all her life had such a thing happened. True, young men had at times attempted to kiss her, but not in this fashion. A rough embrace, a kiss on her cheek, and he had gone. Not a word, not a sign of apology. She could not have been more astounded had a thunder-bolt struck at her feet, nor more bereft of action. She must have sat there fully ten minutes without movement. From Thomas, the guileless, this! What did it mean? She could not understand. Had he instantly begged forgiveness, had he made protestations of sentiment, a glimmering would have been hers. Nothing; he had kissed her and walked away: as he might have kissed Celeste, and had, for all she knew!

When the numbing sense of astonishment passed away, it left her cold with anger. Kitty was a dignified young lady, and she would not tolerate such an affront from any man alive. It was more than an affront; it was a dire catastrophe. What should she do now? What would become of all her wonderfully maneuvered plans?

She went directly to her room and flung herself upon the bed, bewildered and unhappy. And there Killigrew found her. He was a wise old man, deeply versed in humanity, having passed his way up through all sorts and conditions of it to his present peaceful state.

"Kittibudget, what the deuce is all this about? . . . You've been crying!"

"Supposing I have?"--came muffled from the pillows.

"What have you been doing to Thomas?"

"I?" she shot back, sitting up, her eyes blazing. "He kissed me, dad, as he probably kisses his English barmaids."

"Kitty, girl, you're as pretty as a primrose. I don't think Thomas was really accountable."

"Are you defending him?"--blankly.

"No. The strange part of it is, I don't think Thomas wants to be defended. A few minutes ago he came to me and told me what he had done. He is leaving."

The anger went out of her eyes, snuffed--candle-wise. "Leaving?"

"Leaving. He asked me for the motor to the station."

"Leaving! Well, that's about the only possible thing he could do, under the circumstances. He has a good excuse." Excuse! Kitty's nimble mind reached out and touched Thomas' Machiavellian inspiration.

"Hang it, Kitty, I had to run out into the lilacs to laugh! Can't this be smoothed over some way? I like that boy; I don't care if he is a Britisher and sometimes as simple as a fool. When I think of the other light-headed duffers who call themselves gentlemen . . . Pah! They drink my whiskies, smoke my cigars, and dub me an old Mick behind my back. They run around with silly chorus-girls and play poker till sun-up, and never do an honest day's work. It takes a brave man to come to me and frankly say that he has insulted my daughter."

"He said that?" Behind her lips Kitty was already smiling. "You are acting very strangely, dad."

"I know. Ordinarily I'd have taken him by the collar and hustled him into the road. And if it had been one of those young bachelors who are coming down to-night, I'd have done it. I like Thomas; and I don't think he kissed you either to affront or to insult you."

"Indeed!"--icily.

"I dare say I stole a kiss or two in my day."

"Does mother know it?"

"Back in the old country, when I was a lad. It's a normal impulse. There isn't a young man alive who can look upon a pretty girl's face without wishing to kiss it. I don't believe Thomas will repeat the offense. The trouble, girl, is this--you've been living in a false atmosphere, where people hide all their generous impulses because to be natural is not fashionable."

"I marvel at you more and more. Is it generous, then, to kiss a girl without so much as by your leave? If he had been sorry, if he had apologized, I might overlook the deed. But he kissed me and walked away. Do you realize what such an action means to any young woman with pride? Very well, if he apologizes he may stay; but no longer on the basis of friendship. It must be purely business. When my guests arrive I shall not consider it necessary to ask him to join any of our amusements."

"Poor devil! He'll have to pay for that kiss."

"Next, I suppose you'll be wanting me to marry him!" Kitty volleyed. But she wasn't half so angry as she pretended.

"What? Thomas?"

"Ah, that's different, isn't it? There, there; I've promised to overlook the offense on condition that he apologize and keep his place. I have always said that you'd rather have a man about than me."

"Well, perhaps I could understand a man better."

"Go down to breakfast. I hear mother moving about. I'll ring for what I need. I must bathe and dress. Some of the people will motor in for lunch."

Killigrew, subdued and mystified, went in search of Thomas and discovered him in almost the exact spot he had left him; for Thomas, having breakfasted, had returned to the living-room to await the motor.

"Thomas, when Kitty comes down, apologize. And remember this, that you can't kiss a pretty girl just because you happen to want to."

"But, Mr. Killigrew, I didn't want to!" said Thomas.

"Well, I'll be tinker-dammed!"

"I mean . . . Really, sir, it is better that I should return at once to the city. I'm a rotter."

"Don't be a fool! Take your grips back to your room, and don't let's have any more nonsense. Finish up that report from Brazil; and if you handle it right, I'll take you into the office where you'll be away from the women folks."

Thomas' heart went down in despair.

"Mrs. Killigrew can find another secretary for the bureau. I shan't say a word to her, and I'll see that Kitty doesn't. You've had your breakfast. Go and finish up that report. Williams," Killigrew called to the second man, "take Mr. Webb's grips up to his rooms. I'll see you later, Thomas," and Killigrew made off for the breakfast-room, where he chuckled at odd times, much to his wife's curiosity. But he shook his head when she quizzed him.

"You agree with me, Molly, don't you, that Kitty shall marry when and where she pleases?"

"Certainly, Daniel. I don't believe in ready-made matches."

"No more do I. Molly, old girl, I've slathers of money. I could quit now; but I'm healthy and can't play all day. Got to work some of the time. Every one around here shall do as they please. And,"--slyly--"if Kitty should want to marry Thomas . . ."

"Thomas?"

"Anything against the idea?"

"But Thomas couldn't take care of Kitty."

"H'm."

"And Kitty wouldn't marry a man who couldn't."

"Some truth In that. At present Thomas couldn't support an idea. But there's makings in the boy, give a man time and nothing else to do. There's one thing, though; Thomas seems to have the gift of picking out the chaff when it comes to men. A man who can spot a man is worth something to somebody. Where Thomas' niche is, however, I can't tell to date. He'll never get on socially; he has too much regard for other people's feelings."

"And no tact."

"A poor man needs a good deal of that." Killigrew began paring his fourth chop-bone. He hadn't enjoyed himself so much in months. Thomas had kissed Kitty and hadn't wanted to!

It would take a philosopher to dig up the reason for that; or rather a clairvoyant, since philosophers dealt only with logical sequences, and there was nothing logical to Killigrew's mind in Thomas kissing Kitty when he hadn't wanted to!

CHAPTER XVIII

Sugar, coffee and spices. Thomas dipped his pen into the inkwell and went to work. Were all American fathers mad? To condone an affront like this! He could not understand these Americans. He had approached Killigrew with far more courage than the latter suspected. Thomas had read that here men still shot each other on slight provocation. Sugar, coffee and spices. . . . Sao Paulo and valorization committee . . . 10,000,000 bags. What should he do? Whither should he turn? To have offered that affront . . . for nothing! Kitty, whom he revered above all women save one, his mother! . . . Sugar, coffee and spices. Rio number seven, 7 1/2 to 13 1/2 cents. Leaks in the roasting business. . . . Apologize? On his knees, if need be. Caught like a rat in a trap; done for; at the end of his rope. Why hadn't he taken to his heels when he had had the chance? Gone at once to New York and sent for his belongings? . . . Sugar, coffee and spices. . . . The pen slipped from his fingers, and he laid his head on his arms. Monumental ass!

Up suddenly, alert eyed. There was a telephone-booth in the hall. This he sought noiselessly. He remained hidden in the booth for as long as twenty minutes. Then he emerged, wiping the perspiration from his forehead. For the time being he was saved. But he was very miserable.

Sugar, coffee and spices again. Doggedly he recommenced the transcription, adding, deducting, comparing. He heard a slight noise by the portière, and raised his eyes. Kitty stood there like a picture in a frame; pale, calm of eye.

He was on his feet quickly. "Miss Killigrew, I apologize for my unwarranted rudeness. I did not mean it as you thought I did"--which would have made any other woman furious.

"I know it," said Kitty to herself. "You wanted an excuse to run away. All my conjectures are true. I believe I have you, Mr. Thomas, right in the hollow of my hand." To Thomas, however, she was a presentiment of cold and silent indignation.

He blundered on. "You have all been so kind to me . . . I am sorry. I am also quite ready to stay or go, whichever you say."

"We shall say no more about it," she replied coldly; turned on her trim little heels and went out into the rose gardens, where she found fault with the head gardener; and on to the stables, where she rated the head groom for not exercising her favorite mount; and back to the villa, where she upset the cook by ordering a hearty breakfast which she could not eat; and all the time striving to smother her generous impulses and the queer little thrills which stirred in her heart.

Guests began to arrive a little before luncheon. A handsome yacht joined Killigrew's in the offing. Laughter and music began to be heard about the villa.

Thomas took his documents and retired to his room, hoping they would forget all about him. He had luncheon there. About four o'clock he looked out of the window toward the beach. They were in bathing; half a dozen young men and women. The diving-raft bobbed up and down. Only yesterday she had tried to teach him how to swim. After all, he was only a bally haberdasher's clerk; he would never be anything more than that.

More guests for dinner, which Thomas also had in his room, despite Killigrew's protests. The villa would be filled for a whole week, and a merry dance he would have to avoid the guests. At nine, just as he was on the point of going to bed, the second man knocked for admittance.

"Miss Killigrew wishes you to come aboard the visiting yacht at ten, sir."

"Offer Miss Killigrew my excuses. I am very tired."

"Miss Killigrew was decided, sir. Her father's orders. He wishes you to meet his resident partner in Rio Janeiro. Mr. Killigrew and Mr. Savage will be in the smoke-room forward, sir."

"Very well. Tell Miss Killigrew that I shall come aboard."

"Thank you, sir. The motor-boat will be at the jetty at nine-thirty, sir." The servants about the Killigrew home understood Thomas' position. They had known young honorables who had served as private secretaries.

A formal command. There was no way of avoiding it. Resignedly Thomas got into his evening clothes. They might smile at his pumps, the hang of his coat, but there would be no question over the correctness of his collar and cravat. He was very bitter against the world, and more especially against Thomas Webb, late of Hodman, Pelt and Company, "haberdashers to H. H. the Duke of" and so forth and so on.

All the way down to the motor-boat his new pumps sang
"Fool-fool! Rotter-rotter!" He climbed the yacht's ladder and ran
into Kitty and her guests, exactly as she had arranged he
should.

"Mr. Webb," she said; and immediately began introducing
him, leaving Lord Henry Monckton until the last. A cluster of
lights made the spot as bright as day.

Thomas bowed politely and Lord Monckton smiled amiably.

"Mr. Killigrew is in the smoking-room?" Thomas inquired.

"Yes."

Thomas bowed again, indirectly toward the guests and
walked away. Lord Monckton commented on the beauty of the
night.

And Kitty caught the gasp between her teeth, lest it should
be heard. Fog!

CHAPTER XIX

"Rather hot for this time of day," volunteered Lord Monckton, sliding into the Morris chair at the side of Thomas' desk and dangling his legs over the arm.

"Yes, it is," agreed Thomas, folding a sheet of paper and placing the little ivory elephant paper-weight upon it.

"Rippin' doubles this morning. You ought to go into the game. Do you a lot of good."

"I didn't know you played."

"Don't. Watch."

Thomas' gaze was level and steady.

Lord Monckton laughed easily and sought his monocle. He fumbled about the front of his coat and shirt. "By jove! Lost my glass; wonder I can see anything."

Outside, on the veranda, the two men could see the cluster of women of which Kitty was the most animated flower. Voices carried easily.

"Ah--what do you think of these--ah--Americans?" asked Lord Monckton, as one compatriot to another, leaning toward the desk.

"I think them very kindly, very generous people; at least, those I have met. Have you not found them so?"

"Quite so. I am enjoying myself immensely." Lord Monckton swung about in the chair, his back to the veranda.

Thomas loosened his negligee linen-collar.

"Ah, really!" drifted into the room. Lord Monckton sleepily eying Thomas, only heard the voice; he did not see, as Thomas did, the action and gesture which accompanied the phrase. Kitty had put something into her eye, squinted, and twisted an imaginary something a few inches below her dimpled chin. It was a hoydenish trick, but Kitty had enacted it for Lord Monckton's benefit. The women shouted with laughter. Lord Monckton turned in time to see them troop into the gardens. He turned again to Thomas, to find a grin upon that gentleman's face.

"Miss Killigrew is rather an unusual young person," was his comment.

"Uncommon," replied Thomas, scrutinizing the point of his pen.

"For my part, I prefer 'em clinging." Lord Monckton rose.

"Rotter!" breathed Thomas. He rearranged his papers, crackling them suggestively.

"Picnic this afternoon; going along?" asked Lord Monckton, pausing by the portières.

"Really, I am not a guest here; I am only private secretary to Mrs. Killigrew. If they treat me as a human being it is because they believe that charity should not play in grooves."

"Ah! We are all open to a little charity."

"That's true enough. Good morning."

"Beggar!" murmured Lord Monckton as he let the portières fall behind him.

"Blighter!" muttered Thomas, staring malevolently at the empty doorway. He would be glad when Mr. and Mrs. Crawford and the artist came down. Forbes was a chap you could get along with anywhere, under any conditions.

Some time later Kitty came in. She crossed immediately to the desk. As Thomas looked up, she smiled at him. It was the first smile of the kind he had witnessed, coming in his direction, since before that blunder on the tennis-courts.

"I found Lord Monckton's monocle, Mr. Webb. Will you be so kind as to give it to him?"

"Yes, Miss Killigrew." Absently he raised the monocle and squinted through it. "Why, it's plain glass!" he exclaimed.

"So it is," replied Kitty, with a crooked smile. "And I dare say so are most of the monocles we see. A silly affectation, don't you think so?"

He was instantly up in arms. The monocle was a British institution, and he would as soon have denied the divine right of kings as question an Englishman's right to wear what he pleased in his eye.

"It was originally designed for a man whose left eye was weaker than the right. Besides, we don't notice them over there."

"I have often wondered what the wearers do when their noses itch."

"Doubtless they scratch them."

Kitty's laughter bubbled. It subsided instantly. Her hand reached out, then dropped. She had almost said: "Thomas, what have you done with my sapphires?" Urgent as the impulse was, she crushed it back. For deep in her heart she wanted to believe in Thomas; wanted to believe that it was only a mad wager such as Englishmen propose, accept and see to the end. There was not the slightest doubt in her mind that Thomas and Lord Monckton were the two men who had stood on the curb that foggy night in London. One had taken the necklace and the other had wagered he would carry it six months in America before returning it to its owner. The Nana Sahib's ruby she attributed to a real thief, who had known Crawford in former days and, conscience-stricken, had returned it.

Great Britain was an empire of wagerers she knew; they wagered for and against every conceivable thing which had its dependence on chance.

That first night on board the Celtic, when Thomas came to her cabin in the dark, she had recognized his voice. In the light the activity of the eye had dulled the keenness of the ear; but in the dark the ear had found the chord. For days she had been subconsciously waiting to hear one or the other of those voices;

and Thomas' had come with a shock. The words "Aeneid" and "Enid" had so little variation in sound between them that Kitty had found her second man in Lord Monckton. Sooner or later she would trap them.

"Would you like to go to the picnic this afternoon?"--with a spirit which was wholly kind.

"Very much indeed; but I can't"--indicating the stack of papers on his desk.

"Oh," listlessly.

"I am very poor, Miss Killigrew, and perhaps I am ambitious."

Her lips parted expectantly.

"Your father has promised to give me a chance on his coffee plantations in Brazil this autumn, and I wish to show him that I know how to grind. Plug, isn't that the American for it?" He smiled across the desk. "I wish to prove to you all that I am grateful. Your father, who knows something of men, says there is one hidden away in me somewhere, if only I'll take the trouble to dig it out. I should like to be with you and your guests all the time. I like play, and I have been very lonely all my life." He fingered the papers irresolutely. "My place is here, not with your guests; there's the width of the poles between us. I ought not to know anything about the pleasures of idleness till the day comes when I can afford to."

"Perhaps you are right," she admitted. What an agreeable voice he had! Perhaps neither of them was a rogue; only a wild pair of Englishmen embarked on a dangerous frolic. "Don't forget to give Lord Monckton his monocle."

"I shan't."

Kitty departed, smiling. Her thought was: he had kissed her and hadn't wanted to! (Ah, but he had; and not till long hours after did he realize that there had been as much Thomas as Machiavelli in that futile inspiration!)

Report 47, on the difference between the shipments to Europe and America. Very dry, very dull; what with the glorious sunshine outside and the chance to play, Report 47 was damnable. A bird-like peck at the inkwell, and the pen began to scratch-scratch-scratch. He was twenty-four; by the time he was thirty he ought to . . .

"Beg pardon, sir!"

Lord Monckton's valet stood before the desk. Thomas did not
like this man, with his soundless approaches, his thin nervous
fingers, his brilliant roving eyes. Where had he been picked up?
A perfect servant, yes; but it seemed to Thomas that the man
was always expecting some one to come up behind him. Those
quick cat-like glances over his shoulder were not reassuring.
Dark, swarthy; and yet that odd white scar in the scalp above
his ear. That ought to have been dark, logically.

"What is it?"

"Lord Monckton has dropped his glass somewhere, sir, and
he sent me to inquire, sir."

"Oh, here it is. And tell your master to be very careful of it.
Some one might step on it."

"Thank you, sir." The valet departed as noiselessly as he had
entered.

"Really," mused Thomas, "there's a rum chap. I don't like
him around. He gives me the what-d'-y'-call-it."

They needed an extra man at the table that night, so Thomas
came down. He found himself between two jolly young women,
opposite Kitty who divided her time between Lord Monckton and
a young millionaire who, rumor bruited it, was very attentive to
Killigrew's daughter. Still, Thomas enjoyed himself. Nobody
seemed to mind that he was only a clerk in the house. The
simpleton did not realize that he was a personage to these
people; an English private secretary, quite a social stroke on the
part of the Killigrews.

He gathered odd bits of news of what was going on among
the summer colonists. The lady next to Killigrew, a Mrs.
Wilberforce, had had a strange adventure the night before. She
and her maid had been mysteriously overpowered by some
strange fume, and later discovered that her pearls were gone.
She had notified the town police. This brought the conversation
around to the maharajah's emeralds. Hadn't he and his
attendants been overcome in the same manner? Thomas
thought of the sapphires. Since nobody knew he had them, he
stood in no danger. But there was Kitty's great fire-opal, glowing
like a coal on her breast, seeming to breathe as she breathed. It
was almost as large as a crown-piece.

During lulls Thomas dreamed. He was going to give himself
until thirty to make his fortune; and he was going to make it

down there in the wilds of South America. But invariably the
sleepy mocking eyes of Lord Monckton brought him back to
earth, jarringly.

Once, Kitty caught Thomas gazing malevolently at Lord
Monckton. No love lost between them, evidently. It was the
ancient story: to wager, to borrow, to lend, to lose a friend.

Long after midnight Kitty awoke. She awoke hungry. So she
put on her slippers and peignoir and stole down-stairs. The
grills on each side of the entrance to the main hall were open;
that is, the casement windows were thrown back. She heard
voices and naturally paused to learn whose they were. She
would have known them anywhere in the world.

"Tut, tut, Tommy; don't be a bally ass and lose your temper."

"Temper? Lose my temper? I'm not losing it, but I'm jolly
well tired of this rotten business."

"It was you who suggested the wager; I only accepted it."

"I know it."

"And once booked, no Englishman will welch, if he isn't a
cad."

"I'm not thinking of welching. But I don't see what you get
out of it."

"Sport. And a good hand at bridge."

"Remarkably good."

"I say, you don't mean to insinuate . . ."

"I'm not insinuating. I'm just damnably tired. Why the devil
did you take up that monocle business? You never wore one; and
Miss Killigrew found out this morning that it was an ordinary
glass."

"She did?" Lord Monckton chuckled.

"And she laughed over it, too."

"Keen of her. But, what the devil! Stick a monocle in your
eye, and you don't need any letters of introduction. Lucky idea,
your telephoning me that you were here. What a frolic, all
around!"

So that was why her coup had fallen flat? thought Kitty.

"I'll tell you this much," said Thomas. (Kitty heard him tap
his pipe against the veranda railing.) "Play fair or, by the lord,
I'll smash you! I'm going to stick to my end of the bargain, and
see that you walk straight with yours."

"I see what's worrying you. Clear your mind. I would not marry the richest, handsomest woman in all the world, Thomas. There's a dead heart inside of me."

"There's another thing. I'd get rid of that valet."

"Why?"--quickly.

"He's too bally soft on his feet to my liking. I don't like him."

"Neither do I, Thomas!" murmured Kitty, forgetting all about her hunger. Not a word about her sapphires, though. Did she see but the surface of things? Was there something deeper?

She stole back up-stairs. As she reached the upper landing, some one brushed past her, swiftly, noiselessly. With the rush of air which followed the prowler's wake came a peculiar sickish odor. She waited for a while. But there was no sound in all the great house.

"The Carew cottage was entered last night," said Killigrew, "and twenty thousand in diamonds are gone. Getting uncomfortably close. You and your mother, Kitty, had better let me take your jewels into town to-day."

"We have nothing out here but trinkets."

"Trinkets! Do you call that fire-opal a trinket? Better let me take it into town, anyway. I'm Irish enough to be superstitious about opals."

"That's nonsense."

"Maybe."

"Oh, well; if the thought of having it around makes you nervous, I'll give it to you. The Crawfords and Mr. Forbes are coming down this afternoon. You must be home again before dinner. Here's the opal." She took it from around her neck.

"Crawfords? Fine!" Killigrew slipped the gem into his wallet. "I'll bring them back on the yacht if you'll take the trouble to phone them to meet me at the club pier."

"I'll do so at once. Good-by! Mind the street-crossing," she added, mimicking her mother's voice.

"I'll be careful," he laughed, stepping into the launch which immediately swung away toward the beautiful yacht, dazzling white in the early morning sunshine.

Kitty waved her handkerchief, turned and walked slowly back to the villa. Who had passed her in the upper hall? And on what errand? Neither Thomas nor Lord Monckton, for she had left them on the veranda. Perhaps she was worrying unnecessarily. It might have been one of her guests, going down to the library for a book to read.

She met Lord Monckton coming out.

"Fine morning!" he greeted. He made a gesture, palm upward.

A slight shiver touched the nape of Kitty's neck. She had never noticed before how frightfully scarred his thumbs and finger-tips were. He saw the glance.

"Ah! You notice my fingers? Not at all sensitive about them, really. Hunting a few years ago and clumsily fell on the camp-stove. Scar on my shoulder where I struck as I rolled off.

Stupid. Tripped over a case of canned corn. I have fingers now as sensitive as a blind man's."

"I am sorry," she said perfunctorily. "You must tell me of your adventures."

"Had a raft of 'em. Mr. Killigrew gone to New York?"

"For a part of the day. Had your breakfast?"

"No. Nothing to do; thought I'd wait for the rest of them. Read a little. Swim this morning, just about dawn. Refreshing."

"Then I'll see you at breakfast."

He smiled and stepped aside for her to pass. She proved rather a puzzle to him.

Kitty spent several minutes in the telephone booth.

She began to realize that the solution of the Webb-Monckton wager was as far away as ever. Lord Monckton was leaving on the morrow. She must play her cards quickly or throw them away. The fact that neither had in any way referred to the character of the wager left her in a haze. Sometime during the day or evening she must maneuver to get them together and tell them frankly that she knew everything. She wanted her sapphires; more, she wanted the incubus removed from Thomas' shoulders. Mad as March hares, both of them; for they had not the least idea that the sapphires were hers!

Later, she stole to the library door and peered in. Thomas was at his desk. For a long time she watched him. He appeared restless, uneasy. He nibbled the penholder, rumpled his hair, picked up the ivory elephant and balanced it, plunged furiously into work again, paused, stared at the Persian carpet, turned the inkwell around, worked, paused, sighed. Thomas was very unhappy. This state of mind was quite evident to Kitty. Kissed her and hadn't wanted to. He was unlike any young man she knew.

Presently he began to scribble aimlessly on the blotter. All at once he flung down the pen, rose and walked out through the casement-doors, down toward the sea. Kitty's curiosity was irresistible. She ran over to the blotter.

Fool!

Blighter!

Rotter!

Double-dyed ass!

Blockhead!

Kitty Killigrew--(scratched out)!
Nincompoop!
Haberdasher!
Ass!

All of which indicated to the investigator that Thomas for the present had not a high opinion of himself. An ordinary young woman would have laughed herself into hysterics. Kitty tore off the scribbles, not the least sign of laughter in her eyes, and sought the window-seat in the living-room. There was one word which stood out strangely alien: haberdasher. Why that word? Was it a corner of the curtain she had been striving to look behind? Had Thomas been a haberdasher prior to his stewardship? And was he ashamed of the fact?

Haberdasher.

What's the matter with that word? If it irked Thomas it irked Kitty no less. It is a part of youth to crave for high-sounding names and occupations. It is in the mother's milk they feed on. Mothers dream of their babes growing up into presidents or at least ambassadors, if sons; titles and brilliant literary salons, if daughters. What living mother would harbor a dream of a clerkship in a haberdasher's shop? Perish the thought! Myself for years was told that I had as good a chance as anybody of being president of the United States; a far better chance than many, being as I was *my* mother's son.

Irish blood and romance will always be mysteriously intertwined. Haberdasher did not fit in anywhere with Kitty's projects; it was off-key, a jarring note. Whoever heard of a haberdasher's clerk reading *Morte d'Arthur* and writing sonnets? She was reasonably certain that while Thomas had jotted it down in scornful self-flagellation, it occupied a place somewhere in his past.

"They turne out ther trashe   And shew ther haberdashe,
Ther pylde pedlarye."

There's no romance in collars and cuffs and ties and suspenders.

CHAPTER XXI

Meanwhile Killigrew arrived in New York, went to the bank and deposited Kitty's opal, and sought his office.

"There's a Mr. Haggerty in your office, Mr. Killigrew. I told him to wait."

"Haggerty, the detective?"

"Yes. He said you'd be glad to see him. Has news of some sort."

Killigrew hurried into his private office. "Hello, Haggerty! What's the trouble this morning?"

"Got some news for you." Haggerty accepted a cigar. "I've a hunch that I can find Miss Killigrew's sapphires."

"No! I thought they had been sold over the other side."

"Seems not."

"Got your man?"

"Nope. Funny kind of a job, though. Fooled th' customs inspectors. Sapphires 'r here in New York, somewheres."

"A thousand to you, Haggerty, if you recover them."

"A row between two stewards on th' *Celtic* gave me th' clue."

"Why, that's the boat I came over on."

"Sure thing."

"And the thief was on board all the time?"

"Don't think he was when you crossed. I've got t' wait till th' boat docks before I can get particulars. It's like this. Th' chap who took th' sapphires engaged passage as a steward. His cabin-mate saw him lookin' over th' stones. He'd taken 'em out o' their settings. This man Jameson pinches 'em, but his mate follows him up an' has it out with him in a waterfront groggery. Got 'em back. Cool customer. I went on board th' next morning an' quizzed him. An' say, he done me up brown. As unblinkin' a liar 's I ever met. Took me t' his cabin an' showed me what he professed Jameson had swiped. Nothing but a pearl an' coral brooch. He did it so natural that I swallowed th' bull, horns an' hoofs. I've had every pawnshop in New York looked over, but they ain't there. I've been busy on the maharajah's emeralds. There's a case. Cleverest ever. Some drug, atomized through a keyhole, which puts y' t' by-by."

"A drug? Why, say, two of my neighbors have been robbed within the past three days, and they all complained of violent headaches."

"Well, what y' know about that! Say, Mr. Killigrew, any place where I could hang out down there for a couple o' days?"

"Come as my guest, Haggerty. I can tell the folks that you're from the office."

"Fumes! I'll bet a hat it's my maharajah's man. When do you go back?"

"About half-past two, on my yacht. You'll find it at the New York Yacht Club pier. Some old friends of yours will be on board. Crawford, his wife, and Forbes, the artist."

"Fine an' dandy! Forbes is clever at guessing, an' we'll work t'gether. All right I'll hike up t' Bronx an' get some duds. Tell th' chef that corn-beef an' cabbage is my speed-limit," jested the detective as he reached the door.

"By the way, what's the name of that steward who took my daughter's sapphires?"

"His monacker is Webb," said Haggerty; "Thomas Webb, Esquire; an' believe me, he's some smooth guy. Thomas Webb."

For a moment Killigrew sat stiffly upright in his chair; then gradually his body grew limp, his chin sank, his shoulders drooped. "Webb?" he said dully. "Are you sure, Haggerty?"

"No question about it. Y' see, this Jameson chap writes me a sassy letter from Liverpool. Spite. Thomas Webb was th' name. What's th' matter?"

"Haggerty, the very devil is the matter. Thomas Webb, recently a steward on the *Celtic*, has been my wife's private secretary for nearly two months."

"Say that again!" gasped Haggerty, bracing himself against the jamb of the door.

"But I'll wager my right hand that there's some mistake."

"Of all th' gall I ever heard of! Private secretary, an' Miss Killigrew's sapphires stowed away in his trunk, if he ain't sold 'em outside th' pawnshops! Will y' gimme a free hand, Mr. Killigrew?"

"I suppose I'll have to."

"All right. On board you draw me a map o' th' rooms an' where Thomas Webb holds out. I shan't come t' th' house an' meet anybody. While you folks 'r at supper I'll sneak up t' his room an' see what's in his trunk. If I don't find 'em, why, I'll come back t' town an' start a news stand, Forty-second an' Broadway. I'll be on th' yacht at half-past two. I'm on m' way."

The door behind him closed with a bang. It startled every clerk on the huge floor. The door to the boss' office did not bang more than once a year, and that was immediately after the annual meeting of the directors of the Combined Brazilian Coffees. Who was this potentate who dared desecrate the honored quiet of this loft?

Haggerty's news hit Killigrew hard. Thomas. There must be a mistake. He had not studied men all these years without learning to read young and old with creditable accuracy. Thomas was as easy to read as an amateur's scorecard; runs were runs, hits were hits, outs were outs. Why, Thomas wouldn't have stolen an apple from a farmer's orchard--without permission. What, enter a carriage in a fog, steal a necklace, and carry it around with him for months? Never in this world. And private secretary to the very person he had robbed? Of all the fool situations, this was the cap! Imbecility was written all over the face of it. It was simply a coincidence in the matter of names. Yet, steward on the *Celtic*; there was no getting away from that. There could not have been two Thomas Webbs on board. I'm afraid Killigrew swore; distant thunder, off behind the hills there. He struck the desk with his balled fist. He knew it; it was that infernal opal of Kitty's getting in its deadly work. And what would Kitty say? What would she do?

He stood up and pulled down the roller-top violently. The crash of it sent every clerk, bookkeeper and stenographer huddling over his or her work. Two bangs all in one morning? What had happened to the coffee market? As a matter of fact, coffee fell off a quarter point between then and closing; which goes to prove that the stock-market depends upon its business less in the matter of supply and demand than in "signs."

On board the yacht Killigrew laid the affair before Crawford. "What do you believe?"

"I've reached the point," said Crawford, "where I believe in nothing except this young lady," and he laid his hand over his wife's. "For ten years I had a valet named Mason. I would have staked my life on his integrity, his honesty. He turned out to be an accomplished rogue. Went with me into the wilds of Africa and Persia, through deserts, swamps, over mountains; tireless, resourceful, dependable; and saved my life twice. Its knocked a hole in my faith in mankind."

"Listen here," said Haggerty. "Without your knowing it, he always carried a bunch o' first-class skeleton keys. I'm dead sure he was working his game all th' time. He came back for them keys, but he didn't get 'em. He's in New York somewheres. D' y' think y' could recognize him if y' saw him?"

"Instantly."

"A man can change his looks in two years," said Forbes. "Remember File Number 113?"

"This is real life, Mort; not a detective story."

"How would you recognise him?"

"That I'm unable to explain. It's what Haggerty here calls a hunch."

Haggerty nodded. "An' if y' depend on 'em y' generally land. I've made some mistakes in my time, not believing in my hunches. This Webb business goes t' show. I had a hunch that something was wrong, but your Webb had such a kid face, th' hunch pulled for him. Well, if y' ever see Mason again, what'll y' do?"

"I don't know. It's a tough proposition. Somehow or other, I want to be quits with Mason. I want to wipe out those obligations. If I could do that, the next time I saw him I'd hand him over."

"You're a sentimental duffer, Crawffy," said the artist, smiling.

"And I shouldn't love him at all if he wasn't," the wife defended.

"But this Webb affair doesn't add up right," said Killigrew morosely.

"There's th' hull game," declared Haggerty. "It's nothing but adding an' subtracting, this gum-shoe work. Y've got t' keep at it till it adds right. Y' don't realize, Mr. Crawford, how many times I almost put my hand on your shoulder; but y' didn't add up right. I shan't go at Webb like a load o' bricks. I'll nose around first. Take a peek int' his belongings while you folks keep him busy downstairs. No sapphires, no Thomas; I'll let it go at that. But how was this man Jameson t' know anything about sapphires if they wasn't any?"

"I've known Kitty Killigrew ever since she was born," said Killigrew dryly. "I've yet to see her make a mistake in sizing up a man. She picks 'em out the way I do, right off the bat. The minute you dodder about a man or a woman, there's sure to be something' to dodder about. Good lord! you don't suppose he had a hand in these other burglaries?"

"Can't say 's I do," answered Haggerty, reaching for his lemonade. "You wait. I'll have it all cleared up by midnight, 'r they'll be a shake-up at Central t'-morrow. Something's going t' happen; feel it like a sailor feels a storm when they ain't a cloud anywheres. Now, let's see what y' know about auction pinochle, Mr. Killigrew. No use moping."

The yacht dropped anchor off shore at five. The beach was deserted. Doubtless the guests were catnapping or reading. At the Killigrew villa one did as one pleased. Mr. and Mrs. Crawford were shown to their rooms at once, and Haggerty prowled about the stables and garage. Kitty knocked at Mrs. Crawford's door half an hour later.

Introductions were made at dinner. The Crawfords knew most of Kitty's guests and so did Forbes, who was very much interested in Lord Monckton. Here was a romance, if there was any truth at all in the newspapers. What adventures here and there across the world before the title fell to him! He looked like one of R. Caton Woodville's drawings of Indian mutiny officers, with that flowing black beard; very conspicuous among all these smooth chins. Forbes determined to sketch him.

He was rather sorry not to see Thomas at the table. Was Haggerty after him with the third degree? Poor devil! It did not seem possible; yet all the evidence pointed to Thomas. Why should Jameson say that he had seen sapphires if he had not? Still, the thing that did not add up was the position with which Thomas had allied himself to the Killigrews. Hang it, there was a figure missing. Haggerty was right. A man with any sympathy had no business man-hunting.

After dinner Crawford sought Forbes. "Have you any fire-arms with you, Mort?" he whispered.

"A pair of automatics. Why . . ."

"Sh! Please hustle and get them and ask no questions. Hurry!"

CHAPTER XXIII

"Mr. Killigrew," whispered Haggerty, "will you get Miss Kitty an' Thomas int' th' study-end o' th' library?"

"Found anything?"

"Th' sapphires were in his trunk, all right. Tucked away in th' toes of a pair o' shoes. Webb is in th' library now. Jus' get Miss Kitty."

"Very well," replied Killigrew, leaden-hearted.

Thomas had been busy all day. He was growing very tired, and often now the point of his pen sputtered. The second man had brought in his dinner and set it on a small stand which stood at the right of the desk. It was growing cold on the tray. A sound. He glanced up wearily. He saw Kitty and Killigrew, and behind them the sardonic visage of Haggerty. Thomas got up slowly.

"Take it easy, Mr. Webb," warned Haggerty. "Go on, Miss Killigrew, an' we'll see first if you've hit it."

Thomas stared, wide-eyed, from face to face. What in heaven's name had happened? What was this blighter of a detective doing at the villa? And why was Kitty so white?

"Mr. Webb," began Kitty, striving hard to maintain even tones, "on the night of May 13, you and Lord Henry Monckton stood on the curb outside my carriage, near the Garden, where I was blockaded in the fog. I heard your voices. There was talk about a wager. The time imposed upon the fulfilment of this wager was six months. Shortly after, Lord Monckton entered my carriage under the pretense of getting into his own and took my necklace of sapphires. He did it very cleverly. Then they were turned over to you. You were to carry them for six months, find out to whom they belonged, and return them."

"Thousands of miles away," said Haggerty confidently. "Nothing ever happened like that."

"Is it not true?" asked Kitty, ignoring Haggerty's interpolation.

"Miss Killigrew, either I'm dreaming or you are. I haven't the slightest idea what you are talking about." Thomas was now whiter than Kitty. "The talk about a wager is true; but I never knew you had lost any sapphires."

"How about this little chamois-bag which I found in your trunk, Mr. Webb?" asked Haggerty ironically. He tossed the bag on the desk.

The bag hypnotized Thomas. Suddenly he came to life. He snatched up the bag and thrust it into his pocket.

"Those are mine," he said quite calmly. "Mine, by every legal and moral right in the world. Mine!"

Kitty breathed hard and closed her eyes.

"Some brass!" jeered Haggerty, stepping forward.

"Can you prove it, Thomas?" asked Killigrew, hoping against hope.

"Yes, Mr. Killigrew, to your satisfaction, to Miss Killigrew's, and even to Mr. Haggerty's."

Tableau.

Broken by the entrance of Crawford and Forbes, who were also pale and disturbed. Crawford flung a packet of papers on the desk.

"Webb, I fancy that these papers are yours," said Crawford, smiling.

One glance was enough for Thomas.

"Tell them the truth," went on Crawford; "tell them who you are."

"I have wagered . . ."

"Never mind about the wager," put in Forbes. "Crawford and I have just canceled it."

"What has happened?" asked Thomas. The whole world seemed tumbling about his unhappy head.

"Tell Mr. Killigrew here how you have imposed on him and his family," urged Crawford, serious now. "Tell them your name, your full name."

Thomas hesitated a moment. "My name is Henry Thomas Webb-Monckton."

"Ninth Baron of Dimbledon," added Forbes, "and as crazy as a loon!"

CHAPTER XXIV

Meanwhile the whirligig had gone about violently after this fashion.

Forbes, wondering mightily, procured his automatics and gave one to his impatient friend.

"What's the row, Crawffy?"

"Be as silent as you can," said Crawford. "Follow me. We may be too late."

"Anywhere you say."

"The door will be locked. We'll creep around the upper veranda and enter by opposite windows. You keep your eye on the valet. Don't be afraid to shoot if it's necessary."

"What the deuce . . . !"

"Come!"

"But where?"

"Lord Monckton's room."

Blindly and confidently Forbes went out the rear window of the corridor, while Crawford made for the front. They crept soundlessly forward. Lord Monckton? What was up? Shoot the valet if necessary! All right; Crawford knew what he was doing. He generally did. Through his window Forbes saw two men packing suit-cases furiously. The moment Crawford entered the room, Forbes did likewise, without the least idea what it was all about.

"Put up your hands!" said Crawford quietly.

Master and man came about face.

"H'm! The dyed beard and stained skin might fool any one but me, Mason."

Mason! Forbes' hand shook violently.

"I have seen you with a beard before, in the days when we hadn't time for razors. I knew you the instant I laid eyes on you. Now, then, a few words. I do not care to stand in your debt. Haggerty is down-stairs. Upon two occasions you saved my life . . . Keep your eye on your man, Forbes! . . . Twice you saved my life. I'm going to give you a chance in return. An hour's start, perhaps. Forbes, come over to me. That's it. Give me the automatic. There. Now, go through their pockets carefully, and put everything in your own. Leave the money. Mason, a boat leaves to-morrow noon for Liverpool. I'll ship your trunks and grips to the American Express Company there. Do you understand? If I ever see you again, I shan't lift a finger to save you."

The late Lord Henry Monckton shrugged. He had not lived intimately with this quiet-voiced man for ten years without having acquired the knowledge that he never wasted words.

"You're a dangerously clever man, Mason. I noted at dinner that in some manner you had destroyed Haggerty's photograph of your finger-tips. But I recognize you, and know you--your gestures, the turn of your head, every little mannerism. And if you do not do as I bid, I'll take my oath in court as to your identity. Besides,"--with a nod toward the suitcases--"if you're not the man, why this hurry? An hour. I see, fortunately, you have already changed your clothes. Be off!"

"All right. I'm Mason. I knew the game was up the moment I saw you. Any one but you, Mr. Crawford, would pay for this interruption, pistol or no pistol. An hour. So be it. You might tell that fool down-stairs and give him the papers you find in my grip. Miss Killigrew's sapphires, I regret to say, are no more. The mistake I made in London was in returning the Nana Sahib's ruby."

"There is always one mistake," replied Crawford sternly. He felt sad, too.

"Off with you, Tibbets! We can make the train for New York if we hustle."

The man-servant's brilliant eyes flashed evilly.

"Will you make it an hour and a half, sir?" asked Mason, as his valet slid over the window-sill.

It sounded strange to Forbes. Mason had unconsciously fallen into the old tone and mode of address, and he himself recognized him now.

"Till nine-thirty, then. At that time I shall notify Haggerty."

"The boat?"

"Oh, no. I'm giving you that chance without conditions. It's up to Haggerty to find you. There's one question I should like to ask you. Were you in this sort of business while you were serving me?"

Mason laughed. The real man shone in his eyes and smile. "I was. It was very exciting. It was very amusing, too. I valeted you during the day-time and went about my own peculiar business at night. I entered your service to rob you and remained to serve you; ten years. I want you always to remember this: to you I was loyal, that I stood between you and death because you were the only being I was fond of. You are the one bit of sentiment that ever entered my life. Well, I must be off. But I've had a jolly time of it, masquerading as a titled gentleman. What a comedy! How the fools kotowed and simpered while I looked over their jewels and speculated upon how much I could get for them! But I had my code. I never pilfered in the houses of my hosts. I set a fine trap for that simple young man down-stairs, and he fell into it, head-first. Trust an Englishman of his sort to see nothing beyond his nose. I'm off. Good-by, Mr. Crawford. I'm grateful." The man stepped out of the window and vanished into the night.

Crawford glanced at his watch; it was eight-ten.

"Do you hope he'll get away?" asked Forbes breathlessly.

"I don't know what I hope, Mort. I'm rather dazed with the unexpectedness of all this. Let's see what you took from their pockets."

A large diamond brooch, a string of fine pearls, and a bag of wonderful polished emeralds.

"Mort, the man couldn't help it. Why, here's a fortune for a prince; and yet he remained here for more. Well, he's gone; poor beggar."

They burrowed into the suit-cases and trunks. A dark green bottle came to light, Forbes took out the cork and carelessly sniffed. A great black wave of dizziness swept over him, and he would have fallen but for Crawford. The bottle fell. Crawford put Forbes out into the hall and ran back for the bottle, sensing a slight dizziness himself. He recognized the odor. It was Persian. He and Mason had run across it unpleasantly, once upon a time, in Teheran. He was not familiar with the chemistry of the concoction. He corked the bottle tightly. Forbes came in groggily.

"Well! Did you ever see such an ass, Crawford? To open a strange bottle like that and sniff at it!"

"Here's an atomizer. They must have used that. Never touched their victims."

"It evaporates quickly, though. But the effect on a sleeping person would be long. Now, who the deuce is this chap Webb? A confederate?"

"Still dizzy, eh? No; Thomas is a dupe. Don't you get it? He's Lord Monckton. Come on; we'll go down and straighten out the kinks."

So they went down-stairs. And Forbes tells me that when Thomas acknowledged his identity, Kitty did not fall on his neck. Instead, she walked up to him, burning with fury: so pretty that Forbes almost fell in love with her, then and there.

"So! You pretended to be poor, and entered my home to make play behind our backs! Despicable! We took you in without question, generously, kindly, and treated you as one of us; and all the while you were laughing in your sleeve!"

"Kitty!" remonstrated Killigrew, who felt twenty years gone from his shoulders.

"Let me be! I wish him to know exactly what I think of his conduct." She whirled upon the luckless erstwhile haberdasher's clerk; but he held out his hand for silence. He was angry, too.

"Miss Killigrew, I entered your employ honestly. I was poor. I am poor. I have had to work for my bread every day of my life. For seven years I was a clerk in a haberdasher's shop in London. And one day the solicitors came and notified me that I had fallen into the title, two hundred and twenty pounds, and those sapphires. The estate was so small and so heavily mortgaged that I knew I could not live on it. The rents merely paid the interest. I was no better off than before. The cash was all that was saved out of an annuity." From his inner waistcoat pocket he produced a document and dropped it on the desk. "There is the solicitor's statement, relative to the whole transaction. And now I'll tell you the rest of it. I've been a fool. I was always more or less alone. I met this man Cavenaugh, or whatever he calls himself, in a concert-hall about a year ago. We became friendly. He came to me and bought his collars and ties and suspenders."

Kitty found herself retreating from a fury which far outmatched her own; and as he gained in force, hers dwindled correspondingly.

Thomas continued. "He was well-read, traveled; he interested me. When the title came, he was first to congratulate me. Gave me my first real dinner. Naturally I was grateful for this attention. Well, the upshot of it was, we gambled; and I lost. There was wine. I suggested in the spirit of madness that I play the use of my title for six months against the money I had lost. He agreed. And here I am."

His fury evaporated. He sank back into his chair and rested his head in his hands.

"I ain't a detective," murmured Haggerty, breaking in on the silence which ensued. "I'm only fit t' chase dagos selling bananas without licenses. But I'm aching t' see this other chap. I kinda see through his game. He's going t' interest me a hull lot."

Crawford consulted his watch again. Nine. "Haggerty, suppose you and I knock the billiard balls around for half an hour?"

"Huh?"

"Half an hour."

"I got t' see that chap, Mr. Crawford."

"It's a matter of four or five thousand. Do you want to risk it?"

"Come on, Haggerty!" cried Forbes, with good understanding. He caught the detective by the arm and pulled him toward the door. But Haggerty hung back sturdily.

"Is this straight, Mr. Crawford?"

"Half an hour; otherwise not a penny."

"All well an' good; but I'll hold you responsible if anything goes wrong. I'm not seeing things clear."

"You will presently."

"Four thousand for half an hour?"

"To a penny."

"You're on!"

The three of them marched off to the billiard-room. Killigrew touched Kitty's arm and motioned her to follow. She was rather glad to go. She was on the verge of most undignified tears. When she had gone in search of Mrs. Crawford, Killigrew walked over to Thomas and laid a hand on the young man's shoulder.

"Thomas, will you go to Brazil the first week in September?"

"God knows, I'll be glad to," said Thomas, lifting his head. His young face was colorless and haggard. "But you are putting your trust in a double-dyed ass."

"I'll take a chance at that. Now, Thomas, as no doubt you're aware, we are all Irish in this family. Hot-tempered, quick to take affront, but also quick to forgive or admit a wrong. You leave Kitty alone till to-morrow."

"I believe it best for me to leave to-night, sir."

"Nothing of the sort. Come out into the cooler, and we'll have a peg. It won't hurt either of us, after all this racket."

*   *   *   *   *   *

Half after nine. Crawford laid down his cue. From his pocket he took a bottle and gravely handed it to Haggerty.

"Smell of the cork, carefully," Crawford advised.

Haggerty did so. "Th' stuff they put th' maharajah t' sleep with!"

Then Forbes emptied his pockets.

"Th' emeralds!" shouted Haggerty.

Suddenly he stiffened. "I'm wise. I know. It's your man Mason, an' you've bunked me int' letting him have all this time for his get-away!"

CHAPTER XXV

"That is true, Haggerty. I had a debt to pay." Crawford spun a billiard ball down the table.

"Mr. Crawford, I'm going t' show you that I'm a good sport. You've challenged me. All right. I want that man, an' by th' Lord Harry, I'm going t' get him. I'm going t' put my hand on his shoulder an' say 'Come along!' Cash ain't everything, even in my business. I want t' show it's th' game, too. I don't want money in my pockets for winking my eye."

"You'll have hard work."

"How?"

"He has burned the pads of his fingers and thumbs," blurted out Forbes.

Crawford made an angry gesture.

A Homeric laugh from Haggerty. "I don't want his fingers now; this bottle an' these emeralds are enough for me." He stuffed the jewels away. "Where's th' phone?"

"In the hall, under the stairs."

"Good night."

The nights of Poe and the grim realities of Balzac would not serve to describe that chase. The magnificent vitality of that man Haggerty yet fills me with wonder. He borrowed a roadster from Killigrew's garage, and hummed away toward New York. On the way he laid his plans of battle, winnowed the chaff from the grain. He understood the necessity of thinking and acting quickly. A sporting proposition, that was it. He wanted just then not so much the criminal as the joy of finding him against odds and laying his hand on his shoulder: just to show them all that he wasn't a has-been.

His telephone message had thrown a cordon of argus-eyed men around New York. Now, then, what would he, Haggerty, do if he were in Mason's shoes? Make for railroads or boats; for Mason did not belong to New York's underworld, and he would therefore find no haven in the city. Boat or train, then; and of the two, the boat would offer the better security. Once on board, Mason would find it easy to lose his identity, despite the wireless. And it all hung by a hair: would Mason watch? If he hid himself and stayed hidden he was saved.

"Chauffeur, what's your name?" asked Haggerty of Killigrew's man, as the car rolled quietly on to Brooklyn Bridge.

"Harrigan,"--promptly.

"That's good enough for me,"--jovially. "Fill up th' gas-tank. I'm going t' keep y' busy for twenty-four hours, mebbe. An' if I win, a hundred for yours. All y' got t' do is t' act as I say. Let 'er go. Th' Great White Way first, where th' hotels hang out."

Lord Monckton had not returned to the hotel. Good. More telephoning. Yes, the great railroad terminals had ten men each. A black-bearded man with scarred fingers.

Haggerty was really a fine general; he directed his army with shrewdness and little or no waste. The Jersey side was watched, East and North Rivers. The big ships Haggerty himself undertook.

From half after nine that night till noon the next day, without sleep or rest or food, excepting a cup of coffee and a sandwich, which, to a man of Haggerty's build, wasn't food at all, he searched. Each time he left the motor-car, the chauffeur fell asleep. Haggerty reasoned in this wise: There were really but two points of departure for a man in Mason's position, London or South America. Ten men, vigilant and keen-eyed, were watching all fruiters and tramps which sailed for the Caribbean.

It came to the last boat. Haggerty, in each case, had not gone aboard by way of the passengers' gangplank; not he. He got aboard secretly and worked his way up from hold to boat-deck. His chance lay in Mason's curiosity. It would be almost impossible for the man not to watch for his ancient enemy.

At two minutes to twelve, as the whistle boomed its warning to visitors to go ashore, Haggerty put his hard-palmed hand on Mason's shoulder. The man, intent on watching the gangplank, turned quickly, sagged, and fell back against the rail.

"Come along," said Haggerty, not unkindly.

Mason sighed. "One question. Did Mr. Crawford advise you where to look for me?"

"No. I found you myself, Mr. Mason; all alone. It was a sporting proposition; an' you'd have won out if y' hadn't been human like everybody else, an' watched for me. Come along!"

CHAPTER XXVI

It remains for me, then, to relate how Thomas escaped that arm of the law equally as relentless as that of the police--the customs. Perfectly innocent of intent, he was none the less a smuggler.

Killigrew took him before the Collector of the Port, laid the matter before him frankly, paid the duty, and took the gems over to Tiffany's expert, who informed him that these sapphires were the originals from which his daughter's had been copied, and were far more valuable. Twenty-five thousand would not purchase such a string of sapphires these days. All like a nice, calm fairy-story for children.

Immediately upon being informed of his wealth, Thomas became filled with a truly magnanimous idea. But of that, later.

A week later, to be exact.

Around and upon the terrace of the Killigrew villa, with its cool white marble and fresh green strip of lawn, illumined at each end by scarlet poppy-beds, lay the bright beauty of the morning. The sea below was still, the air between, and the heavens above, since no cloud moved up or down the misty blue horizons. Leaning over the baluster was a young woman. She too was still; and her eyes, directed toward the sea, contemplative apparently but introspective in truth, divided in their deeps the blue of the heavens and the green of the sea. Presently a sound broke the hush. It came from a neat little brown shoe. Tap-tap, tap-tap. To the observer of infinite details, a foot is often more expressive than lips or eyes. Moods must find some outlet. One can nearly perfectly control the face and hands; the foot is least guarded.

The young man by the nearest poppy-bed plucked a great scarlet flower. Luckily for him the head gardener was not about. Then slowly he walked over to the young woman. The little foot became still.

"I am sailing day after to-morrow for Rio Janeiro," he said. He laid on the broad marble top of the baluster a little chamois-bag. "Will you have these reset and wear them for me?"

"The sapphires? Why, you mustn't let them go out of the family. They are wonderful heirlooms."

"I do not intend to let them go out of the family," he replied quietly.

Kitty stirred the bag with her fingers. She did not raise her eyes from it. In fact, she would have found it difficult to look elsewhere just then.

"Will you wear them?"

"Yes."

"And some day will you call me Thomas?"

"Yes . . . When you return."

Somewhere back I spoke of Magic Carpets we writer chaps have. A thing of flimsy dreams and fancies! But I forgot the millionaire's. His is real, made of legal-tenders woven intricately, wonderfully. Does he wish a palace, a yacht, a rare jewel? Whiz! There you are, sir. No flowery flourishes; the cold, hard, beautiful facts of reality. Killigrew had his Magic Carpet, and he spread it out and stood on it as he and Mrs. Killigrew viewed the pair out on the terrace. (The millionaire can sometimes wish happiness with his Carpet.)

"Molly, I'm going to send Thomas down to Rio. He'll be worth exactly fifteen hundred the year . . . for years. But I'm going to give him five thousand the first year, ten thousand the next, and twenty thereafter . . . if he sticks. And I think he will. He'll never be any the wiser." He paused tantalizingly.

"Well?" demanded Mrs. Killigrew, smiling.

"Well, neither will Kitty."

The Grand Babylon Hotel
By Arnold Bennett

Originally Published in 1902

THE GRAND BABYLON HOTEL
BY ARNOLD BENNETT

Any journey inevitably involves the arrival at either an interim or a final destination, and one does arrive, it becomes necessary to find accommodations. With the growth of travel that followed the improvements in transportation this no longer meant some haphazard inn or mean lodgings. For the wealthy, at least, it meant staying in an entirely new class of lodgings, the "grand" hotel. These establishments offered rooms and suites fit for any level of wealth including the American millionaire or the crown prince of some German state. Not only were there rooms in the finest style, but restaurants and rooms service offering meals prepared by trained chefs of the highest caliber.

Such is *The Grand Babylon Hotel*, the most luxurious of London hotels, so famous that it has no need to advertise its presence with anything more than the most discrete of signage. It is the height of style and good taste offering only the best to its guests. The kitchens are overseen by the famous Chef Rocco, the dining rooms, lounges and smoking-rooms by the head-waiter Jules. Lord protect the American millionaire who dares to order a "cocktail" or worse, a filleted steak and Bass for dinner. Of course, this is just what Theodore Racksole does. When his requests are refused, he buys the hotel on the spot.

Never having run such an enterprise before, he is unprepared for what he faces, for there have definitely been some strange things going on at The Grand Babylon, and stranger are to come.

About the Author
Enoch Arnold Bennett (May 27, 1867- March 27, 1931) was an English journalist and novelist. Born in Hanley, Staffordshire, his father was a local solicitor, and early on Arnold worked in his father's office. After winning a literary competition in 1889 he took up journalism working for a number of magazines. His early fiction included several magazine serials including *The Grand Babylon Hotel*. He spent much of

the pre-war period in Paris. He wrote nearly forty novels and over a dozen non-fiction books on a variety of subjects. A number of his later novels were set in the "Potteries" district of Staffordshire. Several of these were made into films or television series including *The Card*, which stared Alec Guinness. He was a friend of Lord Beaverbrook and it was on his recommendation that Bennett was appointed as Director of Propaganda for France in the Ministry of Information during World War I. He has the distinction of having an omelet named after him at the Savoy Hotel.

THE GRAND BABYLON HOTEL

CHAPTER I
THE MILLIONAIRE AND THE WAITER

'YES, sir?'

Jules, the celebrated head waiter of the Grand Babylon, was bending formally towards the alert, middle-aged man who had just entered the smoking-room and dropped into a basket-chair in the corner by the conservatory. It was 7.45 on a particularly sultry June night, and dinner was about to be served at the Grand Babylon. Men of all sizes, ages, and nationalities, but every one alike arrayed in faultless evening dress, were dotted about the large, dim apartment. A faint odour of flowers came from the conservatory, and the tinkle of a fountain. The waiters, commanded by Jules, moved softly across the thick Oriental rugs, balancing their trays with the dexterity of jugglers, and receiving and executing orders with that air of profound importance of which only really first-class waiters have the secret. The atmosphere was an atmosphere of serenity and repose, characteristic of the Grand Babylon. It seemed impossible that anything could occur to mar the peaceful, aristocratic monotony of existence in that perfectly-managed establishment. Yet on that night was to happen the mightiest upheaval that the Grand Babylon had ever known.

'Yes, sir?' repeated Jules, and this time there was a shade of august disapproval in his voice: it was not usual for him to have to address a customer twice.

'Oh!' said the alert, middle-aged man, looking up at length. Beautifully ignorant of the identity of the great Jules, he allowed his grey eyes to twinkle as he caught sight of the expression on the waiter's face. 'Bring me an Angel Kiss.'

'Pardon, sir?'

'Bring me an Angel Kiss, and be good enough to lose no time.'

'If it's an American drink, I fear we don't keep it, sir.' The voice of Jules fell icily distinct, and several men glanced round uneasily, as if to deprecate the slightest disturbance of their calm. The appearance of the person to whom Jules was speaking, however, reassured them somewhat, for he had all the look of that expert, the travelled Englishman, who can differentiate between one hotel and another by instinct, and who knows at once where he may make a fuss with propriety, and where it is advisable to behave exactly as at the club. The Grand Babylon was a hotel in whose smoking-room one behaved as though one was at one's club.

'I didn't suppose you did keep it, but you can mix it, I guess, even in this hotel.'

'This isn't an American hotel, sir.' The calculated insolence of the words was cleverly masked beneath an accent of humble submission.

The alert, middle-aged man sat up straight, and gazed placidly at Jules, who was pulling his famous red side-whiskers.

'Get a liqueur glass,' he said, half curtly and half with good-humoured tolerance, 'pour into it equal quantities of maraschino, cream, and crème de menthe. Don't stir it; don't shake it. Bring it to me. And, I say, tell the bar-tender--'

'Bar-tender, sir?'

'Tell the bar-tender to make a note of the recipe, as I shall probably want an Angel Kiss every evening before dinner so long as this weather lasts.'

'I will send the drink to you, sir,' said Jules distantly. That was his parting shot, by which he indicated that he was not as other waiters are, and that any person who treated him with disrespect did so at his own peril.

A few minutes later, while the alert, middle-aged man was tasting the Angel Kiss, Jules sat in conclave with Miss Spencer, who had charge of the bureau of the Grand Babylon. This bureau was a fairly large chamber, with two sliding glass partitions which overlooked the entrance-hall and the smoking-room. Only a small portion of the clerical work of the great hotel was performed there. The place served chiefly as the lair of Miss Spencer, who was as well known and as important as Jules himself. Most modern hotels have a male clerk to superintend the bureau. But the Grand Babylon went its own way. Miss

Spencer had been bureau clerk almost since the Grand Babylon had first raised its massive chimneys to heaven, and she remained in her place despite the vagaries of other hotels. Always admirably dressed in plain black silk, with a small diamond brooch, immaculate wrist-bands, and frizzed yellow hair, she looked now just as she had looked an indefinite number of years ago. Her age--none knew it, save herself and perhaps one other, and none cared. The gracious and alluring contours of her figure were irreproachable; and in the evenings she was a useful ornament of which any hotel might be innocently proud. Her knowledge of Bradshaw, of steamship services, and the programmes of theatres and music-halls was unrivalled; yet she never travelled, she never went to a theatre or a music-hall. She seemed to spend the whole of her life in that official lair of hers, imparting information to guests, telephoning to the various departments, or engaged in intimate conversations with her special friends on the staff, as at present.

'Who's Number 107?' Jules asked this black-robed lady.

Miss Spencer examined her ledgers.

'Mr Theodore Racksole, New York.'

'I thought he must be a New Yorker,' said Jules, after a brief, significant pause, 'but he talks as good English as you or me. Says he wants an "Angel Kiss"--maraschino and cream, if you please--every night. I'll see he doesn't stop here too long.'

Miss Spencer smiled grimly in response. The notion of referring to Theodore Racksole as a 'New Yorker' appealed to her sense of humour, a sense in which she was not entirely deficient. She knew, of course, and she knew that Jules knew, that this Theodore Racksole must be the unique and only Theodore Racksole, the third richest man in the United States, and therefore probably in the world. Nevertheless she ranged herself at once on the side of Jules.

Just as there was only one Racksole, so there was only one Jules, and Miss Spencer instinctively shared the latter's indignation at the spectacle of any person whatsoever, millionaire or Emperor, presuming to demand an 'Angel Kiss', that unrespectable concoction of maraschino and cream, within the precincts of the Grand Babylon. In the world of hotels it was currently stated that, next to the proprietor, there were three gods at the Grand Babylon--Jules, the head waiter, Miss

Spencer, and, most powerful of all, Rocco, the renowned chef, who earned two thousand a year, and had a chalet on the Lake of Lucerne. All the great hotels in Northumberland Avenue and on the Thames Embankment had tried to get Rocco away from the Grand Babylon, but without success. Rocco was well aware that even he could rise no higher than the maître hotel of the Grand Babylon, which, though it never advertised itself, and didn't belong to a limited company, stood an easy first among the hotels of Europe--first in expensiveness, first in exclusiveness, first in that mysterious quality known as 'style'.

Situated on the Embankment, the Grand Babylon, despite its noble proportions, was somewhat dwarfed by several colossal neighbours. It had but three hundred and fifty rooms, whereas there are two hotels within a quarter of a mile with six hundred and four hundred rooms respectively. On the other hand, the Grand Babylon was the only hotel in London with a genuine separate entrance for Royal visitors constantly in use. The Grand Babylon counted that day wasted on which it did not entertain, at the lowest, a German prince or the Maharajah of some Indian State. When Felix Babylon--after whom, and not with any reference to London's nickname, the hotel was christened--when Felix Babylon founded the hotel in 1869 he had set himself to cater for Royalty, and that was the secret of his triumphant eminence.

The son of a rich Swiss hotel proprietor and financier, he had contrived to established a connection with the officials of several European Courts, and he had not spared money in that respect. Sundry kings and not a few princesses called him Felix, and spoke familiarly of the hotel as 'Felix's'; and Felix had found that this was very good for trade. The Grand Babylon was managed accordingly. The 'note' of its policy was discretion, always discretion, and quietude, simplicity, remoteness. The place was like a palace incognito. There was no gold sign over the roof, not even an explanatory word at the entrance. You walked down a small side street off the Strand, you saw a plain brown building in front of you, with two mahogany swing doors, and an official behind each; the doors opened noiselessly; you entered; you were in Felix's. If you meant to be a guest, you, or your courier, gave your card to Miss Spencer. Upon no consideration did you ask for the tariff. It was not good form to mention prices at the Grand

Babylon; the prices were enormous, but you never mentioned them. At the conclusion of your stay a bill was presented, brief and void of dry details, and you paid it without a word. You met with a stately civility, that was all. No one had originally asked you to come; no one expressed the hope that you would come again. The Grand Babylon was far above such manoeuvres; it defied competition by ignoring it; and consequently was nearly always full during the season.

If there was one thing more than another that annoyed the Grand Babylon--put its back up, so to speak--it was to be compared with, or to be mistaken for, an American hotel. The Grand Babylon was resolutely opposed to American methods of eating, drinking, and lodging--but especially American methods of drinking. The resentment of Jules, on being requested to supply Mr Theodore Racksole with an Angel Kiss, will therefore be appreciated.

'Anybody with Mr Theodore Racksole?' asked Jules, continuing his conversation with Miss Spencer. He put a scornful stress on every syllable of the guest's name.

'Miss Racksole--she's in No. 111.'

Jules paused, and stroked his left whisker as it lay on his gleaming white collar.

'She's where?' he queried, with a peculiar emphasis.

'No. 111. I couldn't help it. There was no other room with a bathroom and dressing-room on that floor.' Miss Spencer's voice had an appealing tone of excuse.

'Why didn't you tell Mr Theodore Racksole and Miss Racksole that we were unable to accommodate them?'

'Because Babs was within hearing.'

Only three people in the wide world ever dreamt of applying to Mr Felix Babylon the playful but mean abbreviation--Babs: those three were Jules, Miss Spencer, and Rocco. Jules had invented it. No one but he would have had either the wit or the audacity to do so.

'You'd better see that Miss Racksole changes her room to-night,' Jules said after another pause. 'Leave it to me: I'll fix it. Au revoir! It's three minutes to eight. I shall take charge of the dining-room myself to-night.'

And Jules departed, rubbing his fine white hands slowly and meditatively. It was a trick of his, to rub his hands with a strange, roundabout motion, and the action denoted that some unusual excitement was in the air.

At eight o'clock precisely dinner was served in the immense salle manger, that chaste yet splendid apartment of white and gold. At a small table near one of the windows a young lady sat alone. Her frocks said Paris, but her face unmistakably said New York. It was a self-possessed and bewitching face, the face of a woman thoroughly accustomed to doing exactly what she liked, when she liked, how she liked: the face of a woman who had taught hundreds of gilded young men the true art of fetching and carrying, and who, by twenty years or so of parental spoiling, had come to regard herself as the feminine equivalent of the Tsar of All the Russias. Such women are only made in America, and they only come to their full bloom in Europe, which they imagine to be a continent created by Providence for their diversion.

The young lady by the window glanced disapprovingly at the menu card. Then she looked round the dining-room, and, while admiring the diners, decided that the room itself was rather small and plain. Then she gazed through the open window, and told herself that though the Thames by twilight was passable enough, it was by no means level with the Hudson, on whose shores her father had a hundred thousand dollar country cottage. Then she returned to the menu, and with a pursing of lovely lips said that there appeared to be nothing to eat.

'Sorry to keep you waiting, Nella.' It was Mr Racksole, the intrepid millionaire who had dared to order an Angel Kiss in the smoke-room of the Grand Babylon. Nella--her proper name was Helen--smiled at her parent cautiously, reserving to herself the right to scold if she should feel so inclined.

'You always are late, father,' she said.

'Only on a holiday,' he added. 'What is there to eat?'

'Nothing.'

'Then let's have it. I'm hungry. I'm never so hungry as when I'm being seriously idle.'

'Consommé Britannia,' she began to read out from the menu, 'Saumon d'Ecosse, Sauce Genoise, Aspics de Homard. Oh, heavens! Who wants these horrid messes on a night like this?'

'But, Nella, this is the best cooking in Europe,' he protested.

'Say, father,' she said, with seeming irrelevance, 'had you forgotten it's my birthday to-morrow?'

'Have I ever forgotten your birthday, O most costly daughter?'

'On the whole you've been a most satisfactory dad,' she answered sweetly, 'and to reward you I'll be content this year with the cheapest birthday treat you ever gave me. Only I'll have it to-night.'

'Well,' he said, with the long-suffering patience, the readiness for any surprise, of a parent whom Nella had thoroughly trained, 'what is it?'

'It's this. Let's have filleted steak and a bottle of Bass for dinner to-night. It will be simply exquisite. I shall love it.'

'But my dear Nella,' he exclaimed, 'steak and beer at Felix's! It's impossible! Moreover, young women still under twenty-three cannot be permitted to drink Bass.'

'I said steak and Bass, and as for being twenty-three, shall be going in twenty-four to-morrow.'

Miss Racksole set her small white teeth.

There was a gentle cough. Jules stood over them. It must have been out of a pure spirit of adventure that he had selected this table for his own services. Usually Jules did not personally wait at dinner. He merely hovered observant, like a captain on the bridge during the mate's watch. Regular frequenters of the hotel felt themselves honoured when Jules attached himself to their tables.

Theodore Racksole hesitated one second, and then issued the order with a fine air of carelessness:

'Filleted steak for two, and a bottle of Bass.' It was the bravest act of Theodore Racksole's life, and yet at more than one previous crisis a high courage had not been lacking to him.

'It's not in the menu, sir,' said Jules the imperturbable.

'Never mind. Get it. We want it.'

'Very good, sir.'

Jules walked to the service-door, and, merely affecting to look behind, came immediately back again.

'Mr Rocco's compliments, sir, and he regrets to be unable to serve steak and Bass to-night, sir.'

'Mr Rocco?' questioned Racksole lightly.

'Mr Rocco,' repeated Jules with firmness.

'And who is Mr Rocco?'

'Mr Rocco is our chef, sir.' Jules had the expression of a man who is asked to explain who Shakespeare was.

The two men looked at each other. It seemed incredible that Theodore Racksole, the ineffable Racksole, who owned a thousand miles of railway, several towns, and sixty votes in Congress, should be defied by a waiter, or even by a whole hotel. Yet so it was. When Europe's effete back is against the wall not a regiment of millionaires can turn its flank. Jules had the calm expression of a strong man sure of victory. His face said: 'You beat me once, but not this time, my New York friend!'

As for Nella, knowing her father, she foresaw interesting events, and waited confidently for the steak. She did not feel hungry, and she could afford to wait.

'Excuse me a moment, Nella,' said Theodore Racksole quietly, 'I shall be back in about two seconds,' and he strode out of the salle à manger. No one in the room recognized the millionaire, for he was unknown to London, this being his first visit to Europe for over twenty years. Had anyone done so, and caught the expression on his face, that man might have trembled for an explosion which should have blown the entire Grand Babylon into the Thames.

Jules retired strategically to a corner. He had fired; it was the antagonist's turn. A long and varied experience had taught Jules that a guest who embarks on the subjugation of a waiter is almost always lost; the waiter has so many advantages in such a contest.

CHAPTER II
HOW MR RACKSOLE OBTAINED HIS DINNER

NEVERTHELESS, there are men with a confirmed habit of getting their own way, even as guests in an exclusive hotel: and Theodore Racksole had long since fallen into that useful practice--except when his only daughter Helen, motherless but high-spirited girl, chose to think that his way crossed hers, in which case Theodore capitulated and fell back. But when Theodore and his daughter happened to be going one and the same road, which was pretty often, then Heaven alone might help any obstacle that was so ill-advised as to stand in their path. Jules, great and observant man though he was, had not noticed the terrible projecting chins of both father and daughter, otherwise it is possible he would have reconsidered the question of the steak and Bass.

Theodore Racksole went direct to the entrance-hall of the hotel, and entered Miss Spencer's sanctum.

'I want to see Mr Babylon,' he said, 'without the delay of an instant.'

Miss Spencer leisurely raised her flaxen head.

'I am afraid--,' she began the usual formula. It was part of her daily duty to discourage guests who desired to see Mr Babylon.

'No, no,' said Racksole quickly, 'I don't want any "I'm afraids." This is business. If you had been the ordinary hotel clerk I should have slipped you a couple of sovereigns into your hand, and the thing would have been done. As you are not--as you are obviously above bribes--I merely say to you, I must see Mr Babylon at once on an affair of the utmost urgency. My name is Racksole--Theodore Racksole.'

'Of New York?' questioned a voice at the door, with a slight foreign accent.

The millionaire turned sharply, and saw a rather short, French-looking man, with a bald head, a grey beard, a long and perfectly-built frock coat, eye-glasses attached to a minute silver chain, and blue eyes that seemed to have the transparent innocence of a maid's.

'There is only one,' said Theodore Racksole succinctly.

'You wish to see me?' the new-comer suggested.

'You are Mr Felix Babylon?'

The man bowed.

'At this moment I wish to see you more than anyone else in the world,' said Racksole. 'I am consumed and burnt up with a desire to see you, Mr Babylon. I only want a few minutes' quiet chat. I fancy I can settle my business in that time.'

With a gesture Mr Babylon invited the millionaire down a side corridor, at the end of which was Mr Babylon's private room, a miracle of Louis XV furniture and tapestry: like most unmarried men with large incomes, Mr Babylon had 'tastes' of a highly expensive sort.

The landlord and his guest sat down opposite each other. Theodore Racksole had met with the usual millionaire's luck in this adventure, for Mr Babylon made a practice of not allowing himself to be interviewed by his guests, however distinguished, however wealthy, however pertinacious. If he had not chanced to enter Miss Spencer's office at that precise moment, and if he had not been impressed in a somewhat peculiar way by the physiognomy of the millionaire, not all Mr Racksole's American energy and ingenuity would have availed for a confabulation with the owner of the Grand Babylon Hotel that night. Theodore Racksole, however, was ignorant that a mere accident had served him. He took all the credit to himself.

'I read in the New York papers some months ago,' Theodore started, without even a clearing of the throat, 'that this hotel of yours, Mr Babylon, was to be sold to a limited company, but it appears that the sale was not carried out.'

'It was not,' answered Mr Babylon frankly, 'and the reason was that the middle-men between the proposed company and myself wished to make a large secret profit, and I declined to be a party to such a profit. They were firm; I was firm; and so the affair came to nothing.'

'The agreed price was satisfactory?'

'Quite.'

'May I ask what the price was?'

'Are you a buyer, Mr Racksole?'

'Are you a seller, Mr Babylon?'

'I am,' said Babylon, 'on terms. The price was four hundred thousand pounds, including the leasehold and goodwill. But I sell only on the condition that the buyer does not transfer the property to a limited company at a higher figure.'

'I will put one question to you, Mr Babylon,' said the millionaire. 'What have your profits averaged during the last four years?'

'Thirty-four thousand pounds per annum.'

'I buy,' said Theodore Racksole, smiling contentedly; 'and we will, if you please, exchange contract-letters on the spot.'

'You come quickly to a resolution, Mr Racksole. But perhaps you have been considering this question for a long time?'

'On the contrary,' Racksole looked at his watch, 'I have been considering it for six minutes.'

Felix Babylon bowed, as one thoroughly accustomed to eccentricity of wealth.

'The beauty of being well-known,' Racksole continued, 'is that you needn't trouble about preliminary explanations. You, Mr Babylon, probably know all about me. I know a good deal about you. We can take each other for granted without reference. Really, it is as simple to buy an hotel or a railroad as it is to buy a watch, provided one is equal to the transaction.'

'Precisely,' agreed Mr Babylon smiling. 'Shall we draw up the little informal contract? There are details to be thought of. But it occurs to me that you cannot have dined yet, and might prefer to deal with minor questions after dinner.'

'I have not dined,' said the millionaire, with emphasis, 'and in that connexion will you do me a favour? Will you send for Mr Rocco?'

'You wish to see him, naturally.'

'I do,' said the millionaire, and added, 'about my dinner.'

'Rocco is a great man,' murmured Mr Babylon as he touched the bell, ignoring the last words. 'My compliments to Mr Rocco,' he said to the page who answered his summons, 'and if it is quite convenient I should be glad to see him here for a moment.'

'What do you give Rocco?' Racksole inquired.

'Two thousand a year and the treatment of an Ambassador.'

'I shall give him the treatment of an Ambassador and three thousand.'

'You will be wise,' said Felix Babylon.

At that moment Rocco came into the room, very softly--a man of forty, thin, with long, thin hands, and an inordinately long brown silky moustache.

'Rocco,' said Felix Babylon, 'let me introduce Mr Theodore Racksole, of New York.'

'Sharmed,' said Rocco, bowing. 'Ze--ze, vat you call it, millionaire?'

'Exactly,' Racksole put in, and continued quickly: 'Mr Rocco, I wish to acquaint you before any other person with the fact that I have purchased the Grand Babylon Hotel. If you think well to afford me the privilege of retaining your services I shall be happy to offer you a remuneration of three thousand a year.'

'Tree, you said?'

'Three.'

'Sharmed.'

'And now, Mr Rocco, will you oblige me very much by ordering a plain beefsteak and a bottle of Bass to be served by Jules--I particularly desire Jules--at table No. 17 in the dining-room in ten minutes from now? And will you do me the honour of lunching with me to-morrow?'

Mr Rocco gasped, bowed, muttered something in French, and departed.

Five minutes later the buyer and seller of the Grand Babylon Hotel had each signed a curt document, scribbled out on the hotel note-paper. Felix Babylon asked no questions, and it was this heroic absence of curiosity, of surprise on his part, that more than anything else impressed Theodore Racksole. How many hotel proprietors in the world, Racksole asked himself, would have let that beef-steak and Bass go by without a word of comment.

'From what date do you wish the purchase to take effect?' asked Babylon.

'Oh,' said Racksole lightly, 'it doesn't matter. Shall we say from to-night?'

'As you will. I have long wished to retire. And now that the moment has come--and so dramatically--I am ready. I shall return to Switzerland. One cannot spend much money there, but it is my native land. I shall be the richest man in Switzerland.' He smiled with a kind of sad amusement.

'I suppose you are fairly well off?' said Racksole, in that easy familiar style of his, as though the idea had just occurred to him.

'Besides what I shall receive from you, I have half a million invested.'

'Then you will be nearly a millionaire?'

Felix Babylon nodded.

'I congratulate you, my dear sir,' said Racksole, in the tone of a judge addressing a newly-admitted barrister. 'Nine hundred thousand pounds, expressed in francs, will sound very nice--in Switzerland.'

'Of course to you, Mr Racksole, such a sum would be poverty. Now if one might guess at your own wealth?' Felix Babylon was imitating the other's freedom.

'I do not know, to five millions or so, what I am worth,' said Racksole, with sincerity, his tone indicating that he would have been glad to give the information if it were in his power.

'You have had anxieties, Mr Racksole?'

'Still have them. I am now holiday-making in London with my daughter in order to get rid of them for a time.'

'Is the purchase of hotels your notion of relaxation, then?'

Racksole shrugged his shoulders. 'It is a change from railroads,' he laughed.

'Ah, my friend, you little know what you have bought.'

'Oh! yes I do,' returned Racksole; 'I have bought just the first hotel in the world.'

'That is true, that is true,' Babylon admitted, gazing meditatively at the antique Persian carpet. 'There is nothing, anywhere, like my hotel. But you will regret the purchase, Mr Racksole. It is no business of mine, of course, but I cannot help repeating that you will regret the purchase.'

'I never regret.'

'Then you will begin very soon--perhaps to-night.'

'Why do you say that?'

'Because the Grand Babylon is the Grand Babylon. You think because you control a railroad, or an iron-works, or a line of steamers, therefore you can control anything. But no. Not the Grand Babylon. There is something about the Grand Babylon--' He threw up his hands.

'Servants rob you, of course.'

'Of course. I suppose I lose a hundred pounds a week in that way. But it is not that I mean. It is the guests. The guests are too--too distinguished. The great Ambassadors, the great financiers, the great nobles, all the men that move the world, put up under my roof. London is the centre of everything, and my hotel--your hotel--is the centre of London. Once I had a King and a Dowager Empress staying here at the same time. Imagine that!'

'A great honour, Mr Babylon. But wherein lies the difficulty?'

'Mr Racksole,' was the grim reply, 'what has become of your shrewdness--that shrewdness which has made your fortune so immense that even you cannot calculate it? Do you not perceive that the roof which habitually shelters all the force, all the authority of the world, must necessarily also shelter nameless and numberless plotters, schemers, evil-doers, and workers of mischief? The thing is as clear as day--and as dark as night. Mr Racksole, I never know by whom I am surrounded. I never know what is going forward. Only sometimes I get hints, glimpses of strange acts and strange secrets. You mentioned my servants. They are almost all good servants, skilled, competent. But what are they besides? For anything I know my fourth sub-chef may be an agent of some European Government. For anything I know my invaluable Miss Spencer may be in the pay of a court dressmaker or a Frankfort banker. Even Rocco may be, someone else in addition to Rocco.'

'That makes it all the more interesting,' remarked Theodore Racksole.

'What a long time you have been, Father,' said Nella, when he returned to table No. 17 in the salle manger.

'Only twenty minutes, my dove.'

'But you said two seconds. There is a difference.'

'Well, you see, I had to wait for the steak to cook.'

'Did you have much trouble in getting my birthday treat?'

'No trouble. But it didn't come quite as cheap as you said.'

'What do you mean, Father?'

'Only that I've bought the entire hotel. But don't split.'

'Father, you always were a delicious parent. Shall you give me the hotel for a birthday present?'

'No. I shall run it--as an amusement. By the way, who is that chair for?'

He noticed that a third cover had been laid at the table.

'That is for a friend of mine who came in about five minutes ago. Of course I told him he must share our steak. He'll be here in a moment.'

'May I respectfully inquire his name?'

'Dimmock--Christian name Reginald; profession, English companion to Prince Aribert of Posen. I met him when I was in St Petersburg with cousin Hetty last fall. Oh; here he is. Mr Dimmock, this is my dear father. He has succeeded with the steak.'

Theodore Racksole found himself confronted by a very young man, with deep black eyes, and a fresh, boyish expression. They began to talk.

Jules approached with the steak. Racksole tried to catch the waiter's eye, but could not. The dinner proceeded.

'Oh, Father!' cried Nella, 'what a lot of mustard you have taken!'

'Have I?' he said, and then he happened to glance into a mirror on his left hand between two windows. He saw the reflection of Jules, who stood behind his chair, and he saw Jules give a slow, significant, ominous wink to Mr Dimmock--Christian name, Reginald.

He examined his mustard in silence. He thought that perhaps he had helped himself rather plenteously to mustard.

CHAPTER III
AT THREE A.M.

MR REGINALD DIMMOCK proved himself, despite his extreme youth, to be a man of the world and of experiences, and a practised talker. Conversation between him and Nella Racksole seemed never to flag. They chattered about St Petersburg, and the ice on the Neva, and the tenor at the opera who had been exiled to Siberia, and the quality of Russian tea, and the sweetness of Russian champagne, and various other aspects of Muscovite existence. Russia exhausted, Nella lightly outlined her own doings since she had met the young man in the Tsar's capital, and this recital brought the topic round to London, where it stayed till the final piece of steak was eaten. Theodore Racksole noticed that Mr Dimmock gave very meagre information about his own movements, either past or future. He regarded the youth as a typical hanger-on of Courts, and wondered how he had obtained his post of companion to Prince Aribert of Posen, and who Prince Aribert of Posen might be. The millionaire thought he had once heard of Posen, but he wasn't sure; he rather fancied it was one of those small nondescript German States of which five-sixths of the subjects are Palace officials, and the rest charcoal-burners or innkeepers. Until the meal was nearly over, Racksole said little--perhaps his thoughts were too busy with Jules' wink to Mr Dimmock, but when ices had been followed by coffee, he decided that it might be as well, in the interests of the hotel, to discover something about his daughter's friend. He never for an instant questioned her right to possess her own friends; he had always left her in the most amazing liberty, relying on her inherited good sense to keep her out of mischief; but, quite apart from the wink, he was struck by Nella's attitude towards Mr Dimmock, an attitude in which an amiable scorn was blended with an evident desire to propitiate and please.

'Nella tells me, Mr Dimmock, that you hold a confidential position with Prince Aribert of Posen,' said Racksole. 'You will pardon an American's ignorance, but is Prince Aribert a reigning Prince--what, I believe, you call in Europe, a Prince Regnant?'

'His Highness is not a reigning Prince, nor ever likely to be,' answered Dimmock. 'The Grand Ducal Throne of Posen is occupied by his Highness's nephew, the Grand Duke Eugen.'

'Nephew?' cried Nella with astonishment.

'Why not, dear lady?'

'But Prince Aribert is surely very young?'

'The Prince, by one of those vagaries of chance which occur sometimes in the history of families, is precisely the same age as the Grand Duke. The late Grand Duke's father was twice married. Hence this youthfulness on the part of an uncle.'

'How delicious to be the uncle of someone as old as yourself! But I suppose it is no fun for Prince Aribert. I suppose he has to be frightfully respectful and obedient, and all that, to his nephew?'

'The Grand Duke and my Serene master are like brothers. At present, of course, Prince Aribert is nominally heir to the throne, but as no doubt you are aware, the Grand Duke will shortly marry a near relative of the Emperor's, and should there be a family--' Mr Dimmock stopped and shrugged his straight shoulders. 'The Grand Duke,' he went on, without finishing the last sentence, 'would much prefer Prince Aribert to be his successor. He really doesn't want to marry. Between ourselves, strictly between ourselves, he regards marriage as rather a bore. But, of course, being a German Grand Duke, he is bound to marry. He owes it to his country, to Posen.'

'How large is Posen?' asked Racksole bluntly.

'Father,' Nella interposed laughing, 'you shouldn't ask such inconvenient questions. You ought to have guessed that it isn't etiquette to inquire about the size of a German Dukedom.'

'I am sure,' said Dimmock, with a polite smile, 'that the Grand Duke is as much amused as anyone at the size of his territory. I forget the exact acreage, but I remember that once Prince Aribert and myself walked across it and back again in a single day.'

'Then the Grand Duke cannot travel very far within his own dominions? You may say that the sun does set on his empire?'

'It does,' said Dimmock.

'Unless the weather is cloudy,' Nella put in. 'Is the Grand Duke content always to stay at home?'

'On the contrary, he is a great traveller, much more so than Prince Aribert. I may tell you, what no one knows at present, outside this hotel, that his Royal Highness the Grand Duke, with a small suite, will be here to-morrow.'

'In London?' asked Nella.

'Yes.'

'In this hotel?'

'Yes.'

'Oh! How lovely!'

'That is why your humble servant is here to-night--a sort of advance guard.'

'But I understood,' Racksole said, 'that you were--er--attached to Prince Aribert, the uncle.'

'I am. Prince Aribert will also be here. The Grand Duke and the Prince have business about important investments connected with the Grand Duke's marriage settlement.... In the highest quarters, you understand.'

'For so discreet a person,' thought Racksole, 'you are fairly communicative.' Then he said aloud: 'Shall we go out on the terrace?'

As they crossed the dining-room Jules stopped Mr Dimmock and handed him a letter. 'Just come, sir, by messenger,' said Jules.

Nella dropped behind for a second with her father. 'Leave me alone with this boy a little--there's a dear parent,' she whispered in his ear.

'I am a mere cypher, an obedient nobody,' Racksole replied, pinching her arm surreptitiously. 'Treat me as such. Use me as you like. I will go and look after my hotel' And soon afterwards he disappeared.

Nella and Mr Dimmock sat together on the terrace, sipping iced drinks. They made a handsome couple, bowered amid plants which blossomed at the command of a Chelsea wholesale florist. People who passed by remarked privately that from the look of things there was the beginning of a romance in that conversation. Perhaps there was, but a more intimate acquaintance with the character of Nella Racksole would have been necessary in order to predict what precise form that romance would take.

Jules himself served the liquids, and at ten o'clock he brought another note. Entreating a thousand pardons, Reginald Dimmock, after he had glanced at the note, excused himself on the plea of urgent business for his Serene master, uncle of the Grand Duke of Posen. He asked if he might fetch Mr Racksole, or escort Miss Racksole to her father. But Miss Racksole said gaily that she felt no need of an escort, and should go to bed. She added that her father and herself always endeavoured to be independent of each other.

Just then Theodore Racksole had found his way once more into Mr Babylon's private room. Before arriving there, however, he had discovered that in some mysterious manner the news of the change of proprietorship had worked its way down to the lowest strata of the hotel's cosmos. The corridors hummed with it, and even under-servants were to be seen discussing the thing, just as though it mattered to them.

'Have a cigar, Mr Racksole,' said the urbane Mr Babylon, 'and a mouthful of the oldest cognac in all Europe.'

In a few minutes these two were talking eagerly, rapidly. Felix Babylon was astonished at Racksole's capacity for absorbing the details of hotel management. And as for Racksole he soon realized that Felix Babylon must be a prince of hotel managers. It had never occurred to Racksole before that to manage an hotel, even a large hotel, could be a specially interesting affair, or that it could make any excessive demands upon the brains of the manager; but he came to see that he had underrated the possibilities of an hotel. The business of the Grand Babylon was enormous. It took Racksole, with all his genius for organization, exactly half an hour to master the details of the hotel laundry-work. And the laundry-work was but one branch of activity amid scores, and not a very large one at that. The machinery of checking supplies, and of establishing a mean ratio between the raw stuff received in the kitchen and the number of meals served in the salle à manger and the private rooms, was very complicated and delicate. When Racksole had grasped it, he at once suggested some improvements, and this led to a long theoretical discussion, and the discussion led to digressions, and then Felix Babylon, in a moment of absent-mindedness, yawned.

Racksole looked at the gilt clock on the high mantelpiece.

'Great Scott!' he said. 'It's three o'clock. Mr Babylon, accept my apologies for having kept you up to such an absurd hour.'

'I have not spent so pleasant an evening for many years. You have let me ride my hobby to my heart's content. It is I who should apologize.'

Racksole rose.

'I should like to ask you one question,' said Babylon. 'Have you ever had anything to do with hotels before?'

'Never,' said Racksole.

'Then you have missed your vocation. You could have been the greatest of all hotel-managers. You would have been greater than me, and I am unequalled, though I keep only one hotel, and some men have half a dozen. Mr Racksole, why have you never run an hotel?'

'Heaven knows,' he laughed, 'but you flatter me, Mr Babylon.'

'I? Flatter? You do not know me. I flatter no one, except, perhaps, now and then an exceptionally distinguished guest. In which case I give suitable instructions as to the bill.'

'Speaking of distinguished guests, I am told that a couple of German princes are coming here to-morrow.'

'That is so.'

'Does one do anything? Does one receive them formally-- stand bowing in the entrance-hall, or anything of that sort?'

'Not necessarily. Not unless one wishes. The modern hotel proprietor is not like an innkeeper of the Middle Ages, and even princes do not expect to see him unless something should happen to go wrong. As a matter of fact, though the Grand Duke of Posen and Prince Aribert have both honoured me by staying here before, I have never even set eyes on them. You will find all arrangements have been made.'

They talked a little longer, and then Racksole said good night. 'Let me see you to your room. The lifts will be closed and the place will be deserted.

As for myself, I sleep here,' and Mr Babylon pointed to an inner door.

'No, thanks,' said Racksole; 'let me explore my own hotel unaccompanied. I believe I can discover my room.' When he got fairly into the passages, Racksole was not so sure that he could discover his own room. The number was 107, but he had forgotten whether it was on the first or second floor.

Travelling in a lift, one is unconscious of floors. He passed several lift-doorways, but he could see no glint of a staircase; in all self-respecting hotels staircases have gone out of fashion, and though hotel architects still continue, for old sakes' sake, to build staircases, they are tucked away in remote corners where their presence is not likely to offend the eye of a spoiled and cosmopolitan public. The hotel seemed vast, uncanny, deserted. An electric light glowed here and there at long intervals. On the thick carpets, Racksole's thinly-shod feet made no sound, and he wandered at ease to and fro, rather amused, rather struck by the peculiar senses of night and mystery which had suddenly come over him. He fancied he could hear a thousand snores peacefully descending from the upper realms. At length he found a staircase, a very dark and narrow one, and presently he was on the first floor. He soon discovered that the numbers of the rooms on this floor did not get beyond seventy. He encountered another staircase and ascended to the second floor. By the decoration of the walls he recognized this floor as his proper home, and as he strolled through the long corridor he whistled a low, meditative whistle of satisfaction. He thought he heard a step in the transverse corridor, and instinctively he obliterated himself in a recess which held a service-cabinet and a chair. He did hear a step. Peeping cautiously out, he perceived, what he had not perceived previously, that a piece of white ribbon had been tied round the handle of the door of one of the bedrooms. Then a man came round the corner of the transverse corridor, and Racksole drew back. It was Jules--Jules with his hands in his pockets and a slouch hat over his eyes, but in other respects attired as usual.

Racksole, at that instant, remembered with a special vividness what Felix Babylon had said to him at their first interview. He wished he had brought his revolver. He didn't know why he should feel the desirability of a revolver in a London hotel of the most unimpeachable fair fame, but he did feel the desirability of such an instrument of attack and defence. He privately decided that if Jules went past his recess he would take him by the throat and in that attitude put a few plain questions to this highly dubious waiter. But Jules had stopped. The millionaire made another cautious observation. Jules, with infinite gentleness, was turning the handle of the door to which the white ribbon was attached. The door slowly yielded and

Jules disappeared within the room. After a brief interval, the night-prowling Jules reappeared, closed the door as softly as he had opened it, removed the ribbon, returned upon his steps, and vanished down the transverse corridor.

'This is quaint,' said Racksole; 'quaint to a degree!'

It occurred to him to look at the number of the room, and he stole towards it.

'Well, I'm d--d!' he murmured wonderingly.

The number was 111, his daughter's room! He tried to open it, but the door was locked. Rushing to his own room, No. 107, he seized one of a pair of revolvers (the kind that are made for millionaires) and followed after Jules down the transverse corridor. At the end of this corridor was a window; the window was open; and Jules was innocently gazing out of the window. Ten silent strides, and Theodore Racksole was upon him.

'One word, my friend,' the millionaire began, carelessly waving the revolver in the air. Jules was indubitably startled, but by an admirable exercise of self-control he recovered possession of his faculties in a second.

'Sir?' said Jules.

'I just want to be informed, what the deuce you were doing in No. 111 a moment ago.'

'I had been requested to go there,' was the calm response.

'You are a liar, and not a very clever one. That is my daughter's room. Now--out with it, before I decide whether to shoot you or throw you into the street.'

'Excuse me, sir, No. 111 is occupied by a gentleman.'

'I advise you that it is a serious error of judgement to contradict me, my friend. Don't do it again. We will go to the room together, and you shall prove that the occupant is a gentleman, and not my daughter.'

'Impossible, sir,' said Jules.

'Scarcely that,' said Racksole, and he took Jules by the sleeve. The millionaire knew for a certainty that Nella occupied No. 111, for he had examined the room her, and himself seen that her trunks and her maid and herself had arrived there in safety. 'Now open the door,' whispered Racksole, when they reached No.111.

'I must knock.'

'That is just what you mustn't do. Open it. No doubt you have your pass-key.'

Confronted by the revolver, Jules readily obeyed, yet with a deprecatory gesture, as though he would not be responsible for this outrage against the decorum of hotel life. Racksole entered. The room was brilliantly lighted.

'A visitor, who insists on seeing you, sir,' said Jules, and fled.

Mr Reginald Dimmock, still in evening dress, and smoking a cigarette, rose hurriedly from a table.

'Hello, my dear Mr Racksole, this is an unexpected--ah--pleasure.'

'Where is my daughter? This is her room.'

'Did I catch what you said, Mr Racksole?'

'I venture to remark that this is Miss Racksole's room.'

'My good sir,' answered Dimmock, 'you must be mad to dream of such a thing.

Only my respect for your daughter prevents me from expelling you forcibly, for such an extraordinary suggestion.'

A small spot half-way down the bridge of the millionaire's nose turned suddenly white.

'With your permission,' he said in a low calm voice, 'I will examine the dressing-room and the bath-room.'

'Just listen to me a moment,' Dimmock urged, in a milder tone.

'I'll listen to you afterwards, my young friend,' said Racksole, and he proceeded to search the bath-room, and the dressing-room, without any result whatever. 'Lest my attitude might be open to misconstruction, Mr Dimmock, I may as well tell you that I have the most perfect confidence in my daughter, who is as well able to take care of herself as any woman I ever met, but since you entered it there have been one or two rather mysterious occurrences in this hotel. That is all.' Feeling a draught of air on his shoulder, Racksole turned to the window. 'For instance,' he added, 'I perceive that this window is broken, badly broken, and from the outside. Now, how could that have occurred?'

'If you will kindly hear reason, Mr Racksole,' said Dimmock in his best diplomatic manner, 'I will endeavour to explain things to you. I regarded your first question to me when you entered my room as being offensively put, but I now see that you had some justification.' He smiled politely. 'I was passing along this corridor about eleven o'clock, when I found Miss Racksole in a difficulty with the hotel servants. Miss Racksole was retiring to rest in this room when a large stone, which must have been thrown from the Embankment, broke the window, as you see. Apart from the discomfort of the broken window, she did not care to remain in the room. She argued that where one stone had come another might follow. She therefore insisted on her room being changed. The servants said that there was no other room available with a dressing-room and bath-room attached, and your daughter made a point of these matters. I at once offered to exchange apartments with her. She did me the honour to accept my offer. Our respective belongings were moved--and that is all. Miss Racksole is at this moment, I trust, asleep in No. 124.'

Theodore Racksole looked at the young man for a few seconds in silence.

There was a faint knock at the door.

'Come in,' said Racksole loudly.

Someone pushed open the door, but remained standing on the mat. It was Nella's maid, in a dressing-gown.

'Miss Racksole's compliments, and a thousand excuses, but a book of hers was left on the mantelshelf in this room. She cannot sleep, and wishes to read.'

'Mr Dimmock, I tender my apologies--my formal apologies,' said Racksole, when the girl had gone away with the book. 'Good night.'

'Pray don't mention it,' said Dimmock suavely--and bowed him out.

CHAPTER IV
ENTRANCE OF THE PRINCE

NEVERTHELESS, sundry small things weighed on Racksole's mind. First there was Jules' wink. Then there was the ribbon on the door-handle and Jules' visit to No. 111, and the broken window--broken from the outside. Racksole did not forget that the time was 3 a.m. He slept but little that night, but he was glad that he had bought the Grand Babylon Hotel. It was an acquisition which seemed to promise fun and diversion.

The next morning he came across Mr Babylon early. 'I have emptied my private room of all personal papers,' said Babylon, 'and it is now at your disposal. I purpose, if agreeable to yourself, to stay on in the hotel as a guest for the present. We have much to settle with regard to the completion of the purchase, and also there are things which you might want to ask me. Also, to tell the truth, I am not anxious to leave the old place with too much suddenness. It will be a wrench to me.'

'I shall be delighted if you will stay,' said the millionaire, 'but it must be as my guest, not as the guest of the hotel.'

'You are very kind.'

'As for wishing to consult you, no doubt I shall have need to do so, but I must say that the show seems to run itself.'

'Ah!' said Babylon thoughtfully. 'I have heard of hotels that run themselves. If they do, you may be sure that they obey the laws of gravity and run downwards. You will have your hands full. For example, have you yet heard about Miss Spencer?'

'No,' said Racksole. 'What of her?'

'She has mysteriously vanished during the night, and nobody appears to be able to throw any light on the affair. Her room is empty, her boxes gone. You will want someone to take her place, and that someone will not be very easy to get.'

'H'm!' Racksole said, after a pause. 'Hers is not the only post that falls vacant to-day.'

A little later, the millionaire installed himself in the late owner's private room and rang the bell.

'I want Jules,' he said to the page.

While waiting for Jules, Racksole considered the question of Miss Spencer's disappearance.

'Good morning, Jules,' was his cheerful greeting, when the imperturbable waiter arrived.

'Good morning, sir.'

'Take a chair.'

'Thank you, sir.'

'We have met before this morning, Jules.'

'Yes, sir, at 3 a.m.'

'Rather strange about Miss Spencer's departure, is it not?' suggested Racksole.

'It is remarkable, sir.'

'You are aware, of course, that Mr Babylon has transferred all his interests in this hotel to me?'

'I have been informed to that effect, sir.'

'I suppose you know everything that goes on in the hotel, Jules?'

'As the head waiter, sir, it is my business to keep a general eye on things.'

'You speak very good English for a foreigner, Jules.'

'For a foreigner, sir! I am an Englishman, a Hertfordshire man born and bred. Perhaps my name has misled you, sir. I am only called Jules because the head waiter of any really high-class hotel must have either a French or an Italian name.'

'I see,' said Racksole. 'I think you must be rather a clever person, Jules.'

'That is not for me to say, sir.'

'How long has the hotel enjoyed the advantage of your services?'

'A little over twenty years.'

'That is a long time to be in one place. Don't you think it's time you got out of the rut? You are still young, and might make a reputation for yourself in another and wider sphere.'

Racksole looked at the man steadily, and his glance was steadily returned.

'You aren't satisfied with me, sir?'

'To be frank, Jules, I think--I think you--er--wink too much. And I think that it is regrettable when a head waiter falls into a habit of taking white ribbons from the handles of bedroom doors at three in the morning.'

Jules started slightly.

'I see how it is, sir. You wish me to go, and one pretext, if I may use the term, is as good as another. Very well, I can't say that I'm surprised. It sometimes happens that there is incompatibility of temper between a hotel proprietor and his head waiter, and then, unless one of them goes, the hotel is likely to suffer. I will go, Mr Racksole. In fact, I had already thought of giving notice.'

The millionaire smiled appreciatively. 'What wages do you require in lieu of notice? It is my intention that you leave the hotel within an hour.'

'I require no wages in lieu of notice, sir. I would scorn to accept anything. And I will leave the hotel in fifteen minutes.'

'Good-day, then. You have my good wishes and my admiration, so long as you keep out of my hotel.'

Racksole got up. 'Good-day, sir. And thank you.'

'By the way, Jules, it will be useless for you to apply to any other first-rate European hotel for a post, because I shall take measures which will ensure the rejection of any such application.'

'Without discussing the question whether or not there aren't at least half a dozen hotels in London alone that would jump for joy at the chance of getting me,' answered Jules, 'I may tell you, sir, that I shall retire from my profession.'

'Really! You will turn your brains to a different channel.'

'No, sir. I shall take rooms in Albemarle Street or Jermyn Street, and just be content to be a man-about-town. I have saved some twenty thousand pounds--a mere trifle, but sufficient for my needs, and I shall now proceed to enjoy it. Pardon me for troubling you with my personal affairs. And good-day again.'

That afternoon Racksole went with Felix Babylon first to a firm of solicitors in the City, and then to a stockbroker, in order to carry out the practical details of the purchase of the hotel.

'I mean to settle in England,' said Racksole, as they were coming back. 'It is the only country--' and he stopped.

'The only country?'

'The only country where you can invest money and spend money with a feeling of security. In the United States there is nothing worth spending money on, nothing to buy. In France or Italy, there is no real security.'

'But surely you are a true American?' questioned Babylon.

'I am a true American,' said Racksole, 'but my father, who began by being a bedmaker at an Oxford college, and ultimately made ten million dollars out of iron in Pittsburg--my father took the wise precaution of having me educated in England. I had my three years at Oxford, like any son of the upper middle class! It did me good. It has been worth more to me than many successful speculations. It taught me that the English language is different from, and better than, the American language, and that there is something--I haven't yet found out exactly what--in English life that Americans will never get. Why,' he added, 'in the United States we still bribe our judges and our newspapers. And we talk of the eighteenth century as though it was the beginning of the world. Yes, I shall transfer my securities to London. I shall build a house in Park Lane, and I shall buy some immemorial country seat with a history as long as the A. T. and S. railroad, and I shall calmly and gradually settle down. D'you know--I am rather a good-natured man for a millionaire, and of a social disposition, and yet I haven't six real friends in the whole of New York City. Think of that!'

'And I,' said Babylon, 'have no friends except the friends of my boyhood in Lausanne. I have spent thirty years in England, and gained nothing but a perfect knowledge of the English language and as much gold coin as would fill a rather large box.'

These two plutocrats breathed a simultaneous sigh.

'Talking of gold coin,' said Racksole, 'how much money should you think Jules has contrived to amass while he has been with you?'

'Oh!' Babylon smiled. 'I should not like to guess. He has had unique opportunities--opportunities.'

'Should you consider twenty thousand an extraordinary sum under the circumstances?'

'Not at all. Has he been confiding in you?'

'Somewhat. I have dismissed him.'

'You have dismissed him?'

'Why not?'

'There is no reason why not. But I have felt inclined to dismiss him for the past ten years, and never found courage to do it.'

'It was a perfectly simple proceeding, I assure you. Before I had done with him, I rather liked the fellow.'

'Miss Spencer and Jules--both gone in one day!' mused Felix Babylon.

'And no one to take their places,' said Racksole. 'And yet the hotel continues its way!'

But when Racksole reached the Grand Babylon he found that Miss Spencer's chair in the bureau was occupied by a stately and imperious girl, dressed becomingly in black.

'Heavens, Nella!' he cried, going to the bureau. 'What are you doing here?'

'I am taking Miss Spencer's place. I want to help you with your hotel, Dad. I fancy I shall make an excellent hotel clerk. I have arranged with a Miss Selina Smith, one of the typists in the office, to put me up to all the tips and tricks, and I shall do very well.'

'But look here, Helen Racksole. We shall have the whole of London talking about this thing--the greatest of all American heiresses a hotel clerk! And I came here for quiet and rest!'

'I suppose it was for the sake of quiet and rest that you bought the hotel, Papa?'

'You would insist on the steak,' he retorted. 'Get out of this, on the instant.'

'Here I am, here to stay,' said Nella, and deliberately laughed at her parent.

Just then the face of a fair-haired man of about thirty years appeared at the bureau window. He was very well-dressed, very aristocratic in his pose, and he seemed rather angry.

He looked fixedly at Nella and started back.

'Ach!' he exclaimed. 'You!'

'Yes, your Highness, it is indeed I. Father, this is his Serene Highness Prince Aribert of Posen--one of our most esteemed customers.'

'You know my name, Fräulein?' the new-comer murmured in German.

'Certainly, Prince,' Nella replied sweetly. 'You were plain Count Steenbock last spring in Paris--doubtless travelling incognito--'

'Silence,' he entreated, with a wave of the hand, and his forehead went as white as paper.

IN another moment they were all three talking quite nicely, and with at any rate an appearance of being natural. Prince Aribert became suave, even deferential to Nella, and more friendly towards Nella's father than their respective positions demanded. The latter amused himself by studying this sprig of royalty, the first with whom he had ever come into contact. He decided that the young fellow was personable enough, 'had no frills on him,' and would make an exceptionally good commercial traveller for a first-class firm. Such was Theodore Racksole's preliminary estimate of the man who might one day be the reigning Grand Duke of Posen.

It occurred to Nella, and she smiled at the idea, that the bureau of the hotel was scarcely the correct place in which to receive this august young man. There he stood, with his head half-way through the bureau window, negligently leaning against the woodwork, just as though he were a stockbroker or the manager of a New York burlesque company.

'Is your Highness travelling quite alone?' she asked.

'By a series of accidents I am,' he said. 'My equerry was to have met me at Charing Cross, but he failed to do so--I cannot imagine why.'

'Mr Dimmock?' questioned Racksole.

'Yes, Dimmock. I do not remember that he ever missed an appointment before. You know him? He has been here?'

'He dined with us last night,' said Racksole--'on Nella's invitation,' he added maliciously; 'but to-day we have seen nothing of him. I know, however, that he has engaged the State apartments, and also a suite adjoining the State apartments-- No. 55. That is so, isn't it, Nella?'

'Yes, Papa,' she said, having first demurely examined a ledger. 'Your Highness would doubtless like to be conducted to your room--apartments I mean.' Then Nella laughed deliberately at the Prince, and said, 'I don't know who is the proper person to conduct you, and that's a fact. The truth is that Papa and I are rather raw yet in the hotel line. You see, we only bought the place last night.'

'You have bought the hotel!' exclaimed the Prince.

'That's so,' said Racksole.

'And Felix Babylon has gone?'

'He is going, if he has not already gone.'

'Ah! I see,' said the Prince; 'this is one of your American "strokes". You have bought to sell again, is that not it? You are on your holidays, but you cannot resist making a few thousands by way of relaxation. I have heard of such things.'

'We sha'n't sell again, Prince, until we are tired of our bargain. Sometimes we tire very quickly, and sometimes we don't. It depends--eh? What?'

Racksole broke off suddenly to attend to a servant in livery who had quietly entered the bureau and was making urgent mysterious signs to him.

'If you please, sir,' the man by frantic gestures implored Mr Theodore Racksole to come out.

'Pray don't let me detain you, Mr Racksole,' said the Prince, and therefore the proprietor of the Grand Babylon departed after the servant, with a queer, curt little bow to Prince Aribert.

'Mayn't I come inside?' said the Prince to Nella immediately the millionaire had gone.

'Impossible, Prince,' Nella laughed. 'The rule against visitors entering this bureau is frightfully strict.'

'How do you know the rule is so strict if you only came into possession last night?'

'I know because I made the rule myself this morning, your Highness.'

'But seriously, Miss Racksole, I want to talk to you.'

'Do you want to talk to me as Prince Aribert or as the friend-- the acquaintance--whom I knew in Paris' last year?'

'As the friend, dear lady, if I may use the term.'

'And you are sure that you would not like first to be conducted to your apartments?'

'Not yet. I will wait till Dimmock comes; he cannot fail to be here soon.'

'Then we will have tea served in father's private room--the proprietor's private room, you know.'

'Good!' he said.

Nella talked through a telephone, and rang several bells, and behaved generally in a manner calculated to prove to Princes and to whomever it might concern that she was a young woman of business instincts and training, and then she stepped down from her chair of office, emerged from the bureau, and, preceded by two menials, led Prince Aribert to the Louis XV chamber in which her father and Felix Babylon had had their long confabulation on the previous evening.

'What do you want to talk to me about?' she asked her companion, as she poured out for him a second cup of tea. The Prince looked at her for a moment as he took the proffered cup, and being a young man of sane, healthy, instincts, he could think of nothing for the moment except her loveliness.

Nella was indeed beautiful that afternoon. The beauty of even the most beautiful woman ebbs and flows from hour to hour. Nella's this afternoon was at the flood. Vivacious, alert, imperious, and yet ineffably sweet, she seemed to radiate the very joy and exuberance of life.

'I have forgotten,' he said.

'You have forgotten! That is surely very wrong of you? You gave me to understand that it was something terribly important. But of course I knew it couldn't be, because no man, and especially no Prince, ever discussed anything really important with a woman.'

'Recollect, Miss Racksole, that this afternoon, here, I am not the Prince.'

'You are Count Steenbock, is that it?'

He started. 'For you only,' he said, unconsciously lowering his voice. 'Miss Racksole, I particularly wish that no one here should know that I was in Paris last spring.'

'An affair of State?' she smiled.

'An affair of State,' he replied soberly. 'Even Dimmock doesn't know. It was strange that we should be fellow guests at that quiet out-of-the-way hotel--strange but delightful. I shall never forget that rainy afternoon that we spent together in the Museum of the Trocadéro. Let us talk about that.'

'About the rain, or the museum?'

'I shall never forget that afternoon,' he repeated, ignoring the lightness of her question.

'Nor I,' she murmured corresponding to his mood.

'You, too enjoyed it?' he said eagerly.

'The sculptures were magnificent,' she replied, hastily glancing at the ceiling.

'Ah! So they were! Tell me, Miss Racksole, how did you discover my identity.'

'I must not say,' she answered. 'That is my secret. Do not seek to penetrate it. Who knows what horrors you might discover if you probed too far?' She laughed, but she laughed alone. The Prince remained pensive--as it were brooding.

'I never hoped to see you again,' he said.

'Why not?'

'One never sees again those whom one wishes to see.'

'As for me, I was perfectly convinced that we should meet again.'

'Why?'

'Because I always get what I want.'

'Then you wanted to see me again?'

'Certainly. You interested me extremely. I have never met another man who could talk so well about sculpture as the Count Steenbock.'

'Do you really always get what you want, Miss Racksole?'

'Of course.'

'That is because your father is so rich, I suppose?'

'Oh, no, it isn't!' she said. 'It's simply because I always do get what I want. It's got nothing to do with Father at all.'

'But Mr Racksole is extremely wealthy?'

'Wealthy isn't the word, Count. There is no word. It's positively awful the amount of dollars poor Papa makes. And the worst of it is he can't help it. He told me once that when a man had made ten millions no power on earth could stop those ten millions from growing into twenty. And so it continues. I spend what I can, but I can't come near coping with it; and of course Papa is no use whatever at spending.'

'And you have no mother?'

'Who told you I had no mother?' she asked quietly.

'I--er--inquired about you,' he said, with equal candour and humility.

'In spite of the fact that you never hoped to see me again?'

'Yes, in spite of that.'

'How funny!' she said, and lapsed into a meditative silence.

'Yours must be a wonderful existence,' said the Prince. 'I envy you.'

'You envy me--what? My father's wealth?'

'No,' he said; 'your freedom and your responsibilities.'

'I have no responsibilities,' she remarked.

'Pardon me,' he said; 'you have, and the time is coming when you will feel them.'

'I'm only a girl,' she murmured with sudden simplicity. 'As for you, Count, surely you have sufficient responsibilities of your own?'

'I?' he said sadly. 'I have no responsibilities. I am a nobody--a Serene Highness who has to pretend to be very important, always taking immense care never to do anything that a Serene Highness ought not to do. Bah!'

'But if your nephew, Prince Eugen, were to die, would you not come to the throne, and would you not then have these responsibilities which you so much desire?'

'Eugen die?' said Prince Aribert, in a curious tone. 'Impossible. He is the perfection of health. In three months he will be married. No, I shall never be anything but a Serene Highness, the most despicable of God's creatures.'

'But what about the State secret which you mentioned? Is not that a responsibility?'

'Ah!' he said. 'That is over. That belongs to the past. It was an accident in my dull career. I shall never be Count Steenbock again.'

'Who knows?' she said. 'By the way, is not Prince Eugen coming here to-day? Mr Dimmock told us so.'

'See!' answered the Prince, standing up and bending over her. 'I am going to confide in you. I don't know why, but I am.'

'Don't betray State secrets,' she warned him, smiling into his face.

But just then the door of the room was unceremoniously opened.

'Go right in,' said a voice sharply. It was Theodore Racksole's. Two men entered, bearing a prone form on a stretcher, and Racksole followed them.

Nella sprang up. Racksole stared to see his daughter.

'I didn't know you were in here, Nell. Here,' to the two men, 'out again.'

'Why!' exclaimed Nella, gazing fearfully at the form on the stretcher, 'it's Mr Dimmock!'

'It is,' her father acquiesced. 'He's dead,' he added laconically. 'I'd have broken it to you more gently had I known. Your pardon, Prince.' There was a pause.

'Dimmock dead!' Prince Aribert whispered under his breath, and he kneeled down by the side of the stretcher. 'What does this mean?'

The poor fellow was just walking across the quadrangle towards the portico when he fell down. A commissionaire who saw him says he was walking very quickly. At first I thought it was sunstroke, but it couldn't have been, though the weather certainly is rather warm. It must be heart disease. But anyhow, he's dead. We did what we could. I've sent for a doctor, and for the police. I suppose there'll have to be an inquest.'

Theodore Racksole stopped, and in an awkward solemn silence they all gazed at the dead youth. His features were slightly drawn, and his eyes closed; that was all. He might have been asleep.

'My poor Dimmock!' exclaimed the Prince, his voice broken. 'And I was angry because the lad did not meet me at Charing Cross!'

'Are you sure he is dead, Father?' Nella said.

'You'd better go away, Nella,' was Racksole's only reply; but the girl stood still, and began to sob quietly. On the previous night she had secretly made fun of Reginald Dimmock. She had deliberately set herself to get information from him on a topic in which she happened to be specially interested and she had got it, laughing the while at his youthful crudities--his vanity, his transparent cunning, his absurd airs. She had not liked him; she had even distrusted him, and decided that he was not 'nice'. But now, as he lay on the stretcher, these things were forgotten. She went so far as to reproach herself for them. Such is the strange commanding power of death.

'Oblige me by taking the poor fellow to my apartments,' said the Prince, with a gesture to the attendants. 'Surely it is time the doctor came.'

Racksole felt suddenly at that moment he was nothing but a mere hotel proprietor with an awkward affair on his hands. For a fraction of a second he wished he had never bought the Grand Babylon.

A quarter of an hour later Prince Aribert, Theodore Racksole, a doctor, and an inspector of police were in the Prince's reception-room. They had just come from an ante-chamber, in which lay the mortal remains of Reginald Dimmock.

'Well?' said Racksole, glancing at the doctor.

The doctor was a big, boyish-looking man, with keen, quizzical eyes.

'It is not heart disease,' said the doctor.

'Not heart disease?'

'No.'

'Then what is it?' asked the Prince.

'I may be able to answer that question after the post-mortem,' said the doctor. 'I certainly can't answer it now. The symptoms are unusual to a degree.'

The inspector of police began to write in a note-book.

CHAPTER VI
IN THE GOLD ROOM

AT the Grand Babylon a great ball was given that night in the Gold Room, a huge saloon attached to the hotel, though scarcely part of it, and certainly less exclusive than the hotel itself. Theodore Racksole knew nothing of the affair, except that it was an entertainment offered by a Mr and Mrs Sampson Levi to their friends. Who Mr and Mrs Sampson Levi were he did not know, nor could anyone tell him anything about them except that Mr Sampson Levi was a prominent member of that part of the Stock Exchange familiarly called the Kaffir Circus, and that his wife was a stout lady with an aquiline nose and many diamonds, and that they were very rich and very hospitable. Theodore Racksole did not want a ball in his hotel that evening, and just before dinner he had almost a mind to issue a decree that the Gold Room was to be closed and the ball forbidden, and Mr and Mrs Sampson Levi might name the amount of damages suffered by them. His reasons for such a course were threefold-- first, he felt depressed and uneasy; second, he didn't like the name of Sampson Levi; and, third, he had a desire to show these so-called plutocrats that their wealth was nothing to him, that they could not do what they chose with Theodore Racksole, and that for two pins Theodore Racksole would buy them up, and the whole Kaffir Circus to boot. But something warned him that though such a high-handed proceeding might be tolerated in America, that land of freedom, it would never be tolerated in England. He felt instinctively that in England there are things you can't do, and that this particular thing was one of them. So the ball went forward, and neither Mr nor Mrs Sampson Levi had ever the least suspicion what a narrow escape they had had of looking very foolish in the eyes of the thousand or so guests invited by them to the Gold Room of the Grand Babylon that evening.

The Gold Room of the Grand Babylon was built for a ballroom. A balcony, supported by arches faced with gilt and lapis-lazulo, ran around it, and from this vantage men and maidens and chaperons who could not or would not dance might survey the scene. Everyone knew this, and most people took advantage of it. What everyone did not know--what no one knew-

-was that higher up than the balcony there was a little barred window in the end wall from which the hotel authorities might keep a watchful eye, not only on the dancers, but on the occupants of the balcony itself.

It may seem incredible to the uninitiated that the guests at any social gathering held in so gorgeous and renowned an apartment as the Gold Room of the Grand Babylon should need the observation of a watchful eye. Yet so it was. Strange matters and unexpected faces had been descried from the little window, and more than one European detective had kept vigil there with the most eminently satisfactory results.

At eleven o'clock Theodore Racksole, afflicted by vexation of spirit, found himself gazing idly through the little barred window. Nella was with him.

Together they had been wandering about the corridors of the hotel, still strange to them both, and it was quite by accident that they had lighted upon the small room which had a surreptitious view of Mr and Mrs Sampson Levi's ball. Except for the light of the chandelier of the ball-room the little cubicle was in darkness. Nella was looking through the window; her father stood behind.

'I wonder which is Mrs Sampson Levi?' Nella said, 'and whether she matches her name. Wouldn't you love to have a name like that, Father--something that people could take hold of--instead of Racksole?'

The sound of violins and a confused murmur of voices rose gently up to them.

'Umph!' said Theodore. 'Curse those evening papers!' he added, inconsequently but with sincerity.

'Father, you're very horrid to-night. What have the evening papers been doing?'

'Well, my young madame, they've got me in for one, and you for another; and they're manufacturing mysteries like fun. It's young Dimmock's death that has started 'em.'

'Well, Father, you surely didn't expect to keep yourself out of the papers. Besides, as regards newspapers, you ought to be glad you aren't in New York. Just fancy what the dear old Herald would have made out of a little transaction like yours of last night.'

'That's true,' assented Racksole. 'But it'll be all over New York to-morrow morning, all the same. The worst of it is that Babylon has gone off to Switzerland.'

'Why?'

'Don't know. Sudden fancy, I guess, for his native heath.'

'What difference does it make to you?'

'None. Only I feel sort of lonesome. I feel I want someone to lean up against in running this hotel.'

'Father, if you have that feeling you must be getting ill.'

'Yes,' he sighed, 'I admit it's unusual with me. But perhaps you haven't grasped the fact, Nella, that we're in the middle of a rather queer business.'

'You mean about poor Mr Dimmock?'

'Partly Dimmock and partly other things. First of all, that Miss Spencer, or whatever her wretched name is, mysteriously disappears. Then there was the stone thrown into your bedroom. Then I caught that rascal Jules conspiring with Dimmock at three o'clock in the morning. Then your precious Prince Aribert arrives without any suite--which I believe is a most peculiar and wicked thing for a Prince to do--and moreover I find my daughter on very intimate terms with the said Prince. Then young Dimmock goes and dies, and there is to be an inquest; then Prince Eugen and his suite, who were expected here for dinner, fail to turn up at all--'

'Prince Eugen has not come?'

'He has not; and Uncle Aribert is in a deuce of a stew about him, and telegraphing all over Europe. Altogether, things are working up pretty lively.'

'Do you really think, Dad, there was anything between Jules and poor Mr Dimmock?'

'Think! I know! I tell you I saw that scamp give Dimmock a wink last night at dinner that might have meant--well!'

'So you caught that wink, did you, Dad?'

'Why, did you?'

'Of course, Dad. I was going to tell you about it.'

The millionaire grunted.

'Look here, Father,' Nella whispered suddenly, and pointed to the balcony immediately below them. 'Who's that?' She indicated a man with a bald patch on the back of his head, who was propping himself up against the railing of the balcony and gazing immovable into the ball-room.

'Well, who is it?'

'Isn't it Jules?'

'Gemini! By the beard of the prophet, it is!'

'Perhaps Mr Jules is a guest of Mrs Sampson Levi.'

'Guest or no guest, he goes out of this hotel, even if I have to throw him out myself.'

Theodore Racksole disappeared without another word, and Nella followed him.

But when the millionaire arrived on the balcony floor he could see nothing of Jules, neither there nor in the ball-room itself. Saying no word aloud, but quietly whispering wicked expletives, he searched everywhere in vain, and then, at last, by tortuous stairways and corridors returned to his original post of observation, that he might survey the place anew from the vantage ground. To his surprise he found a man in the dark little room, watching the scene of the ball as intently as he himself had been doing a few minutes before. Hearing footsteps, the man turned with a start.

It was Jules.

The two exchanged glances in the half light for a second.

'Good evening, Mr Racksole,' said Jules calmly. 'I must apologize for being here.'

'Force of habit, I suppose,' said Theodore Racksole drily.

'Just so, sir.'

'I fancied I had forbidden you to re-enter this hotel?'

'I thought your order applied only to my professional capacity. I am here to-night as the guest of Mr and Mrs Sampson Levi.'

'In your new rôle of man-about-town, eh?'

'Exactly.'

'But I don't allow men-about-town up here, my friend.'

'For being up here I have already apologized.'

'Then, having apologized, you had better depart; that is my disinterested advice to you.'

'Good night, sir.'

'And, I say, Mr Jules, if Mr and Mrs Sampson Levi, or any other Hebrews or Christians, should again invite you to my hotel you will oblige me by declining the invitation. You'll find that will be the safest course for you.'

'Good night, sir.'

Before midnight struck Theodore Racksole had ascertained that the invitation-list of Mr and Mrs Sampson Levi, though a somewhat lengthy one, contained no reference to any such person as Jules.

He sat up very late. To be precise, he sat up all night. He was a man who, by dint of training, could comfortably dispense with sleep when he felt so inclined, or when circumstances made such a course advisable. He walked to and fro in his room, and cogitated as few people beside Theodore Racksole could cogitate. At 6 a.m. he took a stroll round the business part of his premises, and watched the supplies come in from Covent Garden, from Smithfield, from Billingsgate, and from other strange places. He found the proceedings of the kitchen department quite interesting, and made mental notes of things that he would have altered, of men whose wages he would increase and men whose wages he would reduce. At 7 a.m. he happened to be standing near the luggage lift, and witnessed the descent of vast quantities of luggage, and its disappearance into a Carter Paterson van.

'Whose luggage is that?' he inquired peremptorily.

The luggage clerk, with an aggrieved expression, explained to him that it was the luggage of nobody in particular, that it belonged to various guests, and was bound for various destinations; that it was, in fact, 'expressed' luggage despatched in advance, and that a similar quantity of it left the hotel every morning about that hour.

Theodore Racksole walked away, and breakfasted upon one cup of tea and half a slice of toast.

At ten o'clock he was informed that the inspector of police desired to see him. The inspector had come, he said, to superintend the removal of the body of Reginald Dimmock to the mortuary adjoining the place of inquest, and a suitable vehicle waited at the back entrance of the hotel.

The inspector had also brought subpoenas for himself and Prince Aribert of Posen and the commissionaire to attend the inquest.

'I thought Mr Dimmock's remains were removed last night,' said Racksole wearily.

'No, sir. The fact is the van was engaged on another job.'

The inspector gave the least hint of a professional smile, and Racksole, disgusted, told him curtly to go and perform his duties.

In a few minutes a message came from the inspector requesting Mr Racksole to be good enough to come to him on the first floor. Racksole went. In the ante-room, where the body of Reginald Dimmock had originally been placed, were the inspector and Prince Aribert, and two policemen.

'Well?' said Racksole, after he and the Prince had exchanged bows. Then he saw a coffin laid across two chairs. 'I see a coffin has been obtained,' he remarked. 'Quite right' He approached it. 'It's empty,' he observed unthinkingly.

'Just so,' said the inspector. 'The body of the deceased has disappeared.

And his Serene Highness Prince Aribert informs me that though he has occupied a room immediately opposite, on the other side of the corridor, he can throw no light on the affair.'

'Indeed, I cannot!' said the Prince, and though he spoke with sufficient calmness and dignity, you could see that he was deeply pained, even distressed.

'Well, I'm--' murmured Racksole, and stopped.

CHAPTER VII
NELLA AND THE PRINCE

IT appeared impossible to Theodore Racksole that so cumbrous an article as a corpse could be removed out of his hotel, with no trace, no hint, no clue as to the time or the manner of the performance of the deed. After the first feeling of surprise, Racksole grew coldly and severely angry. He had a mind to dismiss the entire staff of the hotel. He personally examined the night-watchman, the chambermaids and all other persons who by chance might or ought to know something of the affair; but without avail. The corpse of Reginald Dimmock had vanished utterly--disappeared like a fleshless spirit.

Of course there were the police. But Theodore Racksole held the police in sorry esteem. He acquainted them with the facts, answered their queries with a patient weariness, and expected, nothing whatever from that quarter. He also had several interviews with Prince Aribert of Posen, but though the Prince was suavity itself and beyond doubt genuinely concerned about the fate of his dead attendant, yet it seemed to Racksole that he was keeping something back, that he hesitated to say all he knew. Racksole, with characteristic insight, decided that the death of Reginald Dimmock was only a minor event, which had occurred, as it were, on the fringe of some far more profound mystery. And, therefore, he decided to wait, with his eyes very wide open, until something else happened that would throw light on the business. At the moment he took only one measure--he arranged that the theft of Dimmock's body should not appear in the newspapers. It is astonishing how well a secret can be kept, when the possessors of the secret are handled with the proper mixture of firmness and persuasion. Racksole managed this very neatly. It was a complicated job, and his success in it rather pleased him.

At the same time he was conscious of being temporarily worsted by an unknown group of schemers, in which he felt convinced that Jules was an important item. He could scarcely look Nella in the eyes. The girl had evidently expected him to unmask this conspiracy at once, with a single stroke of the millionaire's magic wand. She was thoroughly accustomed, in the land of her birth, to seeing him achieve impossible feats.

Over there he was a 'boss'; men trembled before his name; when he wished a thing to happen--well, it happened; if he desired to know a thing, he just knew it. But here, in London, Theodore Racksole was not quite the same Theodore Racksole. He dominated New York; but London, for the most part, seemed not to take much interest in him; and there were certainly various persons in London who were capable of snapping their fingers at him--at Theodore Racksole. Neither he nor his daughter could get used to that fact.

As for Nella, she concerned herself for a little with the ordinary business of the bureau, and watched the incomings and outgoings of Prince Aribert with a kindly interest. She perceived, what her father had failed to perceive, that His Highness had assumed an attitude of reserve merely to hide the secret distraction and dismay which consumed him. She saw that the poor fellow had no settled plan in his head, and that he was troubled by something which, so far, he had confided to nobody. It came to her knowledge that each morning he walked to and fro on the Victoria Embankment, alone, and apparently with no object. On the third morning she decided that driving exercise on the Embankment would be good for her health, and thereupon ordered a carriage and issued forth, arrayed in a miraculous putty-coloured gown. Near Blackfriars Bridge she met the Prince, and the carriage was drawn up by the pavement.

'Good morning, Prince,' she greeted him. 'Are you mistaking this for Hyde Park?'

He bowed and smiled.

'I usually walk here in the mornings,' he said.

'You surprise me,' she returned. 'I thought I was the only person in London who preferred the Embankment, with this view of the river, to the dustiness of Hyde Park. I can't imagine how it is that London will never take exercise anywhere except in that ridiculous Park. Now, if they had Central Park--'

'I think the Embankment is the finest spot in all London,' he said.

She leaned a little out of the landau, bringing her face nearer to his.

'I do believe we are kindred spirits, you and I,' she murmured; and then, 'Au revoir, Prince!'

'One moment, Miss Racksole.' His quick tones had a note of entreaty.

'I am in a hurry,' she fibbed; 'I am not merely taking exercise this morning. You have no idea how busy we are.'

'Ah! then I will not trouble you. But I leave the Grand Babylon to-night.'

'Do you?' she said. 'Then will your Highness do me the honour of lunching with me today in Father's room? Father will be out--he is having a day in the City with some stockbroking persons.'

'I shall be charmed,' said the Prince, and his face showed that he meant it.

Nella drove off.

If the lunch was a success that result was due partly to Rocco, and partly to Nella. The Prince said little beyond what the ordinary rules of the conversational game demanded. His hostess talked much and talked well, but she failed to rouse her guest. When they had had coffee he took a rather formal leave of her.

'Good-bye, Prince,' she said, 'but I thought--that is, no I didn't. Good-bye.'

'You thought I wished to discuss something with you. I did; but I have decided that I have no right to burden your mind with my affairs.'

'But suppose--suppose I wish to be burdened?'

'That is your good nature.'

'Sit down,' she said abruptly, 'and tell me everything; mind, everything. I adore secrets.'

Almost before he knew it he was talking to her, rapidly, eagerly.

'Why should I weary you with my confidences?' he said. 'I don't know, I cannot tell; but I feel that I must. I feel that you will understand me better than anyone else in the world. And yet why should you understand me? Again, I don't know. Miss Racksole, I will disclose to you the whole trouble in a word. Prince Eugen, the hereditary Grand Duke of Posen, has disappeared. Four days ago I was to have met him at Ostend. He had affairs in London. He wished me to come with him. I sent Dimmock on in front, and waited for Eugen. He did not arrive. I telegraphed back to Cologne, his last stopping-place, and I learned that he had left there in accordance with his programme; I learned also that he had passed through Brussels. It must have been between Brussels and the railway station at Ostend Quay that he disappeared. He was travelling with a single equerry, and the equerry, too, has vanished. I need not explain to you, Miss Racksole, that when a person of the importance of my nephew contrives to get lost one must proceed cautiously. One cannot advertise for him in the London Times. Such a disappearance must be kept secret. The people at Posen and at Berlin believe that Eugen is in London, here, at this hotel; or, rather, they did so believe. But this morning I received a cypher telegram from--from His Majesty the Emperor, a very peculiar telegram, asking when Eugen might be expected to return to Posen, and requesting that he should go first to Berlin. That telegram was addressed to myself. Now, if the Emperor thought that Eugen was here, why should he have caused the telegram to be addressed to me? I have hesitated for three days, but I can hesitate no longer. I must myself go to the Emperor and acquaint him with the facts.'

'I suppose you've just got to keep straight with him?' Nella was on the point of saying, but she checked herself and substituted, 'The Emperor is your chief, is he not? "First among equals", you call him.'

'His Majesty is our over-lord,' said Aribert quietly.

'Why do you not take immediate steps to inquire as to the whereabouts of your Royal nephew?' she asked simply. The affair seemed to her just then so plain and straightforward.

'Because one of two things may have happened. Either Eugen may have been, in plain language, abducted, or he may have had his own reasons for changing his programme and keeping in the background--out of reach of telegraph and post and railways.'

'What sort of reasons?'

'Do not ask me. In the history of every family there are passages--' He stopped.

'And what was Prince Eugen's object in coming to London?'

Aribert hesitated.

'Money,' he said at length. 'As a family we are very poor-- poorer than anyone in Berlin suspects.'

'Prince Aribert,' Nella said, 'shall I tell you what I think?' She leaned back in her chair, and looked at him out of half-closed eyes. His pale, thin, distinguished face held her gaze as if by some fascination. There could be no mistaking this man for anything else but a Prince.

'If you will,' he said.

'Prince Eugen is the victim of a plot.'

'You think so?'

'I am perfectly convinced of it.'

'But why? What can be the object of a plot against him?'

'That is a point of which you should know more than me,' she remarked drily.

'Ah! Perhaps, perhaps,' he said. 'But, dear Miss Racksole, why are you so sure?'

'There are several reasons, and they are connected with Mr Dimmock. Did you ever suspect, your Highness, that that poor young man was not entirely loyal to you?'

'He was absolutely loyal,' said the Prince, with all the earnestness of conviction.

'A thousand pardons, but he was not.'

'Miss Racksole, if any other than yourself made that assertion, I would--I would--'

'Consign them to the deepest dungeon in Posen?' she laughed, lightly.

'Listen.' And she told him of the incidents which had occurred in the night preceding his arrival in the hotel.

'Do you mean, Miss Racksole, that there was an understanding between poor Dimmock and this fellow Jules?'

'There was an understanding.'

'Impossible!'

'Your Highness, the man who wishes to probe a mystery to its root never uses the word "impossible". But I will say this for young Mr Dimmock. I think he repented, and I think that it was because he repented that he--er--died so suddenly, and that his body was spirited away.'

'Why has no one told me these things before?' Aribert exclaimed.

'Princes seldom hear the truth,' she said.

He was astonished at her coolness, her firmness of assertion, her air of complete acquaintance with the world.

'Miss Racksole,' he said, 'if you will permit me to say it, I have never in my life met a woman like you. May I rely on your sympathy--your support?'

'My support, Prince? But how?'

'I do not know,' he replied. 'But you could help me if you would. A woman, when she has brain, always has more brain than a man.'

'Ah!' she said ruefully, 'I have no brains, but I do believe I could help you.'

What prompted her to make that assertion she could not have explained, even to herself. But she made it, and she had a suspicion--a prescience--that it would be justified, though by what means, through what good fortune, was still a mystery to her.

'Go to Berlin,' she said. 'I see that you must do that; you have no alternative. As for the rest, we shall see. Something will occur. I shall be here. My father will be here. You must count us as your friends.'

He kissed her hand when he left, and afterwards, when she was alone, she kissed the spot his lips had touched again and again. Now, thinking the matter out in the calmness of solitude, all seemed strange, unreal, uncertain to her. Were conspiracies actually possible nowadays? Did queer things actually happen in Europe? And did they actually happen in London hotels? She dined with her father that night.

'I hear Prince Aribert has left,' said Theodore Racksole.

'Yes,' she assented. She said not a word about their interview.

CHAPTER VIII
ARRIVAL AND DEPARTURE OF THE BARONESS

ON the following morning, just before lunch, a lady, accompanied by a maid and a considerable quantity of luggage, came to the Grand Babylon Hotel. She was a plump, little old lady, with white hair and an old-fashioned bonnet, and she had a quaint, simple smile of surprise at everything in general.

Nevertheless, she gave the impression of belonging to some aristocracy, though not the English aristocracy. Her tone to her maid, whom she addressed in broken English--the girl being apparently English--was distinctly insolent, with the calm, unconscious insolence peculiar to a certain type of Continental nobility. The name on the lady's card ran thus: 'Baroness Zerlinski'. She desired rooms on the third floor. It happened that Nella was in the bureau.

'On the third floor, madam?' questioned Nella, in her best clerkly manner.

'I did say on de tird floor,' said the plump little old lady.

'We have accommodation on the second floor.'

'I wish to be high up, out of de dust and in de light,' explained the Baroness.

'We have no suites on the third floor, madam.'

'Never mind, no mattaire! Have you not two rooms that communicate?'

Nella consulted her books, rather awkwardly.

'Numbers 122 and 123 communicate.'

'Or is it 121 and 122? the little old lady remarked quickly, and then bit her lip.

'I beg your pardon. I should have said 121 and 122.'

At the moment Nella regarded the Baroness's correction of her figures as a curious chance, but afterwards, when the Baroness had ascended in the lift, the thing struck her as somewhat strange. Perhaps the Baroness Zerlinski had stayed at the hotel before. For the sake of convenience an index of visitors to the hotel was kept and the index extended back for thirty years. Nella examined it, but it did not contain the name of Zerlinski. Then it was that Nella began to imagine, what had swiftly crossed her mind when first the Baroness presented herself at the bureau, that the features of the Baroness were remotely familiar to her. She thought, not that she had seen the old lady's face before, but that she had seen somewhere, some time, a face of a similar cast. It occurred to Nella to look at the 'Almanach de Gotha'--that record of all the mazes of Continental blue blood; but the 'Almanach de Gotha' made no reference to any barony of Zerlinski. Nella inquired where the Baroness meant to take lunch, and was informed that a table had been reserved for her in the dining-room, and she at once decided to lunch in the dining-room herself. Seated in a corner, half-hidden by a pillar, she could survey all the guests, and watch each group as it entered or left. Presently the Baroness appeared, dressed in black, with a tiny lace shawl, despite the June warmth; very stately, very quaint, and gently smiling. Nella observed her intently. The lady ate heartily, working without haste and without delay through the elaborate menu of the luncheon. Nella noticed that she had beautiful white teeth. Then a remarkable thing happened. A cream puff was served to the Baroness by way of sweets, and Nella was astonished to see the little lady remove the top, and with a spoon quietly take something from the interior which looked like a piece of folded paper. No one who had not been watching with the eye of a lynx would have noticed anything extraordinary in the action; indeed, the chances were nine hundred and ninety-nine to one that it would pass unheeded. But, unfortunately for the Baroness, it was the thousandth chance that happened. Nella jumped up, and walking over to the Baroness, said to her:

'I'm afraid that the tart is not quite nice, your ladyship.'

'Thanks, it is delightful,' said the Baroness coldly; her smile had vanished. 'Who are you? I thought you were de bureau clerk.'

'My father is the owner of this hotel. I thought there was something in the tart which ought not to have been there.'

Nella looked the Baroness full in the face. The piece of folded paper, to which a little cream had attached itself, lay under the edge of a plate.

'No, thanks.' The Baroness smiled her simple smile.

Nella departed. She had noticed one trifling thing besides the paper--namely, that the Baroness could pronounce the English 'th' sound if she chose.

That afternoon, in her own room, Nella sat meditating at the window for long time, and then she suddenly sprang up, her eyes brightening.

'I know,' she exclaimed, clapping her hands. 'It's Miss Spencer, disguised! Why didn't I think of that before?' Her thoughts ran instantly to Prince Aribert. 'Perhaps I can help him,' she said to herself, and gave a little sigh. She went down to the office and inquired whether the Baroness had given any instructions about dinner. She felt that some plan must be formulated. She wanted to get hold of Rocco, and put him in the rack. She knew now that Rocco, the unequalled, was also concerned in this mysterious affair.

'The Baroness Zerlinski has left, about a quarter of an hour ago,' said the attendant.

'But she only arrived this morning.'

'The Baroness's maid said that her mistress had received a telegram and must leave at once. The Baroness paid the bill, and went away in a four-wheeler.'

'Where to? 'The trunks were labelled for Ostend.'

Perhaps it was instinct, perhaps it was the mere spirit of adventure; but that evening Nella was to be seen of all men on the steamer for Ostend which leaves Dover at 11 p.m. She told no one of her intentions--not even her father, who was not in the hotel when she left. She had scribbled a brief note to him to expect her back in a day or two, and had posted this at Dover. The steamer was the Marie Henriette, a large and luxurious boat, whose state-rooms on deck vie with the glories of the Cunard and White Star liners. One of these state-rooms, the best, was evidently occupied, for every curtain of its windows was carefully drawn. Nella did not hope that the Baroness was on board; it was quite possible for the Baroness to have caught the eight o'clock steamer, and it was also possible for the Baroness not to have gone to Ostend at all, but to some other place in an entirely different direction. Nevertheless, Nella had a faint hope that the lady who called herself Zerlinski might be in that curtained stateroom, and throughout the smooth moonlit voyage she never once relaxed her observation of its doors and its windows.

The Maria Henriette arrived in Ostend Harbour punctually at 2 a.m. in the morning. There was the usual heterogeneous, gesticulating crowd on the quay.

Nella kept her post near the door of the state-room, and at length she was rewarded by seeing it open. Four middle-aged Englishmen issued from it. From a glimpse of the interior Nella saw that they had spent the voyage in card-playing.

It would not be too much to say that she was distinctly annoyed. She pretended to be annoyed with circumstances, but really she was annoyed with Nella Racksole. At two in the morning, without luggage, without any companionship, and without a plan of campaign, she found herself in a strange foreign port--a port of evil repute, possessing some of the worst-managed hotels in Europe. She strolled on the quay for a few minutes, and then she saw the smoke of another steamer in the offing. She inquired from an official what that steamer might be, and was told that it was the eight o'clock from Dover, which had broken down, put into Calais for some slight necessary repairs, and was arriving at its destination nearly four hours late. Her mercurial spirits rose again. A minute ago she was regarding herself as no better than a ninny engaged in a wild-goose chase. Now she felt that after all she had been very sagacious and cunning. She was morally sure that she would find the Zerlinski woman on this second steamer, and she took all the credit to herself in advance. Such is human nature.

The steamer seemed interminably slow in coming into harbour. Nella walked on the Digue for a few minutes to watch it the better. The town was silent and almost deserted. It had a false and sinister aspect. She remembered tales which she had heard of this glittering resort, which in the season holds more scoundrels than any place in Europe, save only Monte Carlo. She remembered that the gilded adventures of every nation under the sun forgathered there either for business or pleasure, and that some of the most wonderful crimes of the latter half of the century had been schemed and matured in that haunt of cosmopolitan iniquity.

When the second steamer arrived Nella stood at the end of the gangway, close to the ticket-collector. The first person to step on shore was--not the Baroness Zerlinski, but Miss Spencer herself! Nella turned aside instantly, hiding her face, and Miss

Spencer, carrying a small bag, hurried with assured footsteps to the Custom House. It seemed as if she knew the port of Ostend fairly well. The moon shone like day, and Nella had full opportunity to observe her quarry. She could see now quite plainly that the Baroness Zerlinski had been only Miss Spencer in disguise. There was the same gait, the same movement of the head and of the hips; the white hair was easily to be accounted for by a wig, and the wrinkles by a paint brush and some grease paints. Miss Spencer, whose hair was now its old accustomed yellow, got through the Custom House without difficulty, and Nella saw her call a closed carriage and say something to the driver. The vehicle drove off. Nella jumped into the next carriage--an open one--that came up.

'Follow that carriage,' she said succinctly to the driver in French.

'Bien, madame!' The driver whipped up his horse, and the animal shot forward with a terrific clatter over the cobbles. It appeared that this driver was quite accustomed to following other carriages.

'Now I am fairly in for it!' said Nella to herself. She laughed unsteadily, but her heart was beating with an extraordinary thump.

For some time the pursued vehicle kept well in front. It crossed the town nearly from end to end, and plunged into a maze of small streets far on the south side of the Kursaal. Then gradually Nella's equipage began to overtake it. The first carriage stopped with a jerk before a tall dark house, and Miss Spencer emerged. Nella called to her driver to stop, but he, determined to be in at the death, was engaged in whipping his horse, and he completely ignored her commands. He drew up triumphantly at the tall dark house just at the moment when Miss Spencer disappeared into it. The other carriage drove away. Nella, uncertain what to do, stepped down from her carriage and gave the driver some money. At the same moment a man reopened the door of the house, which had closed on Miss Spencer.

'I want to see Miss Spencer,' said Nella impulsively. She couldn't think of anything else to say.

'Miss Spencer? 'Yes; she's just arrived.'

'It's O.K., I suppose,' said the man.

'I guess so,' said Nella, and she walked past him into the house. She was astonished at her own audacity.

Miss Spencer was just going into a room off the narrow hall. Nella followed her into the apartment, which was shabbily furnished in the Belgian lodging-house style.

'Well, Miss Spencer,' she greeted the former Baroness Zerlinski, 'I guess you didn't expect to see me. You left our hotel very suddenly this afternoon, and you left it very suddenly a few days ago; and so I've just called to make a few inquiries.'

To do the lady justice, Miss Spencer bore the surprising ordeal very well.

She did not flinch; she betrayed no emotion. The sole sign of perturbation was in her hurried breathing.

'You have ceased to be the Baroness Zerlinski,' Nella continued. 'May I sit down?'

'Certainly, sit down,' said Miss Spencer, copying the girl's tone. 'You are a fairly smart young woman, that I will say. What do you want? Weren't my books all straight?'

'Your books were all straight. I haven't come about your books. I have come about the murder of Reginald Dimmock, the disappearance of his corpse, and the disappearance of Prince Eugen of Posen. I thought you might be able to help me in some investigations which I am making.'

Miss Spencer's eyes gleamed, and she stood up and moved swiftly to the mantelpiece.

'You may be a Yankee, but you're a fool,' she said.

She took hold of the bell-rope.

'Don't ring that bell if you value your life,' said Nella.

'If what?' Miss Spencer remarked.

'If you value your life,' said Nella calmly, and with the words she pulled from her pocket a very neat and dainty little revolver.

CHAPTER IX
TWO WOMEN AND THE REVOLVER

'YOU--you're only doing that to frighten me,' stammered Miss Spencer, in a low, quavering voice.

'Am I?' Nella replied, as firmly as she could, though her hand shook violently with excitement, could Miss Spencer but have observed it. 'Am I? You said just now that I might be a Yankee girl, but I was a fool. Well, I am a Yankee girl, as you call it; and in my country, if they don't teach revolver-shooting in boarding-schools, there are at least a lot of girls who can handle a revolver. I happen to be one of them. I tell you that if you ring that bell you will suffer.'

Most of this was simple bluff on Nella's part, and she trembled lest Miss Spencer should perceive that it was simple bluff. Happily for her, Miss Spencer belonged to that order of women who have every sort of courage except physical courage. Miss Spencer could have withstood successfully any moral trial, but persuade her that her skin was in danger, and she would succumb. Nella at once divined this useful fact, and proceeded accordingly, hiding the strangeness of her own sensations as well as she could.

'You had better sit down now,' said Nella, 'and I will ask you a few questions.'

And Miss Spencer obediently sat down, rather white, and trying to screw her lips into a formal smile.

'Why did you leave the Grand Babylon that night?' Nella began her examination, putting on a stern, barrister-like expression.

'I had orders to, Miss Racksole.'

'Whose orders?'

'Well, I'm--I'm--the fact is, I'm a married woman, and it was my husband's orders.'

'Who is your husband? 'Tom Jackson--Jules, you know, head waiter at the Grand Babylon.'

'So Jules's real name is Tom Jackson? Why did he want you to leave without giving notice?'

'I'm sure I don't know, Miss Racksole. I swear I don't know. He's my husband, and, of course, I do what he tells me, as you will some day do what your husband tells you. Please heaven you'll get a better husband than mine!'

Miss Spencer showed a sign of tears.

Nella fingered the revolver, and put it at full cock. 'Well,' she repeated, 'why did he want you to leave?' She was tremendously surprised at her own coolness, and somewhat pleased with it, too.

'I can't tell you, I can't tell you.'

'You've just got to,' Nella said, in a terrible, remorseless tone.

'He--he wished me to come over here to Ostend. Something had gone wrong.

Oh! he's a fearful man, is Tom. If I told you, he'd--'

'Had something gone wrong in the hotel, or over here?'

'Both.'

'Was it about Prince Eugen of Posen?'

'I don't know--that is, yes, I think so.'

'What has your husband to do with Prince Eugen?'

'I believe he has some--some sort of business with him, some money business.'

'And was Mr Dimmock in this business? 'I fancy so, Miss Racksole. I'm telling you all I know, that I swear.'

'Did your husband and Mr Dimmock have a quarrel that night in Room 111?'

'They had some difficulty.'

'And the result of that was that you came to Ostend instantly?'

'Yes; I suppose so.'

'And what were you to do in Ostend? What were your instructions from this husband of yours?'

Miss Spencer's head dropped on her arms on the table which separated her from Nella, and she appeared to sob violently.

'Have pity on me,' she murmured, 'I can't tell you any more.'

'Why?'

'He'd kill me if he knew.'

'You're wandering from the subject,' observed Nella coldly. 'This is the last time I shall warn you. Let me tell you plainly I've got the best reasons for being desperate, and if anything happens to you I shall say I did it in sell-defence. Now, what were you to do in Ostend?'

'I shall die for this anyhow,' whined Miss Spencer, and then, with a sort of fierce despair, 'I had to keep watch on Prince Eugen.'

'Where? In this house?'

Miss Spencer nodded, and, looking up, Nella could see the traces of tears in her face.

'Then Prince Eugen was a prisoner? Some one had captured him at the instigation of Jules?'

'Yes, if you must have it.'

'Why was it necessary for you specially to come to Ostend?'

'Oh! Tom trusts me. You see, I know Ostend. Before I took that place at the Grand Babylon I had travelled over Europe, and Tom knew that I knew a thing or two.'

'Why did you take the place at the Grand Babylon?'

'Because Tom told me to. He said I should be useful to him there.'

'Is your husband an Anarchist, or something of that kind, Miss Spencer?'

'I don't know. I'd tell you in a minute if I knew. But he's one of those that keep themselves to themselves.'

'Do you know if he has ever committed a murder? 'Never!' said Miss Spencer, with righteous repudiation of the mere idea.

'But Mr Dimmock was murdered. He was poisoned. If he had not been poisoned why was his body stolen? It must have been stolen to prevent inquiry, to hide traces. Tell me about that.'

'I take my dying oath,' said Miss Spencer, standing up a little way from the table, 'I take my dying oath I didn't know Mr Dimmock was dead till I saw it in the newspaper.'

'You swear you had no suspicion of it?'

'I swear I hadn't.'

Nella was inclined to believe the statement. The woman and the girl looked at each other in the tawdry, frowsy, lamp-lit room. Miss Spencer nervously patted her yellow hair into shape, as if gradually recovering her composure and equanimity. The whole affair seemed like a dream to Nella, a disturbing, sinister nightmare. She was a little uncertain what to say. She felt that she had not yet got hold of any very definite information. 'Where is Prince Eugen now?' she asked at length.

'I don't know, miss.'

'He isn't in this house?'

'No, miss.'

'Ah! We will see presently.'

'They took him away, Miss Racksole.'

'Who took him away? Some of your husband's friends?'

'Some of his--acquaintances.'

'Then there is a gang of you?'

'A gang of us--a gang! I don't know what you mean,' Miss Spencer quavered.

'Oh, but you must know,' smiled Nella calmly. 'You can't possibly be so innocent as all that, Mrs Tom Jackson. You can't play games with me. You've just got to remember that I'm what you call a Yankee girl. There's one thing that I mean to find out, within the next five minutes, and that is--how your charming husband kidnapped Prince Eugen, and why he kidnapped him. Let us begin with the second question. You have evaded it once.'

Miss Spencer looked into Nella's face, and then her eyes dropped, and her fingers worked nervously with the tablecloth.

'How can I tell you,' she said, 'when I don't know? You've got the whip-hand of me, and you're tormenting me for your own pleasure.' She wore an expression of persecuted innocence.

'Did Mr Tom Jackson want to get some money out of Prince Eugen?'

'Money! Not he! Tom's never short of money.'

'But I mean a lot of money--tens of thousands, hundreds of thousands?'

'Tom never wanted money from anyone,' said Miss Spencer doggedly.

'Then had he some reason for wishing to prevent Prince Eugen from coming to London?'

'Perhaps he had. I don't know. If you kill me, I don't know.' Nella stopped to reflect. Then she raised the revolver. It was a mechanical, unintentional sort of action, and certainly she had no intention of using the weapon, but, strange to say, Miss Spencer again cowered before it. Even at that moment Nella wondered that a woman like Miss Spencer could be so simple as to think the revolver would actually be used. Having absolutely no physical cowardice herself, Nella had the greatest difficulty in imagining that other people could be at the mercy of a bodily fear. Still, she saw her advantage, and used it relentlessly, and with as much theatrical gesture as she could command. She raised the revolver till it was level with Miss Spencer's face, and suddenly a new, queer feeling took hold of her. She knew that she would indeed use that revolver now, if the miserable woman before her drove her too far. She felt afraid--afraid of herself; she was in the grasp of a savage, primeval instinct. In a flash she saw Miss Spencer dead at her feet--the police--a court of justice-- the scaffold. It was horrible.

'Speak,' she said hoarsely, and Miss Spencer's face went whiter.

'Tom did say,' the woman whispered rapidly, awesomely, 'that if Prince Eugen got to London it would upset his scheme.'

'What scheme? What scheme? Answer me.'

'Heaven help me, I don't know.' Miss Spencer sank into a chair. 'He said Mr Dimmock had turned tail, and he should have to settle him and then Rocco--'

'Rocco! What about Rocco?' Nella could scarcely hear herself. Her grip of the revolver tightened.

Miss Spencer's eyes opened wider; she gazed at Nella with a glassy stare.

'Don't ask me. It's death!' Her eyes were fixed as if in horror.

'It is,' said Nella, and the sound of her voice seemed to her to issue from the lips of some third person.

'It's death,' repeated Miss Spencer, and gradually her head and shoulders sank back, and hung loosely over the chair. Nella was conscious of a sudden revulsion. The woman had surely fainted. Dropping the revolver she ran round the table. She was herself again--feminine, sympathetic, the old Nella. She felt immensely relieved that this had happened. But at the same instant Miss Spencer sprang up from the chair like a cat, seized the revolver, and with a wild movement of the arm flung it against the window. It crashed through the glass, exploding as it went, and there was a tense silence.

'I told you that you were a fool,' remarked Miss Spencer slowly, 'coming here like a sort of female Jack Sheppard, and trying to get the best of me. We are on equal terms now. You frightened me, but I knew I was a cleverer woman than you, and that in the end, if I kept on long enough, I should win. Now it will be my turn.'

Dumbfounded, and overcome with a miserable sense of the truth of Miss Spencer's words, Nella stood still. The idea of her colossal foolishness swept through her like a flood. She felt almost ashamed. But even at this juncture she had no fear. She faced the woman bravely, her mind leaping about in search of some plan. She could think of nothing but a bribe--an enormous bribe.

'I admit you've won,' she said, 'but I've not finished yet. Just listen.'

Miss Spencer folded her arms, and glanced at the door, smiling bitterly.

'You know my father is a millionaire; perhaps you know that he is one of the richest men in the world. If I give you my word of honour not to reveal anything that you've told me, what will you take to let me go free?'

'What sum do you suggest?' asked Miss Spencer carelessly.

'Twenty thousand pounds,' said Nella promptly. She had begun to regard the affair as a business operation.

Miss Spencer's lip curled.

'A hundred thousand.'

Again Miss Spencer's lip curled.

'Well, say a million. I can rely on my father, and so may you.'

'You think you are worth a million to him?'

'I do,' said Nella.

'And you think we could trust you to see that it was paid?'

'Of course you could.'

'And we should not suffer afterwards in any way?'

'I would give you my word, and my father's word.'

'Bah!' exclaimed Miss Spencer: 'how do you know I wouldn't let you go free for nothing? You are only a rash, silly girl.'

'I know you wouldn't. I can read your face too well.'

'You are right,' Miss Spencer replied slowly. 'I wouldn't. I wouldn't let you go for all the dollars in America.'

Nella felt cold down the spine, and sat down again in her chair. A draught of air from the broken window blew on her cheek. Steps sounded in the passage; the door opened, but Nella did not turn round. She could not move her eyes from Miss Spencer's. There was a noise of rushing water in her ears. She lost consciousness, and slipped limply to the ground.

CHAPTER X
AT SEA

IT seemed to Nella that she was being rocked gently in a vast cradle, which swayed to and fro with a motion at once slow and incredibly gentle. This sensation continued for some time, and there was added to it the sound of a quick, quiet, muffled beat. Soft, exhilarating breezes wafted her forward in spite of herself, and yet she remained in a delicious calm. She wondered if her mother was kneeling by her side, whispering some lullaby in her childish ears. Then strange colours swam before her eyes, her eyelids wavered, and at last she awoke. For a few moments her gaze travelled to and fro in a vain search for some clue to her surroundings, was aware of nothing except sense of repose and a feeling of relief that some mighty and fatal struggle was over; she cared not whether she had conquered or suffered defeat in the struggle of her soul with some other soul; it was finished, done with, and the consciousness of its conclusion satisfied and contented her. Gradually her brain, recovering from its obsession, began to grasp the phenomena of her surroundings, and she saw that she was on a yacht, and that the yacht was moving. The motion of the cradle was the smooth rolling of the vessel; the beat was the beat of its screw; the strange colours were the cloud tints thrown by the sun as it rose over a distant and receding shore in the wake of the yacht; her mother's lullaby was the crooned song of the man at the wheel. Nella all through her life had had many experiences of yachting. From the waters of the River Hudson to those bluer tides of the Mediterranean Sea, she had yachted in all seasons and all weathers. She loved the water, and now it seemed deliciously right and proper that she should be on the water again. She raised her head to look round, and then let it sink back: she was fatigued, enervated; she desired only solitude and calm; she had no care, no anxiety, no responsibility: a hundred years might have passed since her meeting with Miss Spencer, and the memory of that meeting appeared to have faded into the remotest background of her mind.

It was a small yacht, and her practised eye at once told that it belonged to the highest aristocracy of pleasure craft. As she reclined in the deck-chair (it did not occur to her at that moment to speculate as to the identity of the person who had led her therein) she examined all visible details of the vessel. The deck was as white and smooth as her own hand, and the seams ran along its length like blue veins. All the brass-work, from the band round the slender funnel to the concave surface of the binnacle, shone like gold.

The tapered masts stretched upwards at a rakish angle, and the rigging seemed like spun silk. No sails were set; the yacht was under steam, and doing about seven or eight knots. She judged that it was a boat of a hundred tons or so, probably Clyde-built, and not more than two or three years old.

No one was to be seen on deck except the man at the wheel: this man wore a blue jersey; but there was neither name nor initial on the jersey, nor was there a name on the white life-buoys lashed to the main rigging, nor on the polished dinghy which hung on the starboard davits. She called to the man, and called again, in a feeble voice, but the steerer took no notice of her, and continued his quiet song as though nothing else existed in the universe save the yacht, the sea, the sun, and himself.

Then her eyes swept the outline of the land from which they were hastening, and she could just distinguish a lighthouse and a great white irregular dome, which she recognized as the Kursaal at Ostend, that gorgeous rival of the gaming palace at Monte Carlo. So she was leaving Ostend. The rays of the sun fell on her caressingly, like a restorative. All around the water was changing from wonderful greys and dark blues to still more wonderful pinks and translucent unearthly greens; the magic kaleidoscope of dawn was going forward in its accustomed way, regardless of the vicissitudes of mortals.

Here and there in the distance she descried a sail--the brown sail of some Ostend fishing-boat returning home after a night's trawling. Then the beat of paddles caught her ear, and a steamer blundered past, wallowing clumsily among the waves like a tortoise. It was the Swallow from London. She could see some of its passengers leaning curiously over the aft-rail. A girl in a mackintosh signalled to her, and mechanically she answered the salute with her arm. The officer of the bridge of the Swallow hailed the yacht, but the man at the wheel offered no reply. In another minute the Swallow was nothing but a blot in the distance.

Nella tried to sit straight in the deck-chair, but she found herself unable to do so. Throwing off the rug which covered her, she discovered that she had been tied to the chair by means of a piece of broad webbing. Instantly she was alert, awake, angry; she knew that her perils were not over; she felt that possibly they had scarcely yet begun. Her lazy contentment, her dreamy sense of peace and repose, vanished utterly, and she steeled herself to meet the dangers of a grave and difficult situation.

Just at that moment a man came up from below. He was a man of forty or so, clad in irreproachable blue, with a peaked yachting cap. He raised the cap politely.

'Good morning,' he said. 'Beautiful sunrise, isn't it?' The clever and calculated insolence of his tone cut her like a lash as she lay bound in the chair. Like all people who have lived easy and joyous lives in those fair regions where gold smoothes every crease and law keeps a tight hand on disorder, she found it hard to realize that there were other regions where gold was useless and law without power. Twenty-four hours ago she would have declared it impossible that such an experience as she had suffered could happen to anyone; she would have talked airily about civilization and the nineteenth century, and progress and the police. But her experience was teaching her that human nature remains always the same, and that beneath the thin crust of security on which we good citizens exist the dark and secret forces of crime continue to move, just as they did in the days when you couldn't go from Cheapside to Chelsea without being set upon by thieves. Her experience was in a fair way to teach her this lesson better than she could have learnt it even in the bureaux of the detective police of Paris, London, and St Petersburg.

'Good morning,' the man repeated, and she glanced at him with a sullen, angry gaze.

'You!' she exclaimed, 'You, Mr Thomas Jackson, if that is your name! Loose me from this chair, and I will talk to you.' Her eyes flashed as she spoke, and the contempt in them added mightily to her beauty. Mr Thomas Jackson, otherwise Jules, erstwhile head waiter at the Grand Babylon, considered himself a connoisseur in feminine loveliness, and the vision of Nella Racksole smote him like an exquisite blow.

'With pleasure,' he replied. 'I had forgotten that to prevent you from falling I had secured you to the chair'; and with a quick movement he unfastened the band. Nella stood up, quivering with fiery annoyance and scorn.

'Now,' she said, fronting him, 'what is the meaning of this?'

'You fainted,' he replied imperturbably. 'Perhaps you don't remember.'

The man offered her a deck-chair with a characteristic gesture. Nella was obliged to acknowledge, in spite of herself, that the fellow had distinction, an air of breeding. No one would have guessed that for twenty years he had been an hotel waiter. His long, lithe figure, and easy, careless carriage seemed to be the figure and carriage of an aristocrat, and his voice was quiet, restrained, and authoritative.

'That has nothing to do with my being carried off in this yacht of yours.'

'It is not my yacht,' he said, 'but that is a minor detail. As to the more important matter, forgive me that I remind you that only a few hours ago you were threatening a lady in my house with a revolver.'

'Then it was your house?'

'Why not? May I not possess a house?' He smiled.

'I must request you to put the yacht about at once, instantly, and take me back.' She tried to speak firmly.

'Ah!' he said, 'I am afraid that's impossible. I didn't put out to sea with the intention of returning at once, instantly.' In the last words he gave a faint imitation of her tone.

'When I do get back,' she said, 'when my father gets to know of this affair, it will be an exceedingly bad day for you, Mr Jackson.'

'But supposing your father doesn't hear of it--'

'What?'

'Supposing you never get back?'

'Do you mean, then, to have my murder on your conscience?'

'Talking of murder,' he said, 'you came very near to murdering my friend, Miss Spencer. At least, so she tells me.'

'Is Miss Spencer on board?' Nella asked, seeing perhaps a faint ray of hope in the possible presence of a woman.

'Miss Spencer is not on board. There is no one on board except you and myself and a small crew--a very discreet crew, I may add.'

'I will have nothing more to say to you. You must take your own course.'

Thanks for the permission,' he said. 'I will send you up some breakfast.'

He went to the saloon stairs and whistled, and a Negro boy appeared with a tray of chocolate. Nella took it, and, without the slightest hesitation, threw it overboard. Mr Jackson walked away a few steps and then returned.

'You have spirit,' he said, 'and I admire spirit. It is a rare quality.'

She made no reply. 'Why did you mix yourself up in my affairs at all?' he went on. Again she made no reply, but the question set her thinking: why had she mixed herself up in this mysterious business? It was quite at variance with the usual methods of her gay and butterfly existence to meddle at all with serious things. Had she acted merely from a desire to see justice done and wickedness punished? Or was it the desire of adventure? Or was it, perhaps, the desire to be of service to His Serene Highness Prince Aribert? 'It is no fault of mine that you are in this fix,' Jules continued. 'I didn't bring you into it. You brought yourself into it. You and your father--you have been moving along at a pace which is rather too rapid.'

'That remains to be seen,' she put in coldly.

'It does,' he admitted. 'And I repeat that I can't help admiring you--that is, when you aren't interfering with my private affairs. That is a proceeding which I have never tolerated from anyone-- not even from a millionaire, nor even from a beautiful woman.' He bowed. 'I will tell you what I propose to do. I propose to escort you to a place of safety, and to keep you there till my operations are concluded, and the possibility of interference entirely removed. You spoke just now of murder. What a crude notion that was of yours! It is only the amateur who practises murder--'

'What about Reginald Dimmock?' she interjected quickly.

He paused gravely.

'Reginald Dimmock,' he repeated. 'I had imagined his was a case of heart disease. Let me send you up some more chocolate. I'm sure you're hungry.'

'I will starve before I touch your food,' she said.

'Gallant creature!' he murmured, and his eyes roved over her face. Her superb, supercilious beauty overcame him. 'Ah!' he said, 'what a wife you would make!' He approached nearer to her. 'You and I, Miss Racksole, your beauty and wealth and my brains--we could conquer the world. Few men are worthy of you, but I am one of the few. Listen! You might do worse. Marry me. I am a great man; I shall be greater. I adore you. Marry me, and I will save your life. All shall be well. I will begin again. The past shall be as though there had been no past.'

'This is somewhat sudden--Jules,' she said with biting contempt.

'Did you expect me to be conventional?' he retorted. 'I love you.'

'Granted,' she said, for the sake of the argument. 'Then what will occur to your present wife?'

'My present wife?'

'Yes, Miss Spencer, as she is called.'

'She told you I was her husband?'

'Incidentally she did.'

'She isn't.'

'Perhaps she isn't. But, nevertheless, I think I won't marry you.' Nella stood like a statue of scorn before him.

He went still nearer to her. 'Give me a kiss, then; one kiss--I won't ask for more; one kiss from those lips, and you shall go free. Men have ruined themselves for a kiss. I will.'

'Coward!' she ejaculated.

'Coward!' he repeated. 'Coward, am I? Then I'll be a coward, and you shall kiss me whether you will or not.'

He put a hand on her shoulder. As she shrank back from his lustrous eyes, with an involuntary scream, a figure sprang out of the dinghy a few feet away. With a single blow, neatly directed to Mr Jackson's ear, Mr Jackson was stretched senseless on the deck. Prince Aribert of Posen stood over him with a revolver. It was probably the greatest surprise of Mr Jackson's whole life.

'Don't be alarmed,' said the Prince to Nella, 'my being here is the simplest thing in the world, and I will explain it as soon as I have finished with this fellow.'

Nella could think of nothing to say, but she noticed the revolver in the Prince's hand.

'Why,' she remarked, 'that's my revolver.'

'It is,' he said, 'and I will explain that, too.'

The man at the wheel gave no heed whatever to the scene.

CHAPTER XI
THE COURT PAWNBROKER

'MR SAMPSON LEVI wishes to see you, sir.'

These words, spoken by a servant to Theodore Racksole, aroused the millionaire from a reverie which had been the reverse of pleasant. The fact was, and it is necessary to insist on it, that Mr Racksole, owner of the Grand Babylon Hotel, was by no means in a state of self-satisfaction. A mystery had attached itself to his hotel, and with all his acumen and knowledge of things in general he was unable to solve that mystery. He laughed at the fruitless efforts of the police, but he could not honestly say that his own efforts had been less barren. The public was talking, for, after all, the disappearance of poor Dimmock's body had got noised abroad in an indirect sort of way, and Theodore Racksole did not like the idea of his impeccable hotel being the subject of sinister rumours. He wondered, grimly, what the public and the Sunday newspapers would say if they were aware of all the other phenomena, not yet common property: of Miss Spencer's disappearance, of Jules' strange visits, and of the non-arrival of Prince Eugen of Posen. Theodore Racksole had worried his brain without result. He had conducted an elaborate private investigation without result, and he had spent a certain amount of money without result. The police said that they had a clue; but Racksole remarked that it was always the business of the police to have a clue, that they seldom had more than a clue, and that a clue without some sequel to it was a pretty stupid business. The only sure thing in the whole affair was that a cloud rested over his hotel, his beautiful new toy, the finest of its kind. The cloud was not interfering with business, but, nevertheless, it was a cloud, and he fiercely resented its presence; perhaps it would be more correct to say that he fiercely resented his inability to dissipate it.

'Mr Sampson Levi wishes to see you, sir,' the servant repeated, having received no sign that his master had heard him.

'So I hear,' said Racksole. 'Does he want to see me, personally?'

'He asked for you, sir.'

'Perhaps it is Rocco he wants to see, about a menu or something of that kind?'

'I will inquire, sir,' and the servant made a move to withdraw.

'Stop,' Racksole commanded suddenly. 'Desire Mr Sampson Levi to step this way.'

The great stockbroker of the 'Kaffir Circus' entered with a simple unassuming air. He was a rather short, florid man, dressed like a typical Hebraic financier, with too much watch-chain and too little waistcoat. In his fat hand he held a gold-headed cane, and an absolutely new silk hat--for it was Friday, and Mr Levi purchased a new hat every Friday of his life, holiday times only excepted. He breathed heavily and sniffed through his nose a good deal, as though he had just performed some Herculean physical labour. He glanced at the American millionaire with an expression in which a slight embarrassment might have been detected, but at the same time his round, red face disclosed a certain frank admiration and good nature.

'Mr Racksole, I believe--Mr Theodore Racksole. Proud to meet you, sir.'

Such were the first words of Mr Sampson Levi. In form they were the greeting of a third-rate chimney-sweep, but, strangely enough, Theodore Racksole liked their tone. He said to himself that here, precisely where no one would have expected to find one, was an honest man.

'Good day,' said Racksole briefly. 'To what do I owe the pleasure--'

'I expect your time is limited,' answered Sampson Levi. 'Anyhow, mine is, and so I'll come straight to the point, Mr Racksole. I'm a plain man. I don't pretend to be a gentleman or any nonsense of that kind. I'm a stockbroker, that's what I am, and I don't care who knows it. The other night I had a ball in this hotel. It cost me a couple of thousand and odd pounds, and, by the way, I wrote out a cheque for your bill this morning. I don't like balls, but they're useful to me, and my little wife likes 'em, and so we give 'em. Now, I've nothing to say against the hotel management as regards that ball: it was very decently done, very decently, but what I want to know is this--Why did you have a private detective among my guests?'

'A private detective?' exclaimed Racksole, somewhat surprised at this charge.

'Yes,' Mr Sampson Levi said firmly, fanning himself in his chair, and gazing at Theodore Racksole with the direct earnest expression of a man having a grievance. 'Yes; a private detective. It's a small matter, I know, and I dare say you think you've got a right, as proprietor of the show, to do what you like in that line; but I've just called to tell you that I object. I've called as a matter of principle. I'm not angry; it's the principle of the thing.'

'My dear Mr Levi,' said Racksole, 'I assure you that, having let the Gold Room to a private individual for a private entertainment, I should never dream of doing what you suggest.'

'Straight?' asked Mr Sampson Levi, using his own picturesque language.

'Straight,' said Racksole smiling.

'There was a gent present at my ball that I didn't ask. I've got a wonderful memory for faces, and I know. Several fellows asked me afterwards what he was doing there. I was told by someone that he was one of your waiters, but I didn't believe that. I know nothing of the Grand Babylon; it's not quite my style of tavern, but I don't think you'd send one of your own waiters to watch my guests--unless, of course, you sent him as a waiter; and this chap didn't do any waiting, though he did his share of drinking.'

'Perhaps I can throw some light on this mystery,' said Racksole. 'I may tell you that I was already aware that man had attended your ball uninvited.'

'How did you get to know?'

'By pure chance, Mr Levi, and not by inquiry. That man was a former waiter at this hotel--the head waiter, in fact--Jules. No doubt you have heard of him.'

'Not I,' said Mr Levi positively.

'Ah!' said Racksole, 'I was informed that everyone knew Jules, but it appears not. Well, be that as it may, previously to the night of your ball, I had dismissed Jules. I had ordered him never to enter the Babylon again. But on that evening I encountered him here--not in the Gold Room, but in the hotel itself. I asked him to explain his presence, and he stated he was your guest. That is all I know of the matter, Mr Levi, and I am extremely sorry that you should have thought me capable of the enormity of placing a private detective among your guests.'

'This is perfectly satisfactory to me,' Mr Sampson Levi said, after a pause.

'I only wanted an explanation, and I've got it. I was told by some pals of mine in the City I might rely on Mr Theodore Racksole going straight to the point, and I'm glad they were right. Now as to that feller Jules, I shall make my own inquiries as to him. Might I ask you why you dismissed him?'

'I don't know why I dismissed him.'

'You don't know? Oh! come now! I'm only asking because I thought you might be able to give me a hint why he turned up uninvited at my ball. Sorry if I'm too inquisitive.'

'Not at all, Mr Levi; but I really don't know. I only sort of felt that he was a suspicious character. I dismissed him on instinct, as it were. See?'

Without answering this question Mr Levi asked another. 'If this Jules is such a well-known person,' he said, 'how could the feller hope to come to my ball without being recognized?'

'Give it up,' said Racksole promptly.

'Well, I'll be moving on,' was Mr Sampson Levi's next remark. 'Good day, and thank ye. I suppose you aren't doing anything in Kaffirs?'

Mr Racksole smiled a negative.

'I thought not,' said Levi. Well, I never touch American rails myself, and so I reckon we sha'n't come across each other. Good day.'

'Good day,' said Racksole politely, following Mr Sampson Levi to the door.

With his hand on the handle of the door, Mr Levi stopped, and, gazing at Theodore Racksole with a shrewd, quizzical expression, remarked:

'Strange things been going on here lately, eh?'

The two men looked very hard at each other for several seconds.

'Yes,' Racksole assented. 'Know anything about them?'

'Well--no, not exactly,' said Mr Levi. 'But I had a fancy you and I might be useful to each other; I had a kind of fancy to that effect.'

'Come back and sit down again, Mr Levi,' Racksole said, attracted by the evident straightforwardness of the man's tone. 'Now, how can we be of service to each other? I flatter myself I'm something of a judge of character, especially financial character, and I tell you--if you'll put your cards on the table, I'll do ditto with mine.'

'Agreed,' said Mr Sampson Levi. 'I'll begin by explaining my interest in your hotel. I have been expecting to receive a summons from a certain Prince Eugen of Posen to attend him here, and that summons hasn't arrived. It appears that Prince Eugen hasn't come to London at all. Now, I could have taken my dying davy that he would have been here yesterday at the latest.'

'Why were you so sure?'

'Question for question,' said Levi. 'Let's clear the ground first, Mr Racksole. Why did you buy this hotel? That's a conundrum that's been puzzling a lot of our fellows in the City for some days past. Why did you buy the Grand Babylon? And what is the next move to be?'

'There is no next move,' answered Racksole candidly, 'and I will tell you why I bought the hotel; there need be no secret about it. I bought it because of a whim.' And then Theodore Racksole gave this little Jew, whom he had begun to respect, a faithful account of the transaction with Mr Felix Babylon. 'I suppose,' he added, 'you find a difficulty in appreciating my state of mind when I did the deal.'

'Not a bit,' said Mr Levi. 'I once bought an electric launch on the Thames in a very similar way, and it turned out to be one of the most satisfactory purchases I ever made. Then it's a simple accident that you own this hotel at the present moment?'

'A simple accident--all because of a beefsteak and a bottle of Bass.'

'Um!' grunted Mr Sampson Levi, stroking his triple chin.

'To return to Prince Eugen,' Racksole resumed. 'I was expecting His Highness here. The State apartments had been prepared for him. He was due on the very afternoon that young Dimmock died. But he never came, and I have not heard why he has failed to arrive; nor have I seen his name in the papers. What his business was in London, I don't know.'

'I will tell you,' said Mr Sampson Levi, 'he was coming to arrange a loan.'

'A State loan?'

'No--a private loan.'

'Whom from?'

'From me, Sampson Levi. You look surprised. If you'd lived in London a little longer, you'd know that I was just the person the Prince would come to. Perhaps you aren't aware that down Throgmorton Street way I'm called "The Court Pawnbroker", because I arrange loans for the minor, second-class Princes of Europe. I'm a stockbroker, but my real business is financing some of the little Courts of Europe. Now, I may tell you that the Hereditary Prince of Posen particularly wanted a million, and he wanted it by a certain date, and he knew that if the affair wasn't fixed up by a certain time here he wouldn't be able to get it by that certain date. That's why I'm surprised he isn't in London.'

'What did he need a million for?'

'Debts,' answered Sampson Levi laconically.

'His own?'

'Certainly.'

'But he isn't thirty years of age?'

'What of that? He isn't the only European Prince who has run up a million of debts in a dozen years. To a Prince the thing is as easy as eating a sandwich.'

'And why has he taken this sudden resolution to liquidate them?'

'Because the Emperor and the lady's parents won't let him marry till he has done so! And quite right, too! He's got to show a clean sheet, or the Princess Anna of Eckstein-Schwartzburg will never be Princess of Posen. Even now the Emperor has no idea how much Prince Eugen's debts amount to. If he had--!'

'But would not the Emperor know of this proposed loan?'

'Not necessarily at once. It could be so managed. Twig?' Mr Sampson Levi laughed. 'I've carried these little affairs through before. After marriage it might be allowed to leak out. And you know the Princess Anna's fortune is pretty big! Now, Mr Racksole,' he added, abruptly changing his tone, 'where do you suppose Prince Eugen has disappeared to? Because if he doesn't turn up to-day he can't have that million. To-day is the last day. To-morrow the money will be appropriated, elsewhere. Of course, I'm not alone in this business, and my friends have something to say.'

'You ask me where I think Prince Eugen has disappeared to?'

'I do.'

'Then you think it's a disappearance?'

Sampson Levi nodded. 'Putting two and two together,' he said, 'I do. The Dimmock business is very peculiar--very peculiar, indeed. Dimmock was a left-handed relation of the Posen family. Twig? Scarcely anyone knows that. He was made secretary and companion to Prince Aribert, just to keep him in the domestic circle. His mother was an Irishwoman, whose misfortune was that she was too beautiful. Twig?' (Mr Sampson Levi always used this extraordinary word when he was in a communicative mood.) 'My belief is that Dimmock's death has something to do with the disappearance of Prince Eugen. The only thing that passes me is this: Why should anyone want to make Prince Eugen disappear? The poor little Prince hasn't an enemy in the world. If he's been "copped", as they say, why has he been "copped"? It won't do anyone any good.'

'Won't it?' repeated Racksole, with a sudden flash.

'What do you mean?' asked Mr Levi.

'I mean this: Suppose some other European pauper Prince was anxious to marry Princess Anna and her fortune, wouldn't that Prince have an interest in stopping this loan of yours to Prince Eugen? Wouldn't he have an interest in causing Prince Eugen to disappear--at any rate, for a time?'

Sampson Levi thought hard for a few moments.

'Mr Theodore Racksole,' he said at length, 'I do believe you have hit on something.'

ON the afternoon of the same day--the interview just described had occurred in the morning--Racksole was visited by another idea, and he said to himself that he ought to have thought of it before. The conversation with Mr Sampson Levi had continued for a considerable time, and the two men had exchanged various notions, and agreed to meet again, but the theory that Reginald Dimmock had probably been a traitor to his family--a traitor whose repentance had caused his death--had not been thoroughly discussed; the talk had tended rather to Continental politics, with a view to discovering what princely family might have an interest in the temporary disappearance of Prince Eugen. Now, as Racksole considered in detail the particular affair of Reginald Dimmock, deceased, he was struck by one point especially, to wit: Why had Dimmock and Jules manoeuvred to turn Nella Racksole out of Room No. 111 on that first night? That they had so manoeuvred, that the broken window-pane was not a mere accident, Racksole felt perfectly sure. He had felt perfectly sure all along; but the significance of the facts had not struck him. It was plain to him now that there must be something of extraordinary and peculiar importance about Room No. 111. After lunch he wandered quietly upstairs and looked at Room No. 111; that is to say, he looked at the outside of it; it happened to be occupied, but the guest was leaving that evening. The thought crossed his mind that there could be no object in gazing blankly at the outside of a room; yet he gazed; then he wandered quickly down again to the next floor, and in passing along the corridor of that floor he stopped, and with an involuntary gesture stamped his foot.

'Great Scott!' he said, 'I've got hold of something--No. 111 is exactly over the State apartments.'

He went to the bureau, and issued instructions that No. 111 was not to be re-let to anyone until further orders. At the bureau they gave him Nella's note, which ran thus:

Dearest Papa,--I am going away for a day or two on the trail of a due.

If I'm not back in three days, begin to inquire for me at Ostend. Till then leave me alone.--Your sagacious daughter, NELL.

These few words, in Nella's large scrawling hand, filled one side of the paper. At the bottom was a P.T.O. He turned over, and read the sentence, underlined, 'P.S.--Keep an eye on Rocco.'

'I wonder what the little creature is up to?' he murmured, as he tore the letter into small fragments, and threw them into the waste-paper basket.

Then, without any delay, he took the lift down to the basement, with the object of making a preliminary inspection of Rocco in his lair. He could scarcely bring himself to believe that this suave and stately gentleman, this enthusiast of gastronomy, was concerned in the machinations of Jules and other rascals unknown. Nevertheless, from habit, he obeyed his daughter, giving her credit for a certain amount of perspicuity and cleverness.

The kitchens of the Grand Babylon Hotel are one of the wonders of Europe.

Only three years before the events now under narration Felix Babylon had had them newly installed with every device and patent that the ingenuity of two continents could supply. They covered nearly an acre of superficial space.

They were walled and floored from end to end with tiles and marble, which enabled them to be washed down every morning like the deck of a man-of-war.

Visitors were sometimes taken to see the potato-paring machine, the patent plate-dryer, the Babylon-spit (a contrivance of Felix Babylon's own), the silver-grill, the system of connected stock-pots, and other amazing phenomena of the department. Sometimes, if they were fortunate, they might also see the artist who sculptured ice into forms of men and beasts for table ornaments, or the first napkin-folder in London, or the man who daily invented fresh designs for pastry and blancmanges. Twelve chefs pursued their labours in those kitchens, helped by ninety assistant chefs, and a further army of unconsidered menials. Over all these was Rocco, supreme and unapproachable. Half-way along the suite of kitchens, Rocco had an apartment of his own, wherein he thought out those magnificent combinations, those marvellous feats of succulence and originality, which had given him his fame. Visitors never caught a glimpse of Rocco in the kitchens, though sometimes, on a special night, he would stroll nonchalantly through the dining-room, like the great man he was, to receive the compliments of the hotel habitués--people of insight who recognized his uniqueness.

Theodore Racksole's sudden and unusual appearance in the kitchen caused a little stir. He nodded to some of the chefs, but said nothing to anyone, merely wandering about amid the maze of copper utensils, and white-capped workers. At length he saw Rocco, surrounded by several admiring chefs. Rocco was bending over a freshly-roasted partridge which lay on a blue dish. He plunged a long fork into the back of the bird, and raised it in the air with his left hand. In his right he held a long glittering carving-knife. He was giving one of his world-famous exhibitions of carving. In four swift, unerring, delicate, perfect strokes he cleanly severed the limbs of the partridge. It was a wonderful achievement--how wondrous none but the really skilful carver can properly appreciate. The chefs emitted a hum of applause, and Rocco, long, lean, and graceful, retired to his own apartment. Racksole followed him. Rocco sat in a chair, one hand over his eyes; he had not noticed Theodore Racksole.

'What are you doing, M. Rocco?' the millionaire asked smiling. 'Ah!' exclaimed Rocco, starting up with an apology. 'Pardon! I was inventing a new mayonnaise, which I shall need for a certain menu next week.'

'Do you invent these things without materials, then?' questioned Racksole.

'Certainly. I do dem in my mind. I tink dem. Why should I want materials? I know all flavours. I tink, and tink, and tink, and it is done. I write down. I give the recipe to my best chef-- dere you are. I need not even taste, I know how it will taste. It is like composing music. De great composers do not compose at de piano.'

'I see,' said Racksole.

'It is because I work like dat dat you pay me three thousand a year,' Rocco added gravely.

'Heard about Jules?' said Racksole abruptly.

'Jules?'

'Yes. He's been arrested in Ostend,' the millionaire continued, lying cleverly at a venture. 'They say that he and

several others are implicated in a murder case--the murder of
Reginald Dimmock.'

'Truly?' drawled Rocco, scarcely hiding a yawn. His
indifference was so superb, so gorgeous, that Racksole instantly
divined that it was assumed for the occasion.

'It seems that, after all, the police are good for something.
But this is the first time I ever knew them to be worth their salt.
There is to be a thorough and systematic search of the hotel to-
morrow,' Racksole went on. 'I have mentioned it to you to warn
you that so far as you are concerned the search is of course
merely a matter of form. You will not object to the detectives
looking through your rooms?'

'Certainly not,' and Rocco shrugged his shoulders.

'I shall ask you to say nothing about this to anyone,' said
Racksole. 'The news of Jules' arrest is quite private to myself.
The papers know nothing of it. You comprehend?'

Rocco smiled in his grand manner, and Rocco's master
thereupon went away.

Racksole was very well satisfied with the little conversation.
It was perhaps dangerous to tell a series of mere lies to a clever
fellow like Rocco, and Racksole wondered how he should
ultimately explain them to this great master-chef if his and
Nella's suspicions should be unfounded, and nothing came of
them. Nevertheless, Rocco's manner, a strange elusive
something in the man's eyes, had nearly convinced Racksole that
he was somehow implicated in Jules' schemes--and probably in
the death of Reginald Dimmock and the disappearance of Prince
Eugen of Posen.

That night, or rather about half-past one the next morning,
when the last noises of the hotel's life had died down, Racksole
made his way to Room 111 on the second floor. He locked the
door on the inside, and proceeded to examine the place, square
foot by square foot. Every now and then some creak or other
sound startled him, and he listened intently for a few seconds.
The bedroom was furnished in the ordinary splendid style of
bedrooms at the Grand Babylon Hotel, and in that respect called
for no remark. What most interested Racksole was the flooring.
He pulled up the thick Oriental carpet, and peered along every
plank, but could discover nothing unusual.

Then he went to the dressing-room, and finally to the bathroom, both of which opened out of the main room. But in neither of these smaller chambers was he any more successful than in the bedroom itself. Finally he came to the bath, which was enclosed in a panelled casing of polished wood, after the manner of baths. Some baths have a cupboard beneath the taps, with a door at the side, but this one appeared to have none. He tapped the panels, but not a single one of them gave forth that 'curious hollow sound' which usually betokens a secret place. Idly he turned the cold-tap of the bath, and the water began to rush in. He turned off the cold-tap and turned on the waste-tap, and as he did so his knee, which was pressing against the panelling, slipped forward. The panelling had given way, and he saw that one large panel was hinged from the inside, and caught with a hasp, also on the inside. A large space within the casing of the end of the bath was thus revealed. Before doing anything else, Racksole tried to repeat the trick with the waste-tap, but he failed; it would not work again, nor could he in any way perceive that there was any connection between the rod of the waste-tap and the hasp of the panel. Racksole could not see into the cavity within the casing, and the electric light was fixed, and could not be moved about like a candle. He felt in his pockets, and fortunately discovered a box of matches. Aided by these, he looked into the cavity, and saw nothing; nothing except a rather large hole at the far end--some three feet from the casing. With some difficulty he squeezed himself through the open panel, and took a half-kneeling, half-sitting posture within. There he struck a match, and it was a most unfortunate thing that in striking, the box being half open, he set fire to all the matches, and was half smothered in the atrocious stink of phosphorus which resulted. One match burned clear on the floor of the cavity, and, rubbing his eyes, Racksole picked it up, and looked down the hole which he had previously descried. It was a hole apparently bottomless, and about eighteen inches square. The curious part about the hole was that a rope-ladder hung down it. When he saw that rope-ladder Racksole smiled the smile of a happy man.

The match went out.

Should he make a long journey, perhaps to some distant corner of the hotel, for a fresh box of matches, or should he attempt to descend that rope-ladder in the dark? He decided on the latter course, and he was the more strongly moved thereto as he could now distinguish a faint, a very faint tinge of light at the bottom of the hole.

With infinite care he compressed himself into the well-like hole, and descended the latter. At length he arrived on firm ground, perspiring, but quite safe and quite excited. He saw now that the tinge of light came through a small hole in the wood. He put his eye to the wood, and found that he had a fine view of the State bathroom, and through the door of the State bathroom into the State bedroom. At the massive marble-topped washstand in the State bedroom a man was visible, bending over some object which lay thereon.

The man was Rocco!

CHAPTER XIII
IN THE STATE BEDROOM

IT was of course plain to Racksole that the peculiar passageway which he had, at great personal inconvenience, discovered between the bathroom of No. 111 and the State bathroom on the floor below must have been specially designed by some person or persons for the purpose of keeping a nefarious watch upon the occupants of the State suite of apartments. It was a means of communication at once simple and ingenious. At that moment he could not be sure of the precise method employed for it, but he surmised that the casing of the waterpipes had been used as a 'well', while space for the pipes themselves had been found in the thickness of the ample brick walls of the Grand Babylon. The eye-hole, through which he now had a view of the bedroom, was a very minute one, and probably would scarcely be noticed from the exterior. One thing he observed concerning it, namely, that it had been made for a man somewhat taller than himself; he was obliged to stand on tiptoe in order to get his eye in the correct position. He remembered that both Jules and Rocco were distinctly above the average height; also that they were both thin men, and could have descended the well with comparative ease. Theodore Racksole, though not stout, was a well-set man with large bones.

These things flashed through his mind as he gazed, spellbound, at the mysterious movements of Rocco. The door between the bathroom and the bedroom was wide open, and his own situation was such that his view embraced a considerable portion of the bedroom, including the whole of the immense and gorgeously-upholstered bedstead, but not including the whole of the marble washstand. He could see only half of the washstand, and at intervals Rocco passed out of sight as his lithe hands moved over the object which lay on the marble. At first Theodore Racksole could not decide what this object was, but after a time, as his eyes grew accustomed to the position and the light, he made it out.

It was the body of a man. Or, rather, to be more exact, Racksole could discern the legs of a man on that half of the table which was visible to him. Involuntarily he shuddered, as the conviction forced itself upon him that Rocco had some unconscious human being helpless on that cold marble surface. The legs never moved. Therefore, the hapless creature was either asleep or under the influence of an anaesthetic--or (horrible thought!) dead.

Racksole wanted to call out, to stop by some means or other the dreadful midnight activity which was proceeding before his astonished eyes; but fortunately he restrained himself.

On the washstand he could see certain strangely-shaped utensils and instruments which Rocco used from time to time. The work seemed to Racksole to continue for interminable hours, and then at last Rocco ceased, gave a sign of satisfaction, whistled several bars from 'Cavalleria Rusticana', and came into the bath-room, where he took off his coat, and very quietly washed his hands. As he stood calmly and leisurely wiping those long fingers of his, he was less than four feet from Racksole, and the cooped-up millionaire trembled, holding his breath, lest Rocco should detect his presence behind the woodwork. But nothing happened, and Rocco returned unsuspectingly to the bedroom. Racksole saw him place some sort of white flannel garment over the prone form on the table, and then lift it bodily on to the great bed, where it lay awfully still. The hidden watcher was sure now that it was a corpse upon which Rocco had been exercising his mysterious and sinister functions.

But whose corpse? And what functions? Could this be a West End hotel, Racksole's own hotel, in the very heart of London, the best-policed city in the world? It seemed incredible, impossible; yet so it was. Once more he remembered what Felix Babylon had said to him and realized the truth of the saying anew. The proprietor of a vast and complicated establishment like the Grand Babylon could never know a tithe of the extraordinary and queer occurrences which happened daily under his very nose; the atmosphere of such a caravanserai must necessarily be an atmosphere of mystery and problems apparently inexplicable. Nevertheless, Racksole thought that Fate was carrying things with rather a high hand when she permitted his chef to spend the night hours over a man's corpse in his State bedroom, this sacred apartment which was supposed to be occupied only by individuals of Royal Blood. Racksole would not have objected to a certain amount of mystery, but he decidedly thought that there was a little too much mystery here for his taste. He thought that even Felix Babylon would have been surprised at this.

The electric chandelier in the centre of the ceiling was not lighted; only the two lights on either side of the washstand were switched on, and these did not sufficiently illuminate the features of the man on the bed to enable Racksole to see them clearly. In vain the millionaire strained his eyes; he could only make out that the corpse was probably that of a young man. Just as he was wondering what would be the best course of action to pursue, he saw Rocco with a square-shaped black box in his hand. Then the chef switched off the two electric lights, and the State bedroom was in darkness. In that swift darkness Racksole heard Rocco spring on to the bed. Another half-dozen moments of suspense, and there was a blinding flash of white, which endured for several seconds, and showed Rocco standing like an evil spirit over the corpse, the black box in one hand and a burning piece of aluminium wire in the other. The aluminium wire burnt out, and darkness followed blacker than before.

Rocco had photographed the corpse by flashlight.

But the dazzling flare which had disclosed the features of the dead man to the insensible lens of the camera had disclosed them also to Theodore Racksole. The dead man was Reginald Dimmock!

Stung into action by this discovery, Racksole tried to find the exit from his place of concealment. He felt sure that there existed some way out into the State bathroom, but he sought for it fruitlessly, groping with both hands and feet. Then he decided that he must ascend the rope-ladder, make haste for the first-floor corridor, and intercept Rocco when he left the State apartments. It was a painful and difficult business to ascend that thin and yielding ladder in such a confined space, but Racksole was managing it very nicely, and had nearly reached the top, when, by some untoward freak of chance, the ladder broke above his weight, and he slipped ignominiously down to the bottom of the wooden tube. Smothering an excusable curse, Racksole crouched, baffled. Then he saw that the force of his fall had somehow opened a trap-door at his feet. He squeezed through, pushed open another tiny door, and in another second stood in the State bathroom. He was dishevelled, perspiring, rather bewildered; but he was there. In the next second he had resumed absolute command of all his faculties.

Strange to say, he had moved so quietly that Rocco had apparently not heard him. He stepped noiselessly to the door between the bathroom and the bedroom, and stood there in silence. Rocco had switched on again the lights over the washstand and was busy with his utensils.

Racksole deliberately coughed.

ROCCO turned round with the swiftness of a startled tiger, and gave Theodore Racksole one long piercing glance.

'D--n!' said Rocco, with as pure an Anglo-Saxon accent and intonation as Racksole himself could have accomplished.

The most extraordinary thing about the situation was that at this juncture Theodore Racksole did not know what to say. He was so dumbfounded by the affair, and especially by Rocco's absolute and sublime calm, that both speech and thought failed him.

'I give in,' said Rocco. 'From the moment you entered this cursed hotel I was afraid of you. I told Jules I was afraid of you. I knew there would be trouble with a man of your kidney, and I was right; confound it! I tell you I give in. I know when I'm beaten. I've got no revolver and no weapons of any kind. I surrender. Do what you like.'

And with that Rocco sat down on a chair. It was magnificently done. Only a truly great man could have done it. Rocco actually kept his dignity.

For answer, Racksole walked slowly into the vast apartment, seized a chair, and, dragging it up to Rocco's chair, sat down opposite to him. Thus they faced each other, their knees almost touching, both in evening dress. On Rocco's right hand was the bed, with the corpse of Reginald Dimmock. On Racksole's right hand, and a little behind him, was the marble washstand, still littered with Rocco's implements. The electric light shone on Rocco's left cheek, leaving the other side of his face in shadow. Racksole tapped him on the knee twice.

'So you're another Englishman masquerading as a foreigner in my hotel,'

Racksole remarked, by way of commencing the interrogation.

'I'm not,' answered Rocco quietly. 'I'm a citizen of the United States.'

'The deuce you are!' Racksole exclaimed.

'Yes, I was born at West Orange, New Jersey, New York State. I call myself an Italian because it was in Italy that I first made a name as a chef--at Rome. It is better for a great chef like me to be a foreigner. Imagine a great chef named Elihu P.

Rucker. You can't imagine it. I changed my nationality for the same reason that my friend and colleague, Jules, otherwise Mr Jackson, changed his.'

'So Jules is your friend and colleague, is he?'

'He was, but from this moment he is no longer. I began to disapprove of his methods no less than a week ago, and my disapproval will now take active form.'

'Will it?' said Racksole. 'I calculate it just won't, Mr Elihu P. Rucker, citizen of the United States. Before you are very much older you'll be in the kind hands of the police, and your activities, in no matter what direction, will come to an abrupt conclusion.'

'It is possible,' sighed Rocco.

'In the meantime, I'll ask you one or two questions for my own private satisfaction. You've acknowledged that the game is up, and you may as well answer them with as much candour as you feel yourself capable of. See?'

'I see,' replied Rocco calmly, 'but I guess I can't answer all questions.

I'll do what I can.'

'Well,' said Racksole, clearing his throat, 'what's the scheme all about? Tell me in a word.'

'Not in a thousand words. It isn't my secret, you know.'

'Why was poor little Dimmock poisoned?' The millionaire's voice softened as he looked for an instant at the corpse of the unfortunate young man.

'I don't know,' said Rocco. 'I don't mind informing you that I objected to that part of the business. I wasn't made aware of it till after it was done, and then I tell you it got my dander up considerable.'

'You mean to say you don't know why Dimmock was done to death?'

'I mean to say I couldn't see the sense of it. Of course he--er-- died, because he sort of cried off the scheme, having previously taken a share of it. I don't mind saying that much, because you probably guessed it for yourself. But I solemnly state that I have a conscientious objection to murder.'

'Then it was murder?'

'It was a kind of murder,' Rocco admitted. Who did it?'

'Unfair question,' said Rocco.

'Who else is in this precious scheme besides Jules and yourself?'

'Don't know, on my honour.'

'Well, then, tell me this. What have you been doing to Dimmock's body?'

'How long were you in that bathroom?' Rocco parried with sublime impudence.

'Don't question me, Mr Rucker,' said Theodore Racksole. 'I feel very much inclined to break your back across my knee. Therefore I advise you not to irritate me. What have you been doing to Dimmock's body?'

'I've been embalming it.'

'Em--balming it.'

'Certainly; Richardson's system of arterial fluid injection, as improved by myself. You weren't aware that I included the art of embalming among my accomplishments. Nevertheless, it is so.'

'But why?' asked Racksole, more mystified than ever. 'Why should you trouble to embalm the poor chap's corpse?'

'Can't you see? Doesn't it strike you? That corpse has to be taken care of. It contains, or rather, it did contain, very serious evidence against some person or persons unknown to the police. It may be necessary to move it about from place to place. A corpse can't be hidden for long; a corpse betrays itself. One couldn't throw it in the Thames, for it would have been found inside twelve hours. One couldn't bury it--it wasn't safe. The only thing was to keep it handy and movable, ready for emergencies. I needn't inform you that, without embalming, you can't keep a corpse handy and movable for more than four or five days. It's the kind of thing that won't keep. And so it was suggested that I should embalm it, and I did. Mind you, I still objected to the murder, but I couldn't go back on a colleague, you understand. You do understand that, don't you? Well, here you are, and here it is, and that's all.'

Rocco leaned back in his chair as though he had said everything that ought to be said. He closed his eyes to indicate that so far as he was concerned the conversation was also closed. Theodore Racksole stood up.

'I hope,' said Rocco, suddenly opening his eyes, 'I hope you'll call in the police without any delay. It's getting late, and I don't like going without my night's rest.'

'Where do you suppose you'll get a night's rest?' Racksole asked.

'In the cells, of course. Haven't I told you I know when I'm beaten. I'm not so blind as not to be able to see that there's at any rate a prima facie case against me. I expect I shall get off with a year or two's imprisonment as accessory after the fact--I think that's what they call it. Anyhow, I shall be in a position to prove that I am not implicated in the murder of this unfortunate nincompoop.' He pointed, with a strange, scornful gesture of his elbow, to the bed. 'And now, shall we go? Everyone is asleep, but there will be a policeman within call of the watchman in the portico. I am at your service. Let us go down together, Mr Racksole. I give you my word to go quietly.'

'Stay a moment,' said Theodore Racksole curtly; 'there is no hurry. It won't do you any harm to forego another hour's sleep, especially as you will have no work to do to-morrow. I have one or two more questions to put to you.'

'Well?' Rocco murmured, with an air of tired resignation, as if to say, 'What must be must be.'

'Where has Dimmock's corpse been during the last three or four days, since he--died?'

'Oh!' answered Rocco, apparently surprised at the simplicity of the question. 'It's been in my room, and one night it was on the roof; once it went out of the hotel as luggage, but it came back the next day as a case of Demerara sugar. I forgot where else it has been, but it's been kept perfectly safe and treated with every consideration.'

'And who contrived all these manoeuvres?' asked Racksole as calmly as he could.

'I did. That is to say, I invented them and I saw that they were carried out. You see, the suspicions of your police obliged me to be particularly spry.'

'And who carried them out?'

'Ah! that would be telling tales. But I don't mind assuring you that my accomplices were innocent accomplices. It is absurdly easy for a man like me to impose on underlings--absurdly easy.'

'What did you intend to do with the corpse ultimately?' Racksole pursued his inquiry with immovable countenance.

'Who knows?' said Rocco, twisting his beautiful moustache. 'That would have depended on several things--on your police, for instance. But probably in the end we should have restored this mortal clay'--again he jerked his elbow--'to the man's sorrowing relatives.'

'Do you know who the relatives are?'

'Certainly. Don't you? If you don't I need only hint that Dimmock had a Prince for his father.'

'It seems to me,' said Racksole, with cold sarcasm, 'that you behaved rather clumsily in choosing this bedroom as the scene of your operations.'

'Not at all,' said Rocco. 'There was no other apartment so suitable in the whole hotel. Who would have guessed that anything was going on here? It was the very place for me.'

'I guessed,' said Racksole succinctly.

'Yes, you guessed, Mr Racksole. But I had not counted on you. You are the only smart man in the business. You are an American citizen, and I hadn't reckoned to have to deal with that class of person.'

'Apparently I frightened you this afternoon?'

'Not in the least.'

'You were not afraid of a search?'

'I knew that no search was intended. I knew that you were trying to frighten me. You must really credit me with a little sagacity and insight, Mr Racksole. Immediately you began to talk to me in the kitchen this afternoon I felt you were on the track. But I was not frightened. I merely decided that there was no time to be lost--that I must act quickly. I did act quickly, but, it seems, not quickly enough. I grant that your rapidity exceeded mine. Let us go downstairs, I beg.'

Rocco rose and moved towards the door. With an instinctive action Racksole rushed forward and seized him by the shoulder.

'No tricks!' said Racksole. 'You're in my custody and don't forget it.'

Rocco turned on his employer a look of gentle, dignified scorn. 'Have I not informed you,' he said, 'that I have the intention of going quietly?'

Racksole felt almost ashamed for the moment. It flashed across him that a man can be great, even in crime.

'What an ineffable fool you were,' said Racksole, stopping him at the threshold, 'with your talents, your unique talents, to get yourself mixed up in an affair of this kind. You are ruined. And, by Jove! you were a great man in your own line.'

'Mr Racksole,' said Rocco very quickly, 'that is the truest word you have spoken this night. I was a great man in my own line. And I am an ineffable fool. Alas!' He brought his long arms to his sides with a thud.

'Why did you do it?'

'I was fascinated--fascinated by Jules. He, too, is a great man. We had great opportunities, here in the Grand Babylon. It was a great game. It was worth the candle. The prizes were enormous. You would admit these things if you knew the facts. Perhaps some day you will know them, for you are a fairly clever person at getting to the root of a matter. Yes, I was blinded, hypnotized.'

'And now you are ruined.'

'Not ruined, not ruined. Afterwards, in a few years, I shall come up again. A man of genius like me is never ruined till he is dead. Genius is always forgiven. I shall be forgiven. Suppose I am sent to prison. When I emerge I shall be no gaol-bird. I shall be Rocco--the great Rocco. And half the hotels in Europe will invite me to join them.'

'Let me tell you, as man to man, that you have achieved your own degradation. There is no excuse.'

'I know it,' said Rocco. 'Let us go.'

Racksole was distinctly and notably impressed by this man-- by this master spirit to whom he was to have paid a salary at the rate of three thousand pounds a year. He even felt sorry for him. And so, side by side, the captor and the captured, they passed into the vast deserted corridor of the hotel.

Rocco stopped at the grating of the first lift.

'It will be locked,' said Racksole. 'We must use the stairs to-night.'

'But I have a key. I always carry one,' said Rocco, and he pulled one out of his pocket, and, unfastening the iron screen, pushed it open. Racksole smiled at his readiness and aplomb.

'After you,' said Rocco, bowing in his finest manner, and Racksole stepped into the lift.

With the swiftness of lighting Rocco pushed forward the iron screen, which locked itself automatically. Theodore Racksole was hopelessly a prisoner within the lift, while Rocco stood free in the corridor.

'Good-bye, Mr Racksole,' he remarked suavely, bowing again, lower than before. 'Good-bye: I hate to take a mean advantage of you in this fashion, but really you must allow that you have been very simple. You are a clever man, as I have already said, up to a certain point. It is past that point that my own cleverness comes in. Again, good-bye. After all, I shall have no rest to-night, but perhaps even that will be better that sleeping in a police cell. If you make a great noise you may wake someone and ultimately get released from this lift. But I advise you to compose yourself, and wait till morning. It will be more dignified. For the third time, good-bye.'

And with that Rocco, without hastening, walked down the corridor and so out of sight.

Racksole said never a word. He was too disgusted with himself to speak. He clenched his fists, and put his teeth together, and held his breath. In the silence he could hear the dwindling sound of Rocco's footsteps on the thick carpet.

It was the greatest blow of Racksole's life.

The next morning the high-born guests of the Grand Babylon were aroused by a rumour that by some accident the millionaire proprietor of the hotel had remained all night locked up m the lift. It was also stated that Rocco had quarrelled with his new master and incontinently left the place. A duchess said that Rocco's departure would mean the ruin of the hotel, whereupon her husband advised her not to talk nonsense.

As for Racksole, he sent a message for the detective in charge of the Dimmock affair, and bravely told him the happenings of the previous night.

The narration was a decided ordeal to a man of Racksole's temperament.

'A strange story!' commented Detective Marshall, and he could not avoid a smile. 'The climax was unfortunate, but you have certainly got some valuable facts.'

Racksole said nothing.

'I myself have a clue,' added the detective. When your message arrived I was just coming up to see you. I want you to accompany me to a certain spot not far from here. Will you come, now, at once?'

'With pleasure,' said Racksole.

At that moment a page entered with a telegram. Racksole opened it read:

'Please come instantly. Nella. Hotel Wellington, Ostend.'

He looked at his watch.

'I can't come,' he said to the detective. I'm going to Ostend.'

'To Ostend?'

'Yes, now.'

'But really, Mr Racksole,' protested the detective. 'My business is urgent.'

'So's mine,' said Racksole.

In ten minutes he was on his way to Victoria Station.

CHAPTER XV
END OF THE YACHT ADVENTURE

WE must now return to Nella Racksole and Prince Aribert of Posen on board the yacht without a name. The Prince's first business was to make Jules, otherwise Mr Tom Jackson, perfectly secure by means of several pieces of rope. Although Mr Jackson had been stunned into a complete unconsciousness, and there was a contused wound under his ear, no one could say how soon he might not come to himself and get very violent. So the Prince, having tied his arms and legs, made him fast to a stanchion.

'I hope he won't die,' said Nella. 'He looks very white.'

'The Mr Jacksons of this world,' said Prince Aribert sententiously, 'never die till they are hung. By the way, I wonder how it is that no one has interfered with us. Perhaps they are discreetly afraid of my revolver--of your revolver, I mean.'

Both he and Nella glanced up at the imperturbable steersman, who kept the yacht's head straight out to sea. By this time they were about a couple of miles from the Belgian shore.

Addressing him in French, the Prince ordered the sailor to put the yacht about, and make again for Ostend Harbour, but the fellow took no notice whatever of the summons. The Prince raised the revolver, with the idea of frightening the steersman, and then the man began to talk rapidly in a mixture of French and Flemish. He said that he had received Jules' strict orders not to interfere in any way, no matter what might happen on the deck of the yacht. He was the captain of the yacht, and he had to make for a certain English port, the name of which he could not divulge: he was to keep the vessel at full steam ahead under any and all circumstances. He seemed to be a very big, a very strong, and a very determined man, and the Prince was at a loss what course of action to pursue. He asked several more questions, but the only effect of them was to render the man taciturn and ill-humoured.

In vain Prince Aribert explained that Miss Nella Racksole, daughter of millionaire Racksole, had been abducted by Mr Tom Jackson; in vain he flourished the revolver threateningly; the surly but courageous captain said merely that that had nothing to do with him; he had instructions, and he should carry them out. He sarcastically begged to remind his interlocutor that he was the captain of the yacht.

'It won't do to shoot him, I suppose,' said the Prince to Nella. 'I might bore a hole into his leg, or something of that kind.'

'It's rather risky, and rather hard on the poor captain, with his extraordinary sense of duty,' said Nella. 'And, besides, the whole crew might turn on us. No, we must think of something else.'

'I wonder where the crew is,' said the Prince.

Just then Mr Jackson, prone and bound on the deck, showed signs of recovering from his swoon. His eyes opened, and he gazed vacantly around. At length he caught sight of the Prince, who approached him with the revolver well in view.

'It's you, is it?' he murmured faintly. 'What are you doing on board? Who's tied me up like this?'

'See here!' replied the Prince, 'I don't want to have any arguments, but this yacht must return to Ostend at once, where you will be given up to the authorities.'

'Really!' snarled Mr Tom Jackson. 'Shall I!' Then he called out in French to the man at the wheel, 'Hi André! let these two be put off in the dinghy.'

It was a peculiar situation. Certain of nothing but the possession of Nella's revolver, the Prince scarcely knew whether to carry the argument further, and with stronger measures, or to accept the situation with as much dignity as the circumstances would permit.

'Let us take the dinghy,' said Nella; 'we can row ashore in an hour.'

He felt that she was right. To leave the yacht in such a manner seemed somewhat ignominious, and it certainly involved the escape of that profound villain, Mr Thomas Jackson. But what else could be done? The Prince and Nella constituted one party on the vessel; they knew their own strength, but they did not know the strength of their opponents. They held the hostile ringleader bound and captive, but this man had proved himself capable of giving orders, and even to gag him would not help them if the captain of the yacht persisted in his obstinate course. Moreover, there was a distinct objection to promiscuous shooting; the Prince felt that; there was no knowing how promiscuous shooting might end.

'We will take the dinghy,' said the Prince quickly, to the captain.

A bell rang below, and a sailor and the Negro boy appeared on deck. The pulsations of the screw grew less rapid. The yacht stopped. The dinghy was lowered. As the Prince and Nella prepared to descend into the little cock-boat Mr Tom Jackson addressed Nella, all bound as he lay.

'Good-bye,' he said, 'I shall see you again, never fear.'.

In another moment they were in the dinghy, and the dinghy was adrift. The yacht's screw chumed the water, and the beautiful vessel slipped away from them. As it receded a figure appeared at the stem. It was Mr Thomas Jackson.

He had been released by his minions. He held a white handkerchief to his ear, and offered a calm, enigmatic smile to the two forlorn but victorious occupants of the dinghy. Jules had been defeated for once in his life; or perhaps it would be more just to say that he had been out-manoeuvred. Men like Jules are incapable of being defeated. It was characteristic of his luck that now, in the very hour when he had been caught red-handed in a serious crime against society, he should be effecting a leisurely escape--an escape which left no clue behind.

The sea was utterly calm and blue in the morning sun. The dinghy rocked itself lazily in the swell of the yacht's departure. As the mist cleared away the outline of the shore became more distinct, and it appeared as if Ostend was distant scarcely a cable's length. The white dome of the great Kursaal glittered in the pale turquoise sky, and the smoke of steamers in the harbour could be plainly distinguished. On the offing was a crowd of brown-sailed fishing luggers returning with the night's catch. The many-hued bathing-vans could be counted on the distant beach. Everything seemed perfectly normal. It was difficult for either Nella or her companion to realize that anything extraordinary had happened within the last hour. Yet there was the yacht, not a mile off, to prove to them that something very extraordinary had, in fact, happened. The yacht was no vision, nor was that sinister watching figure at its stern a vision, either.

'I suppose Jules was too surprised and too feeble to inquire how I came to be on board his yacht,' said the Prince, taking the oars.

'Oh! How did you?' asked Nella, her face lighting up. 'Really, I had almost forgotten that part of the affair.'

'I must begin at the beginning and it will take some time,' answered the Prince. 'Had we not better postpone the recital till we get ashore?'

'I will row and you shall talk,' said Nella. 'I want to know now.'

He smiled happily at her, but gently declined to yield up the oars.

'Is it not sufficient that I am here?' he said.

'It is sufficient, yes,' she replied, 'but I want to know.'

With a long, easy stroke he was pulling the dinghy shorewards. She sat in the stern-sheets.

'There is no rudder,' he remarked, 'so you must direct me. Keep the boat's head on the lighthouse. The tide seems to be running in strongly; that will help us. The people on shore will think that we have only been for a little early morning excursion.'

'Will you kindly tell me how it came about that you were able to save my life, Prince?' she said.

'Save your life, Miss Racksole? I didn't save your life; I merely knocked a man down.'

'You saved my life,' she repeated. 'That villain would have stopped at nothing. I saw it in his eye.'

'Then you were a brave woman, for you showed no fear of death.' His admiring gaze rested full on her. For a moment the oars ceased to move.

She gave a gesture of impatience.

'It happened that I saw you last night in your carriage,' he said. 'The fact is, I had not had the audacity to go to Berlin with my story. I stopped in Ostend to see whether I could do a little detective work on my own account.

It was a piece of good luck that I saw you. I followed the carriage as quickly as I could, and I just caught a glimpse of you as you entered that awful house. I knew that Jules had something to do with that house. I guessed what you were doing. I was afraid for you. Fortunately I had surveyed the house pretty thoroughly. There is an entrance to it at the back, from a narrow lane. I made my way there. I got into the yard at the back, and I stood under the window of the room where you had the interview with Miss Spencer. I heard everything that was said. It was a courageous enterprise on your part to follow Miss Spencer from the Grand Babylon to Ostend. Well, I dared not force an entrance, lest I might precipitate matters too suddenly, and involve both of us in a difficulty. I merely kept watch. Ah, Miss Racksole! you were magnificent with Miss Spencer; as I say, I could hear every word, for the window was slightly open. I felt that you needed no assistance from me. And then she cheated you with a trick, and the revolver came flying through the window. I picked it up, I thought it would probably be useful. There was a silence. I did not guess at first that you had fainted. I thought that you had escaped. When I found out the truth it was too late for me to intervene. There were two men, both desperate, besides Miss Spencer--'

'Who was the other man?' asked Nella.

'I do not know. It was dark. They drove away with you to the harbour. Again I followed. I saw them carry you on board. Before the yacht weighed anchor I managed to climb unobserved into the dinghy. I lay down full length in it, and no one suspected that I was there. I think you know the rest.'

'Was the yacht all ready for sea?'

'The yacht was all ready for sea. The captain fellow was on the bridge, and steam was up.'

'Then they expected me! How could that be?'

'They expected some one. I do not think they expected you.'

'Did the second man go on board?'

'He helped to carry you along the gangway, but he came back again to the carriage. He was the driver.'

'And no one else saw the business?'

'The quay was deserted. You see, the last steamer had arrived for the night.'

There was a brief silence, and then Nella ejaculated, under her breath.

'Truly, it is a wonderful world!'

And it was a wonderful world for them, though scarcely perhaps, in the sense which Nella Racksole had intended. They had just emerged from a highly disconcerting experience. Among other minor inconveniences, they had had no breakfast. They were out in the sea in a tiny boat. Neither of them knew what the day might bring forth. The man, at least, had the most

serious anxieties for the safety of his Royal nephew. And yet--
and yet--neither of them wished that that voyage of the little
boat on the summer tide should come to an end. Each, perhaps
unconsciously, had a vague desire that it might last for ever, he
lazily pulling, she directing his course at intervals by a
movement of her distractingly pretty head. How was this
condition of affairs to be explained? Well, they were both young;
they both had superb health, and all the ardour of youth; and--
they were together.

The boat was very small indeed; her face was scarcely a yard
from his. She, in his eyes, surrounded by the glamour of beauty
and vast wealth; he, in her eyes, surrounded by the glamour of
masculine intrepidity and the brilliance of a throne.

But all voyages come to an end, either at the shore or at the
bottom of the sea, and at length the dinghy passed between the
stone jetties of the harbour. The Prince rowed to the nearest
steps, tied up the boat, and they landed. It was six o'clock in the
morning, and a day of gorgeous sunlight had opened. Few people
were about at that early hour.

'And now, what next?' said the Prince. 'I must take you to an
hotel.'

'I am in your hands,' she acquiesced, with a smile which sent
the blood racing through his veins. He perceived now that she
was tired and overcome, suffering from a sudden and natural
reaction.

At the Hotel Wellington the Prince told the sleepy door-
keeper that they had come by the early train from Bruges, and
wanted breakfast at once. It was absurdly early, but a common
English sovereign will work wonders in any Belgian hotel, and
in a very brief time Nella and the Prince were breakfasting on
the verandah of the hotel upon chocolate that had been specially
and hastily brewed for them.

'I never tasted such excellent chocolate,' claimed the Prince.

The statement was wildly untrue, for the Hotel Wellington is
not celebrated for its chocolate. Nevertheless Nella replied
enthusiastically, 'Nor I.'

Then there was a silence, and Nella, feeling possibly that she
had been too ecstatic, remarked in a very matter-of-fact tone: 'I
must telegraph to Papa instantly.'

Thus it was that Theodore Racksole received the telegram which drew him away from Detective Marshall.

CHAPTER XVI
THE WOMAN WITH THE RED HAT

'THERE is one thing, Prince, that we have just got to settle straight off,' said Theodore Racksole.

They were all three seated--Racksole, his daughter, and Prince Aribert--round a dinner table in a private room at the Hotel Wellington. Racksole had duly arrived by the afternoon boat, and had been met on the quay by the other two. They had dined early, and Racksole had heard the full story of the adventures by sea and land of Nella and the Prince. As to his own adventure of the previous night he said very little, merely explaining, with as little detail as possible, that Dimmock's body had come to light.

'What is that?' asked the Prince, in answer to Racksole's remark.

'We have got to settle whether we shall tell the police at once all that has occurred, or whether we shall proceed on our own responsibility. There can be no doubt as to which course we ought to pursue. Every consideration of prudence points to the advisability of taking the police into our confidence, and leaving the matter entirely in their hands.'

'Oh, Papa!' Nella burst out in her pouting, impulsive way. 'You surely can't think of such a thing. Why, the fun has only just begun.'

'Do you call last night fun?' questioned Racksole, gazing at her solemnly.

'Yes, I do,' she said promptly. 'Now.'

'Well, I don't,' was the millionaire's laconic response; but perhaps he was thinking of his own situation in the lift.

'Do you not think we might investigate a little further,' said the Prince judiciously, as he cracked a walnut, 'just a little further--and then, if we fail to accomplish anything, there would still be ample opportunity to consult the police?'

'How do you suggest we should begin?' asked Racksole.

'Well, there is the house which Miss Racksole so intrepidly entered last evening'--he gave her the homage of an admiring glance; 'you and I, Mr Racksole, might examine that abode in detail.'

'To-night?'

'Certainly. We might do something.'

'We might do too much.'

'For example?'

'We might shoot someone, or get ourselves mistaken for burglars. If we outstepped the law, it would be no excuse for us that we had been acting in a good cause.'

'True,' said the Prince. 'Nevertheless--' He stopped.

'Nevertheless you have a distaste for bringing the police into the business. You want the hunt all to yourself. You are on fire with the ardour of the chase. Is not that it? Accept the advice of an older man, Prince, and sleep on this affair. I have little fancy for nocturnal escapades two nights together. As for you, Nella, off with you to bed. The Prince and I will have a yarn over such fluids as can be obtained in this hole.'

'Papa,' she said, 'you are perfectly horrid to-night.'

'Perhaps I am,' he said. 'Decidedly I am very cross with you for coming over here all alone. It was monstrous. If I didn't happen to be the most foolish of parents--There! Good-night. It's nine o'clock. The Prince, I am sure, will excuse you.'

If Nella had not really been very tired Prince Aribert might have been the witness of a good-natured but stubborn conflict between the millionaire and his spirited offspring. As it was, Nella departed with surprising docility, and the two men were left alone.

'Now,' said Racksole suddenly, changing his tone, 'I fancy that after all I'm your man for a little amateur investigation to-night. And, if I must speak the exact truth, I think that to sleep on this affair would be about the very worst thing we could do. But I was anxious to keep Nella out of harm's way at any rate till to-morrow. She is a very difficult creature to manage, Prince, and I may warn you,' he laughed grimly, 'that if we do succeed in doing anything to-night we shall catch it from her ladyship in the morning. Are you ready to take that risk?'

'I am,' the Prince smiled. 'But Miss Racksole is a young lady of quite remarkable nerve.'

'She is,' said Racksole drily. 'I wish sometimes she had less.'

'I have the highest admiration for Miss Racksole,' said the Prince, and he looked Miss Racksole's father full in the face.

'You honour us, Prince,' Racksole observed. 'Let us come to business. Am I right in assuming that you have a reason for keeping the police out of this business, if it can possibly be done?'

'Yes,' said the Prince, and his brow clouded. 'I am very much afraid that my poor nephew has involved himself in some scrape that he would wish not to be divulged.'

'Then you do not believe that he is the victim of foul play?'

'I do not.'

'And the reason, if I may ask it?'

'Mr Racksole, we speak in confidence--is it not so? Some years ago my foolish nephew had an affair--an affair with a feminine star of the Berlin stage. For anything I know, the lady may have been the very pattern of her sex, but where a reigning Prince is concerned scandal cannot be avoided in such a matter. I had thought that the affair was quite at an end, since my nephew's betrothal to Princess Anna of Eckstein-Schwartzburg is shortly to be announced. But yesterday I saw the lady to whom I have referred driving on the Digue. The coincidence of her presence here with my nephew's disappearance is too extraordinary to be disregarded.'

'But how does this theory square with the murder of Reginald Dimmock?'

'It does not square with it. My idea is that the murder of poor Dimmock and the disappearance of my nephew are entirely unconnected--unless, indeed, this Berlin actress is playing into the hands of the murderers. I had not thought of that.'

'Then what do you propose to do to-night?'

'I propose to enter the house which Miss Racksole entered last night and to find out something definite.'

'I concur,' said Racksole. 'I shall heartily enjoy it. But let me tell you, Prince, and pardon me for speaking bluntly, your surmise is incorrect. I would wager a hundred thousand dollars that Prince Eugen has been kidnapped.'

'What grounds have you for being so sure?'

'Ah! said Racksole, 'that is a long story. Let me begin by asking you this. Are you aware that your nephew, Prince Eugen, owes a million of money?'

'A million of money!' cried Prince Aribert astonished. 'It is impossible!'

'Nevertheless, he does,' said Racksole calmly. Then he told him all he had learnt from Mr Sampson Levi.

'What have you to say to that?' Racksole ended. Prince Aribert made no reply.

'What have you to say to that?' Racksole insisted.

'Merely that Eugen is ruined, even if he is alive.'

'Not at all,' Racksole returned with cheerfulness. 'Not at all. We shall see about that. The special thing that I want to know just now from you is this:

Has any previous application ever been made for the hand of the Princess Anna?'

'Yes. Last year. The King of Bosnia sued for it, but his proposal was declined.'

'Why?'

'Because my nephew was considered to be a more suitable match for her.'

'Not because the personal character of his Majesty of Bosnia is scarcely of the brightest?'

'No. Unfortunately it is usually impossible to consider questions of personal character when a royal match is concerned.'

'Then, if for any reason the marriage of Princess Anna with your nephew was frustrated, the King of Bosnia would have a fair chance in that quarter?'

'He would. The political aspect of things would be perfectly satisfactory.'

'Thanks!' said Racksole. 'I will wager another hundred thousand dollars that someone in Bosnia--I don't accuse the King himself--is at the bottom of this business. The methods of Balkan politicians have always been half-Oriental. Let us go.'

'Where?'

'To this precious house of Nella's adventure.'

'But surely it is too early?'

'So it is,' said Racksole, 'and we shall want a few things, too. For instance, a dark lantern. I think I will go out and forage for a lantern.'

'And a revolver?' suggested Prince Aribert.

'Does it mean revolvers?' The millionaire laughed. 'It may come to that.' 'Here you are, then, my friend,' said Racksole, and he pulled one out of his hip pocket. 'And yours?'

'I,' said the Prince, 'I have your daughter's.'

'The deuce you have!' murmured Racksole to himself.

It was then half past nine. They decided that it would be impolitic to begin their operations till after midnight. There were three hours to spare.

'Let us go and see the gambling,' Racksole suggested. 'We might encounter the Berlin lady.'

The suggestion, in the first instance, was not made seriously, but it appeared to both men that they might do worse than spend the intervening time in the gorgeous saloon of the Kursaal, where, in the season, as much money is won and lost as at Monte Carlo. It was striking ten o'clock as they entered the rooms. There was a large company present--a company which included some of the most notorious persons in Europe. In that multifarious assemblage all were equal. The electric light shone coldly and impartially on the just and on the unjust, on the fool and the knave, on the European and the Asiatic. As usual, women monopolized the best places at the tables.

The scene was familiar enough to Prince Aribert, who had witnessed it frequently at Monaco, but Theodore Racksole had never before entered any European gaming palace; he had only the haziest idea of the rules of play, and he was at once interested. For some time they watched the play at the table which happened to be nearest to them. Racksole never moved his lips.

With his eyes glued on the table, and ears open for every remark, of the players and the croupier, he took his first lesson in roulette. He saw a mere youth win fifteen thousand francs, which were stolen in the most barefaced mariner by a rouged girl scarcely older than the youth; he saw two old gamesters stake their coins, and lose, and walk quietly out of the place; he saw the bank win fifty thousand francs at a single turn.

'This is rather good fun,' he said at length, 'but the stakes are too small to make it really exciting. I'll try my luck, just for the experience. I'm bound to win.'

'Why?' asked the Prince.

'Because I always do, in games of chance,' Racksole answered with gay confidence. 'It is my fate. Then to-night, you must remember, I shall be a beginner, and you know the tyro's luck.'

In ten minutes the croupier of that table was obliged to suspend operations pending the arrival of a further supply of coin.

'What did I tell you?' said Racksole, leading the way to another table further up the room. A hundred curious glances went after him. One old woman, whose gay attire suggested a false youthfulness, begged him in French to stake a five-franc piece for her. She offered him the coin. He took it, and gave her a hundred-franc note in exchange. She clutched the crisp rustling paper, and with hysterical haste scuttled back to her own table.

At the second table there was a considerable air of excitement. In the forefront of the players was a woman in a low-cut evening dress of black silk and a large red picture hat. Her age appeared to be about twenty-eight; she had dark eyes, full lips, and a distinctly Jewish nose. She was handsome, but her beauty was of that forbidding, sinister order which is often called Junoesque. This woman was the centre of attraction. People said to each other that she had won a hundred and sixty thousand francs that day at the table.

'You were right,' Prince Aribert whispered to Theodore Racksole; 'that is the Berlin lady.'

'The deuce she is! Has she seen you? Will she know you?'

'She would probably know me, but she hasn't looked up yet.'

'Keep behind her, then. I propose to find her a little occupation.' By dint of a carefully-exercised diplomacy, Racksole manoeuvred himself into a seat opposite to the lady in the red hat. The fame of his success at the other table had followed him, and people regarded him as a serious and formidable player. In the first turn the lady put a thousand francs on double zero; Racksole put a hundred on number nineteen and a thousand on the odd numbers.

Nineteen won. Racksole received four thousand four hundred francs. Nine times in succession Racksole backed number nineteen and the odd numbers; nine times the lady backed double zero. Nine times Racksole won and the lady lost. The other players, perceiving that the affair had resolved itself into a duel, stood back for the most part and watched those two. Prince Aribert never stirred from his position behind the great red hat. The game continued. Racksole lost trifles from time to time, but ninety-nine hundredths of the luck was with him. As an English spectator at the table remarked, 'he couldn't do wrong.' When midnight struck the lady in the red hat was reduced to a thousand francs. Then she fell into a winning vein for half an hour, but at one o'clock her resources were exhausted. Of the hundred and sixty thousand francs which she was reputed to have had early in the evening, Racksole held about ninety thousand, and the bank had the rest.

It was a calamity for the Juno of the red hat. She jumped up, stamped her foot, and hurried from the room. At a discreet distance Racksole and the Prince pursued her.

'It might be well to ascertain her movements,' said Racksole.

Outside, in the glare of the great arc lights, and within sound of the surf which beats always at the very foot of the Kursaal, the Juno of the red hat summoned a fiacre and drove rapidly away. Racksole and the Prince took an open carriage and started in pursuit. They had not, however, travelled more than half a mile when Prince Aribert stopped the carriage, and, bidding Racksole get out, paid the driver and dismissed him.

'I feel sure I know where she is going,' he explained, 'and it will be better for us to follow on foot.'

'You mean she is making for the scene of last night's affair?' said Racksole.

'Exactly. We shall--what you call, kill two birds with one stone.'

Prince Aribert's guess was correct. The lady's carriage stopped in front of the house where Nella Racksole and Miss Spencer had had their interview on the previous evening, and the lady vanished into the building just as the two men appeared at the end of the street. Instead of proceeding along that street, the Prince led Racksole to the lane which gave on to the backs of the houses, and he counted the houses as they went up the lane. In a few minutes they had burglariously climbed over a wall, and crept, with infinite caution, up a long, narrow piece of ground--half garden, half paved yard, till they crouched under a window--a window which was shielded by curtains, but which had been left open a little.

'Listen,' said the Prince in his lightest whisper, 'they are talking.'

'Who?'

'The Berlin lady and Miss Spencer. I'm sure it's Miss Spencer's voice.'

Racksole boldly pushed the french window a little wider open, and put his ear to the aperture, through which came a beam of yellow light.

'Take my place,' he whispered to the Prince, 'they're talking German. You'll understand better.'

Silently they exchanged places under the window, and the Prince listened intently.

'Then you refuse?' Miss Spencer's visitor was saying.

There was no answer from Miss Spencer.

'Not even a thousand francs? I tell you I've lost the whole twenty-five thousand.'

Again no answer.

'Then I'll tell the whole story,' the lady went on, in an angry rush of words. 'I did what I promised to do. I enticed him here, and you've got him safe in your vile cellar, poor little man, and you won't give me a paltry thousand francs.'

'You have already had your price.' The words were Miss Spencer's. They fell cold and calm on the night air.

'I want another thousand.'

'I haven't it.'

'Then we'll see.'

Prince Aribert heard a rustle of flying skirts; then another movement--a door banged, and the beam of light through the aperture of the window suddenly disappeared. He pushed the window wide open. The room was in darkness, and apparently empty.

'Now for that lantern of yours,' he said eagerly to Theodore Racksole, after he had translated to him the conversation of the two women, Racksole produced the dark lantern from the capacious pocket of his dust coat, and lighted it. The ray flashed about the ground.

'What is it?' exclaimed Prince Aribert with a swift cry, pointing to the ground. The lantern threw its light on a perpendicular grating at their feet, through which could be discerned a cellar. They both knelt down, and peered into the subterranean chamber. On a broken chair a young man sat listlessly with closed eyes, his head leaning heavily forward on his chest.

In the feeble light of the lantern he had the livid and ghastly appearance of a corpse.

'Who can it be?' said Racksole.

'It is Eugen,' was the Prince's low answer.

CHAPTER XVII
THE RELEASE OF PRINCE EUGEN

'EUGEN,' Prince Aribert called softly. At the sound of his own name the young man in the cellar feebly raised his head and stared up at the grating which separated him from his two rescuers. But his features showed no recognition. He gazed in an aimless, vague, silly manner for a few seconds, his eyes blinking under the glare of the lantern, and then his head slowly drooped again on to his chest. He was dressed in a dark tweed travelling suit, and Racksole observed that one sleeve--the left--was torn across the upper part of the cuff, and that there were stains of dirt on the left shoulder. A soiled linen collar, which had lost all its starch and was half unbuttoned, partially encircled the captive's neck; his brown boots were unlaced; a cap, a handkerchief, a portion of a watch-chain, and a few gold coins lay on the floor. Racksole flashed the lantern into the corners of the cellar, but he could discover no other furniture except the chair on which the Hereditary Prince of Posen sat and a small deal table on which were a plate and a cup.

'Eugen,' cried Prince Aribert once more, but this time his forlorn nephew made no response whatever, and then Aribert added in a low voice to Racksole: 'Perhaps he cannot see us clearly.'

'But he must surely recognize your voice,' said Racksole, in a hard, gloomy tone. There was a pause, and the two men above ground looked at each other hesitatingly. Each knew that they must enter that cellar and get Prince Eugen out of it, and each was somehow afraid to take the next step.

'Thank God he is not dead!' said Aribert.

'He may be worse than dead!' Racksole replied.

'Worse than--What do you mean?'

'I mean--he may be mad.'

'Come,' Aribert almost shouted, with a sudden access of energy--a wild impulse for action. And, snatching the lantern from Racksole, he rushed into the dark room where they had heard the conversation of Miss Spencer and the lady in the red hat. For a moment Racksole did not stir from the threshold of the window. 'Come,' Prince Aribert repeated, and there was an imperious command in his utterance. 'What are you afraid of?'

'I don't know,' said Racksole, feeling stupid and queer; 'I don't know.'

Then he marched heavily after Prince Aribert into the room. On the mantelpiece were a couple of candles which had been blown out, and in a mechanical, unthinking way, Racksole lighted them, and the two men glanced round the room. It presented no peculiar features: it was just an ordinary room, rather small, rather mean, rather shabby, with an ugly wallpaper and ugly pictures in ugly frames. Thrown over a chair was a man's evening-dress jacket. The door was closed. Prince Aribert turned the knob, but he could not open it.

'It's locked,' he said. 'Evidently they know we're here.'

'Nonsense,' said Racksole brusquely; 'how can they know?' And, taking hold of the knob, he violently shook the door, and it opened. 'I told you it wasn't locked,' he added, and this small success of opening the door seemed to steady the man. It was a curious psychological effect, this terrorizing (for it amounted to that) of two courageous full-grown men by the mere apparition of a helpless creature in a cellar. Gradually they both recovered from it. The next moment they were out in the passage which led to the front door of the house. The front door stood open. They looked into the street, up and down, but there was not a soul in sight. The street, lighted by three gas-lamps only, seemed strangely sinister and mysterious.

'She has gone, that's clear,' said Racksole, meaning the woman with the red hat.

'And Miss Spencer after her, do you think?' questioned Aribert.

'No. She would stay. She would never dare to leave. Let us find the cellar steps.'

The cellar steps were happily not difficult to discover, for in moving a pace backwards Prince Aribert had a narrow escape of precipitating himself to the bottom of them. The lantern showed that they were built on a curve.

Silently Racksole resumed possession of the lantern and went first, the Prince close behind him. At the foot was a short passage, and in this passage crouched the figure of a woman. Her eyes threw back the rays of the lantern, shining like a cat's at midnight. Then, as the men went nearer, they saw that it was Miss Spencer who barred their way. She seemed half to kneel on the stone floor, and in one hand she held what at first appeared to be a dagger, but which proved to be nothing more romantic than a rather long bread-knife.

'I heard you, I heard you,' she exclaimed. 'Get back; you mustn't come here.'

There was a desperate and dangerous look on her face, and her form shook with scarcely controlled passionate energy.

'Now see here, Miss Spencer,' Racksole said calmly, 'I guess we've had enough of this fandango. You'd better get up and clear out, or we'll just have to drag you off.'

He went calmly up to her, the lantern in his hand. Without another word she struck the knife into his arm, and the lantern fell extinguished. Racksole gave a cry, rather of angry surprise than of pain, and retreated a few steps. In the darkness they could still perceive the glint of her eyes.

'I told you you mustn't come here,' the woman said. 'Now get back.'

Racksole positively laughed. It was a queer laugh, but he laughed, and he could not help it. The idea of this woman, this bureau clerk, stopping his progress and that of Prince Aribert by means of a bread-knife aroused his sense of humour. He struck a match, relighted the candle, and faced Miss Spencer once more.

'I'll do it again,' she said, with a note of hard resolve.

'Oh, no, you won't, my girl,' said Racksole; and he pulled out his revolver, cocked it, raised his hand.

'Put down that plaything of yours,' he said firmly.

'No,' she answered.

'I shall shoot.'

She pressed her lips together.

'I shall shoot,' he repeated. 'One--two--three.'

Bang, bang! He had fired twice, purposely missing her. Miss Spencer never blenched. Racksole was tremendously surprised-- and he would have been a thousandfold more surprised could he have contrasted her behaviour now with her abject terror on the previous evening when Nella had threatened her.

'You've got a bit of pluck,' he said, 'but it won't help you. Why won't you let us pass?'

As a matter of fact, pluck was just what she had not, really; she had merely subordinated one terror to another. She was desperately afraid of Racksole's revolver, but she was much more afraid of something else.

'Why won't you let us pass?'

'I daren't,' she said, with a plaintive tremor; 'Tom put me in charge.'

That was all. The men could see tears running down her poor wrinkled face.

Theodore Racksole began to take off his light overcoat.

'I see I must take my coat off to you,' he said, and he almost smiled. Then, with a quick movement, he threw the coat over Miss Spencer's head and flew at her, seizing both her arms, while Prince Aribert assisted.

Her struggles ceased--she was beaten.

'That's all right,' said Racksole: 'I could never have used that revolver--to mean business with it, of course.'

They carried her, unresisting, upstairs and on to the upper floor, where they locked her in a bedroom. She lay in the bed as if exhausted.

'Now for my poor Eugen,' said Prince Aribert.

'Don't you think we'd better search the house first?' Racksole suggested; 'it will be safer to know just how we stand. We can't afford any ambushes or things of that kind, you know.'

The Prince agreed, and they searched the house from top to bottom, but found no one. Then, having locked the front door and the french window of the sitting-room, they proceeded again to the cellar.

Here a new obstacle confronted them. The cellar door was, of course, locked; there was no sign of a key, and it appeared to be a heavy door. They were compelled to return to the bedroom where Miss Spencer was incarcerated, in order to demand the key of the cellar from her. She still lay without movement on the bed.

'Tom's got it,' she replied, faintly, to their question: 'Tom's got it, I swear to you. He took it for safety.'

'Then how do you feed your prisoner?' Racksole asked sharply.

'Through the grating,' she answered.

Both men shuddered. They felt she was speaking the truth. For the third time they went to the cellar door. In vain Racksole thrust himself against it; he could do no more than shake it.

'Let's try both together,' said Prince Aribert. 'Now!' There was a crack.

'Again,' said Prince Aribert. There was another crack, and then the upper hinge gave way. The rest was easy. Over the wreck of the door they entered Prince Eugen's prison.

The captive still sat on his chair. The terrific noise and bustle of breaking down the door seemed not to have aroused him from his lethargy, but when Prince Aribert spoke to him in German he looked at his uncle.

'Will you not come with us, Eugen?' said Prince Aribert; 'you needn't stay here any longer, you know.'

'Leave me alone,' was the strange reply; 'leave me alone. What do you want?'

'We are here to get you out of this scrape,' said Aribert gently. Racksole stood aside.

'Who is that fellow?' said Eugen sharply.

'That is my friend Mr Racksole, an Englishman--or rather, I should say, an American--to whom we owe a great deal. Come and have supper, Eugen.'

'I won't,' answered Eugen doggedly. 'I'm waiting here for her. You didn't think anyone had kept me here, did you, against my will? I tell you I'm waiting for her. She said she'd come.'

'Who is she?' Aribert asked, humouring him.

'She! Why, you know! I forgot, of course, you don't know. You mustn't ask. Don't pry, Uncle Aribert. She was wearing a red hat.'

'I'll take you to her, my dear Eugen.' Prince Aribert put his hands on the other's shoulder, but Eugen shook him off violently, stood up, and then sat down again.

Aribert looked at Racksole, and they both looked at Prince Eugen. The latter's face was flushed, and Racksole observed that the left pupil was more dilated than the right. The man started, muttered odd, fragmentary scraps of sentences, now grumbling, now whining.

'His mind is unhinged,' Racksole whispered in English.

'Hush!' said Prince Aribert. 'He understands English.' But Prince Eugen took no notice of the brief colloquy.

'We had better get him upstairs, somehow,' said Racksole.

'Yes,' Aribert assented. 'Eugen, the lady with the red hat, the lady you are waiting for, is upstairs. She has sent us down to ask you to come up. Won't you come?'

'Himmel!' the poor fellow exclaimed, with a kind of weak anger. 'Why did you not say this before?'

He rose, staggered towards Aribert, and fell headlong on the floor. He had swooned. The two men raised him, carried him up the stone steps, and laid him with infinite care on a sofa. He lay, breathing queerly through the nostrils, his eyes closed, his fingers contracted; every now and then a convulsion ran through his frame.

'One of us must fetch a doctor,' said Prince Aribert.

'I will,' said Racksole. At that moment there was a quick, curt rap on the french window, and both Racksole and the Prince glanced round startled. A girl's face was pressed against the large window-pane. It was Nella's.

Racksole unfastened the catch, and she entered.

'I have found you,' she said lightly; 'you might have told me. I couldn't sleep. I inquired from the hotel-folks if you had retired, and they said no; so I slipped out. I guessed where you were.' Racksole interrupted her with a question as to what she meant by this escapade, but she stopped him with a careless gesture. What's this?' She pointed to the form on the sofa.

'That is my nephew, Prince Eugen,' said Aribert.

'Hurt?' she inquired coldly. 'I hope not.'

'He is ill,' said Racksole, 'his brain is turned.'

Nella began to examine the unconscious Prince with the expert movements of a girl who had passed through the best hospital course to be obtained in New York.

'He has got brain fever,' she said. 'That is all, but it will be enough. Do you know if there is a bed anywhere in this remarkable house?'

CHAPTER XVIII
IN THE NIGHT-TIME

'HE must on no account be moved,' said the dark little Belgian doctor, whose eyes seemed to peer so quizzically through his spectacles; and he said it with much positiveness.

That pronouncement rather settled their plans for them. It was certainly a professional triumph for Nella, who, previous to the doctor's arrival, had told them the very same thing. Considerable argument had passed before the doctor was sent for. Prince Aribert was for keeping the whole affair a deep secret among their three selves. Theodore Racksole agreed so far, but he suggested further that at no matter what risk they should transport the patient over to England at once. Racksole had an idea that he should feel safer in that hotel of his, and better able to deal with any situation that might arise. Nella scorned the idea. In her quality of an amateur nurse, she assured them that Prince Eugen was much more seriously ill than either of them suspected, and she urged that they should take absolute possession of the house, and keep possession till Prince Eugen was convalescent.

'But what about the Spencer female?' Racksole had said.

'Keep her where she is. Keep her a prisoner. And hold the house against all comers. If Jules should come back, simply defy him to enter--that is all. There are two of you, so you must keep an eye on the former occupiers, if they return, and on Miss Spencer, while I nurse the patient. But first, you must send for a doctor.'

'Doctor!' Prince Aribert had said, alarmed. 'Will it not be necessary to make some awkward explanation to the doctor?'

'Not at all!' she replied. 'Why should it be? In a place like Ostend doctors are far too discreet to ask questions; they see too much to retain their curiosity. Besides, do you want your nephew to die?'

Both the men were somewhat taken aback by the girl's sagacious grasp of the situation, and it came about that they began to obey her like subordinates.

She told her father to sally forth in search of a doctor, and he went. She gave Prince Aribert certain other orders, and he promptly executed them.

By the evening of the following day, everything was going smoothly. The doctor came and departed several times, and sent medicine, and seemed fairly optimistic as to the issue of the illness. An old woman had been induced to come in and cook and clean. Miss Spencer was kept out of sight on the attic floor, pending some decision as to what to do with her. And no one outside the house had asked any questions. The inhabitants of that particular street must have been accustomed to strange behaviour on the part of their neighbours, unaccountable appearances and disappearances, strange flittings and arrivals. This strong-minded and active trio--Racksole, Nella, and Prince Aribert--might have been the lawful and accustomed tenants of the house, for any outward evidence to the contrary.

On the afternoon of the third day Prince Eugen was distinctly and seriously worse. Nella had sat up with him the previous night and throughout the day.

Her father had spent the morning at the hotel, and Prince Aribert had kept watch. The two men were never absent from the house at the same time, and one of them always did duty as sentinel at night. On this afternoon Prince Aribert and Nella sat together in the patient's bedroom. The doctor had just left. Theodore Racksole was downstairs reading the New York Herald. The Prince and Nella were near the window, which looked on to the back-garden.

It was a queer shabby little bedroom to shelter the august body of a European personage like Prince Eugen of Posen. Curiously enough, both Nella and her father, ardent democrats though they were, had been somehow impressed by the royalty and importance of the fever-stricken Prince--impressed as they had never been by Aribert. They had both felt that here, under their care, was a species of individuality quite new to them, and different from anything they had previously encountered. Even the gestures and tones of his delirium had an air of abrupt yet condescending command--an imposing mixture of suavity and haughtiness. As for Nella, she had been first struck by the beautiful 'E' over a crown on the sleeves of his linen, and by the signet ring on his pale, emaciated hand. After all, these trifling outward signs are at least as effective as others of deeper but less obtrusive significance. The Racksoles, too, duly marked the attitude of Prince Aribert to his nephew: it was at once paternal and reverential; it disclosed clearly that Prince Aribert continued, in spite of everything, to regard his nephew as his sovereign lord and master, as a being surrounded by a natural and inevitable pomp and awe. This attitude, at the beginning, seemed false and unreal to the Americans; it seemed to them to be assumed; but gradually they came to perceive that they were mistaken, and that though America might have cast out 'the monarchial superstition', nevertheless that 'superstition' had vigorously survived in another part of the world.

'You and Mr Racksole have been extraordinarily kind to me,' said Prince Aribert very quietly, after the two had sat some time in silence.

'Why? How?' she asked unaffectedly. 'We are interested in this affair ourselves, you know. It began at our hotel--you mustn't forget that, Prince.'

'I don't,' he said. 'I forget nothing. But I cannot help feeling that I have led you into a strange entanglement. Why should you and Mr Racksole be here--you who are supposed to be on a holiday!--hiding in a strange house in a foreign country, subject to all sorts of annoyances and all sorts of risks, simply because I am anxious to avoid scandal, to avoid any sort of talk, in connection with my misguided nephew? It is nothing to you that the Hereditary Prince of Posen should be liable to a public disgrace. What will it matter to you if the throne of Posen becomes the laughing-stock of Europe?'

'I really don't know, Prince,' Nella smiled roguishly. 'But we Americans have, a habit of going right through with anything we have begun.'

'Ah!' he said, 'who knows how this thing will end? All our trouble, our anxieties, our watchfulness, may come to nothing. I tell you that when I see Eugen lying there, and think that we cannot learn his story until he recovers, I am ready to go mad. We might be arranging things, making matters smooth, preparing for the future, if only we knew--knew what he can tell us. I tell you that I am ready to go mad. If anything should happen to you, Miss Racksole, I would kill myself.'

'But why?' she questioned. 'Supposing, that is, that anything could happen to me--which it can't.'

'Because I have dragged you into this,' he replied, gazing at her. 'It is nothing to you. You are only being kind.'

'How do you know it is nothing to me, Prince?' she asked him quickly.

Just then the sick man made a convulsive movement, and Nella flew to the bed and soothed him. From the head of the bed she looked over at Prince Aribert, and he returned her bright, excited glance. She was in her travelling-frock, with a large white Belgian apron tied over it. Large dark circles of fatigue and sleeplessness surrounded her eyes, and to the Prince her cheek seemed hollow and thin; her hair lay thick over the temples, half covering the ears. Aribert gave no answer to her query--merely gazed at her with melancholy intensity.

'I think I will go and rest,' she said at last. 'You will know all about the medicine.'

'Sleep well,' he said, as he softly opened the door for her. And then he was alone with Eugen. It was his turn that night to watch, for they still half-expected some strange, sudden visit, or onslaught, or move of one kind or another from Jules. Racksole slept in the parlour on the ground floor.

Nella had the front bedroom on the first floor; Miss Spencer was immured in the attic; the last-named lady had been singularly quiet and incurious, taking her food from Nella and asking no questions, the old woman went at nights to her own abode in the purlieus of the harbour. Hour after hour Aribert sat silent by his nephew's bed-side, attending mechanically to his wants, and every now and then gazing hard into the vacant, anguished face, as if trying to extort from that mask the secrets which it held. Aribert was tortured by the idea that if he could have only half an hour's, only a quarter of an hour's, rational speech with Prince Eugen, all might be cleared up and put right, and by the fact that that rational talk was absolutely impossible on Eugen's part until the fever had run its course. As the minutes crept on to midnight the watcher, made nervous by the intense, electrical atmosphere which seems always to surround a person who is dangerously ill, grew more and more a prey to vague and terrible apprehensions. His mind dwelt hysterically on the most fatal possibilities.

He wondered what would occur if by any ill-chance Eugen should die in that bed--how he would explain the affair to Posen and to the Emperor, how he would justify himself. He saw himself being tried for murder, sentenced (him--a Prince of the blood!), led to the scaffold... a scene unparalleled in Europe for over a century! ... Then he gazed anew at the sick man, and thought he saw death in every drawn feature of that agonized face. He could have screamed aloud. His ears heard a peculiar resonant boom. He started--it was nothing but the city clock striking twelve. But there was another sound--a mysterious shuffle at the door. He listened; then jumped from his chair. Nothing now! Nothing! But still he felt drawn to the door, and after what seemed an interminable interval he went and opened it, his heart beating furiously. Nella lay in a heap on the door mat. She was fully dressed, but had apparently lost consciousness. He clutched at her slender body, picked her up, carried her to the chair by the fire-place, and laid her in it. He had forgotten all about Eugen.

'What is it, my angel?' he whispered, and then he kissed her-- kissed her twice. He could only look at her; he did not know what to do to succour her.

At last she opened her eyes and sighed.

'Where am I?' she asked vaguely, in a tremulous tone as she recognized him. 'Is it you? Did I do anything silly? Did I faint?'

'What has happened? Were you ill?' he questioned anxiously. He was kneeling at her feet, holding her hand tight.

'I saw Jules by the side of my bed,' she murmured; 'I'm sure I saw him; he laughed at me. I had not undressed. I sprang up, frightened, but he had gone, and then I ran downstairs--to you.'

'You were dreaming,' he soothed her.

'Was I?'

'You must have been. I have not heard a sound. No one could have entered.

But if you like I will wake Mr Racksole.'

'Perhaps I was dreaming,' she admitted. 'How foolish!'

'You were over-tired,' he said, still unconsciously holding her hand. They gazed at each other. She smiled at him.

'You kissed me,' she said suddenly, and he blushed red and stood up before her. 'Why did you kiss me?'

'Ah! Miss Racksole,' he murmured, hurrying the words out. 'Forgive me. It is unforgivable, but forgive me. I was overpowered by my feelings. I did not know what I was doing.'

'Why did you kiss me?' she repeated.

'Because--Nella! I love you. I have no right to say it.'

'Why have you no right to say it?'

'If Eugen dies, I shall owe a duty to Posen--I shall be its ruler.'

'Well!' she said calmly, with an adorable confidence. 'Papa is worth forty millions. Would you not abdicate?'

'Ah!' he gave a low cry. 'Will you force me to say these things? I could not shirk my duty to Posen, and the reigning Prince of Posen can only marry a Princess.'

'But Prince Eugen will live,' she said positively, 'and if he lives--'

'Then I shall be free. I would renounce all my rights to make you mine, if--if--'

'If what, Prince?'

'If you would deign to accept my hand.'

'Am I, then, rich enough?'

'Nella!' He bent down to her.

Then there was a crash of breaking glass. Aribert went to the window and opened it. In the starlit gloom he could see that a ladder had been raised against the back of the house. He thought he heard footsteps at the end of the garden.

'It was Jules,' he exclaimed to Nella, and without another word rushed upstairs to the attic. The attic was empty. Miss Spencer had mysteriously vanished.

CHAPTER XIX
ROYALTY AT THE GRAND BABYLON

THE Royal apartments at the Grand Babylon are famous in the world of hotels, and indeed elsewhere, as being, in their own way, unsurpassed. Some of the palaces of Germany, and in particular those of the mad Ludwig of Bavaria, may possess rooms and saloons which outshine them in gorgeous luxury and the mere wild fairy-like extravagance of wealth; but there is nothing, anywhere, even on Eighth Avenue, New York, which can fairly be called more complete, more perfect, more enticing, or--not least important--more comfortable.

The suite consists of six chambers--the ante-room, the saloon or audience chamber, the dining-room, the yellow drawing-room (where Royalty receives its friends), the library, and the State bedroom--to the last of which we have already been introduced. The most important and most impressive of these is, of course, the audience chamber, an apartment fifty feet long by forty feet broad, with a superb outlook over the Thames, the Shot Tower, and the higher signals of the South-Western Railway. The decoration of this room is mainly in the German taste, since four out of every six of its Royal occupants are of Teutonic blood; but its chief glory is its French ceiling, a masterpiece by Fragonard, taken bodily from a certain famous palace on the Loire. The walls are of panelled oak, with an eight-foot dado of Arras cloth imitated from unique Continental examples. The carpet, woven in one piece, is an antique specimen of the finest Turkish work, and it was obtained, a bargain, by Felix Babylon, from an impecunious Roumanian Prince. The silver candelabra, now fitted with electric light, came from the Rhine, and each had a separate history. The Royal chair--it is not etiquette to call it a throne, though it amounts to a throne--was looted by Napoleon from an Austrian city, and bought by Felix Babylon at the sale of a French collector. At each corner of the room stands a gigantic grotesque vase of German faïence of the sixteenth century. These were presented to Felix Babylon by William the First of Germany, upon the conclusion of his first incognito visit to London in connection with the French trouble of 1875.

There is only one picture in the audience chamber. It is a portrait of the luckless but noble Dom Pedro, Emperor of the

Brazils. Given to Felix Babylon by Dom Pedro himself, it hangs there solitary and sublime as a reminder to Kings and Princes that Empires may pass away and greatness fall. A certain Prince who was occupying the suite during the Jubilee of 1887--when the Grand Babylon had seven persons of Royal blood under its roof--sent a curt message to Felix that the portrait must be removed. Felix respectfully declined to remove it, and the Prince left for another hotel, where he was robbed of two thousand pounds' worth of jewellery. The Royal audience chamber of the Grand Babylon, if people only knew it, is one of the sights of London, but it is never shown, and if you ask the hotel servants about its wonders they will tell you only foolish facts concerning it, as that the Turkey carpet costs fifty pounds to clean, and that one of the great vases is cracked across the pedestal, owing to the rough treatment accorded to it during a riotous game of Blind Man's Buff, played one night by four young Princesses, a Balkan King, and his aides-de-camp.

In one of the window recesses of this magnificent apartment, on a certain afternoon in late July, stood Prince Aribert of Posen. He was faultlessly dressed in the conventional frock-coat of English civilization, with a gardenia in his button-hole, and the indispensable crease down the front of the trousers. He seemed to be fairly amused, and also to expect someone, for at frequent intervals he looked rapidly over his shoulder in the direction of the door behind the Royal chair. At last a little wizened, stooping old man, with a distinctly German cast of countenance, appeared through the door, and laid some papers on a small table by the side of the chair.

'Ah, Hans, my old friend!' said Aribert, approaching the old man. 'I must have a little talk with you about one or two matters. How do you find His Royal Highness?'

The old man saluted, military fashion. 'Not very well, your Highness,' he answered. 'I've been valet to your Highness's nephew since his majority, and I was valet to his Royal father before him, but I never saw--' He stopped, and threw up his wrinkled hands deprecatingly.

'You never saw what?' Aribert smiled affectionately on the old fellow. You could perceive that these two, so sharply differentiated in rank, had been intimate in the past, and would be intimate again.

'Do you know, my Prince,' said the old man, 'that we are to receive the financier, Sampson Levi--is that his name?--in the audience chamber? Surely, if I may humbly suggest, the library would have been good enough for a financier?'

'One would have thought so,' agreed Prince Aribert, 'but perhaps your master has a special reason. Tell me,' he went on, changing the subject quickly, 'how came it that you left the Prince, my nephew, at Ostend, and returned to Posen?'

'His orders, Prince,' and old Hans, who had had a wide experience of Royal whims and knew half the secrets of the Courts of Europe, gave Aribert a look which might have meant anything. 'He sent me back on an--an errand, your Highness.'

'And you were to rejoin him here?'

'Just so, Highness. And I did rejoin him here, although, to tell the truth, I had begun to fear that I might never see my master again.'

'The Prince has been very ill in Ostend, Hans.'

'So I have gathered,' Hans responded drily, slowly rubbing his hands together. 'And his Highness is not yet perfectly recovered.'

'Not yet. We despaired of his life, Hans, at one time, but thanks to an excellent constitution, he came safely through the ordeal.'

'We must take care of him, your Highness.'

'Yes, indeed,' said Aribert solemnly, 'his life is very precious to Posen.'

At that moment, Eugen, Hereditary Prince of Posen, entered the audience chamber. He was pale and languid, and his uniform seemed to be a trouble to him. His hair had been slightly ruffled, and there was a look of uneasiness, almost of alarmed unrest, in his fine dark eyes. He was like a man who is afraid to look behind him lest he should see something there which ought not to be there. But at the same time, here beyond doubt was Royalty. Nothing could have been more striking than the contrast between Eugen, a sick man in the shabby house at Ostend, and this Prince Eugen in the Royal apartments of the Grand Babylon Hotel, surrounded by the luxury and pomp which modern civilization can offer to those born in high places. All the desperate episode of Ostend was now hidden, passed over. It was supposed never to have occurred. It existed only like a secret shame in the hearts of those who had witnessed it. Prince Eugen had recovered; at any rate, he was convalescent, and he had been removed to London, where he took up again the dropped thread of his princely life. The lady with the red hat, the incorruptible and savage Miss Spencer, the unscrupulous and brilliant Jules, the dark, damp cellar, the horrible little bedroom--these things were over. Thanks to Prince Aribert and the Racksoles, he had emerged from them in safety. He was able to resume his public and official career. The Emperor had been informed of his safe arrival in London, after an unavoidable delay in Ostend; his name once more figured in the Court chronicle of the newspapers. In short, everything was smothered over. Only--only Jules, Rocco, and Miss Spencer were still at large; and the body of Reginald Dimmock lay buried in the domestic mausoleum of the palace at Posen; and Prince Eugen had still to interview Mr Sampson Levi.

That various matters lay heavy on the mind of Prince Eugen was beyond question. He seemed to have withdrawn within himself. Despite the extraordinary experiences through which he had recently passed, events which called aloud for explanations and confidence between the nephew and the uncle, he would say scarcely a word to Prince Aribert. Any allusion, however direct, to the days at Ostend, was ignored by him with more or less ingenuity, and Prince Aribert was really no nearer a full solution of the mystery of Jules' plot than he had been on the night when he and Racksole visited the gaming tables at Ostend. Eugen was well aware that he had been kidnapped through the agency of the woman in the red hat, but, doubtless ashamed at having been her dupe, he would not proceed in any way with the clearing-up of the matter.

'You will receive in this room, Eugen?' Aribert questioned him.

'Yes,' was the answer, given pettishly. 'Why not? Even if I have no proper retinue here, surely that is no reason why I should not hold audience in a proper manner?... Hans, you can go.' The old valet promptly disappeared.

'Aribert,' the Hereditary Prince continued, when they were alone in the chamber, 'you think I am mad.'

'My dear Eugen,' said Prince Aribert, startled in spite of himself. 'Don't be absurd.'

'I say you think I am mad. You think that that attack of brain fever has left its permanent mark on me. Well, perhaps I am mad. Who can tell? God knows that I have been through enough lately to drive me mad.'

Aribert made no reply. As a matter of strict fact, the thought had crossed his mind that Eugen's brain had not yet recovered its normal tone and activity. This speech of his nephew's, however, had the effect of immediately restoring his belief in the latter's entire sanity. He felt convinced that if only he could regain his nephew's confidence, the old brotherly confidence which had existed between them since the years when they played together as boys, all might yet be well. But at present there appeared to be no sign that Eugen meant to give his confidence to anyone.

The young Prince had come up out of the valley of the shadow of death, but some of the valley's shadow had clung to him, and it seemed he was unable to dissipate it.

'By the way,' said Eugen suddenly, 'I must reward these Racksoles, I suppose. I am indeed grateful to them. If I gave the girl a bracelet, and the father a thousand guineas--how would that meet the case?'

'My dear Eugen!' exclaimed Aribert aghast. 'A thousand guineas! Do you know that Theodore Racksole could buy up all Posen from end to end without making himself a pauper. A thousand guineas! You might as well offer him sixpence.'

'Then what must I offer?'

'Nothing, except your thanks. Anything else would be an insult. These are no ordinary hotel people.'

'Can't I give the little girl a bracelet?' Prince Eugen gave a sinister laugh.

Aribert looked at him steadily. 'No,' he said.

'Why did you kiss her--that night?' asked Prince Eugen carelessly.

'Kiss whom?' said Aribert, blushing and angry, despite his most determined efforts to keep calm and unconcerned.

'The Racksole girl.'

'When do you mean?'

'I mean,' said Prince Eugen, 'that night in Ostend when I was ill. You thought I was in a delirium. Perhaps I was. But somehow I remember that with extraordinary distinctness. I remember raising my head for a fraction of an instant, and just in that fraction of an instant you kissed her. Oh, Uncle Aribert!'

'Listen, Eugen, for God's sake. I love Nella Racksole. I shall marry her.'

'You!' There was a long pause, and then Eugen laughed. 'Ah!' he said. 'They all talk like that to start with. I have talked like that myself, dear uncle; it sounds nice, and it means nothing.'

'In this case it means everything, Eugen,' said Aribert quietly. Some accent of determination in the latter's tone made Eugen rather more serious.

'You can't marry her,' he said. 'The Emperor won't permit a morganatic marriage.'

'The Emperor has nothing to do with the affair. I shall renounce my rights. I shall become a plain citizen.'

'In which case you will have no fortune to speak of.'

'But my wife will have a fortune. Knowing the sacrifices which I shall have made in order to marry her, she will not hesitate to place that fortune in my hands for our mutual use,' said Aribert stiffly.

'You will decidedly be rich,' mused Eugen, as his ideas dwelt on Theodore Racksole's reputed wealth. 'But have you thought of this,' he asked, and his mild eyes glowed again in a sort of madness. 'Have you thought that I am unmarried, and might die at any moment, and then the throne will descend to you--to you, Aribert?'

'The throne will never descend to me, Eugen,' said Aribert softly, 'for you will live. You are thoroughly convalescent. You have nothing to fear.'

'It is the next seven days that I fear,' said Eugen.

'The next seven days! Why?'

'I do not know. But I fear them. If I can survive them--'

'Mr Sampson Levi, sire,' Hans announced in a loud tone.

CHAPTER XX
MR SAMPSON LEVI BIDS PRINCE EUGEN GOOD MORNING

PRINCE EUGEN started. 'I will see him,' he said, with a gesture to Hans as if to indicate that Mr Sampson Levi might enter at once.

'I beg one moment first,' said Aribert, laying a hand gently on his nephew's arm, and giving old Hans a glance which had the effect of precipitating that admirably trained servant through the doorway.

'What is it?' asked Prince Eugen crossly. 'Why this sudden seriousness? Don't forget that I have an appointment with Mr Sampson Levi, and must not keep him waiting. Someone said that punctuality is the politeness of princes.'

'Eugen,' said Aribert, 'I wish you to be as serious as I am. Why cannot we have faith in each other? I want to help you. I have helped you. You are my titular Sovereign; but on the other hand I have the honour to be your uncle:

'I have the honour to be the same age as you, and to have been your companion from youth up. Give me your confidence. I thought you had given it me years ago, but I have lately discovered that you had your secrets, even then. And now, since your illness, you are still more secretive.'

'What do you mean, Aribert?' said Eugen, in a tone which might have been either inimical or friendly. 'What do you want to say?'

'Well, in the first place, I want to say that you will not succeed with the estimable Mr Sampson Levi.'

'Shall I not?' said Eugen lightly. 'How do you know what my business is with him?'

'Suffice it to say that I know. You will never get that million pounds out of him.'

Prince Eugen gasped, and then swallowed his excitement. 'Who has been talking? What million?' His eyes wandered uneasily round the room. 'Ah!' he said, pretending to laugh. 'I see how it is. I have been chattering in my delirium. You mustn't take any notice of that, Aribert. When one has a fever one's ideas become grotesque and fanciful.'

'You never talked in your delirium,' Aribert replied; 'at least not about yourself. I knew about this projected loan before I saw you in Ostend.'

'Who told you?' demanded Eugen fiercely.

'Then you admit that you are trying to raise a loan?'

'I admit nothing. Who told you?'

'Theodore Racksole, the millionaire. These rich men have no secrets from each other. They form a coterie, closer than any coterie of ours. Eugen, and far more powerful. They talk, and in talking they rule the world, these millionaires. They are the real monarchs.'

'Curse them!' said Eugen.

'Yes, perhaps so. But let me return to your case. Imagine my shame, my disgust, when I found that Racksole could tell me more about your affairs than I knew myself. Happily, he is a good fellow; one can trust him; otherwise I should have been tempted to do something desperate when I discovered that all your private history was in his hands. Eugen, let us come to the point; why do you want that million? Is it actually true that you are so deeply in debt? I have no desire to improve the occasion. I merely ask.'

'And what if I do owe a million?' said Prince Eugen with assumed valour.

'Oh, nothing, my dear Eugen, nothing. Only it is rather a large sum to have scattered in ten years, is it not? How did you manage it?'

'Don't ask me, Aribert. I've been a fool. But I swear to you that the woman whom you call "the lady in the red hat" is the last of my follies. I am about to take a wife, and become a respectable Prince.'

'Then the engagement with Princess Anna is an accomplished fact?'

'Practically so. As soon as I have settled with Levi, all will be smooth.

Aribert, I wouldn't lose Anna for the Imperial throne. She is a good and pure woman, and I love her as a man might love an angel.'

'And yet you would deceive her as to your debts, Eugen?'

'Not her, but her absurd parents, and perhaps the Emperor. They have heard rumours, and I must set those rumours at rest by presenting to them a clean sheet.'

'I am glad you have been frank with me, Eugen,' said Prince Aribert, 'but I will be plain with you. You will never marry the Princess Anna.'

'And why?' said Eugen, supercilious again.

'Because her parents will not permit it. Because you will not be able to present a clean sheet to them. Because this Sampson Levi will never lend you a million.'

'Explain yourself.'

'I propose to do so. You were kidnapped--it is a horrid word, but we must use it--in Ostend.'

'True.'

'Do you know why?'

'I suppose because that vile old red-hatted woman and her accomplices wanted to get some money out of me. Fortunately, thanks to you, they didn't.'

'Not at all,' said Aribert. 'They wanted no money from you. They knew well enough that you had no money. They knew you were the naughty schoolboy among European Princes, with no sense of responsibility or of duty towards your kingdom. Shall I tell you why they kidnapped you?'

'When you have done abusing me, my dear uncle.'

'They kidnapped you merely to keep you out of England for a few days, merely to compel you to fail in your appointment with Sampson Levi. And it appears to me that they succeeded. Assuming that you don't obtain the money from Levi, is there another financier in all Europe from whom you can get it--on such strange security as you have to offer?'

'Possibly there is not,' said Prince Eugen calmly. 'But, you see, I shall get it from Sampson Levi. Levi promised it, and I know from other sources that he is a man of his word. He said that the money, subject to certain formalities, would be available till--'

'Till?'

'Till the end of June.'

'And it is now the end of July.'

'Well, what is a month? He is only too glad to lend the money. He will get excellent interest. How on earth have you got into your sage old head this notion of a plot against me? The idea is ridiculous. A plot against me? What for?'

'Have you ever thought of Bosnia?' asked Aribert coldly.

'What of Bosnia?'

'I need not tell you that the King of Bosnia is naturally under obligations to Austria, to whom he owes his crown. Austria is anxious for him to make a good influential marriage.'

'Well, let him.'

'He is going to. He is going to marry the Princess Anna.'

'Not while I live. He made overtures there a year ago, and was rebuffed.'

'Yes; but he will make overtures again, and this time he will not be rebuffed. Oh, Eugen! can't you see that this plot against you is being engineered by some persons who know all about your affairs, and whose desire is to prevent your marriage with Princess Anna? Only one man in Europe can have any motive for wishing to prevent your marriage with Princess Anna, and that is the man who means to marry her himself.' Eugen went very pale.

'Then, Aribert, do you mean to convey to me that my detention in Ostend was contrived by the agents of the King of Bosnia?'

'I do.'

'With a view to stopping my negotiations with Sampson Levi, and so putting an end to the possibility of my marriage with Anna?'

Aribert nodded.

'You are a good friend to me, Aribert. You mean well. But you are mistaken. You have been worrying about nothing.'

'Have you forgotten about Reginald Dimmock?'

'I remember you said that he had died.'

'I said nothing of the sort. I said that he had been assassinated. That was part of it, my poor Eugen.'

'Pooh!' said Eugen. 'I don't believe he was assassinated. And as for Sampson Levi, I will bet you a thousand marks that he and I come to terms this morning, and that the million is in my hands before I leave London.' Aribert shook his head.

'You seem to be pretty sure of Mr Levi's character. Have you had much to do with him before?'

'Well,' Eugen hesitated a second, 'a little. What young man in my position hasn't had something to do with Mr Sampson Levi at one time or another?'

'I haven't,' said Aribert.

'You! You are a fossil.' He rang a silver bell. 'Hans! I will receive Mr Sampson Levi.'

Whereupon Aribert discreetly departed, and Prince Eugen sat down in the great velvet chair, and began to look at the papers which Hans had previously placed upon the table.

'Good morning, your Royal Highness,' said Sampson Levi, bowing as he entered. 'I trust your Royal Highness is well.'

'Moderately, thanks,' returned the Prince.

In spite of the fact that he had had as much to do with people of Royal blood as any plain man in Europe, Sampson Levi had never yet learned how to be at ease with these exalted individuals during the first few minutes of an interview. Afterwards, he resumed command of himself and his faculties, but at the beginning he was invariably flustered, scarlet of face, and inclined to perspiration.

'We will proceed to business at once,' said Prince Eugen. 'Will you take a seat, Mr Levi?'

'I thank your Royal Highness.'

'Now as to that loan which we had already practically arranged--a million, I think it was,' said the Prince airily.

'A million,' Levi acquiesced, toying with his enormous watch chain.

'Everything is now in order. Here are the papers and I should like to finish the matter up at once.'

'Exactly, your Highness, but--'

'But what? You months ago expressed the warmest satisfaction at the security, though I am quite prepared to admit that the security, is of rather an unusual nature. You also agreed to the rate of interest. It is not everyone, Mr Levi, who can lend out a million at 5-1/2 per cent. And in ten years the whole amount will be paid back. I--er--I believe I informed you that the fortune of Princess Anna, who is about to accept my hand, will ultimately amount to something like fifty millions of marks, which is over two million pounds in your English money.' Prince Eugen stopped. He had no fancy for talking in this confidential manner to financiers, but he felt that circumstances demanded it.

'You see, it's like this, your Royal Highness,' began Mr Sampson Levi, in his homely English idiom. 'It's like this. I said I could keep that bit of money available till the end of June, and you were to give me an interview here before that date. Not having heard from your Highness, and not knowing your Highness's address, though my German agents made every inquiry, I concluded, that you had made other arrangements, money being so cheap this last few months.'

'I was unfortunately detained at Ostend,' said Prince Eugen, with as much haughtiness as he could assume, 'by--by important business. I have made no other arrangements, and I shall have need of the million. If you will be so good as to pay it to my London bankers--'

'I'm very sorry,' said Mr Sampson Levi, with a tremendous and dazzling air of politeness, which surprised even himself, 'but my syndicate has now lent the money elsewhere. It's in South America--I don't mind telling your Highness that we've lent it to the Chilean Government.'

'Hang the Chilean Government, Mr Levi,' exclaimed the Prince, and he went white. 'I must have that million. It was an arrangement.'

'It was an arrangement, I admit,' said Mr Sampson Levi, 'but your Highness broke the arrangement.'

There was a long silence.

'Do you mean to say,' began the Prince with tense calmness, 'that you are not in a position to let me have that million?'

'I could let your Highness have a million in a couple of years' time.'

The Prince made a gesture of annoyance. 'Mr Levi,' he said, 'if you do not place the money in my hands to-morrow you will ruin one of the oldest of reigning families, and, incidentally, you will alter the map of Europe. You are not keeping faith, and I had relied on you.'

'Pardon me, your Highness,' said little Levi, rising in resentment, 'it is not I who have not kept faith. I beg to repeat that the money is no longer at my disposal, and to bid your Highness good morning.'

And Mr Sampson Levi left the audience chamber with an awkward, aggrieved bow. It was a scene characteristic of the end of the nineteenth century--an overfed, commonplace, pursy little man who had been born in a Brixton semi-detached villa, and whose highest idea of pleasure was a Sunday up the river in an expensive electric launch, confronting and utterly routing, in a hotel belonging to an American millionaire, the representative of a race of men who had fingered every page of European history for centuries, and who still, in their native castles, were surrounded with every outward circumstance of pomp and power.

'Aribert,' said Prince Eugen, a little later, 'you were right. It is all over. I have only one refuge--'

'You don't mean--' Aribert stopped, dumbfounded.

'Yes, I do,' he said quickly. 'I can manage it so that it will look like an accident.'

ON the evening of Prince Eugen's fateful interview with Mr Sampson Levi, Theodore Racksole was wandering somewhat aimlessly and uneasily about the entrance hail and adjacent corridors of the Grand Babylon. He had returned from Ostend only a day or two previously, and had endeavoured with all his might to forget the affair which had carried him there--to regard it, in fact, as done with. But he found himself unable to do so. In vain he remarked, under his breath, that there were some things which were best left alone: if his experience as a manipulator of markets, a contriver of gigantic schemes in New York, had taught him anything at all, it should surely have taught him that. Yet he could not feel reconciled to such a position. The mere presence of the princes in his hotel roused the fighting instincts of this man, who had never in his whole career been beaten. He had, as it were, taken up arms on their side, and if the princes of Posen would not continue their own battle, nevertheless he, Theodore Racksole, wanted to continue it for them. To a certain extent, of course, the battle had been won, for Prince Eugen had been rescued from an extremely difficult and dangerous position, and the enemy--consisting of Jules, Rocco, Miss Spencer, and perhaps others--had been put to flight. But that, he conceived, was not enough; it was very far from being enough. That the criminals, for criminals they decidedly were, should still be at large, he regarded as an absurd anomaly. And there was another point: he had said nothing to the police of all that had occurred. He disdained the police, but he could scarcely fail to perceive that if the police should by accident gain a clue to the real state of the case he might be placed rather awkwardly, for the simple reason that in the eyes of the law it amounted to a misdemeanour to conceal as much as he had concealed. He asked himself, for the thousandth time, why he had adopted a policy of concealment from the police, why he had become in any way interested in the Posen matter, and why, at this present moment, he should be so anxious to prosecute it further? To the first two questions he replied, rather lamely, that he had been influenced by Nella, and also by a natural spirit of adventure; to the third he replied that he had always been in the habit of carrying things through, and was now actuated by a mere childish, obstinate desire to carry this one through. Moreover, he was splendidly conscious of his perfect ability to carry it through. One additional impulse he had, though he did not admit it to himself, being by nature adverse to big words, and that was an abstract love of justice, the Anglo-Saxon's deep-found instinct for helping the right side to conquer, even when grave risks must thereby be run, with no corresponding advantage.

He was turning these things over in his mind as he walked about the vast hotel on that evening of the last day in July. The Society papers had been stating for a week past that London was empty, but, in spite of the Society papers, London persisted in seeming to be just as full as ever. The Grand Babylon was certainly not as crowded as it had been a month earlier, but it was doing a very passable business. At the close of the season the gay butterflies of the social community have a habit of hovering for a day or two in the big hotels before they flutter away to castle and country-house, meadow and moor, lake and stream. The great basket-chairs in the portico were well filled by old and middle-aged gentlemen engaged in enjoying the varied delights of liqueurs, cigars, and the full moon which floated so serenely above the Thames. Here and there a pretty woman on the arm of a cavalier in immaculate attire swept her train as she turned to and fro in the promenade of the terrace. Waiters and uniformed commissionaires and gold-braided doorkeepers moved noiselessly about; at short intervals the chief of the doorkeepers blew his shrill whistle and hansoms drove up with tinkling bell to take away a pair of butterflies to some place of amusement or boredom; occasionally a private carriage drawn by expensive and self-conscious horses put the hansoms to shame by its mere outward glory. It was a hot night, a night for the summer woods, and save for the vehicles there was no rapid movement of any kind. It seemed as though the world--the world, that is to say, of the Grand Babylon--was fully engaged in the solemn processes of digestion and small-talk. Even the long row of the Embankment gas-lamps, stretching right and left, scarcely trembled in the still, warm, caressing air. The stars overhead looked down with many blinkings upon the enormous pile of the Grand Babylon, and the moon regarded it with bland and changeless face; what they thought of it and its inhabitants cannot, unfortunately, be

368 Resurrected Press Mystery Series

recorded. What Theodore Racksole thought of the moon can be recorded: he thought it was a nuisance. It somehow fascinated his gaze with its silly stare, and so interfered with his complex meditations. He glanced round at the well-dressed and satisfied people--his guests, his customers. They appeared to ignore him absolutely.

Probably only a very small percentage of them had the least idea that this tall spare man, with the iron-grey hair and the thin, firm, resolute face, who wore his American-cut evening clothes with such careless ease, was the sole proprietor of the Grand Babylon, and possibly the richest man in Europe. As has already been stated, Racksole was not a celebrity in England.

The guests of the Grand Babylon saw merely a restless male person, whose restlessness was rather a disturber of their quietude, but with whom, to judge by his countenance, it would be inadvisable to remonstrate. Therefore Theodore Racksole continued his perambulations unchallenged, and kept saying to himself, 'I must do something.' But what? He could think of no course to pursue.

At last he walked straight through the hotel and out at the other entrance, and so up the little unassuming side street into the roaring torrent of the narrow and crowded Strand. He jumped on a Putney bus, and paid his fair to Putney, fivepence, and then, finding that the humble occupants of the vehicle stared at the spectacle of a man in evening dress but without a dustcoat, he jumped off again, oblivious of the fact that the conductor jerked a thumb towards him and winked at the passengers as who should say, 'There goes a lunatic.' He went into a tobacconist's shop and asked for a cigar. The shopman mildly inquired what price.

'What are the best you've got?' asked Theodore Racksole.

'Five shillings each, sir,' said the man promptly.

'Give me a penny one,' was Theodore Racksole's laconic request, and he walked out of the shop smoking the penny cigar. It was a new sensation for him.

He was inhaling the aromatic odours of Eugène Rimmel's establishment for the sale of scents when a gentleman, walking slowly in the opposite direction, accosted him with a quiet, 'Good evening, Mr Racksole.' The millionaire did not at first recognize his interlocutor, who wore a travelling overcoat, and was carrying a handbag. Then a slight, pleased smile passed over his features, and he held out his hand.

'Well, Mr Babylon,' he greeted the other, 'of all persons in the wide world you are the man I would most have wished to meet.'

'You flatter me,' said the little Anglicized Swiss.

'No, I don't,' answered Racksole; 'it isn't my custom, any more than it's yours. I wanted to have a real good long yarn with you, and lo! here you are! Where have you sprung from?'

'From Lausanne,' said Felix Babylon. 'I had finished my duties there, I had nothing else to do, and I felt homesick. I felt the nostalgia of London, and so I came over, just as you see,' and he raised the handbag for Racksole's notice. 'One toothbrush, one razor, two slippers, eh?' He laughed. 'I was wondering as I walked along where I should stay--me, Felix Babylon, homeless in London.'

'I should advise you to stay at the Grand Babylon,' Racksole laughed back. It is a good hotel, and I know the proprietor personally.'

'Rather expensive, is it not?' said Babylon.

'To you, sir,' answered Racksole, 'the inclusive terms will be exactly half a crown a week. Do you accept?'

'I accept,' said Babylon, and added, 'You are very good, Mr Racksole.'

They strolled together back to the hotel, saying nothing in particular, but feeling very content with each other's company.

'Many customers?' asked Felix Babylon.

'Very tolerable,' said Racksole, assuming as much of the air of the professional hotel proprietor as he could. 'I think I may say in the storekeeper's phrase, that if there is any business about I am doing it.

To-night the people are all on the terrace in the portico--it's so confoundedly hot--and the consumption of ice is simply enormous--nearly as large as it would be in New York.'

'In that case,' said Babylon politely, 'let me offer you another cigar.'

'But I have not finished this one.'

'That is just why I wish to offer you another one. A cigar such as yours, my good friend, ought never to be smoked within the precincts of the Grand Babylon, not even by the proprietor of the

Grand Babylon, and especially when all the guests are assembled in the portico. The fumes of it would ruin any hotel.'

Theodore Racksole laughingly lighted the Rothschild Havana which Babylon gave him, and they entered the hotel arm in arm. But no sooner had they mounted the steps than little Felix became the object of numberless greetings. It appeared that he had been highly popular among his quondam guests. At last they reached the managerial room, where Babylon was regaled on a chicken, and Racksole assisted him in the consumption of a bottle of Heidsieck Monopole, Carte d'Or.

'This chicken is almost perfectly grilled,' said Babylon at length. 'It is a credit to the house. But why, my dear Racksole, why in the name of Heaven did you quarrel with Rocco?'

'Then you have heard?'

'Heard! My dear friend, it was in every newspaper on the Continent. Some journals prophesied that the Grand Babylon would have to close its doors within half a year now that Rocco had deserted it. But of course I knew better. I knew that you must have a good reason for allowing Rocco to depart, and that you must have made arrangements in advance for a substitute.'

'As a matter of fact, I had not made arrangements in advance,' said Theodore Racksole, a little ruefully; 'but happily we have found in our second sous-chef an artist inferior only to Rocco himself. That, however, was mere good fortune.'

'Surely,' said Babylon, 'it was indiscreet to trust to mere good fortune in such a serious matter?'

'I didn't trust to mere good fortune. I didn't trust to anything except Rocco, and he deceived me.'

'But why did you quarrel with him?'

'I didn't quarrel with him. I found him embalming a corpse in the State bedroom one night--'

'You what?' Babylon almost screamed.

'I found him embalming a corpse in the State bedroom,' repeated Racksole in his quietest tones.

The two men gazed at each other, and then Racksole replenished Babylon's glass.

'Tell me,' said Babylon, settling himself deep in an easy chair and lighting a cigar.

And Racksole thereupon recounted to him the whole of the Posen episode, with every circumstantial detail so far as he knew it. It was a long and complicated recital, and occupied about an hour. During that time little Felix never spoke a word, scarcely moved a muscle; only his small eyes gazed through the bluish haze of smoke. The clock on the mantelpiece tinkled midnight.

'Time for whisky and soda,' said Racksole, and got up as if to ring the bell; but Babylon waved him back.

'You have told me that this Sampson Levi had an audience of Prince Eugen to-day, but you have not told me the result of that audience,' said Babylon.

'Because I do not yet know it. But I shall doubtless know to-morrow. In the meantime, I feel fairly sure that Levi declined to produce Prince Eugen's required million. I have reason to believe that the money was lent elsewhere.'

'H'm!' mused Babylon; and then, carelessly, 'I am not at all surprised at that arrangement for spying through the bathroom of the State apartments.'

'Why are you not surprised?'

'Oh!' said Babylon, 'it is such an obvious dodge--so easy to carry out. As for me, I took special care never to involve myself in these affairs. I knew they existed; I somehow felt that they existed. But I also felt that they lay outside my sphere. My business was to provide board and lodging of the most sumptuous kind to those who didn't mind paying for it; and I did my business. If anything else went on in the hotel, under the rose, I long determined to ignore it unless it should happen to be brought before my notice; and it never was brought before my notice. However, I admit that there is a certain pleasurable excitement in this kind of affair and doubtless you have experienced that.'

'I have,' said Racksole simply, 'though I believe you are laughing at me.'

'By no means,' Babylon replied. 'Now what, if I may ask the question, is going to be your next step?'

'That is just what I desire to know myself,' said Theodore Racksole.

'Well,' said Babylon, after a pause, 'let us begin. In the first place, it is possible you may be interested to hear that I happened to see Jules to-day.'

'You did!' Racksole remarked with much calmness. 'Where?'

'Well, it was early this morning, in Paris, just before I left there. The meeting was quite accidental, and Jules seemed rather surprised at meeting me. He respectfully inquired where I was going, and I said that I was going to Switzerland. At that moment I thought I was going to Switzerland. It had occurred to me that after all I should be happier there, and that I had better turn back and not see London any more. However, I changed my mind once again, and decided to come on to London, and accept the risks of being miserable there without my hotel. Then I asked Jules whither he was bound, and he told me that he was off to Constantinople, being interested in a new French hotel there. I wished him good luck, and we parted.'

'Constantinople, eh!' said Racksole. 'A highly suitable place for him, I should say.'

'But,' Babylon resumed, 'I caught sight of him again.'

'Where?'

'At Charing Cross, a few minutes before I had the pleasure of meeting you.

Mr Jules had not gone to Constantinople after all. He did not see me, or I should have suggested to him that in going from Paris to Constantinople it is not usual to travel via London.'

'The cheek of the fellow!' exclaimed Theodore Racksole. 'The gorgeous and colossal cheek of the fellow!'

CHAPTER XXII
IN THE WINE CELLARS OF THE GRAND BABYLON

'DO you know anything of the antecedents of this Jules,' asked Theodore Racksole, helping himself to whisky.

'Nothing whatever,' said Babylon. 'Until you told me, I don't think I was aware that his true name was Thomas Jackson, though of course I knew that it was not Jules. I certainly was not aware that Miss Spencer was his wife, but I had long suspected that their relations were somewhat more intimate than the nature of their respective duties in the hotel absolutely demanded. All that I do know of Jules--he will always be called Jules--is that he gradually, by some mysterious personal force, acquired a prominent position in the hotel. Decidedly he was the cleverest and most intellectual waiter I have ever known, and he was specially skilled in the difficult task of retaining his own dignity while not interfering with that of other people.'

'I'm afraid this information is a little too vague to be of any practical assistance in the present difficulty.'

'What is the present difficulty?' Racksole queried, with a simple air.

'I should imagine that the present difficulty is to account for the man's presence in London.'

'That is easily accounted for,' said Racksole.

'How? Do you suppose he is anxious to give himself up to justice, or that the chains of habit bind him to the hotel?'

'Neither,' said Racksole. 'Jules is going to have another try--that's all.'

'Another try at what?'

'At Prince Eugen. Either at his life or his liberty. Most probably the former this time; almost certainly the former. He has guessed that we are somewhat handicapped by our anxiety to keep Prince Eugen's predicament quite quiet, and he is taking advantage, of that fact. As he already is fairly rich, on his own admission, the reward which has been offered to him must be enormous, and he is absolutely determined to get it. He has several times recently proved himself to be a daring fellow; unless I am mistaken he will shortly prove himself to be still more daring.'

'But what can he do? Surely you don't suggest that he will attempt the life of Prince Eugen in this hotel?'

'Why not? If Reginald Dimmock fell on mere suspicion that he would turn out unfaithful to the conspiracy, why not Prince Eugen?'

'But it would be an unspeakable crime, and do infinite harm to the hotel!'

'True!' Racksole admitted, smiling. Little Felix Babylon seemed to brace himself for the grasping of his monstrous idea.

'How could it possibly be done?' he asked at length.

'Dimmock was poisoned.'

'Yes, but you had Rocco here then, and Rocco was in the plot. It is conceivable that Rocco could have managed it--barely conceivable. But without Rocco I cannot think it possible. I cannot even think that Jules would attempt it. You see, in a place like the Grand Babylon, as probably I needn't point out to you, food has to pass through so many hands that to poison one person without killing perhaps fifty would be a most delicate operation. Moreover, Prince Eugen, unless he has changed his habits, is always served by his own attendant, old Hans, and therefore any attempt to tamper with a cooked dish immediately before serving would be hazardous in the extreme.'

'Granted,' said Racksole. 'The wine, however, might be more easily got at. Had you thought of that?'

'I had not,' Babylon admitted. 'You are an ingenious theorist, but I happen to know that Prince Eugen always has his wine opened in his own presence. No doubt it would be opened by Hans. Therefore the wine theory is not tenable, my friend.'

'I do not see why,' said Racksole. 'I know nothing of wine as an expert, and I very seldom drink it, but it seems to me that a bottle of wine might be tampered with while it was still in the cellar, especially if there was an accomplice in the hotel.'

'You think, then, that you are not yet rid of all your conspirators?'

'I think that Jules might still have an accomplice within the building.'

'And that a bottle of wine could be opened and recorked without leaving any trace of the operation?' Babylon was a trifle sarcastic.

'I don't see the necessity of opening the bottle in order to poison the wine,' said Racksole. 'I have never tried to poison anybody by means of a bottle of wine, and I don't lay claim to any natural talent as a poisoner, but I think I could devise several ways of managing the trick. Of course, I admit I may be entirely mistaken as to Jules' intentions.'

'Ah!' said Felix Babylon. 'The wine cellars beneath us are one of the wonders of London. I hope you are aware, Mr Racksole, that when you bought the Grand Babylon you bought what is probably the finest stock of wines in England, if not in Europe. In the valuation I reckoned them at sixty thousand pounds. And I may say that I always took care that the cellars were properly guarded. Even Jules would experience a serious difficulty in breaking into the cellars without the connivance of the wine-clerk, and the wine-clerk is, or was, incorruptible.'

'I am ashamed to say that I have not yet inspected my wines,' smiled Racksole; 'I have never given them a thought. Once or twice I have taken the trouble to make a tour of the hotel, but I omitted the cellars in my excursions.'

'Impossible, my dear fellow!' said Babylon, amused at such a confession, to him--a great connoisseur and lover of fine wines-- almost incredible. 'But really you must see them to-morrow. If I may, I will accompany you.'

'Why not to-night?' Racksole suggested, calmly.

'To-night! It is very late: Hubbard will have gone to bed.'

'And may I ask who is Hubbard? I remember the name but dimly.'

'Hubbard is the wine-clerk of the Grand Babylon,' said Felix, with a certain emphasis. 'A sedate man of forty. He has the keys of the cellars. He knows every bottle of every bin, its date, its qualities, its value. And he's a teetotaler. Hubbard is a curiosity. No wine can leave the cellars without his knowledge, and no person can enter the cellars without his knowledge. At least, that is how it was in my time,' Babylon added.

'We will wake him,' said Racksole.

'But it is one o'clock in the morning,' Babylon protested.

'Never mind--that is, if you consent to accompany me. A cellar is the same by night as by day. Therefore, why not now?'

Babylon shrugged his shoulders. 'As you wish,' he agreed, with his indestructible politeness.

'And now to find this Mr Hubbard, with his key of the cupboard,' said Racksole, as they walked out of the room together. Although the hour was so late, the hotel was not, of course, closed for the night. A few guests still remained about in the public rooms, and a few fatigued waiters were still in attendance. One of these latter was despatched in search of the singular Mr Hubbard, and it fortunately turned out that this gentleman had not actually retired, though he was on the point of doing so. He brought the keys to Mr Racksole in person, and after he had had a little chat with his former master, the proprietor and the ex-proprietor of the Grand Babylon Hotel proceeded on their way to the cellars.

These cellars extend over, or rather under, quite half the superficial areas of the whole hotel--the longitudinal half which lies next to the Strand.

Owing to the fact that the ground slopes sharply from the Strand to the river, the Grand Babylon is, so to speak, deeper near the Strand than it is near the Thames. Towards the Thames there is, below the entrance level, a basement and a sub-basement. Towards the Strand there is basement, sub-basement, and the huge wine cellars beneath all. After descending the four flights of the service stairs, and traversing a long passage running parallel with the kitchen, the two found themselves opposite a door, which, on being unlocked, gave access to another flight of stairs. At the foot of this was the main entrance to the cellars. Outside the entrance was the wine-lift, for the ascension of delicious fluids to the upper floors, and, opposite, Mr Hubbard's little office. There was electric light everywhere.

Babylon, who, as being most accustomed to them, held the bunch of keys, opened the great door, and then they were in the first cellar--the first of a suite of five. Racksole was struck not only by the icy coolness of the place, but also by its vastness. Babylon had seized a portable electric handlight, attached to a long wire, which lay handy, and, waving it about, disclosed the dimensions of the place. By that flashing illumination the subterranean chamber looked unutterably weird and mysterious, with its rows of numbered bins, stretching away into the distance till the radiance was reduced to the occasional far gleam of the light on the shoulder of a bottle. Then Babylon switched on the fixed electric lights, and Theodore Racksole entered upon a personally-conducted tour of what was quite the most interesting part of his own property.

To see the innocent enthusiasm of Felix Babylon for these stores of exhilarating liquid was what is called in the North 'a sight for sair een'.

He displayed to Racksole's bewildered gaze, in their due order, all the wines of three continents--nay, of four, for the superb and luscious Constantia wine of Cape Colony was not wanting in that most catholic collection of vintages. Beginning with the unsurpassed products of Burgundy, he continued with the clarets of Médoc, Bordeaux, and Sauterne; then to the champagnes of Ay, Hautvilliers, and Pierry; then to the hocks and moselles of Germany, and the brilliant imitation champagnes of Main, Neckar, and Naumburg; then to the famous and adorable Tokay of Hungary, and all the Austrian varieties of French wines, including Carlowitz and Somlauer; then to the dry sherries of Spain, including purest Manzanilla, and Amontillado, and Vino de Pasto; then to the wines of Malaga, both sweet and dry, and all the 'Spanish reds' from Catalonia, including the dark 'Tent' so often used sacramentally; then to the renowned port of Oporto. Then he proceeded to the Italian cellar, and descanted upon the excellence of Barolo from Piedmont, of Chianti from Tuscany, of Orvieto from the Roman States, of the 'Tears of Christ' from Naples, and the commoner Marsala from Sicily. And so on, to an extent and with a fullness of detail which cannot be rendered here.

At the end of the suite of cellars there was a glazed door, which, as could be seen, gave access to a supplemental and smaller cellar, an apartment about fifteen or sixteen feet square.

'Anything special in there?' asked Racksole curiously, as they stood before the door, and looked within at the seined ends of bottles.

'Ah!' exclaimed Babylon, almost smacking his lips, 'therein lies the cream of all.'

'The best champagne, I suppose?' said Racksole.

'Yes,' said Babylon, 'the best champagne is there--a very special Sillery, as exquisite as you will find anywhere. But I see, my friend, that you fall into the common error of putting champagne first among wines. That distinction belongs to

Burgundy. You have old Burgundy in that cellar, Mr Racksole, which cost me--how much do you think?--eighty pounds a bottle. Probably it will never be drunk,' he added with a sigh. 'It is too expensive even for princes and plutocrats.'

'Yes, it will,' said Racksole quickly. 'You and I will have a bottle up to-morrow.'

'Then,' continued Babylon, still riding his hobby-horse, 'there is a sample of the Rhine wine dated 1706 which caused such a sensation at the Vienna Exhibition of 1873. There is also a singularly glorious Persian wine from Shiraz, the like of which I have never seen elsewhere. Also there is an unrivalled vintage of Romanée-Conti, greatest of all modern Burgundies. If I remember right Prince Eugen invariably has a bottle when he comes to stay here. It is not on the hotel wine list, of course, and only a few customers know of it. We do not precisely hawk it about the dining-room.'

'Indeed!' said Racksole. 'Let us go inside.'

They entered the stone apartment, rendered almost sacred by the preciousness of its contents, and Racksole looked round with a strangely intent and curious air. At the far side was a grating, through which came a feeble light.

'What is that?' asked the millionaire sharply.

'That is merely a ventilation grating. Good ventilation is absolutely essential.'

'Looks broken, doesn't it?' Racksole suggested and then, putting a finger quickly on Babylon's shoulder, 'there's someone in the cellar. Can't you hear breathing, down there, behind that bin?'

The two men stood tense and silent for a while, listening, under the ray of the single electric light in the ceiling. Half the cellar was involved in gloom. At length Racksole walked firmly down the central passage-way between the bins and turned to the corner at the right.

'Come out, you villain!' he said in a low, well-nigh vicious tone, and dragged up a cowering figure.

He had expected to find a man, but it was his own daughter, Nella Racksole, upon whom he had laid angry hands.

'WELL, Father,' Nella greeted her astounded parent. 'You should make sure that you have got hold of the right person before you use all that terrible muscular force of yours. I do believe you have broken my shoulder bone.' She rubbed her shoulder with a comical expression of pain, and then stood up before the two men. The skirt of her dark grey dress was torn and dirty, and the usually trim Nella looked as though she had been shot down a canvas fire-escape. Mechanically she smoothed her frock, and gave a straightening touch to her hair.

'Good evening, Miss Racksole,' said Felix Babylon, bowing formally. 'This is an unexpected pleasure.' Felix 's drawing-room manners never deserted him upon any occasion whatever.

'May I inquire what you are doing in my wine cellar, Nella Racksole?' said the millionaire a little stiffly He was certainly somewhat annoyed at having mistaken his daughter for a criminal; moreover, he hated to be surprised, and upon this occasion he had been surprised beyond any ordinary surprise; lastly, he was not at all pleased that Nella should be observed in that strange predicament by a stranger.

'I will tell you,' said Nella. 'I had been reading rather late in my room--the night was so close. I heard Big Ben strike half-past twelve, and then I put the book down, and went out on to the balcony of my window for a little fresh air before going to bed. I leaned over the balcony very quietly--you will remember that I am on the third floor now--and looked down below into the little sunk yard which separates the wall of the hotel from Salisbury Lane. I was rather astonished to see a figure creeping across the yard. I knew there was no entrance into the hotel from that yard, and besides, it is fifteen or twenty feet below the level of the street. So I watched. The figure went close up against the wall, and disappeared from my view. I leaned over the balcony as far as I dared, but I couldn't see him. I could hear him, however.'

'What could you hear?' questioned Racksole sharply.

'It sounded like a sawing noise,' said Nella; 'and it went on for quite a long time--nearly a quarter of an hour, I should think--a rasping sort of noise.'

'Why on earth didn't you come and warn me or someone else in the hotel?' asked Racksole.

'Oh, I don't know, Dad,' she replied sweetly. 'I had got interested in it, and I thought I would see it out myself. Well, as I was saying, Mr. Babylon,' she continued, addressing her remarks to Felix, with a dazzling smile, 'that noise went on for quite a long time. At last it stopped, and the figure reappeared from under the wall, crossed the yard, climbed up the opposite wall by some means or other, and so over the railings into Salisbury Lane. I felt rather relieved then, because I knew he hadn't actually broken into the hotel. He walked down Salisbury Lane very slowly. A policeman was just coming up. "Goodnight, officer," I heard him say to the policeman, and he asked him for a match. The policeman supplied the match, and the other man lighted a cigarette, and proceeded further down the lane. By cricking your neck from my window, Mr Babylon, you can get a glimpse of the Embankment and the river. I saw the man cross the Embankment, and lean over the river wall, where he seemed to be talking to some one. He then walked along the Embankment to Westminster and that was the last I saw of him. I waited a minute or two for him to come back, but he didn't come back, and so I thought it was about time I began to make inquiries into the affair. I went downstairs instantly, and out of the hotel, through the quadrangle, into Salisbury Lane, and I looked over those railings. There was a ladder on the other side, by which it was perfectly easy--once you had got over the railings--to climb down into the yard. I was horribly afraid lest someone might walk up Salisbury Lane and catch me in the act of negotiating those railings, but no one did, and I surmounted them, with no worse damage than a torn skirt. I crossed the yard on tiptoe, and I found that in the wall, close to the ground and almost exactly under my window, there was an iron grating, about one foot by fourteen inches. I suspected, as there was no other ironwork near, that the mysterious visitor must have been sawing at this grating for private purposes of his own. I gave it a good shake, and I was not at all surprised that a good part of it came off in my hand, leaving just enough room for a person to creep through. I decided that I would creep through, and now wish I hadn't. I don't know, Mr Babylon, whether you have ever tried to creep through a small hole with a skirt on. Have you?'

'I have not had that pleasure,' said little Felix, bowing again, and absently taking up a bottle which lay to his hand.

'Well, you are fortunate,' the imperturbable Nella resumed. 'For quite three minutes I thought I should perish in that grating, Dad, with my shoulder inside and the rest of me outside. However, at last, by the most amazing and agonizing efforts, I pulled myself through and fell into this extraordinary cellar more dead than alive. Then I wondered what I should do next. Should I wait for the mysterious visitor to return, and stab him with my pocket scissors if he tried to enter, or should I raise an alarm? First of all I replaced the broken grating, then I struck a match, and I saw that I had got landed in a wilderness of bottles. The match went out, and I hadn't another one. So I sat down in the corner to think. I had just decided to wait and see if the visitor returned, when I heard footsteps, and then voices; and then you came in. I must say I was rather taken aback, especially as I recognized the voice of Mr Babylon. You see, I didn't want to frighten you.

If I had bobbed up from behind the bottles and said "Booh!" you would have had a serious shock. I wanted to think of a way of breaking my presence gently to you. But you saved me the trouble, Dad. Was I really breathing so loudly that you could hear me?'

The girl ended her strange recital, and there was a moment's silence in the cellar. Racksole merely nodded an affirmative to her concluding question.

'Well, Nell, my girl,' said the millionaire at length, 'we are much obliged for your gymnastic efforts--very much obliged. But now, I think you had better go off to bed. There is going to be some serious trouble here, I'll lay my last dollar on that?'

'But if there is to be a burglary I should so like to see it, Dad,' Nella pleaded. 'I've never seen a burglar caught red-handed.'

'This isn't a burglary, my dear. I calculate it's something far worse than a burglary.'

'What?' she cried. 'Murder? Arson? Dynamite plot? How perfectly splendid!'

'Mr Babylon informs me that Jules is in London,' said Racksole quietly.

'Jules!' she exclaimed under her breath, and her tone changed instantly to the utmost seriousness. 'Switch off the light, quick!' Springing to the switch, she put the cellar in darkness.

'What's that for?' said her father.

'If he comes back he would see the light, and be frightened away,' said Nella. 'That wouldn't do at all.'

'It wouldn't, Miss Racksole,' said Babylon, and there was in his voice a note of admiration for the girl's sagacity which Racksole heard with high paternal pride.

'Listen, Nella,' said the latter, drawing his daughter to him in the profound gloom of the cellar. 'We fancy that Jules may be trying to tamper with a certain bottle of wine--a bottle which might possibly be drunk by Prince Eugen. Now do you think that the man you saw might have been Jules?'

'I hadn't previously thought of him as being Jules, but immediately you mentioned the name I somehow knew that he was. Yes, I am sure it was Jules.'

'Well, just hear what I have to say. There is no time to lose. If he is coming at all he will be here very soon--and you can help.' Racksole explained what he thought Jules' tactics might be. He proposed that if the man returned he should not be interfered with, but merely watched from the other side of the glass door.

'You want, as it were, to catch Mr Jules alive?' said Babylon, who seemed rather taken aback at this novel method of dealing with criminals. 'Surely,' he added, 'it would be simpler and easier to inform the police of your suspicion, and to leave everything to them.'

'My dear fellow,' said Racksole, 'we have already gone much too far without the police to make it advisable for us to call them in at this somewhat advanced stage of the proceedings. Besides, if you must know it, I have a particular desire to capture the scoundrel myself. I will leave you and Nella here, since Nella insists on seeing everything, and I will arrange things so that once he has entered the cellar Jules will not get out of it again-- at any rate through the grating. You had better place yourselves on the other side of the glass door, in the big cellar; you will be in a position to observe from there, I will skip off at once. All you have to do is to take note of what the fellow does. If he has any accomplices within the hotel we shall probably be able by that means to discover who the accomplice is.'

Lighting a match and shading it with his hands, Racksole showed them both out of the little cellar. 'Now if you lock this glass door on the outside he can't escape this way: the panes of glass are too small, and the woodwork too stout. So, if he comes into the trap, you two will have the pleasure of actually seeing him frantically writhe therein, without any personal danger; but perhaps you'd better not show yourselves.'

In another moment Felix Babylon and Nella were left to themselves in the darkness of the cellar, listening to the receding footfalls of Theodore Racksole. But the sound of these footfalls had not died away before another sound greeted their ears--the grating of the small cellar was being removed.

'I hope your father will be in time,' whispered Felix

'Hush!' the girl warned him, and they stooped side by side in tense silence.

A man cautiously but very neatly wormed his body through the aperture of the grating. The watchers could only see his form indistinctly in the darkness.

Then, being fairly within the cellar, he walked without the least hesitation to the electric switch and turned on the light. It was unmistakably Jules, and he knew the geography of the cellar very well. Babylon could with difficulty repress a start as he saw this bold and unscrupulous ex-waiter moving with such an air of assurance and determination about the precious cellar. Jules went directly to a small bin which was numbered 17, and took there from the topmost bottle.

'The Romanee-Conti--Prince Eugen's wine!' Babylon exclaimed under his breath.

Jules neatly and quickly removed the seal with an instrument which he had clearly brought for the purpose. He then took a little flat box from his pocket, which seemed to contain a sort of black salve. Rubbing his finger in this, he smeared the top of the neck of the bottle with it, just where the cork came against the glass. In another instant he had deftly replaced the seal and restored the bottle to its position. He then turned off the light, and made for the aperture. When he was half-way through Nella exclaimed, 'He will escape, after all. Dad has not had time--we must stop him.'

But Babylon, that embodiment of caution, forcibly, but nevertheless politely, restrained this Yankee girl, whom he

deemed so rash and imprudent, and before she could free herself
the lithe form of Jules had disappeared.

CHAPTER XXIV
THE BOTTLE OF WINE

AS regards Theodore Racksole, who was to have caught his man from the outside of the cellar, he made his way as rapidly as possible from the wine-cellars, up to the ground floor, out of the hotel by the quadrangle, through the quadrangle, and out into the top of Salisbury Lane. Now, owing to the vastness of the structure of the Grand Babylon, the mere distance thus to be traversed amounted to a little short of a quarter of a mile, and, as it included a number of stairs, about two dozen turnings, and several passages which at that time of night were in darkness more or less complete, Racksole could not have been expected to accomplish the journey in less than five minutes. As a matter of fact, six minutes had elapsed before he reached the top of Salisbury Lane, because he had been delayed nearly a minute by some questions addressed to him by a muddled and whisky-laden guest who had got lost in the corridors. As everybody knows, there is a sharp short bend in Salisbury Lane near the top. Racksole ran round this at good racing speed, but he was unfortunate enough to run straight up against the very policeman who had not long before so courteously supplied Jules with a match. The policeman seemed to be scarcely in so pliant a mood just then.

'Hullo!' he said, his naturally suspicious nature being doubtless aroused by the spectacle of a bareheaded man in evening dress running violently down the lane. 'What's this? Where are you for in such a hurry?' and he forcibly detained Theodore Racksole for a moment and scrutinized his face.

'Now, officer,' said Racksole quietly, 'none of your larks, if you please. I've no time to lose.'

'Beg your pardon, sir,' the policeman remarked, though hesitatingly and not quite with good temper, and Racksole was allowed to proceed on his way. The millionaire's scheme for trapping Jules was to get down into the little sunk yard by means of the ladder, and then to secrete himself behind some convenient abutment of brickwork until Mr Tom Jackson should have got into the cellar. He therefore nimbly surmounted the railings--the railings of his own hotel--and was gingerly descending the ladder, when lo! a rough hand seized him by the coat-collar and with a ferocious jerk urged him backwards. The fact was, Theodore Racksole had counted without the policeman. That guardian of the peace, mistrusting Racksole's manner, quietly followed him down the lane. The sight of the millionaire climbing the railings had put him on his mettle, and the result was the ignominious capture of Racksole. In vain Theodore expostulated, explained, anathematized. Only one thing would satisfy the stolid policeman--namely, that Racksole should return with him to the hotel and there establish his identity. If Racksole then proved to be Racksole, owner of the Grand Babylon, well and good--the policeman promised to apologize. So Theodore had no alternative but to accept the suggestion. To prove his identity was, of course, the work of only a few minutes, after which Racksole, annoyed, but cool as ever, returned to his railings, while the policeman went off to another part of his beat, where he would be likely to meet a comrade and have a chat.

In the meantime, our friend Jules, sublimely unconscious of the altercation going on outside, and of the special risk which he ran, was of course actually in the cellar, which he had reached before Racksole got to the railings for the first time. It was, indeed, a happy chance for Jules that his exit from the cellar coincided with the period during which Racksole was absent from the railings. As Racksole came down the lane for the second time, he saw a figure walking about fifty yards in front of him towards the Embankment. Instantly he divined that it was Jules, and that the policeman had thrown him just too late. He ran, and Jules, hearing the noise of pursuit, ran also. The ex-waiter was fleet; he made direct for a certain spot in the Embankment wall, and, to the intense astonishment of Racksole, jumped clean over the wall, as it seemed, into the river. 'Is he so desperate as to commit suicide?' Racksole exclaimed as he ran, but a second later the puff and snort of a steam launch told him that Jules was not quite driven to suicide. As the millionaire crossed the Embankment roadway he saw the funnel of the launch move out from under the river-wall. It swerved into midstream and headed towards London Bridge. There was a silent mist over the river. Racksole was helpless....

Although Racksole had now been twice worsted in a contest of wits within the precincts of the Grand Babylon, once by Rocco and once by Jules, he could not fairly blame himself for the present miscarriage of his plans--a miscarriage due to the meddlesomeness of an extraneous person, combined with pure ill-fortune. He did not, therefore, permit the accident to interfere with his sleep that night.

On the following day he sought out Prince Aribert, between whom and himself there now existed a feeling of unmistakable, frank friendship, and disclosed to him the happenings of the previous night, and particularly the tampering with the bottle of Romanée-Conti.

'I believe you dined with Prince Eugen last night?'

'I did. And curiously enough we had a bottle of Romanée-Conti, an admirable wine, of which Eugen is passionately fond.'

'And you will dine with him to-night?'

'Most probably. To-day will, I fear, be our last day here. Eugen wishes to return to Posen early to-morrow.'

'Has it struck you, Prince,' said Racksole, 'that if Jules had succeeded in poisoning your nephew, he would probably have succeeded also in poisoning you?'

'I had not thought of it,' laughed Aribert, 'but it would seem so. It appears that so long as he brings down his particular quarry, Jules is careless of anything else that may be accidentally involved in the destruction. However, we need have no fear on that score now. You know the bottle, and you can destroy it at once.'

'But I do not propose to destroy it,' said Racksole calmly. 'If Prince Eugen asks for Romanée-Conti to be served to-night, as he probably will, I propose that that precise bottle shall be served to him--and to you.'

'Then you would poison us in spite of ourselves?'

'Scarcely,' Racksole smiled. 'My notion is to discover the accomplices within the hotel. I have already inquired as to the wine-clerk, Hubbard. Now does it not occur to you as extraordinary that on this particular day Mr Hubbard should be ill in bed? Hubbard, I am informed, is suffering from an attack of stomach poisoning, which has supervened during the night. He says that he does not know what can have caused it. His place in the wine cellars will be taken to-day by his assistant, a mere youth, but to all appearances a fairly smart youth. I need not say that we shall keep an eye on that youth.'

'One moment,' Prince Aribert interrupted. 'I do not quite understand how you think the poisoning was to have been effected.'

'The bottle is now under examination by an expert, who has instructions to remove as little as possible of the stuff which Jules put on the rim of the mouth of it. It will be secretly replaced in its bin during the day. My idea is that by the mere action of pouring out the wine takes up some of the poison, which I deem to be very strong, and thus becomes fatal as it enters the glass.'

'But surely the servant in attendance would wipe the mouth of the bottle?'

'Very carelessly, perhaps. And moreover he would be extremely unlikely to wipe off all the stuff; some of it has been ingeniously placed just on the inside edge of the rim. Besides, suppose he forgot to wipe the bottle?'

'Prince Eugen is always served at dinner by Hans. It is an honour which the faithful old fellow reserves for himself.'

'But suppose Hans--' Racksole stopped.

'Hans an accomplice! My dear Racksole, the suggestion is wildly impossible.'

That night Prince Aribert dined with his august nephew in the superb dining-room of the Royal apartments. Hans served, the dishes being brought to the door by other servants. Aribert found his nephew despondent and taciturn. On the previous day, when, after the futile interview with Sampson Levi, Prince Eugen had despairingly threatened to commit suicide, in such a manner as to make it 'look like an accident', Aribert had compelled him to give his word of honour not to do so.

'What wine will your Royal Highness take?' asked old Hans in his soothing tones, when the soup was served.

'Sherry,' was Prince Eugen's curt order.

'And Romanée-Conti afterwards?' said Hans. Aribert looked up quickly.

'No, not to-night. I'll try Sillery to-night,' said Prince Eugen.

'I think I'll have Romanée-Conti, Hans, after all,' he said. 'It suits me better than champagne.'

The famous and unsurpassable Burgundy was served with the roast. Old Hans brought it tenderly in its wicker cradle, inserted the corkscrew with mathematical precision, and drew the cork, which he offered for his master's inspection. Eugen nodded, and told him to put it down. Aribert watched with intense interest. He could not for an instant believe that Hans was not the very soul of fidelity, and yet, despite himself, Racksole's words had caused him a certain uneasiness. At that moment Prince Eugen murmured across the table:

'Aribert, I withdraw my promise. Observe that, I withdraw it.' Aribert shook his head emphatically, without removing his gaze from Hans. The white-haired servant perfunctorily dusted his napkin round the neck of the bottle of Romanée-Conti, and poured out a glass. Aribert trembled from head to foot.

Eugen took up the glass and held it to the light.

'Don't drink it,' said Aribert very quietly. 'It is poisoned.'

'Poisoned!' exclaimed Prince Eugen.

'Poisoned, sire!' exclaimed old Hans, with an air of profound amazement and concern, and he seized the glass. 'Impossible, sire. I myself opened the bottle. No one else has touched it, and the cork was perfect.'

'I tell you it is poisoned,' Aribert repeated.

'Your Highness will pardon an old man,' said Hans, 'but to say that this wine is poison is to say that I am a murderer. I will prove to you that it is not poisoned. I will drink it.' And he raised the glass to his trembling lips. In that moment Aribert saw that old Hans, at any rate, was not an accomplice of Jules. Springing up from his seat, he knocked the glass from the aged servitor's hands, and the fragments of it fell with a light tinkling crash partly on the table and partly on the floor. The Prince and the servant gazed at one another in a distressing and terrible silence.

There was a slight noise, and Aribert looked aside. He saw that Eugen's body had slipped forward limply over the left arm of his chair; the Prince's arms hung straight and lifeless; his eyes were closed; he was unconscious.

'Hans!' murmured Aribert. 'Hans! What is this?'

CHAPTER XXV
THE STEAM LAUNCH

MR TOM JACKSON's notion of making good his escape from the hotel by means of a steam launch was an excellent one, so far as it went, but Theodore Racksole, for his part, did not consider that it went quite far enough.

Theodore Racksole opined, with peculiar glee, that he now had a tangible and definite clue for the catching of the Grand Babylon's ex-waiter. He knew nothing of the Port of London, but he happened to know a good deal of the far more complicated, though somewhat smaller, Port of New York, and he was sure there ought to be no extraordinary difficulty in getting hold of Jules' steam launch. To those who are not thoroughly familiar with it the River Thames and its docks, from London Bridge to Gravesend, seems a vast and uncharted wilderness of craft--a wilderness in which it would be perfectly easy to hide even a three-master successfully. To such people the idea of looking for a steam launch on the river would be about equivalent to the idea of looking for a needle in a bundle of hay. But the fact is, there are hundreds of men between St Katherine's Wharf and Blackwall who literally know the Thames as the suburban householder knows his back-garden--who can recognize thousands of ships and put a name to them at a distance of half a mile, who are informed as to every movement of vessels on the great stream, who know all the captains, all the engineers, all the lightermen, all the pilots, all the licensed watermen, and all the unlicensed scoundrels from the Tower to Gravesend, and a lot further. By these experts of the Thames the slightest unusual event on the water is noticed and discussed--a wherry cannot change hands but they will guess shrewdly upon the price paid and the intentions of the new owner with regard to it. They have a habit of watching the river for the mere interest of the sight, and they talk about everything like housewives gathered of an evening round the cottage door. If the first mate of a Castle Liner gets the sack they will be able to tell you what he said to the captain, what the old man said to him, and what both said to the Board, and having finished off that affair they will cheerfully turn to discussing whether Bill Stevens sank his barge outside the West Indian No.2 by accident or on purpose.

Theodore Racksole had no satisfactory means of identifying the steam launch which carried away Mr Tom Jackson. The sky had clouded over soon after midnight, and there was also a slight mist, and he had only been able to make out that it was a low craft, about sixty feet long, probably painted black. He had personally kept a watch all through the night on vessels going upstream, and during the next morning he had a man to take his place who warned him whenever a steam launch went towards Westminster. At noon, after his conversation with Prince Aribert, he went down the river in a hired row-boat as far as the Custom House, and poked about everywhere, in search of any vessel which could by any possibility be the one he was in search of.

But he found nothing. He was, therefore, tolerably sure that the mysterious launch lay somewhere below the Custom House. At the Custom House stairs, he landed, and asked for a very high official--an official inferior only to a Commissioner--whom he had entertained once in New York, and who had met him in London on business at Lloyd's. In the large but dingy office of this great man a long conversation took place--a conversation in which Racksole had to exercise a certain amount of persuasive power, and which ultimately ended in the high official ringing his bell.

'Desire Mr Hazell--room No. 332--to speak to me,' said the official to the boy who answered the summons, and then, turning to Racksole: 'I need hardly repeat, my dear Mr Racksole, that this is strictly unofficial.'

'Agreed, of course,' said Racksole.

Mr Hazell entered. He was a young man of about thirty, dressed in blue serge, with a pale, keen face, a brown moustache and a rather handsome brown beard.

'Mr Hazell,' said the high official, 'let me introduce you to Mr Theodore Racksole--you will doubtless be familiar with his name. Mr Hazell,' he went on to Racksole, 'is one of our outdoor staff--what we call an examining officer. Just now he is doing night duty. He has a boat on the river and a couple of men, and the right to board and examine any craft whatever. What Mr Hazell and his crew don't know about the Thames between here and Gravesend isn't knowledge.'

'Glad to meet you, sir,' said Racksole simply, and they shook hands.

Racksole observed with satisfaction that Mr Hazell was entirely at his ease.

'Now, Hazell,' the high official continued, 'Mr Racksole wants you to help in a little private expedition on the river to-night. I will give you a night's leave. I sent for you partly because I thought you would enjoy the affair and partly because I think I can rely on you to regard it as entirely unofficial and not to talk about it. You understand? I dare say you will have no cause to regret having obliged Mr Racksole.'

'I think I grasp the situation,' said Hazell, with a slight smile.

'And, by the way,' added the high official, 'although the business is unofficial, it might be well if you wore your official overcoat. See?'

'Decidedly,' said Hazell; 'I should have done so in any case.'

'And now, Mr Hazell,' said Racksole, 'will you do me the pleasure of lunching with me? If you agree, I should like to lunch at the place you usually frequent.'

So it came to pass that Theodore Racksole and George Hazell, outdoor clerk in the Customs, lunched together at 'Thomas's Chop-House', in the city of London, upon mutton-chops and coffee. The millionaire soon discovered that he had got hold of a keen-witted man and a person of much insight.

'Tell me,' said Hazell, when they had reached the cigarette stage, 'are the magazine writers anything like correct?'

'What do you mean?' asked Racksole, mystified.

'Well, you're a millionaire--"one of the best", I believe. One often sees articles on and interviews with millionaires, which describe their private railroad cars, their steam yachts on the Hudson, their marble stables, and so on, and so on. Do you happen to have those things?'

'I have a private car on the New York Central, and I have a two thousand ton schooner-yacht--though it isn't on the Hudson. It happens just now to be on East River. And I am bound to admit that the stables of my uptown place are fitted with marble.' Racksole laughed.

'Ah!' said Hazell. 'Now I can believe that I am lunching with a millionaire. It's strange how facts like those--unimportant in themselves--appeal to the imagination. You seem to me a real millionaire now. You've given me some personal information; I'll give you some in return. I earn three hundred a year, and perhaps sixty pounds a year extra for overtime. I live by myself in two rooms in Muscovy Court. I've as much money as I need, and I always do exactly what I like outside office. As regards the office, I do as little work as I can, on principle--it's a fight between us and the Commissioners who shall get the best. They try to do us down, and we try to do them down--it's pretty even on the whole. All's fair in war, you know, and there ain't no ten commandments in a Government office.'

Racksole laughed. 'Can you get off this afternoon?' he asked.

'Certainly,' said Hazell; 'I'll get one of my pals to sign on for me, and then I shall be free.'

'Well,' said Racksole, 'I should like you to come down with me to the Grand Babylon. Then we can talk over my little affair at length. And may we go on your boat? I want to meet your crew.'

'That will be all right,' Hazell remarked. 'My two men are the idlest, most soul-less chaps you ever saw. They eat too much, and they have an enormous appetite for beer; but they know the river, and they know their business, and they will do anything within the fair game if they are paid for it, and aren't asked to hurry.'

That night, just after dark, Theodore Racksole embarked with his new friend George Hazell in one of the black-painted Customs wherries, manned by a crew of two men--both the later freemen of the river, a distinction which carries with it certain privileges unfamiliar to the mere landsman. It was a cloudy and oppressive evening, not a star showing to illumine the slow tide, now just past its flood. The vast forms of steamers at anchor-- chiefly those of the General Steam Navigation and the Aberdeen Line--heaved themselves high out of the water, straining sluggishly at their mooring buoys. On either side the naked walls of warehouses rose like grey precipices from the stream, holding forth quaint arms of steam-cranes. To the west the Tower Bridge spanned the river with its formidable arch, and above that its suspended footpath--a hundred and fifty feet from earth.

Down towards the east and the Pool of London a forest of funnels and masts was dimly outlined against the sinister sky.

Huge barges, each steered by a single man at the end of a pair of giant oars, lumbered and swirled down-stream at all angles. Occasionally a tug snorted busily past, flashing its red and green signals and dragging an unwieldy tail of barges in its wake. Then a Margate passenger steamer, its electric lights gleaming from every porthole, swerved round to anchor, with its load of two thousand fatigued excursionists. Over everything brooded an air of mystery--a spirit and feeling of strangeness, remoteness, and the inexplicable. As the broad flat little boat bobbed its way under the shadow of enormous hulks, beneath stretched hawsers, and past buoys covered with green slime, Racksole could scarcely believe that he was in the very heart of London--the most prosaic city in the world. He had a queer idea that almost anything might happen in this seeming waste of waters at this weird hour of ten o'clock. It appeared incredible to him that only a mile or two away people were sitting in theatres applauding farces, and that at Cannon Street Station, a few yards off, other people were calmly taking the train to various highly respectable suburbs whose names he was gradually learning. He had the uplifting sensation of being in another world which comes to us sometimes amid surroundings violently different from our usual surroundings. The most ordinary noises--of men calling, of a chain running through a slot, of a distant siren--translated themselves to his ears into terrible and haunting sounds, full of portentous significance. He looked over the side of the boat into the brown water, and asked himself what frightful secrets lay hidden in its depth. Then he put his hand into his hip-pocket and touched the stock of his Colt revolver--that familiar substance comforted him.

The oarsmen had instructions to drop slowly down to the Pool, as the wide reach below the Tower is called. These two men had not been previously informed of the precise object of the expedition, but now that they were safely afloat Hazell judged it expedient to give them some notion of it. 'We expect to come across a rather suspicious steam launch,' he said. 'My friend here is very anxious to get a sight of her, and until he has seen her nothing definite can be done.'

'What sort of a craft is she, sir?' asked the stroke oar, a fat-faced man who seemed absolutely incapable of any serious exertion.

'I don't know,' Racksole replied; 'but as near as I can judge, she's about sixty feet in length, and painted black. I fancy I shall recognize her when I see her.'

'Not much to go by, that,' exclaimed the other man curtly. But he said no more. He, as well as his mate, had received from Theodore Racksole one English sovereign as a kind of preliminary fee, and an English sovereign will do a lot towards silencing the natural sarcastic tendencies and free speech of a Thames waterman.

'There's one thing I noticed,' said Racksole suddenly, 'and I forgot to tell you of it, Mr Hazell. Her screw seemed to move with a rather irregular, lame sort of beat.'

Both watermen burst into a laugh.

'Oh,' said the fat rower, 'I know what you're after, sir--it's Jack Everett's launch, commonly called "Squirm". She's got a four-bladed propeller, and one blade is broken off short.'

'Ay, that's it, sure enough,' agreed the man in the bows. 'And if it's her you want, I seed her lying up against Cherry Gardens Pier this very morning.'

'Let us go to Cherry Gardens Pier by all means, as soon as possible,'

Racksole said, and the boat swung across stream and then began to creep down by the right bank, feeling its way past wharves, many of which, even at that hour, were still busy with their cranes, that descended empty into the bellies of ships and came up full. As the two watermen gingerly manoeuvred the boat on the ebbing tide, Hazell explained to the millionaire that the 'Squirm' was one of the most notorious craft on the river. It appeared that when anyone had a nefarious or underhand scheme afoot which necessitated river work Everett's launch was always available for a suitable monetary consideration. The 'Squirm' had got itself into a thousand scrapes, and out of those scrapes again with safety, if not precisely with honour. The river police kept a watchful eye on it, and the chief marvel about the whole thing was that old Everett, the owner, had never yet been seriously compromised in any illegal escapade. Not once had the officer of the law been able to prove anything definite against the proprietor of the 'Squirm', though several of its quondam hirers were at that very moment in various of Her Majesty's prisons throughout the country. Latterly, however, the launch, with its damaged propeller, which Everett consistently refused to have repaired, had acquired an evil reputation, even among evil-doers, and this fraternity had gradually come to abandon it for less easily recognizable craft.

'Your friend, Mr Tom Jackson,' said Hazell to Racksole, 'committed an error of discretion when he hired the "Squirm". A scoundrel of his experience and calibre ought certainly to have known better than that. You cannot fail to get a clue now.'

By this time the boat was approaching Cherry Gardens Pier, but unfortunately a thin night-fog had swept over the river, and objects could not be discerned with any clearness beyond a distance of thirty yards. As the Customs boat scraped down past the pier all its occupants strained eyes for a glimpse of the mysterious launch, but nothing could be seen of it. The boat continued to float idly down-stream, the men resting on their oars.

Then they narrowly escaped bumping a large Norwegian sailing vessel at anchor with her stem pointing down-stream. This ship they passed on the port side. Just as they got clear of her bowsprit the fat man cried out excitedly, 'There's her nose!' and he put the boat about and began to pull back against the tide. And surely the missing 'Squirm' was comfortably anchored on the starboard quarter of the Norwegian ship, hidden neatly between the ship and the shore. The men pulled very quietly alongside.

'I'LL board her to start with,' said Hazell, whispering to Racksole. 'I'll make out that I suspect they've got dutiable goods on board, and that will give me a chance to have a good look at her.'

Dressed in his official overcoat and peaked cap, he stepped, rather jauntily as Racksole thought, on to the low deck of the launch. 'Anyone aboard?'

Racksole heard him cry out, and a woman's voice answered. 'I'm a Customs examining officer, and I want to search the launch,' Hazell shouted, and then disappeared down into the little saloon amidships, and Racksole heard no more. It seemed to the millionaire that Hazell had been gone hours, but at length he returned.

'Can't find anything,' he said, as he jumped into the boat, and then privately to Racksole: 'There's a woman on board. Looks as if she might coincide with your description of Miss Spencer. Steam's up, but there's no engineer. I asked where the engineer was, and she inquired what business that was of mine, and requested me to get through with my own business and clear off. Seems rather a smart sort. I poked my nose into everything, but I saw no sign of any one else. Perhaps we'd better pull away and lie near for a bit, just to see if anything queer occurs.'

'You're quite sure he isn't on board?' Racksole asked.

'Quite,' said Hazell positively: 'I know how to search a vessel. See this,' and he handed to Racksole a sort of steel skewer, about two feet long, with a wooden handle. 'That,' he said, 'is one of the Customs' aids to searching.'

'I suppose it wouldn't do to go on board and carry off the lady?' Racksole suggested doubtfully.

'Well,' Hazell began, with equal doubtfulness, 'as for that--'

'Where's 'e orf?' It was the man in the bows who interrupted Hazell.

Following the direction of the man's finger, both Hazell and Racksole saw with more or less distinctness a dinghy slip away from the forefoot of the Norwegian vessel and disappear downstream into the mist.

'It's Jules, I'll swear,' cried Racksole. 'After him, men. Ten pounds apiece if we overtake him!'

'Lay down to it now, boys!' said Hazell, and the heavy Customs boat shot out in pursuit.

'This is going to be a lark,' Racksole remarked.

'Depends on what you call a lark,' said Hazell; 'it's not much of a lark tearing down midstream like this in a fog. You never know when you mayn't be in kingdom come with all these barges knocking around. I expect that chap hid in the dinghy when he first caught sight of us, and then slipped his painter as soon as I'd gone.'

The boat was moving at a rapid pace with the tide. Steering was a matter of luck and instinct more than anything else. Every now and then Hazell, who held the lines, was obliged to jerk the boat's head sharply round to avoid a barge or an anchored vessel. It seemed to Racksole that vessels were anchored all over the stream. He looked about him anxiously, but for a long time he could see nothing but mist and vague nautical forms. Then suddenly he said, quietly enough, 'We're on the right road; I can see him ahead.

'We're gaining on him.' In another minute the dinghy was plainly visible, not twenty yards away, and the sculler--sculling frantically now--was unmistakably Jules--Jules in a light tweed suit and a bowler hat.

'You were right,' Hazell said; 'this is a lark. I believe I'm getting quite excited. It's more exciting than playing the trombone in an orchestra. I'll run him down, eh?--and then we can drag the chap in from the water.'

Racksole nodded, but at that moment a barge, with her red sails set, stood out of the fog clean across the bows of the Customs boat, which narrowly escaped instant destruction. When they got clear, and the usual interchange of calm, nonchalant swearing was over, the dinghy was barely to be discerned in the mist, and the fat man was breathing in such a manner that his sighs might almost have been heard on the banks. Racksole wanted violently to do something, but there was nothing to do; he could only sit supine by Hazell's side in the stern-sheets. Gradually they began again to overtake the dinghy, whose one-man crew was evidently tiring. As they came up, hand over fist, the dinghy's nose swerved aside, and the tiny craft passed down a water-lane between two anchored mineral barges, which lay black and deserted about fifty yards from the Surrey shore. 'To starboard,' said Racksole. 'No, man!'

Hazell replied; 'we can't get through there. He's bound to come Out below; it's only a feint. I'll keep our nose straight ahead.'

And they went on, the fat man pounding away, with a face which glistened even in the thick gloom. It was an empty dinghy which emerged from between the two barges and went drifting and revolving down towards Greenwich.

The fat man gasped a word to his comrade, and the Customs boat stopped dead.

"E's all right,' said the man in the bows. 'If it's 'im you want, 'e's on one o' them barges, so you've only got to step on and take 'im orf.'

'That's all,' said a voice out of the depths of the nearest barge, and it was the voice of Jules, otherwise known as Mr Tom Jackson.

"Ear 'im?' said the fat man smiling. "E's a good 'un, 'e is. But if I was you, Mr Hazell, or you, sir, I shouldn't step on to that barge so quick as all that.'

They backed the boat under the stem of the nearest barge and gazed upwards.

'It's all right,' said Racksole to Hazell; 'I've got a revolver. How can I clamber up there?'

'Yes, I dare say you've got a revolver all right,' Hazell replied sharply. 'But you mustn't use it. There mustn't be any noise. We should have the river police down on us in a twinkling if there was a revolver shot, and it would be the ruin of me. If an inquiry was held the Commissioners wouldn't take any official notice of the fact that my superior officer had put me on to this job, and I should be requested to leave the service.'

'Have no fear on that score,' said Racksole. 'I shall, of course, take all responsibility.'

'It wouldn't matter how much responsibility you took,' Hazell retorted; 'you wouldn't put me back into the service, and my career would be at an end.'

'But there are other careers,' said Racksole, who was really anxious to lame his ex-waiter by means of a judiciously-aimed bullet. 'There are other careers.'

'The Customs is my career,' said Hazell, 'so let's have no shooting. We'll wait about a bit; he can't escape. You can have my skewer if you like'--and he gave Racksole his searching instrument. 'And you can do what you please, provided you do it neatly and don't make a row over it.'

For a few moments the four men were passive in the boat, surrounded by swirling mist, with black water beneath them, and towering above them a half-loaded barge with a desperate and resourceful man on board. Suddenly the mist parted and shrivelled away in patches, as though before the breath of some monster. The sky was visible; it was a clear sky, and the moon was shining. The transformation was just one of those meteorological quick-changes which happen most frequently on a great river.

'That's a sight better,' said the fat man. At the same moment a head appeared over the edge of the barge. It was Jules' face-- dark, sinister and leering.

'Is it Mr Racksole in that boat?' he inquired calmly; 'because if so, let Mr Racksole step up. Mr Racksole has caught me, and he can have me for the asking. Here I am.' He stood up to his full height on the barge, tall against the night sky, and all the occupants of the boat could see that he held firmly clasped in his right hand a short dagger. 'Now, Mr Racksole, you've been after me for a long time,' he continued; 'here I am. Why don't you step up? If you haven't got the pluck yourself, persuade someone else to step up in your place ... the same fair treatment will be accorded to all.' And Jules laughed a low, penetrating laugh.

He was in the midst of this laugh when he lurched suddenly forward.

'What'r' you doing of aboard my barge? Off you goes!' It was a boy's small shrill voice that sounded in the night. A ragged boy's small form had appeared silently behind Jules, and two small arms with a vicious shove precipitated him into the water. He fell with a fine gurgling splash. It was at once obvious that swimming was not among Jules' accomplishments. He floundered wildly and sank. When he reappeared he was dragged into the Customs boat. Rope was produced, and in a minute or two the man lay ignominiously bound in the bottom of the boat. With the aid of a mudlark--a mere barge boy, who probably had no more right on the barge than Jules himself--

Racksole had won his game. For the first time for several weeks the millionaire experienced a sensation of equanimity and satisfaction. He leaned over the prostrate form of Jules, Hazell's professional skewer in his hand.

'What are you going to do with him now?' asked Hazell.

'We'll row up to the landing steps in front of the Grand Babylon. He shall be well lodged at my hotel, I promise him.'

Jules spoke no word.

Before Racksole parted company with the Customs man that night Jules had been safely transported into the Grand Babylon Hotel and the two watermen had received their £10 apiece.

'You will sleep here?' said the millionaire to Mr George Hazell. 'It is late.'

'With pleasure,' said Hazell. The next morning he found a sumptuous breakfast awaiting him, and in his table-napkin was a Bank of England note for a hundred pounds. But, though he did not hear of them till much later, many things had happened before Hazell consumed that sumptuous breakfast.

CHAPTER XXVII
THE CONFESSION OF MR TOM JACKSON

IT happened that the small bedroom occupied by Jules during the years he was head-waiter at the Grand Babylon had remained empty since his sudden dismissal by Theodore Racksole. No other head-waiter had been formally appointed in his place; and, indeed, the absence of one man--even the unique Jules--could scarcely have been noticed in the enormous staff of a place like the Grand Babylon. The functions of a head-waiter are generally more ornamental, spectacular, and morally impressive than useful, and it was so at the great hotel on the Embankment. Racksole accordingly had the excellent idea of transporting his prisoner, with as much secrecy as possible, to this empty bedroom. There proved to be no difficulty in doing so; Jules showed himself perfectly amenable to a show of superior force.

Racksole took upstairs with him an old commissionaire who had been attached to the outdoor service of the hotel for many years--a grey-haired man, wiry as a terrier and strong as a mastiff. Entering the bedroom with Jules, whose hands were bound, he told the commissionaire to remain outside the door.

Jules' bedroom was quite an ordinary apartment, though perhaps slightly superior to the usual accommodation provided for servants in the caravanserais of the West End. It was about fourteen by twelve. It was furnished with a bedstead, a small wardrobe, a--mall washstand and dressing-table, and two chairs. There were two hooks behind the door, a strip of carpet by the bed, and some cheap ornaments on the iron mantelpiece. There was also one electric light. The window was a little square one, high up from the floor, and it looked on the inner quadrangle.

The room was on the top storey--the eighth--and from it you had a view sheer to the ground. Twenty feet below ran a narrow cornice about a foot wide; three feet or so above the window another and wider cornice jutted out, and above that was the high steep roof of the hotel, though you could not see it from the window. As Racksole examined the window and the outlook, he said to himself that Jules could not escape by that exit, at any rate. He gave a glance up the chimney, and saw that the flue was far too small to admit a man's body.

Then he called in the commissionaire, and together they bound Jules firmly to the bedstead, allowing him, however, to lie down. All the while the captive never opened his mouth--merely smiled a smile of disdain. Finally Racksole removed the ornaments, the carpet, the chairs and the hooks, and wrenched away the switch of the electric light. Then he and the commissionaire left the room, and Racksole locked the door on the outside and put the key in his pocket.

'You will keep watch here,' he said to the commissionaire, 'through the night. You can sit on this chair. Don't go to sleep. If you hear the slightest noise in the room blow your cab-whistle; I will arrange to answer the signal. If there is no noise do nothing whatever. I don't want this talked about, you understand. I shall trust you; you can trust me.'

'But the servants will see me here when they get up to-morrow,' said the commissionaire, with a faint smile, 'and they will be pretty certain to ask what I'm doing of up here. What shall I say to 'em?'

'You've been a soldier, haven't you?' asked Racksole.

'I've seen three campaigns, sir,' was the reply, and, with a gesture of pardonable pride, the grey-haired fellow pointed to the medals on his breast.

'Well, supposing you were on sentry duty and some meddlesome person in camp asked you what you were doing--what should you say?'

'I should tell him to clear off or take the consequences, and pretty quick too.'

'Do that to-morrow morning, then, if necessary,' said Racksole, and departed.

It was then about one o'clock a.m. The millionaire retired to bed--not his own bed, but a bed on the seventh storey. He did not, however, sleep very long. Shortly after dawn he was wide awake, and thinking busily about Jules.

He was, indeed, very curious to know Jules' story, and he determined, if the thing could be done at all, by persuasion or otherwise, to extract it from him. With a man of Theodore Racksole's temperament there is no time like the present, and at six o'clock, as the bright morning sun brought gaiety into the window, he dressed and went upstairs again to the eighth storey. The commissionaire sat stolid, but alert on his chair, and, at the sight of his master, rose and saluted.

'Anything happened?' Racksole asked.

'Nothing, sir.'

'Servants say anything?'

'Only a dozen or so of 'em are up yet, sir. One of 'em asked what I was playing at, and so I told her I was looking after a bull bitch and a litter of pups that you was very particular about, sir.'

'Good,' said Racksole, as he unlocked the door and entered the room. All was exactly as he had left it, except that Jules who had been lying on his back, had somehow turned over and was now lying on his face. He gazed silently, scowling at the millionaire. Racksole greeted him and ostentatiously took a revolver from his hip-pocket and laid it on the dressing-table. Then he seated himself on the dressing-table by the side of the revolver, his legs dangling an inch or two above the floor.

'I want to have a talk to you, Jackson,' he began.

'You can talk to me as much as you like,' said Jules. 'I shan't interfere, you may bet on that.'

'I should like you to answer some questions.'

'That's different,' said Jules. 'I'm not going to answer any questions while I'm tied up like this. You may bet on that, too.'

'It will pay you to be reasonable,' said Racksole.

'I'm not going to answer any questions while I'm tied up.'

'I'll unfasten your legs, if you like,' Racksole suggested politely, 'then you can sit up. It's no use you pretending you've been uncomfortable, because I know you haven't. I calculate you've been treated very handsomely, my son. There you are!' and he loosened the lower extremities of his prisoner from their bonds. 'Now I repeat you may as well be reasonable. You may as well admit that you've been fairly beaten in the game and act accordingly. I was determined to beat you, by myself, without the police, and I've done it.'

'You've done yourself,' retorted Jules. 'You've gone against the law. If you'd had any sense you wouldn't have meddled; you'd have left everything to the police. They'd have muddled about for a year or two, and then done nothing. Who's going to tell the police now? Are you? Are you going to give me up to 'em, and say, "Here, I've caught him for you". If you do they'll ask you to explain several things, and then you'll look foolish. One crime doesn't excuse another, and you'll find that out.'

With unerring insight, Jules had perceived exactly the difficulty of Racksole's position, and it was certainly a difficulty which Racksole did not attempt to minimize to himself. He knew well that it would have to be faced. He did not, however, allow Jules to guess his thoughts.

'Meanwhile,' he said calmly to the other, 'you're here and my prisoner. You've committed a variegated assortment of crimes, and among them is murder. You are due to be hung. You know that. There is no reason why I should call in the police at all. It will be perfectly easy for me to finish you off, as you deserve, myself. I shall only be carrying out justice, and robbing the hangman of his fee. Precisely as I brought you into the hotel, I can take you out again. A few days ago you borrowed or stole a steam yacht at Ostend. What you have done with it I don't know, nor do I care. But I strongly suspect that my daughter had a narrow escape of being murdered on your steam yacht. Now I have a steam yacht of my own. Suppose I use it as you used yours! Suppose I smuggle you on to it, steam out to sea, and then ask you to step off it into the ocean one night. Such things have been done.

Such things will be done again. If I acted so, I should at least, have the satisfaction of knowing that I had relieved society from the incubus of a scoundrel.'

'But you won't,' Jules murmured.

'No,' said Racksole steadily, 'I won't--if you behave yourself this morning. But I swear to you that if you don't I will never rest till you are dead, police or no police. You don't know Theodore Racksole.'

'I believe you mean it,' Jules exclaimed, with an air of surprised interest, as though he had discovered something of importance.

'I believe I do,' Racksole resumed. 'Now listen. At the best, you will be given up to the police. At the worst, I shall deal with you myself. With the police you may have a chance--you may get off with twenty years' penal servitude, because, though it is absolutely certain that you murdered Reginald Dimmock, it would be a little difficult to prove the case against you. But with me you would have no chance whatever. I have a few questions to put to you, and it will depend on how you answer them whether I give you up to the police or take the law into my own hands. And let me tell you that the latter course would be much simpler for me. And I would take it, too, did I not feel that you were a very clever and exceptional man; did I not have a sort of sneaking admiration for your detestable skill and ingenuity.'

'You think, then, that I am clever?' said Jules. 'You are right. I am. I should have been much too clever for you if luck had not been against me. You owe your victory, not to skill, but to luck.'

'That is what the vanquished always say. Waterloo was a bit of pure luck for the English, no doubt, but it was Waterloo all the same.'

Jules yawned elaborately. 'What do you want to know?' he inquired, with politeness.

'First and foremost, I want to know the names of your accomplices inside this hotel.'

'I have no more,' said Jules. 'Rocco was the last.'

'Don't begin by lying to me. If you had no accomplice, how did you contrive that one particular bottle of Romanée-Conti should be served to his Highness Prince Eugen?'

'Then you discovered that in time, did you?' said Jules. 'I was afraid so. Let me explain that that needed no accomplice. The bottle was topmost in the bin, and naturally it would be taken. Moreover, I left it sticking out a little further than the rest.'

'You did not arrange, then, that Hubbard should be taken ill the night before last?'

'I had no idea,' said Jules, 'that the excellent Hubbard was not enjoying his accustomed health.'

'Tell me,' said Racksole, 'who or what is the origin of your vendetta against the life of Prince Eugen?'

'I had no vendetta against the life of Prince Eugen,' said Jules, 'at least, not to begin with. I merely undertook, for a consideration, to see that Prince Eugen did not have an interview with a certain Mr Sampson Levi in London before a certain date, that was all. It seemed simple enough. I had been engaged in far more complicated transactions before. I was convinced that I could manage it, with the help of Rocco and Em--and Miss Spencer.'

'Is that woman your wife?'

'She would like to be,' he sneered. 'Please don't interrupt. I had completed my arrangements, when you so inconsiderately bought the hotel. I don't mind admitting now that from the very moment when you came across me that night in the corridor I was secretly afraid of you, though I scarcely admitted the fact even to myself then. I thought it safer to shift the scene of our operations to Ostend. I had meant to deal with Prince Eugen in this hotel, but I decided, then, to intercept him on the Continent, and I despatched Miss Spencer with some instructions. Troubles never come singly, and it happened that just then that fool Dimmock, who had been in the swim with us, chose to prove refractory. The slightest hitch would have upset everything, and I was obliged to--to clear him off the scene. He wanted to back out--he had a bad attack of conscience, and violent measures were essential. I regret his untimely decease, but he brought it on himself. Well, everything was going serenely when you and your brilliant daughter, apparently determined to meddle, turned up again among us at Ostend. Only twenty-four hours, however, had to elapse before the date which had been mentioned to me by my employers. I kept poor little Eugen for the allotted time, and then you managed to get hold of him. I do not deny that you scored there, though, according to my original instructions, you scored too late. The time had passed, and so, so far as I knew, it didn't matter a pin whether Prince Eugen saw Mr Sampson Levi or not. But my employers were still uneasy. They were uneasy even after little Eugen had lain ill in Ostend for several weeks. It appears that they feared that even at that date an interview between Prince Eugen and Mr Sampson Levi might work harm to them. So they applied to me again. This time they wanted Prince Eugen to be--em--finished off entirely. They offered high terms.'

'What terms?'

'I had received fifty thousand pounds for the first job, of which Rocco had half. Rocco was also to be made a member of a certain famous European order, if things went right. That was what he coveted far more than the money--the vain fellow! For the second job I was offered a hundred thousand. A tolerably large sum. I regret that I have not been able to earn it.'

'Do you mean to tell me,' asked Racksole, horror-struck by this calm confession, in spite of his previous knowledge, 'that you were offered a hundred thousand pounds to poison Prince Eugen?'

'You put it rather crudely,' said Jules in reply. 'I prefer to say that I was offered a hundred thousand pounds if Prince Eugen should die within a reasonable time.'

'And who were your damnable employers?'

'That, honestly, I do not know.'

'You know, I suppose, who paid you the first fifty thousand pounds, and who promised you the hundred thousand.'

'Well,' said Jules, 'I know vaguely. I know that he came via Vienna from--em--Bosnia. My impression was that the affair had some bearing, direct or indirect, on the projected marriage of the King of Bosnia. He is a young monarch, scarcely out of political leading-strings, as it were, and doubtless his Ministers thought that they had better arrange his marriage for him. They tried last year, and failed because the Princess whom they had in mind had cast her sparkling eyes on another Prince. That Prince happened to be Prince Eugen of Posen. The Ministers of the King of Bosnia knew exactly the circumstances of Prince Eugen. They knew that he could not marry without liquidating his debts, and they knew that he could only liquidate his debts through this Jew, Sampson Levi. Unfortunately for me, they ultimately wanted to make too sure of Prince Eugen. They were afraid he might after all arrange his marriage without the aid of Mr Sampson Levi, and so--well, you know the rest.... It is a pity that the poor little innocent King of Bosnia can't have the Princess of his Ministers' choice.'

'Then you think that the King himself had no part in this abominable crime?'

'I think decidedly not.'

'I am glad of that,' said Racksole simply. 'And now, the name of your immediate employer.'

'He was merely an agent. He called himself Sleszak--S-l-e-s-z-a-k. But I imagine that that wasn't his real name. I don't know his real name. An old man, he often used to be found at the Hotel Ritz, Paris.'

'Mr Sleszak and I will meet,' said Racksole.

'Not in this world,' said Jules quickly. 'He is dead. I heard only last night--just before our little tussle.'

There was a silence.

'It is well,' said Racksole at length. 'Prince Eugen lives, despite all plots. After all, justice is done.'

'Mr Racksole is here, but he can see no one, Miss.' The words came from behind the door, and the voice was the commissionaire's. Racksole started up, and went towards the door.

'Nonsense,' was the curt reply, in feminine tones. 'Move aside instantly.'

The door opened, and Nella entered. There were tears in her eyes.

'Oh! Dad,' she exclaimed, 'I've only just heard you were in the hotel. We looked for you everywhere. Come at once, Prince Eugen is dying--' Then she saw the man sitting on the bed, and stopped.

Later, when Jules was alone again, he remarked to himself, 'I may get that hundred thousand.'

CHAPTER XXVIII
THE STATE BEDROOM ONCE MORE

WHEN, immediately after the episode of the bottle of Romanée-Conti in the State dining-room, Prince Aribert and old Hans found that Prince Eugen had sunk in an unconscious heap over his chair, both the former thought, at the first instant, that Eugen must have already tasted the poisoned wine. But a moment's reflection showed that this was not possible. If the Hereditary Prince of Posen was dying or dead, his condition was due to some other agency than the Romanée-Conti. Aribert bent over him, and a powerful odour from the man's lips at once disclosed the cause of the disaster: it was the odour of laudanum. Indeed, the smell of that sinister drug seemed now to float heavily over the whole table. Across Aribert's mind there flashed then the true explanation. Prince Eugen, taking advantage of Aribert's attention being momentarily diverted; and yielding to a sudden impulse of despair, had decided to poison himself, and had carried out his intention on the spot.

The laudanum must have been already in his pocket, and this fact went to prove that the unfortunate Prince had previously contemplated such a proceeding, even after his definite promise. Aribert remembered now with painful vividness his nephew's words: 'I withdraw my promise. Observe that--I withdraw it.' It must have been instantly after the utterance of that formal withdrawal that Eugen attempted to destroy himself.

'It's laudanum, Hans,' Aribert exclaimed, rather helplessly.

'Surely his Highness has not taken poison?' said Hans. 'It is impossible!'

'I fear it is only too possible,' said the other. 'It's laudanum. What are we to do? Quick, man!'

'His Highness must be roused, Prince. He must have an emetic. We had better carry him to the bedroom.'

They did, and laid him on the great bed; and then Aribert mixed an emetic of mustard and water, and administered it, but without any effect. The sufferer lay motionless, with every muscle relaxed. His skin was ice-cold to the touch, and the eyelids, half-drawn, showed that the pupils were painfully contracted.

'Go out, and send for a doctor, Hans. Say that Prince Eugen has been suddenly taken ill, but that it isn't serious. The truth must never be known.'

'He must be roused, sire,' Hans said again, as he hurried from the room.

Aribert lifted his nephew from the bed, shook him, pinched him, flicked him cruelly, shouted at him, dragged him about, but to no avail. At length he desisted, from mere physical fatigue, and laid the Prince back again on the bed. Every minute that elapsed seemed an hour. Alone with the unconscious organism in the silence of the great stately chamber, under the cold yellow glare of the electric lights, Aribert became a prey to the most despairing thoughts. The tragedy of his nephew's career forced itself upon him, and it occurred to him that an early and shameful death had all along been inevitable for this good-natured, weak-purposed, unhappy child of a historic throne. A little good fortune, and his character, so evenly balanced between right and wrong, might have followed the proper path, and Eugen might have figured at any rate with dignity on the European stage. But now it appeared that all was over, the last stroke played. And in this disaster Aribert saw the ruin of his own hopes. For Aribert would have to occupy his nephew's throne, and he felt instinctively that nature had not cut him out for a throne. By a natural impulse he inwardly rebelled against the prospect of monarchy. Monarchy meant so much for which he knew himself to be entirely unfitted. It meant a political marriage, which means a forced marriage, a union against inclination. And then what of Nella--Nella!

Hans returned. 'I have sent for the nearest doctor, and also for a specialist,' he said.

'Good,' said Aribert. 'I hope they will hurry.' Then he sat down and wrote a card. 'Take this yourself to Miss Racksole. If she is out of the hotel, ascertain where she is and follow her. Understand, it is of the first importance.'

Hans bowed, and departed for the second time, and Aribert was alone again.

He gazed at Eugen, and made another frantic attempt to rouse him from the deadly stupor, but it was useless. He walked away to the window: through the opened casement he could hear the tinkle of passing hansoms on the Embankment below, whistles of door-keepers, and the hoot of steam tugs on the river. The world went on as usual, it appeared. It was an absurd world.

He desired nothing better than to abandon his princely title, and live as a plain man, the husband of the finest woman on earth.... But now!...

Pah! How selfish he was, to be thinking of himself when Eugen lay dying. Yet--Nella!

The door opened, and a man entered, who was obviously the doctor. A few curt questions, and he had grasped the essentials of the case. 'Oblige me by ringing the bell, Prince. I shall want some hot water, and an able-bodied man and a nurse.'

'Who wants a nurse?' said a voice, and Nella came quietly in. 'I am a nurse,' she added to the doctor, 'and at your orders.'

The next two hours were a struggle between life and death. The first doctor, a specialist who followed him, Nella, Prince Aribert, and old Hans formed, as it were, a league to save the dying man. None else in the hotel knew the real seriousness of the case. When a Prince falls ill, and especially by his own act, the precise truth is not issued broadcast to the universe.

According to official intelligence, a Prince is never seriously ill until he is dead. Such is statecraft.

The worst feature of Prince Eugen's case was that emetics proved futile.

Neither of the doctors could explain their failure, but it was only too apparent. The league was reduced to helplessness. At last the great specialist from Manchester Square gave it out that there was no chance for Prince Eugen unless the natural vigour of his constitution should prove capable of throwing off the poison unaided by scientific assistance, as a drunkard can sleep off his potion. Everything had been tried, even to artificial respiration and the injection of hot coffee. Having emitted this pronouncement, the great specialist from Manchester Square left. It was one o'clock in the morning. By one of those strange and futile coincidences which sometimes startle us by their subtle significance, the specialist met Theodore Racksole and his captive as they were entering the hotel. Neither had the least suspicion of the other's business.

In the State bedroom the small group of watchers surrounded the bed. The slow minutes filed away in dreary procession. Another hour passed. Then the figure on the bed, hitherto so motionless, twitched and moved; the lips parted.

'There is hope,' said the doctor, and administered a stimulant which was handed to him by Nella.

In a quarter of an hour the patient had regained consciousness. For the ten thousandth time in the history of medicine a sound constitution had accomplished a miracle impossible to the accumulated medical skill of centuries.

In due course the doctor left, saying that Prince Eugen was 'on the high road to recovery,' and promising to come again within a few hours. Morning had dawned. Nella drew the great curtains, and let in a flood of sunlight.

Old Hans, overcome by fatigue, dozed in a chair in a far corner of the room.

The reaction had been too much for him. Nella and Prince Aribert looked at each other. They had not exchanged a word about themselves, yet each knew what the other had been thinking. They clasped hands with a perfect understanding. Their brief love-making had been of the silent kind, and it was silent now. No word was uttered. A shadow had passed from over them, but only their eyes expressed relief and joy.

'Aribert!' The faint call came from the bed. Aribert went to the bedside, while Nella remained near the window.

'What is it, Eugen?' he said. 'You are better now.'

'You think so?' murmured the other. 'I want you to forgive me for all this, Aribert. I must have caused you an intolerable trouble. I did it so clumsily; that is what annoys me. Laudanum was a feeble expedient; but I could think of nothing else, and I daren't ask anyone for advice. I was obliged to go out and buy the stuff for myself. It was all very awkward. But, thank goodness, it has not been ineffectual.'

'What do you mean, Eugen? You are better. In a day or so you will be perfectly recovered.'

'I am dying,' said Eugen quietly. 'Do not be deceived. I die because I wish to die. It is bound to be so. I know by the feel of my heart. In a few hours it will be over. The throne of Posen will be yours, Aribert. You will fill it more worthily than I have done. Don't let them know over there that I poisoned myself. Swear Hans to secrecy; swear the doctors to secrecy; and breathe no word yourself. I have been a fool, but I do not wish it to be known that I was also a coward. Perhaps it is not cowardice; perhaps it is courage, after all--courage to cut the knot. I could not have survived the disgrace of any revelations, Aribert, and revelations would have been sure to come. I have made a fool of myself, but I am ready to pay for it. We of Posen--we always pay--everything except our debts. Ah! those debts! Had it not been for those I could have faced her who was to have been my wife, to have shared my throne. I could have hidden my past, and begun again. With her help I really could have begun again. But Fate has been against me--always! always! By the way, what was that plot against me, Aribert? I forget, I forget.'

His eyes closed. There was a sudden noise. Old Hans had slipped from his chair to the floor. He picked himself up, dazed, and crept shamefacedly out of the room.

Aribert took his nephew's hand.

'Nonsense, Eugen! You are dreaming. You will be all right soon. Pull yourself together.'

'All because of a million,' the sick man moaned. 'One miserable million English pounds. The national debt of Posen is fifty millions, and I, the Prince of Posen, couldn't borrow one. If I could have got it, I might have held my head up again. Good-bye, Aribert.... Who is that girl?'

Aribert looked up. Nella was standing silent at the foot of the bed, her eyes moist. She came round to the bedside, and put her hand on the patient's heart. Scarcely could she feel its pulsation, and to Aribert her eyes expressed a sudden despair.

At that moment Hans re-entered the room and beckoned to her.

'I have heard that Herr Racksole has returned to the hotel,' he whispered, 'and that he has captured that man Jules, who they say is such a villain.'

Several times during the night Nella inquired for her father, but could gain no knowledge of his whereabouts. Now, at half-past six in the morning, a rumour had mysteriously spread among the servants of the hotel about the happenings of the night before. How it had originated no one could have determined, but it had originated.

'Where is my father?' Nella asked of Hans.

He shrugged his shoulders, and pointed upwards. 'Somewhere at the top, they say.'

Nella almost ran out of the room. Her interruption of the interview between Jules and Theodore Racksole has already been described. As she came downstairs with her father she said again, 'Prince Eugen is dying--but I think you can save him.'

'I?' exclaimed Theodore.

'Yes,' she repeated positively. 'I will tell you what I want you to do, and you must do it.'

AS Nella passed downstairs from the top storey with her father--the lifts had not yet begun to work--she drew him into her own room, and closed the door.

'What's this all about?' he asked, somewhat mystified, and even alarmed by the extreme seriousness of her face.

'Dad,' the girl began, 'you are very rich, aren't you? very, very rich?' She smiled anxiously, timidly. He did not remember to have seen that expression on her face before. He wanted to make a facetious reply, but checked himself.

'Yes,' he said, 'I am. You ought to know that by this time.'

'How soon could you realize a million pounds?'

'A million--what?' he cried. Even he was staggered by her calm reference to this gigantic sum. 'What on earth are you driving at?'

'A million pounds, I said. That is to say, five million dollars. How soon could you realize as much as that?'

'Oh!' he answered, 'in about a month, if I went about it neatly enough. I could unload as much as that in a month without scaring Wall Street and other places. But it would want some arrangement.'

'Useless!' she exclaimed. 'Couldn't you do it quicker, if you really had to?'

'If I really had to, I could fix it in a week, but it would make things lively, and I should lose on the job.'

'Couldn't you,' she persisted, 'couldn't you go down this morning and raise a million, somehow, if it was a matter of life and death?'

He hesitated. 'Look here, Nella,' he said, 'what is it you've got up your sleeve?'

'Just answer my question, Dad, and try not to think that I'm a stark, staring lunatic.'

'I rather expect I could get a million this morning, even in London. But it would cost pretty dear. It might cost me fifty thousand pounds, and there would be the dickens of an upset in New York--a sort of grand universal slump in my holdings.'

'Why should New York know anything about it?'

'Why should New York know anything about it!' he repeated. 'My girl, when anyone borrows a million sovereigns the whole world knows about it. Do you reckon that I can go up to the Governors of the Bank of England and say, "Look here, lend Theodore Racksole a million for a few weeks, and he'll give you an IOU and a covering note on stocks"?'

'But you could get it?' she asked again.

'If there's a million in London I guess I could handle it,' he replied.

'Well, Dad,' and she put her arms round his neck, 'you've just got to go out and fix it. See? It's for me. I've never asked you for anything really big before. But I do now. And I want it so badly.'

He stared at her. 'I award you the prize,' he said, at length. 'You deserve it for colossal and immense coolness. Now you can tell me the true inward meaning of all this rigmarole. What is it?'

'I want it for Prince Eugen,' she began, at first hesitatingly, with pauses.

'He's ruined unless he can get a million to pay off his debts. He's dreadfully in love with a Princess, and he can't marry her because of this. Her parents wouldn't allow it. He was to have got it from Sampson Levi, but he arrived too late--owing to Jules.'

'I know all about that--perhaps more than you do. But I don't see how it affects you or me.'

'The point is this, Dad,' Nella continued. 'He's tried to commit suicide--he's so hipped. Yes, real suicide. He took laudanum last night. It didn't kill him straight off--he's got over the first shock, but he's in a very weak state, and he means to die. And I truly believe he will die. Now, if you could let him have that million, Dad, you would save his life.'

Nella's item of news was a considerable and disconcerting surprise to Racksole, but he hid his feelings fairly well.

'I haven't the least desire to save his life, Nell. I don't overmuch respect your Prince Eugen. I've done what I could for him--but only for the sake of seeing fair play, and because I object to conspiracies and secret murders.

It's a different thing if he wants to kill himself. What I say is: Let him.

Who is responsible for his being in debt to the tune of a million pounds? He's only got himself and his bad habits to thank for that. I suppose if he does happen to peg out, the throne of Posen will go to Prince Aribert. And a good thing, too! Aribert is worth twenty of his nephew.'

'That's just it, Dad,' she said, eagerly following up her chance. 'I want you to save Prince Eugen just because Aribert-- Prince Aribert--doesn't wish to occupy the throne. He'd much prefer not to have it.'

'Much prefer not to have it! Don't talk nonsense. If he's honest with himself, he'll admit that he'll be jolly glad to have it. Thrones are in his blood, so to speak.'

'You are wrong, Father. And the reason is this: If Prince Aribert ascended the throne of Posen he would be compelled to marry a Princess.'

'Well! A Prince ought to marry a Princess.'

'But he doesn't want to. He wants to give up all his royal rights, and live as a subject. He wants to marry a woman who isn't a Princess.'

'Is she rich?'

'Her father is,' said the girl. 'Oh, Dad! can't you guess? He-- he loves me.' Her head fell on Theodore's shoulder and she began to cry.

The millionaire whistled a very high note. 'Nell!' he said at length. 'And you? Do you sort of cling to him?'

'Dad,' she answered, 'you are stupid. Do you imagine I should worry myself like this if I didn't?' She smiled through her tears. She knew from her father's tone that she had accomplished a victory.

'It's a mighty queer arrangement,' Theodore remarked. 'But of course if you think it'll be of any use, you had better go down and tell your Prince Eugen that that million can be fixed up, if he really needs it. I expect there'll be decent security, or Sampson Levi wouldn't have mixed himself up in it.'

'Thanks, Dad. Don't come with me; I may manage better alone.'

She gave a formal little curtsey and disappeared. Racksole, who had the talent, so necessary to millionaires, of attending to several matters at once, the large with the small, went off to give orders about the breakfast and the remuneration of his assistant of the evening before, Mr George Hazell. He then sent an invitation to Mr Felix Babylon's room, asking that gentleman to take breakfast with him. After he had related to Babylon the history of Jules' capture, and had a long discussion with him upon several points of hotel management, and especially as to the guarding of wine-cellars, Racksole put on his hat, sallied forth into the Strand, hailed a hansom, and was driven to the City. The order and nature of his operations there were, too complex and technical to be described here.

When Nella returned to the State bedroom both the doctor and the great specialist were again in attendance. The two physicians moved away from the bedside as she entered, and began to talk quietly together in the embrasure of the window.

'A curious case!' said the specialist.

'Yes. Of course, as you say, it's a neurotic temperament that's at the bottom of the trouble. When you've got that and a vigorous constitution working one against the other, the results are apt to be distinctly curious. Do you consider there is any hope, Sir Charles?'

'If I had seen him when he recovered consciousness I should have said there was hope. Frankly, when I left last night, or rather this morning, I didn't expect to see the Prince alive again--let alone conscious, and able to talk. According to all the rules of the game, he ought to get over the shock to the system with perfect ease and certainty. But I don't think he will. I don't think he wants to. And moreover, I think he is still under the influence of suicidal mania. If he had a razor he would cut his throat. You must keep his strength up. Inject, if necessary. I will come in this afternoon. I am due now at St James's Palace.' And the specialist hurried away, with an elaborate bow and a few hasty words of polite reassurances to Prince Aribert.

When he had gone Prince Aribert took the other doctor aside. 'Forget everything, doctor,' he said, 'except that I am one man and you are another, and tell me the truth. Shall you be able to save his Highness? Tell me the truth.'

'There is no truth,' was the doctor's reply. 'The future is not in our hands, Prince.'

'But you are hopeful? Yes or no.'

The doctor looked at Prince Aribert. 'No!' he said shortly. 'I am not. I am never hopeful when the patient is not on my side.'

'You mean--?'

'I mean that his Royal Highness has no desire to live. You must have observed that.'

'Only too well,' said Aribert.

'And you are aware of the cause?'

Aribert nodded an affirmative.

'But cannot remove it?'

'No,' said Aribert. He felt a touch on his sleeve. It was Nella's finger.

With a gesture she beckoned him towards the ante-room.

'If you choose,' she said, when they were alone, 'Prince Eugen can be saved. I have arranged it.'

'You have arranged it?' He bent over her, almost with an air of alarm. 'Go and tell him that the million pounds which is so necessary to his happiness will be forthcoming. Tell him that it will be forthcoming today, if that will be any satisfaction to him.'

'But what do you mean by this, Nella?'

'I mean what I say, Aribert,' and she sought his hand and took it in hers.

'Just what I say. If a million pounds will save Prince Eugen's life, it is at his disposal.'

'But how--how have you managed it? By what miracle?'

'My father,' she replied softly, 'will do anything that I ask him. Do not let us waste time. Go and tell Eugen it is arranged, that all will be well. Go!'

'But we cannot accept this--this enormous, this incredible favour. It is impossible.'

'Aribert,' she said quickly, 'remember you are not in Posen holding a Court reception. You are in England and you are talking to an American girl who has always been in the habit of having her own way.'

The Prince threw up his hands and went back in to the bedroom. The doctor was at a table writing out a prescription. Aribert approached the bedside, his heart beating furiously. Eugen greeted him with a faint, fatigued smile.

'Eugen,' he whispered, 'listen carefully to me. I have news. With the assistance of friends I have arranged to borrow that million for you. It is quite settled, and you may rely on it. But you must get better. Do you hear me?'

Eugen almost sat up in bed. 'Tell me I am not delirious,' he exclaimed.

'Of course you aren't,' Aribert replied. 'But you mustn't sit up. You must take care of yourself.'

'Who will lend the money?' Eugen asked in a feeble, happy whisper.

'Never mind. You shall hear later. Devote yourself now to getting better.'

The change in the patient's face was extraordinary. His mind seemed to have put on an entirely different aspect. The doctor was startled to hear him murmur a request for food. As for Aribert, he sat down, overcome by the turmoil of his own thoughts. Till that moment he felt that he had never appreciated the value and the marvellous power of mere money, of the lucre which philosophers pretend to despise and men sell their souls for. His heart almost burst in its admiration for that extraordinary Nella, who by mere personal force had raised two men out of the deepest slough of despair to the blissful heights of hope and happiness. 'These Anglo-Saxons,' he said to himself, 'what a race!'

By the afternoon Eugen was noticeably and distinctly better. The physicians, puzzled for the third time by the progress of the case, announced now that all danger was past. The tone of the announcement seemed to Aribert to imply that the fortunate issue was due wholly to unrivalled medical skill, but perhaps Aribert was mistaken. Anyhow, he was in a most charitable mood, and prepared to forgive anything.

'Nella,' he said a little later, when they were by themselves again in the ante-chamber, 'what am I to say to you? How can I thank you? How can I thank your father?'

'You had better not thank my father,' she said. 'Dad will affect to regard the thing as a purely business transaction, as, of course, it is. As for me, you can--you can--'

'Well?'

'Kiss me,' she said. 'There! Are you sure you've formally proposed to me, mon prince?'

'Ah! Nell!' he exclaimed, putting his arms round her again. 'Be mine! That is all I want!'

'You'll find,' she said, 'that you'll want Dad's consent too!'

'Will he make difficulties? He could not, Nell--not with you!'

'Better ask him,' she said sweetly.

A moment later Racksole himself entered the room. 'Going on all right?' he enquired, pointing to the bedroom. 'Excellently,' the lovers answered together, and they both blushed.

'Ah!' said Racksole. 'Then, if that's so, and you can spare a minute, I've something to show you, Prince.'

CHAPTER XXX
CONCLUSION

'I'VE a great deal to tell you, Prince,' Racksole began, as soon as they were out of the room, 'and also, as I said, something to show you. Will you come to my room? We will talk there first. The whole hotel is humming with excitement.'

'With pleasure,' said Aribert.

'Glad his Highness Prince Eugen is recovering,' Racksole said, urged by considerations of politeness.

'Ah! As to that--' Aribert began. 'If you don't mind, we'll discuss that later, Prince,' Racksole interrupted him.

They were in the proprietor's private room.

'I want to tell you all about last night,' Racksole resumed, 'about my capture of Jules, and my examination of him this morning.' And he launched into a full account of the whole thing, down to the least details. 'You see,' he concluded, 'that our suspicions as to Bosnia were tolerably correct. But as regards Bosnia, the more I think about it, the surer I feel that nothing can be done to bring their criminal politicians to justice.'

'And as to Jules, what do you propose to do?'

'Come this way,' said Racksole, and led Aribert to another room. A sofa in this room was covered with a linen cloth. Racksole lifted the cloth--he could never deny himself a dramatic moment--and disclosed the body of a dead man.

It was Jules, dead, but without a scratch or mark on him.

'I have sent for the police--not a street constable, but an official from Scotland Yard,' said Racksole.

'How did this happen?' Aribert asked, amazed and startled. 'I understood you to say that he was safely immured in the bedroom.'

'So he was,' Racksole replied. 'I went up there this afternoon, chiefly to take him some food. The commissionaire was on guard at the door. He had heard no noise, nothing unusual. Yet when I entered the room Jules was gone.

'He had by some means or other loosened his fastenings; he had then managed to take the door off the wardrobe. He had moved the bed in front of the window, and by pushing the wardrobe door three parts out of the window and lodging the inside end of it under the rail at the head of the bed, he had provided himself with a sort of insecure platform outside the window. All this he did without making the least sound. He must then have got through the window, and stood on the little platform. With his fingers he would just be able to reach the outer edge of the wide cornice under the roof of the hotel. By main strength of arms he had swung himself on to this cornice, and so got on to the roof proper. He would then have the run of the whole roof.

'At the side of the building facing Salisbury Lane there is an iron fire-escape, which runs right down from the ridge of the roof into a little sunk yard level with the cellars. Jules must have thought that his escape was accomplished. But it unfortunately happened that one rung in the iron escape-ladder had rusted rotten through being badly painted. It gave way, and Jules, not expecting anything of the kind, fell to the ground. That was the end of all his cleverness and ingenuity.'

As Racksole ceased, speaking he replaced the linen cloth with a gesture from which reverence was not wholly absent.

When the grave had closed over the dark and tempestuous career of Tom Jackson, once the pride of the Grand Babylon, there was little trouble for the people whose adventures we have described. Miss Spencer, that yellow-haired, faithful slave and attendant of a brilliant scoundrel, was never heard of again. Possibly to this day she survives, a mystery to her fellow-creatures, in the pension of some cheap foreign boarding-house. As for Rocco, he certainly was heard of again. Several years after the events set down, it came to the knowledge of Felix Babylon that the unrivalled Rocco had reached Buenos Aires, and by his culinary skill was there making the fortune of a new and splendid hotel. Babylon transmitted the information to Theodore Racksole, and Racksole might, had he chosen, have put the forces of the law in motion against him. But Racksole, seeing that everything pointed to the fact that Rocco was now pursuing his vocation honestly, decided to leave him alone. The one difficulty which Racksole experienced after the demise of Jules-- and it was a difficulty which he had, of course, anticipated--was connected with the police. The police, very properly, wanted to know things. They desired to be informed what Racksole had been doing in the Dimmock affair, between his first visit to Ostend and his sending for them to take charge of Jules' dead body. And Racksole was by no means inclined to tell them everything. Beyond question he had transgressed the laws of England, and possibly also the laws of Belgium; and the moral excellence of his motives in doing so was, of course, in the eyes of legal justice, no excuse for such conduct. The inquest upon Jules aroused some bother; and about ninety-and-nine separate and distinct rumours. In the end, however, a compromise was arrived at. Racksole's first aim was to pacify the inspector whose clue, which by the way was a false one, he had so curtly declined to follow up. That done, the rest needed only tact and patience. He proved to the satisfaction of the authorities that he had acted in a perfectly honest spirit, though with a high hand, and that substantial justice had been done. Also, he subtly indicated that, if it came to the point, he should defy them to do their worst. Lastly, he was able, through the medium of the United States Ambassador, to bring certain soothing influences to bear upon the situation.

One afternoon, a fortnight after the recovery of the Hereditary Prince of Posen, Aribert, who was still staying at the Grand Babylon, expressed a wish to hold converse with the millionaire. Prince Eugen, accompanied by Hans and some Court officials whom he had sent for, had departed with immense éclat, armed with the comfortable million, to arrange formally for his betrothal.

Touching the million, Eugen had given satisfactory personal security, and the money was to be paid off in fifteen years.

'You wish to talk to me, Prince,' said Racksole to Aribert, when they were seated together in the former's room.

'I wish to tell you,' replied Aribert, 'that it is my intention to renounce all my rights and titles as a Royal Prince of Posen, and to be known in future as Count Hartz--a rank to which I am entitled through my mother.

Also that I have a private income of ten thousand pounds a year, and a château and a town house in Posen. I tell you this because I am here to ask the hand of your daughter in marriage. I love her, and I am vain enough to believe that she loves me. I have already asked her to be my wife, and she has consented. We await your approval.'

'You honour us, Prince,' said Racksole with a slight smile, 'and in more ways than one, May I ask your reason for renouncing your princely titles?'

'Simply because the idea of a morganatic marriage would be as repugnant to me as it would be to yourself and to Nella.'

'That is good.' The Prince laughed. 'I suppose it has occurred to you that ten thousand pounds per annum, for a man in your position, is a somewhat small income. Nella is frightfully extravagant. I have known her to spend sixty thousand dollars in a single year, and have nothing to show for it at the end. Why! she would ruin you in twelve months.'

'Nella must reform her ways,' Aribert said.

'If she is content to do so,' Racksole went on, 'well and good! I consent.'

'In her name and my own, I thank you,' said Aribert gravely.

'And,' the millionaire continued, 'so that she may not have to reform too fiercely, I shall settle on her absolutely, with reversion to your children, if you have any, a lump sum of fifty million dollars, that is to say, ten million pounds, in sound, selected railway stock. I reckon that is about half my fortune. Nella and I have always shared equally.'

Aribert made no reply. The two men shook hands in silence, and then it happened that Nella entered the room.

That night, after dinner, Racksole and his friend Felix Babylon were walking together on the terrace of the Grand Babylon Hotel.

Felix had begun the conversation.

'I suppose, Racksole,' he had said, 'you aren't getting tired of the Grand Babylon?'

'Why do you ask?'

'Because I am getting tired of doing without it. A thousand times since I sold it to you I have wished I could undo the bargain. I can't bear idleness. Will you sell?'

'I might,' said Racksole, 'I might be induced to sell.'

'What will you take, my friend?' asked Felix

'What I gave,' was the quick answer.

'Eh!' Felix exclaimed. 'I sell you my hotel with Jules, with Rocco, with Miss Spencer. You go and lose all those three inestimable servants, and then offer me the hotel without them at the same price! It is monstrous.' The little man laughed heartily at his own wit. 'Nevertheless,' he added, 'we will not quarrel about the price. I accept your terms.'

And so was brought to a close the complex chain of events which had begun when Theodore Racksole ordered a steak and a bottle of Bass at the table d'hôte of the Grand Babylon Hotel.

AVAILABLE FROM RESURRECTED PRESS!

THE EDWARDIAN DETECTIVES
LITERARY SLEUTHS OF THE EDWARDIAN ERA

The exploits of the great Victorian Detectives, Poe's C. Auguste Dupin, Gaboriau's Lecoq, and most famously, Arthur Conan Doyle's Sherlock Holmes, are well known. But what of those fictional detectives that came after, those of the Edwardian Age? The period between the death of Queen Victoria and the First World War had been called the Golden Age of the detective short story, but how familiar is the modern reader with the sleuths of this era? And such an extraordinary group they were, including in their numbers an unassuming English priest, a blind man, a master of disguises, a lecturer in medical jurisprudence, a noble woman working for Scotland Yard, and a savant so brilliant he was known as "The Thinking Machine."

To introduce readers to these detectives, Resurrected Press has assembled a collection of stories featuring these and other remarkable sleuths in The Edwardian Detectives.

- The Case of Laker, Absconded by Arthur Morrison
- The Fenchurch Street Mystery by Baroness Orczy
- The Crime of the French Café by Nick Carter
- The Man with Nailed Shoes by R Austin Freeman
- The Blue Cross by G. K. Chesterton
- The Case of the Pocket Diary Found in the Snow by Augusta Groner
- The Ninescore Mystery by Baroness Orczy
- The Riddle of the Ninth Finger by Thomas W. Hanshew
- The Knight's Cross Signal Problem by Ernest Bramah
- The Problem of Cell 13 by Jacques Futrelle
- The Conundrum of the Golf Links by Percy James Brebner
- The Silkworms of Florence by Clifford Ashdown
- The Gateway of the Monster by William Hope Hodgson
- The Affair at the Semiramis Hotel by A. E. W. Mason
- The Affair of the Avalanche Bicycle & Tyre Co., LTD by Arthur Morrison

RESURRECTED PRESS CLASSIC MYSTERY CATALOGUE

E. C. Bentley
Trent's Last Case: The Woman in Black

Ernest Bramah
Max Carrados Resurrected:
The Detective Stories of Max Carrados

Agatha Christie
The Secret Adversary
The Mysterious Affair at Styles

Octavus Roy Cohen
Midnight

Freeman Wills Croft
The Ponson Case
The Pit Prop Syndicate

J. S. Fletcher
The Herapath Property
The Rayner-Slade Amalgamation
The Chestermarke Instinct
The Paradise Mystery
Dead Men's Money
The Middle of Things
Ravensdene Court
Scarhaven Keep
The Orange-Yellow Diamond
The Middle Temple Murder
The Tallyrand Maxim
The Borough Treasurer
In the Mayor's Parlour
The Saftey Pin

R. Austin Freeman
The Mystery of 31 New Inn from the Dr. Thorndyke Series
John Thorndyke's Cases from the Dr. Thorndyke Series
The Red Thumb Mark from The Dr. Thorndyke Series
The Eye of Osiris from The Dr. Thorndyke Series
A Silent Witness from the Dr. John Thorndyke Series
The Cat's Eye from the Dr. John Thorndyke Series
Helen Vardon's Confession: A Dr. John Thorndyke Story
As a Thief in the Night: A Dr. John Thorndyke Story
Mr. Pottermack's Oversight: A Dr. John Thorndyke Story
Dr. Thorndyke Intervenes: A Dr. John Thorndyke Story
The Singing Bone: The Adventures of Dr. Thorndyke
The Stoneware Monkey: A Dr. John Thorndyke Story
The Great Portrait Mystery, and Other Stories: A Collection of
Dr. John Thorndyke and Other Stories
The Penrose Mystery: A Dr. John Thorndyke Story
The Uttermost Farthing: A Savant's Vendetta

Arthur Griffiths
The Passenger From Calais
The Rome Express

Fergus Hume
The Mystery of a Hansom Cab
The Green Mummy
The Silent House
The Secret Passage

Edgar Jepson
The Loudwater Mystery

A. E. W. Mason
At the Villa Rose

A. A. Milne
The Red House Mystery

Baroness Emma Orczy
The Old Man in the Corner

Carolyn Wells
Vicky Van
The Man Who Fell Through the Earth
In the Onyx Lobby
Raspberry Jam
The Clue
The Room with the Tassels
The Vanishing of Betty Varian
The Mystery Girl
The White Alley
The Curved Blades
Anybody but Anne
The Bride of a Moment
Faulkner's Folly
The Diamond Pin
The Gold Bag
The Mystery of the Sycamore
The Come Backy

Raoul Whitfield
Death in a Bowl

Mildred A. Wirt
The Clock Strikes Thirteen
Clue of the Silken Ladder
The Cry at Midnight
Ghost Beyond the Gate
Guilt of the Brass Thieves
Hoofbeats on the Turnpike
The Secret Pact
Saboteurs on the River
Signal in the Dark
Voice from the Cave
Whispering Walls
The Wishing Well

And much more!
Visit ResurrectedPress.com for our complete
catalogue

About Resurrected Press

A division of Intrepid Ink, LLC, Resurrected Press is dedicated to bringing high quality, vintage books back into publication. See our entire catalogue and find out more at www.ResurrectedPress.com.

About Intrepid Ink, LLC

Intrepid Ink, LLC provides full publishing services to authors of fiction and non-fiction books, eBooks and websites. From editing to formatting, from publishing to marketing, Intrepid Ink gets your creative works into the hands of the people who want to read them. Find out more at www.IntrepidInk.com.